THE AIKI CHRONICLES
SKILL

24/06/06

For Stephen

Please read and enjoy this new edition

Next one on the way

Gadi

Gadiel Shorr first went to Japan in 1989, motivated and determined to study the martial art of Aikido. In Tokyo he joined the Yoshinkan Aikido headquarters where he successfully completed an intensive course with the Japanese Riot Police. Later he became one of the foreign instructors at the Yoshinkan Aikido headquarters.
Gadiel Shorr currently lives in England with his wife Tessa and daughters, Robyn and Megan.

References

The Great Onisaburo Deguchi by Kyotaro Deguchi
Aikido Master – by Stanely A Pranin
The Essence of Aikido – by John Stevens
Budo – by Morihei Ueshiba
Abundant Peace – by John Stevens
Budo Training in Aikido – by Morihei Ueshiba
Dueling with O Sensei – by Ellis Amdur
And thousands of internet pages…

SKILL

Gadiel Shorr

Teromega

Published by Teromega
Watford Lodge, 1 Sandy Lodge Road,
Rickmansworth, Hertfordshire, WD3 1LP
UK

Second edition published 2006
First published in 2006

Copyright © Gadiel Shorr 2006
Copyright © Tessa Shorr 2006

The moral rights of Gadiel Shorr and Tessa Shorr to be identified as author and cover illustrator of this work have been asserted.

All rights reserved to the author Gadiel Shorr. No part of this publication may be reproduced, stored in a retrieval system, or transmitted, in any form or by any means, electronic, mechanical, photocopying, recording or otherwise, without the prior written permission of the author Gadiel Shorr.

This book is sold subject to the condition that it shall not, by way of trade or otherwise, be lent, re-sold, hired out or otherwise circulated without the author's prior consent in any form of binding other than that in which it is published and without a similar condition including this condition being imposed on the subsequent purchaser.

ISBN-13: 978-0-9552438-0-6
ISBN-10: 0-9552438-0-7

TIMELINE

22 August 1871	Onisaburo Deguchi is born
14 December 1883	Morihei Ueshiba is born in Tanabe
March 1912	Ueshiba moves to Hokaido, Shirataki
Winter 1915	Ueshiba meets Master Sokaku Takeda
December 1919	Ueshiba meets Deguchi in Ayabe
2 January 1920	Ueshiba's father, Yoroku, dies aged 76
1920 - 1928	Ueshiba lives in Ayabe
August 1920	Ueshiba's son, Takemori, dies aged 3
September 1920	Ueshiba's son, Kuniharu, dies aged 1
13 February 1924	Deguchi & Ueshiba begin their journey to Mongolia
21 June 1924	Deguchi & Ueshiba are arrested in Tongliao
25 July 1924	Deguchi & Ueshiba return to Japan
Spring 1925	Ueshiba reaches enlightenment
8 December 1935	Second Omoto incident, Deguchi is arrested
7 August 1942	Deguchi is released from prison
19 January 1948	Deguchi dies
26 April 1969	Ueshiba dies
15 May 2016	Jacques Patye performs his demonstration
20 December 2157	Jerome is born
2172	Jerome is kidnapped and begins life at the School of Aikilibrium

Contents

Prologue
1 Jerome
2 Max
3 The Dojo
4 An Introduction to the Skill
5 Building the Foundations: Dai Ichi Kihon
6 Stomach Aches
7 Locks and Throws: Dai Ichi Kihon
8 A Bitter Day of Nikyo
9 The Quest
10 The Day Before the Test: Dai Ichi Kihon
11 The Search for the Lost Book
12 Senseless Aggression
13 Second-Level Techniques: Dai Ni Kihon
14 Recollection
15 Misogi
16 Misogi No Jo
17 The Search for the Book: Part 2
18 An Assault by Night
19 String Theory
20 The Song of Creation
21 Ki: Katana Blue
22 Shaking Up the Su

23 The Mirror of Amaterasu
24 Reflection
25 Third Level of Techniques: Dai San Kihon
26 The Spark
27 A World of Shadows and Sounds
28 The Eight Powers
29 Division and Unification
30 Windows of Opportunity
31 The Thirst for Detachment
32 The Ring Fighter
33 The Evaluation
34 Second Shaking of the Su
35 The Stunt
36 The Rehearsal
37 The Demonstration
38 Sealing the Process
39 The Final Act
Epilogue
Glossary

For Tessa

Sometimes the unplanned becomes visible,
Sometimes it is planned but cannot be perceived.
The way that life takes one character,
And changes through him the things to be.
(from *The Book of the Catalyst*)

Prologue

Ayabe, Japan, 1919

MASTER ONISABURO DEGUCHI was sitting one evening at his headquarters in Ayabe, deeply consumed in meditation. It was, he knew, a time of visions, a time to call upon his powers to foresee the future. The early winter of November 1919 had a chill air that penetrated the colourful robes of the master who was, as ever, dressed like a peacock. His eyes were closed, meaty lips quietly chanting the holy scripts, his body shaking. There was a role for him to play, the conclusion far into the future, long after his ashes scattered away in the wind, and he was eager to get started.

A vision came to mind of a man, a single man soon to arrive in Ayabe, the *Omoto Kyo* religion headquarters. A man to bring about the next step in the evolution of humankind, a man who would bind the knowledge that had been collected through history and add his own decisive contribution. Master Deguchi knew that he would need to prepare this successor and that he would have to be his mentor as well.

Japan was at war and in turmoil. In this time of great changes, the man who was to come would bring the message of the higher arts through the work of warriors and their martial techniques. Onisaburo stood up and walked the *tatami* floor to the outer room and the hallway. The *tatami* mats were made by the finest weavers and were coated in silk sheets to keep them intact and allow minimum friction.

He slipped into his boots and put on his overcoat. A student rushed to help him and the master brushed him away with a wave of his hand. He was not angry with him, but just slightly disturbed – after all, the youngster was only doing his duty. He walked outside and swiftly moved out of the major pathways, hiding from the attention of his followers. Sitting momentarily behind one of the temples he tightened his exotic hat, warming his ears against the cold. His never resting mind started to compose a *waka* – a song for the warrior to come. It was ironic to think that the higher arts would be acquired by a man of *Budo*, but he couldn't argue with the strong vision he had. He sensed that it was going to be soon, perhaps in a few weeks, and there were plenty of things to prepare. He would have to guide him along the paths of the *Omoto* and make sure that he excelled in his studies. He would help him conceive, grow and name his findings; build the network for this new stranger to spread his art.

Master Deguchi's eyes closed and his body rocked: once more a vision was coming. He sensed the clouds parting and the shining body of the Dragon King burst through the opening, tainting the night's sky in burning embers of crimson. With the vision Onisaburo learned the identity of the newcomer, and came to understand what he truly was.

Opening his eyes he walked to the highest point in the farming settlement, ignoring those who recognised him and fussed around. Someone had the good sense to realise his desire for privacy and she called the crowds away. Deguchi reached the top and looked to the east, searching with his eyes beyond the neat squares that marked the boundaries of the fields, following them all the way to the mountains. He couldn't see him as yet but he could tell that the whole play was in motion.

'Let the great plot begin!' he cried, more to himself than to anyone else and promptly composed another *waka*.

Soon, he knew, it would start. Very soon.

1   Jerome

Paris, 2172

JEROME WOKE UP and instinctively raised an arm to protect his head. His eyes moved in all directions, chin tucked in and back pressed against the wall. There was no attack coming, he was safe. He breathed out in relief and stood up cautiously, pushing off the cardboard he used as a blanket. A puddle on the ground caught his reflection and he stepped back in alarm; a fifteen-year-old boy, strong, agile and very skinny, just under five and a half feet in height yet never stretching fully, black hair and sharp black eyes, peering beneath the eyebrows, a shadow by day and night. He could have been considered handsome but there was a hardness in his features that prevented the softness and beauty from surfacing, thus serving as a shield behind which he faced the world.

He brushed at his matted hair and lifted up his head, inspecting the blue slit of skies above the alley. The air was chilled but it was bound to warm up soon; it was going to be a nice day. His gaze shifted to the roofs that bordered with the blue and he frowned at the memory of last night's incident with the stalker. Jerome was angry with himself, falling asleep on his guard – he could have paid dearly.

The thoughts went back to the stalker, the stranger who had been hunting him for the past week and yesterday almost took him by surprise on one of the roofs.

'How could I have been so careless?'

It was a miracle what had happened up there: he had somehow sensed the presence of the man and managed to jump to the next roof, no less than four metres away. He couldn't comprehend how he had done it and didn't ponder on it for too long; three years' experience of surviving the streets had taught him not to question good luck. People who had the time to question good luck probably didn't need it. Jerome was not one of those.

Wiping his frosty nostrils on a sleeve, he winced at the smell that penetrated his nose, frowning at the alley where he had slept. It was not the best place for him to have used, and it reeked of something whose origins he didn't dare imagine.

No wonder he couldn't find me, he thought sarcastically of the stalker. *It smells worse than me in here.*

The alley was just off Rue de Rivoli, with office buildings towering over his little hideout. Business would start soon and it was time to go. He had to get some food if he was to survive, yet he was holding back, afraid of the demented stalker.

'Maybe I should go back home.'

He smiled bitterly: painful memories that dulled with time would still come flashing into his mind, briefly rekindling soft, comforting feelings.

Early childhood had been a cherished time when he had experienced a warm, stable and healthy family life. Jerome had been happy and like most fortunate kids he foolishly took it for granted. Christmas trees were present, hugs and kisses a daily routine; home provided love and comfort, sheltering him from the world. As usual the pacifying images didn't last long, but gave way to painful memories, reminding him of the need to avoid personal history altogether.

Fate lashed out at him when he was five years old, when his mother had lost her job and was forced to stay at home. His father worked hard, trying to support the family, leaving his mother alone and depressed, seeking support and compassion in her immediate surroundings. A 'kind' neighbour offered her a substitute for happiness in the shape of a needle. She took it and paid dearly in both her vitality and health. The once large, clear eyes turned to pinpoint pupils, soft and smooth skin was altered by bumpy puncture scars and bluish bloodshot marks. His father tried to cope and help, but couldn't handle his mother and although he appeared to tolerate her increasingly abusive ways, the day came when he left the family home and never returned.

Jerome was able to watch his memories in a detached way, as if they belonged to someone else; he saw a little boy, staring out of a stained window, pressing his face to the cold glass, waiting for his protective giant to come back, waiting days and nights.

'Father …' the boy chanted quietly, tears drawing patterns on the glass. 'Father …'

Mother felt betrayed and could not cope financially; and to make matters worse she blamed Jerome for her misfortune. His life became a living hell as beatings and shouts in the day were replaced by strange men who came home at night, smelling of alcohol and sweat, cursing, grunting and terrifying young Jerome. He was forced to spend much of his time out on the streets, keeping himself hidden from home and gradually learning how to endure life on his own. Occasionally he would spy on his mother, whenever he missed her warmth. The memory of the beatings and pain dulled with time, convincing him that she did it out of love and that it was all his fault – that he was a bad son. Her love, however, hurt him in a dangerous way.

On the street it wasn't too safe, but unfortunate incidents were far less frequent. That had all recently changed, however, with the stalker's almost daily attacks.

Jerome tidied up his ragged clothes and stepped out of the alley into the Parisian morning. He turned right on Rue de Rivoli and then left next to the Hôtel de Ville, the city hall. When he was close to the river bank he turned right and walked parallel to the Seine. It was not hot enough for the smog to form just yet and a gentle breeze, fresh and awakening, blew off the river. He stood and closed his eyes, enjoying a moment of partial calm before the hectic daily routines began.

A rumbling noise alarmed him and he froze momentarily, yet a second later he was smiling. It was only his stomach demanding food.

I knew I'd forgotten something.

Hunger was a trusted friend and he was used to the feeling, at times forced to forget all about food as other, more pressing issues preoccupied him.

Jerome's attention shifted, the calming meditation gone; he was once again a street cat, searching for the opportunity to score. It was not going to be easy as he so often avoided the day and practised at night. There were places in the city where he could get a free meal but he preferred to stay away from most of them. He was young and the volunteers at the shelters could send him to an orphanage. He was terrified of their good intentions.

No, thank you. That would be worse than home.

He knew how to beg and he knew how to steal. He would rather have worked but at his age it could have led to other legal problems he didn't need. Jerome was not at all proud of the way he was making his living, especially when it involved aggression. He was never mean enough to do anything that would dent his soul, but he was capable of protecting himself if he had to.

He moved away from the river, turning right at the Quai du Louvre, walking by hordes of tourists that gathered in front of the museum.

'Paris is one of the most magnificent cities in the world,' he overheard a guide addressing a band of elderly tourists. 'Nothing can go wrong around here.'

Sure, Jerome thought, rubbing his way through them, *just keep your hands on top of your valuables!*

A dark smile crossed his face when he remembered how Alan, another homeless kid, had tried to teach him to pick pockets.

'It's easy, my friend,' he had told him. 'All you need is the right touch.' Jerome had tried a few times but was forced to quit early on.

'You make a very bad thief,' Alan concluded after Jerome was twice caught red-handed. 'You look so guilty everyone knows you're up to no good.'

There was no pride in the trade of the beggar and Jerome shamelessly peeped into rubbish bins and brushed at their contents, reacting to anything that resembled food.

He passed a little alley on his right, gave it a quick glance and a movement there caught his attention. He stopped and peered in, intrigued by the unusual sight. The alley itself was typically narrow and blocked at its end by a high brick wall. Two garbage trolleys and emergency staircases further minimised and shaped the space, giving the boy he saw there quite a few options for his extraordinary performance; if that indeed was what it was …

The boy jumped from a garbage trolley to a railing on the wall opposite, somersaulting backwards to the stairs and climbing like a spider from window ledge to window ledge. Jerome was mesmerised and it took him a while to realise that the boy had stopped moving and was actually staring right back at him.

He had piercing blue eyes that pinned Jerome to the spot, making him hold his breath. Vaguely, he sensed the boy getting closer – really close. He did not move but focused ahead of him, eyelids heavy and swaying on his feet. The space around the stranger was blurring in a mist, disorientating and confusing, but Jerome was too taken by the nuclei of the eyes to pull away. Then, a hand touched his shoulder and the spell was broken. He shook his head and inhaled deeply, as if coming out of the deep blue sea.

2   Max

'ARE YOU OK?' asked the strange boy as Jerome looked at him with a fixed expression, trying to analyse what had just happened. 'Does it ever close?' the boy grinned, pointing at Jerome's open mouth.

'Sorry.'

He closed his mouth, senses returning to their normal function.

The boy in front of him was about his age, maybe a year senior. They were both of the same height and almost the same build, yet the strange boy had unusually developed muscles, fair skin and honey colour hair in contrast to Jerome's. All in all, he looked like a healthy version of Jerome. Then Jerome noticed the boy's clothes and the boy in turn, so it seemed, became aware of the staring eyes.

'Yes,' he said. 'We shop at the same clothes shop!'

To emphasise his words, the boy held out his trousers from the sides and gave a mock curtsey. It was so comical that Jerome burst out laughing and the boy joined in. He had a deep, hearty rolling laughter. The ice was broken and the boy stretched out his hand, offering it to Jerome.

'Max,' he said and winked, waiting patiently for Jerome to take his hand and shake it. 'What is it then?' he asked, enjoying Jerome's embarrassment.

'What is what?'

'What is your name?'

'Jerome,' he answered shyly.

'Jerome,' the boy repeated the name. 'Nice name. Where do you live, Jerome?'

A bit too direct, a bit too soon. Jerome was not about to reveal all his cards yet. He looked behind his shoulder and absently pulled on his lips, not comfortable with the question.

'I live around,' he finally said.

Max nodded in understanding. 'I live on the street too; I can tell you've been to the shelters.'

Jerome smiled at Max. 'What were you up to over there?' he said, trying to change the subject. 'It was quite amazing.'

'Oh, that,' Max indicated with his thumb at the alley. 'That was a practical exercise. You would be surprised how handy it can be, especially when you're out shopping.' He gave Jerome another wink.

There was a loud rumble and Max shook his head, stepping back, eyes widening in fright. Jerome smiled and Max grinned back.

'Sorry about that,' Jerome said. 'Haven't eaten for some time. My stomach is protesting.'

Max nodded in understanding. 'Say!' he called out. 'Want to come with me and score some food?'

Jerome's eyes instantly narrowed with suspicion.

'Forget it,' Max said immediately, reading the reserved expression on Jerome's face. 'Didn't mean to frighten you. It's my twisted nature to be so direct.' He tapped Jerome on the shoulder with a knowing smile.

'Sorry,' Jerome said again.

'Yes, I got you,' Max chuckled. 'You are constantly sorry. I tell you what, Jerome: I know this lovely bakery not too far from here. I'm going there to score some hot fresh bread. Why don't you come with me? You don't have to do anything, just have a look and if you'd like some bread, maybe we can work something out together.'

That was a fair offer and Jerome took him up on it. 'Let's go,' he said and Max led the way.

It was a good decision since there was safety in numbers and the madman was bound to appear at some point. They headed down Rue des Petits, pushing their way through the pedestrians who were hurrying to work and leisure.

'Look at them,' called Max. 'Just like ants.'

He mischievously bumped into them, poking his tongue out and making hilarious faces. Gradually Jerome relaxed and started to have fun. He couldn't remember the last time he had felt at such ease with anyone. When they got to an intersection, Max stopped Jerome by pressing his hand against his chest.

'In a few steps you will absorb the inimitable scent of the bread,' he mock warned him. 'I hope that you'll be able to control yourself.' Jerome smiled back at him.

'I will do my best,' he promised.

They walked a hundred more metres and then the smell hit them. Max stopped him in front of a little path that ran behind the shops.

'Inhale, my friend,' he ordered Jerome. 'Enjoy.'

'Stop it, you mean bastard.'

The smell didn't pacify the empty ache in his stomach. It only increased the pain, producing new rumbles from his pit. Jerome's mouth filled with juices, crazed by the proximity of the food.

'What do you want me to do?' he asked, shifting weight from leg to leg, the hunger jolting away precaution.

'Good boy,' Max smiled, absently brushing at the wall with his palm, sensing the texture. 'Now, don't you worry. I've done it before. There is a window facing on to this little path. I will climb in there and take some bread. All you have to do is keep the baker busy.'

'What if you get caught?' Whenever anyone told him not to worry he immediately started to do just that.

'Relax, "J",' Max stroked his shoulder, already giving him a nickname. 'You are absolutely risk free. The worst that can happen is that I get caught and you take your leave. Remember, all you are doing is talking to the guy.'

'Agreed,' Jerome finally nodded, exhaling heavily like a boxer before a fight. They shook hands on it. It sounded reasonably safe to Jerome and he needed that meal.

In the most amazing display of balance, Max suddenly spiralled backwards, connecting his right foot to the wall and pushing himself away on impact. He disappeared behind the corner of the bakery and Jerome peered around to find him sitting, smiling, on the window ledge. Max winked and motioned with his palm for Jerome to get a move on.

He went back to the main road to face the front door of the bakery. He was suddenly seized with panic as he recognised the stalker looking at him from across the road. Taking a deep breath, Jerome stepped in, now finding a new reason to follow the plan. A bell rang and the door shut loudly behind him. It was surprisingly spacious inside, shelves stuffed with fresh bread covering the walls and a large counter blocking the door-less opening to the oven room, which was even bigger than the wide shop floor.

Jerome took a glimpse at the baker and swallowed hard. The man was enormous, tall and muscular. He twisted his nose at the newcomer, large floury palms rubbing on his apron. Jerome's eyes ran in all directions, fidgeting where he stood, his cheeks burning with shame. Perhaps that was what Alan meant when he had said Jerome wasn't cut out for theft.

'Yes?' said the baker, looking at Jerome's clothes. 'What do you want?'

Behind the man, in the oven room, the silhouette of Max moved quietly around.

It won't be too long, Jerome thought. 'I want … er … I …' he began to mumble feebly when the entrance door swung open, the ringing bell taking his words away. A man dressed in black entered the shop.

I'm trapped. Jerome tightened his jaw.

To make matters worse, a noise came from the room behind the baker. The three of them turned to look. The baker was the first to react as he came from behind his counter, cursing and grabbing hold of Jerome's shirt.

'I know all about your tricks,' he called and dragged the frightened boy into the oven room, looking up to find Max sitting comfortably on a high shelf, chewing on a fresh bread roll, smiling and feeling completely at ease.

'Get down here,' yelled the baker. 'I've got your accomplice with me.'

Max was obviously not too impressed with the baker's threatening gestures. He glanced down at him with a taunting look in his eyes, perhaps knowing that the baker had no chance of catching him.

'Only met him today,' he masticated his words through the fresh roll, breadcrumbs decorating his face. 'I don't really care about him.' Jerome hoped it to be a diversionary technique. He shook his head and his palms tightened into fists. *You'd better not hand me to the baker, partner,* he thought, grinding his teeth.

Whether or not Max was intentionally diverting the attention away from Jerome, the baker in his fury let go of the boy and instead grabbed a heavy broom. Taking a position under Max he swung the wooden broom sharply, trying to pull him down – but without success. Max effortlessly manoeuvred first to one side then to the other, teasing the baker to a new level of fury.

'Wait till I get my hands on you,' the baker huffed and sweated, swinging wildly and aggressively.

Jerome was absorbed by the chase, forgetting the man in black who stood beside him. A movement to his right startled him and reminded him of the stranger. Turning his head to look, he jumped back in fright.

'What the hell?' he cried as the man in black forcefully coiled into himself.

It was totally surreal, something Jerome had never witnessed before. The vitality seemed to drain out of the man's limbs as he crumpled and swayed gently on his feet, the energy collecting at his core. He froze on the spot momentarily and then he shot out and upwards; extending himself like a liberated giant spring, releasing his compressed energy. In an instant the man landed next to the spot where the overconfident boy was standing.

Max looked surprised but he didn't lose his grip. He sprang out instead, hovering upward and connecting with the railings that were running parallel to the ceiling. He hung there, legs dangling beneath, looking straight at the stranger.

Jerome watched Max as he arrogantly stared back at the man in black. His new friend was very bold, if not very clever and Jerome knew with conviction that he didn't stand a chance.

The stranger coiled into his centre and moved out again, fast and incomprehensible, a blur to the eyes. The next instant he was standing on the railing, his feet almost touching Max's hands. Max realised how desperate the situation was becoming. He might have been a good, even great acrobat, but he was no match for the unnatural abilities of the stranger. He tried one last move to freedom, aiming at the window at the back of the shop, but it was a very weak move.

The man in black stretched his hand out, quick as a whiplash, and disrupted the flow of Max's flight. With a twirl in the air, the boy crashed; landing ungracefully on the floor. The baker's hands, eager for the catch, got hold of Max.

'Now I've got you,' he said joyfully and pulled at Max's hair.

Here was a gap that Jerome could have used for his escape. The baker was busy giving Max some rough treatment and the man in black was still up there on the railings. He couldn't leave though, circumstances made him stay. He felt a responsibility to his new friend and he felt guilty for playing a part in the crime. His own well-being had far less importance than the hope for friendship and loyalty.

'Nice one!' he grumbled at his twisted morals. 'Some kind of survivor I am.'

The stranger landed next to him and the moment was over.

The boys were taken into the shop and the baker held them behind the counter while serving the stranger.

'I thank you, my friend,' the baker told the man in black, handing him the change and a bag full of bread. 'It's about time somebody did something about these criminals. They are everywhere nowadays.'

Jerome wanted the stranger to stay in the shop, dreading what the baker might do to them once he left. The man finished his shopping and turned to leave and the baker pulled on Max's hair, his face twisted in a vengeful grin. Max screeched in pain and Jerome instinctively said, 'Please sir, don't hurt him, he was only doing it for me. It's all my fault.'

The baker didn't care much for Jerome's words, which were accompanied by confirming bobs of Max's head. The stranger, however, stopped his hand that was just reaching for the doorknob. He turned around silently and faced them, making his presence felt even more palpably.

'Yes?' said the baker angrily. He had already thanked the stranger and didn't wish to be disturbed.

'I will take these two with me,' the stranger said in a soft voice and the baker snorted a laugh.

'Don't concern yourself with these boys, sir. I promise you that they'll get what they deserve.'

'I don't doubt it,' replied the stranger, 'but I would still like to take them with me.'

The baker shook his head in determination. 'They are staying here.'

'I am Yves Bertrand, Head of the School of Aikilibrium,' the stranger lifted his chin proudly, 'and I promise you that they will be dealt with.'

A new kind of hostility shone in the baker's eyes. 'I know all about you heathens,' he foamed, swinging his arms in the air. 'I prefer not to be associated with you. Get out or get hurt.'

'Come on kids,' Yves encouraged the boys, ignoring the large man.

The kids started towards the door yet the baker stepped forward and blocked their way. His right hand was holding a rolling pin high, and it was cutting down sharply at his customer.

'You asked for it!' he shouted.

Yves moved in, fast and low, ending up almost on the same spot on which the baker stood. He offset the balance of the startled man, connecting his arm to the large body and throwing it to the floor. Yves stood victorious, his feet tucked beneath the baker's back, keeping him unbalanced, muscles twitching randomly on the floor.

'I thank you, sir.' Yves bowed politely and walked the kids out of the bakery.

3   The Dojo

YVES LED THEM out of the shop and down towards the Seine, tightly holding Max by the shirt. It was nearing noon and the streets were filled with cheerful tourists, frowning, stiff locals on their way to lunch, and of course the cars, the smelly noisy beasts that sullied the otherwise fresh air. They walked on Quai des Tuileries, just on the waterfront and further down on Cours de la Reine, rushing as they crossed the fast and busy road.

Jerome slowed down, allowing the two to walk ahead as he looked over his shoulder. He saw the shadow of the man that prowled behind and he hurriedly joined the others, accidentally bumping into Max who tripped and tried to use it for an escape. Yves didn't lose his grip, sharply jerking Max onwards, aggressively convincing him to stay.

They crossed the river on one of the many bridges and the last familiar point for Jerome was Hôtel des Invalides, which long ago had been a shelter for the disabled. From there on he was in unfamiliar territory, the south part of the city. They followed Yves obediently and quietly; even Max stopped struggling.

Should I stay with them? Jerome thought and tried to reason it out.

The man had saved them from the baker's punishment, but he was also the one who had caught Max and delivered him to the same assailant. Jerome measured Yves for any special features, something to explain his extraordinary performance but the man had none; looking like any other Parisian Jerome had seen – apart, maybe, from the eccentric clothing. Yves was of average height, around 5ft 10in. He had fair hair and skin and an athletic body that radiated strength. There was a parental air about him – at least it felt that way to Jerome and that feeling strengthened his decision to stay.

They stopped at the entrance to a large building and looking up, Jerome saw above the thick glass doors, engraved in bold letters: **THE SCHOOL OF AIKILIBRIUM**. Yves gestured with his hand for them to enter and Jerome scanned the streets and spotted the man who stalked him. He sighed and went in, spine rigid and shoulders held high.

If the finely decorated exterior made an impression on the boys then it was nothing compared to the richness they witnessed on the inside. The whole reception room was made from marble, shiny patterns of white and creamy colours that gave a sense of space and stability. The ceiling was high and the distance to either side of the hall was at least 30 metres. Far across from the entrance was the reception desk and two large oak doors behind it suggested that the hall stretched more deeply than the eye could see. Two men stood next to the reception desk. They wore Aikido training gear, looking serious and severe.

'*Osu*!' they shouted in greeting and rushed towards the newcomers. They stopped in front of Yves and bowed deeply. Yves returned an informal bow, showing his authority.

'Looks like a mental institute to me,' remarked Max. 'See how they are all dressed in white and behaving silly.' He was tidying his shirt, straightening the creases where he was held by Yves.

One of the men in training gear gave him a warning look. Max snorted a laugh and eyed the man. 'I'm afraid that I was right. All we need to do, J, is sew their sleeves together to complete the picture.'

Max had ignored his first warning completely and one of the *aikidoka* – the aikido practitioners – grabbed hold of his hair at the side of his temple, pulling and twisting. He fell screaming.

Yves hardly looked at Max as he explained, 'In our school we demand a high level of discipline and manners. Try to maintain it and we will get along just fine. Misbehave and you will suffer the consequences.' The man holding Max's hair gave an extra twist on Yves' final words and left Max sitting on the floor, cursing to himself.

'Follow me please, gentlemen,' Yves ordered and the two obeyed.

Yves headed to the reception desk where he gave some orders to the man behind the counter. His two disciples stayed next to Jerome and Max, keeping them restrained and quiet. After a few minutes Yves finished and turned to face the two.

'Welcome to my school,' he said. 'This is the most acclaimed institute in the world for Aikilibrium, one of the highest *Skills* of Aikido.' Here Yves stopped to look at the two, judging whether they knew what he was talking about.

'School?' Max raised his voice. 'I'm not going to join any bloody school. You can't make me, Yves.'

Yves sighed, and it might have been a hint for one of the men, who immediately kicked Max in the ribs. 'Raise your hand, please, if you would like to ask a question. And don't call me by my first name.' Yves pointed a finger in warning. 'From now on you shall refer to me as *Sensei*, which means teacher in Japanese.' He waited a second and asked, 'Do you understand?'

'Yes, *Sensei*,' replied Jerome.

'Yes, yes,' answered Max and was rewarded with another kick in the ribs.

'Don't forget to say *Sensei*,' Yves smiled and waited for Max to comply.

'Understood, *Sensei*,' he said with clenched teeth and the *sensei* nodded his head, pleased with the response. He then ordered them to answer all the receptionist's questions.

They were asked about their family and other personal information that Jerome didn't care to reveal. He had left that part of his life long ago. What worried him was the same thing that worried Max, only Jerome was clever enough to conceal it. The last thing he needed was living in an orphanage and the place certainly looked like one.

He inspected the hall and the doors leading to the street while the receptionist was busy with Max. There were no fences or barbed wire outside and the hall was open and vast, not threatening or confining; he didn't think it would be difficult to escape if he had to. He had done it before and, besides, for the time being he wanted to stay, intrigued by the events unfolding.

The receptionist finished his interview and Yves *Sensei* had a few quiet words with him.

'OK boys,' Yves announced as he turned around. 'You are now official property of the school. Please don't try to escape, it would be pointless. You will get caught and punished severely.'

Max's face was contorted in concentration, his chest heaving in quick respiration and his eyes were darting around the hall; a caged animal, surveying his options.

'Follow me please,' Yves ordered, opening one of the oak doors behind the desk. They had to follow, the two men in training gear made sure.

'You bastards!' Max cursed at the guards who encouraged him through the opening with a kick.

Beyond the doors the space was divided differently. There was a long corridor with sliding paper doors along its sides. They walked fast through it, being pushed constantly by their guards. Jerome heard shouts and commotion coming from the doors but he only caught a brief glimpse of the action within; two people dressed in training gear practising some fighting moves. It was interesting to watch but soon he was dragged along the corridor. At the end of the long walk there was another door. This one was very different from the decorated doors they had seen before. It was made of thick iron and looked heavy to open. Yves, with the help of one of the disciples, opened the door and waited for them to move in. He closed the door behind them and rechecked that it was locked.

'Welcome to your future home,' he told the boys. 'Here you will spend quite a bit of time; the duration will be determined by your performance. But I will get into that later on. First let me congratulate you on joining our school. This will be your home and here, hopefully, one of you will excel. This room is the living room, a place you will use for your meditation and reading.' He looked at them questioningly. 'You do know how to read, don't you?'

Max scowled. 'I can read better than you, *Sensei*,' he said irritably.

Yves ignored the attitude; one of his disciples didn't. He smacked Max on the earlobe, causing him to grimace.

'What about you, Jerome?' Yves asked, ignoring the fuss around Max.

'I can read well enough, *Sensei*.'

'Very well then,' Yves smiled. He placed three large books on the table. 'Study these ones like a priest studies the Bible,' he said. 'It's not often that we get youngsters that can read and write. We usually have to teach it verbally and consequently it takes a long time. I hope you will take your studies seriously and do as you are told.'

Max spat on the floor, lips curled in resentment. 'What if we don't get along? You can't make us do a thing. Perhaps it would be better if you let us out of here altogether.'

Jerome was shaking on his feet uncomfortably and biting his lower lip. He liked his friend and didn't want to see him getting in trouble. Yves materialised Jerome's fears as he approached Max without a word, his stare cold and deadly. His right arm reached out, grabbing Max by the shirt and driving forward, picking momentum, forcing Max's legs to lift high in the air. The wall blocked their advance, bringing Max to a sharp halt, speared at the chest by Yves' arm.

'You will never be able to leave,' the *sensei* whispered in a disturbing voice, loud enough for Jerome to hear. 'I only need one of you. The other will serve as stimulation along the way. Like a rabbit in a dog race, something to tempt the runner, to force his progress.' He winked at Max in understanding. 'I know what you are thinking; you think that you won't try too hard. You're thinking you will deliberately do badly in order to be released.'

The pressure of Yves arm was agonising, Max coughed in pain yet managed to defiantly smile back.

'Like I said,' Yves continued, 'all I need is one. The other is expendable, and will be killed.' He looked straight into Max's eyes, like a wolf at his prey. 'The only thing to keep you alive at the moment is the fact that I haven't decided which of you is going to be killed.' The *sensei*'s lips lined tensely. 'I won't hesitate to execute the one that fails to hold the lead, even if he is almost as good as the other.'

4   An Introduction to the Skill

JEROME'S HEART was pounding in his chest. He could not believe his ears. This man, someone he had just met, had promised to execute him or his friend. This was not happening; it didn't feel real. Jerome knew all about parental cruelty; he knew about the harshness of life on the street. This was his first encounter with the professional, methodical malice of institutional abuse. It was very powerful! He wondered if following Yves wasn't the biggest mistake of his life, one that would end his life altogether.

Yves twisted his hips in a move that caused his arm to jerk. At the same instant he let go of Max. It was abrupt and surprising, yet beautifully done, almost artistic. Max's body turned in the air and then landed on top of his shoulders, legs dangling over his head. The master walked back towards the door. He then turned to face them.

'I will revive the *Skill* in the one I choose, beat it out of him if I have to, make him bleed if it will serve the cause. In the end he shall thank me. And as for the other?' he smiled viciously. 'Well, the other will never know, will he?'

Jerome swallowed hard; the man was a total psychopath.

'Tomorrow you shall start training,' Yves continued, 'and I demand that tonight you read the first chapter in the book titled: *Introduction to the Skill*. It will give you a clue as to what you will learn and what can help you achieve it.' He stopped talking and let the two guards step forwards.

'The two men in training gear, or as we call it *dogi*, are your instructors. You shall refer to them as *Sensei* and they will guide you through your studies of the *Skill*. The one on the right is called Henri and the other is George.'

Yves stopped talking as the two men bowed to the boys.

'You will have to do better than your best in order to survive, boys. Tomorrow is a long day and you have reading to do as well as getting acquainted with your new home. We are always watching you so don't embarrass yourselves or us.'

He looked at them one final time. 'Read the first chapter in your book, you might like it. Good night, boys, and welcome to a world of pain!'

Yves and one of his companions bowed and left the room. The other companion, the one named Henri, was left behind.

'Over here, boys,' he called when they had gone, waiting for them to stand by him. 'I will give you a brief description of your new home. You will not physically train here, but you shall use it for your studies and rest.' He ran his arm around the room. 'Here, as Yves *Sensei* told you, is where you will do your reading. Don't you dare damage the furniture.' Max raised an eyebrow in amusement.

'Furniture?' he asked, staring at the two rigid metal chairs and the heavy table. 'We wouldn't be able to damage it even if we wanted to.'

Henri ignored him altogether, leading the way to a door opposite the one they came through. The next room was the bedroom. It was very small, a couple of plain army beds and a little night table that had three drawers and a lamp on top. The walls were white and shiny; Jerome felt chilled and exposed, longing for the streets, for the hazards he was familiar with. Max plainly thought otherwise, licking his lips as if staring at a juicy meal. Beyond the bedroom they saw the bathroom and toilet.

'You must keep this place clean at all times and you must clean it yourself. This is a respectable school; we don't raise pigs here.' It sounded like Henri was enjoying the sound of his own voice and Max comically moved his mouth behind the *sensei's* back, mimicking an endless speech. The last door led to a staircase.

'This is the door to the interview room. Every evening you will go there and report to Yves *Sensei*. The stairs can only be used at designated times or on special request. The rest of the time the door remains shut.'

'What are we to report about, *Sensei*?' asked Jerome.

Henri eyed him distastefully; Jerome could read the hostility there.

Maybe it would be better to behave like Max.

Henri sucked some air between his clenched teeth.

'Every day you will train and report to Yves *Sensei*. Every day he wants to know about your progress and he wants to hear it from you.' He thought for a moment longer. 'Use your time to get acquainted with the place, eat, and study what Yves *Sensei* instructed you to read. It will give you the necessary background for what we do tomorrow. You are about to study the first level of techniques, the ones that will teach you the base for Aikido and the *Skill*. Good night boys. Please do as you are told.'

And that was it! Henri left the room and the boys to wonder what to do next.

Jerome broke the silence. 'I'll take a shower now,' he blurred, 'and then I am going to read that chapter.'

He went to the bedroom and got a towel from the drawer next to his bed. Each boy had his own name tag on every piece of clothing. In the drawers they had a couple of *dogi* or training suits, *yukata* or Japanese robes, some other clothes and creams to soothe aching muscles.

Jerome took off his ragged clothes and threw them in the laundry basket. He went out to the shower, passing by Max, who looked fairly depressed.

'Are you all right?' he asked softly.

'Oh yes, couldn't be better.' It was an obvious lie.

After the shower Jerome returned to the bedroom and saw that Max was missing. He walked into the study room and found him reading.

'Any good?' he asked. He couldn't wait to have a read himself.

'Excellent stuff,' Max answered excitedly, not lifting his eyes from the open page. The reading seemed to have elevated his spirits. 'Get dressed and have a look. I've almost finished the chapter myself.'

Jerome rushed back to the room and got dressed in the *yukata*, not fully dry as yet. All the clothes that he would wear in school from now on would be school issued. All that he wore, ate and used from that time on would be school property. Including himself.

Jerome finished dressing and quickly walked back to the study. Max had closed the book and was on his way out for a shower.

'It's very interesting, I must admit,' he told Jerome and wrapped a towel around his waist. Jerome sat in the metal chair and looked at the cover of the book. It was old but in good condition. He opened the heavy cover, skipped the introduction, and revealed the first chapter. Taking a deep breath he started to read. 'A Brief History of Aikido Relevant to the Development of the *Skill*' was the long title of the first chapter.

There is no way of understanding the *Skill* without a proper historical background as it is a main factor in obtaining the higher arts.

Aikido was invented in the twentieth century by Morihei Ueshiba, also named O Sensei, or the Great Teacher. He was born in 1883 to a well-respected family in the farming village of Tanabe, Japan, and as a child was tutored in *Budo*, martial arts, and spiritual studies, both creating huge impact on the boy and serving as the base for his later findings. As he grew up he continued to practise the ancient arts passionately but failed to generate the same kind of enthusiasm when participating in business ventures, showing difficulties in finding his place in the modern materialistic Japan.

His interest in *Budo* compelled him to join the army in the war against Russia where he excelled in bayonet fighting. He was pleased with his achievements but as he returned home he was troubled yet again by anxiousness and unfulfilled feelings.

In the year 1912 he led an expedition of fifty families to the northern island of Hokaido where they established a village called Shirataki. There he studied martial arts under the notorious *Daito Ryu* master Sokaku Takeda, but was left unaccomplished spiritually.

At the end of 1919 he left Hokaido and returned to his home town, where his father had fallen seriously ill. On the way to Tanabe he was motivated to make a detour and meet Master Onisaburo Deguchi, the director of the new religion *Omoto Kyo* and he spent a few days with him, engrossed in reflection and meditating. When he returned home he learned that his father had passed away and he was left unstable, roaming the mountain surrounding his home town like a mad man.

In 1920 he moved to live in Ayabe, the *Omoto Kyo* religion headquarters, feeling the need for spiritual guidance. Master Deguchi received him warmly, opened a *dojo*, martial art school, for him and ordered Ueshiba to compose a new form of *Budo* using the philosophical principles of the *Omoto Kyo*.

Many adventures and tragedies befell Ueshiba during this time, such as losing two of his children to disease in 1920 and the persecution of *Omoto Kyo* members by the authorities in 1921. Yet the most significant incident for his development occurred in 1924, when he took a trip to Mongolia, serving as a bodyguard to his mentor, on a quest to establish the New Jerusalem. Although the trip itself was a shambles with almost tragic consequences, it still presented Ueshiba with the biggest discovery of his life.

There was more to read on the next page but that wasn't part of Jerome's assignment for the night. Instead he looked at some of the diagrams at the back of the book, the ones referring to the bit he had just read. They showed all kinds of exercises and techniques. Jerome couldn't figure out much from them, but they all shared one thing he could spot straight away: an abundance of circular motions.

The door to the bathroom burst open and a smiling Max came out dripping water. Jerome closed the book and went to the bedroom. They stayed awake for a long time, sharing an excitement that was mixed with fear and worries, and it was late when they finally fell asleep.

* * *

'Boys,' said Henri. 'Pay attention please. Today we will start to learn essential Aikido skills. In those I refer to breakfalls, strikes, and the turning of the body's centre. In addition you will learn how to connect to your centre. This is only the beginning, the basics. Remember, Aikido uses the opponent's power for execution of techniques such as throws and locks. Aikilibrium, the higher *Skill*, uses all the immediate powers surrounding.'

'*Osu, Sensei*,' shouted Max, miming a respectful expression. He felt that Henri was talking too much. If they had to be there then he preferred to get on with it.

Henri sensed the insulting attitude. He reacted immediately, punishing the rude youngster. His right hand connected, open palm, with Max's left cheek. Max was quick but couldn't anticipate the move in time to counter. The sound of the slap echoed across the empty training room. Max rubbed his cheek, his mouth twisted in pain and anger.

'Calm down,' whispered Jerome, dreading Max's temper.

'No problem, J,' Max smiled. He was staring at Henri murderously and Jerome thought that Henri was actually frightened.

They were in the room nicknamed the Plain *Dojo*, for the very reason that the space was mainly vacant. Near the wall they saw a few punch and kick pads, a weapon rack and that was all. It was designed intentionally empty, to avoid any external stimulation that might distract the students from their goal. The simplicity in the School of Aikilibrium, however, didn't come cheap as was demonstrated by the high quality of the materials composing the room. The walls were covered with smooth planks of wood that sweetly scented the well-ventilated hall, a remnant of living nature. A narrow and decorated tiled patch, at the entrance of the room led to a floor covered with *tatami* mats.

It was not a large *dojo*, only a hundred metres square but it was big enough for two. *Skilled* fighters were used to training in small secretive halls, although Jerome was certain that Yves would have put them on display if it brought him profit. The whole place stank of money and greed. Yves kept them hidden and Jerome was positive the reason was to conceal their identity and to minimise their chances of escape.

The walls of the Plain *Dojo* were padded one metre up from the floor to give extra protection for the fighting drills. Students of the *Skill* were an expensive investment. Simply maintaining the special equipment and paying the rent were substantially costly. Understandably Yves took many measures to keep practice controlled and protected, not wanting his protégés hurt. Not unless it was done deliberately by him or at his command. Nobody in the school dared to hurt his students without permission. Henri was one who had that permission.

Max stopped rubbing his cheek and clenched his jaw. There was a red patch, resembling the large palm of Henri, on his face. If any instructor had to hurt a student, they had to do it just as Henri did, superficially and painfully. Enough to sting the flesh and the pride. Enough to bring about discipline. Jerome kicked Max when Henri was not watching. He shook his head at him, signalling with a finger across his sealed lips. He didn't like to see Max getting hurt.

Henri demonstrated a forward breakfall, starting with a low and round fall.

'The main objective of this drill is not to get hurt while falling. It is the most basic breakfall.' Max copied him with ease, his natural acrobatic skills coming in handy. Jerome managed to roll but it took him a little longer.

'Come on, J,' Max teased. 'We'll never make it to lunch like that.'

Henri approached and slapped him across the face. This time on the other cheek.

'No one speaks during training. No one apart from the *sensei*.'

Max nodded in conformation, his eyes flushed with tears of pain.

'Do I make myself clear?' Henri asked, loud and sharp.

'*Osu, Sensei*,' answered Max, tightening his lips.

They went through the low breakfall exercise for an hour.

When the time came to train on the high breakfall, Henri ordered them to sit as he explained. 'The high breakfall, like everything else in Aikido, is carried out with emphasis on the centre of the body.'

He stopped to demonstrate how he stretched his head and spine, creating the right sensation for practice.

'You must practise a lot of these drills and indeed you shall in the days to come. It is the basis for the whole art.'

They rolled constantly, dazed and nauseated, the bony ridge of their lower backs swelling up. Henri stopped them for an hour's lunch break, taking them back to their quarters.

'Enjoy the little breather,' he grumbled and left.

They ate, replaced their sweaty *dogi* with clean ones and lay briefly on the hard floor. Before they knew it Henri came back and led them to the Plain *Dojo*.

'In order to create a circular motion, a person needs a good centre, an axis to rotate upon. You will practise how to create awareness of that centre and once you have mastered that you will have to learn where to place it.' Jerome raised his hand to ask a question. Henri allowed him to speak.

'What do you mean by saying "where to place our centre", *Sensei*?'

Henri seemed to like that question. Henri seemed to like talking the best.

'You will learn to place your centre and bodyweight on different places of your feet, like your heel or the ball of the foot. Later on you will learn where to place it in relation to your opponent's position. Another important matter, as it can determine the outcome of your technical execution.' To emphasise his words, Henri stopped explaining and demonstrated two kinds of pivots, one using the heel as an axis and the other the ball of the foot.

'We will start with these turns,' Henri ordered and once again they resumed training.

As before, Max was doing exceptionally well, performing with ease and confidence. Jerome struggled a bit, but he got there soon enough. Next they practised strikes and the way to deliver them from the centre.

'It is vital that your strikes be derived from your core. You might be able to extract a lot of power with your limbs but it is a very different level of energy when it comes from your centre.'

He ordered Jerome to pick up a square punching pad and to rest it against his body. Henri placed his fist on the pad. He concentrated a minute and then a shudder went through his body. He didn't really punch, his hand didn't lose contact with the pad. Jerome, however, felt a huge power surging into the pad and through it to his body. His legs lifted off the floor and he flew backwards. The padded wall stopped his flight and with a grunt he dropped to the floor. Max laughed heartily, tears in his eyes and Henri looked quite pleased with himself.

A fine bunch of sadists, Jerome grimaced. *Does everyone here have to be that cruel?*

It was a question he would repeat to himself on numerous occasions during the following days.

They waited for Jerome to return and then they started to practise. Henri worked them tirelessly, hardly allowing them any break.

'You will need to be a warrior to survive. Don't you dare stop before I tell you to.' They didn't, concentrating firmly on their training, well behaved over all. Discipline, however, didn't come that easily to Max; he got smacked twice more before the day ended. When they were done, Henri escorted them back to their living quarters and locked the door.

'This is heaven, I tell you,' Max shouted and jumped on top of his bed.

'What about a shower?' Jerome reminded him. Yves ordered them to shower daily and it was a task Jerome liked. He kept that fact a secret because he knew how much Max hated it.

'Come on,' he called. 'You'll feel much better afterwards.' He didn't wait for him though and a moment later Jerome was standing under the steaming water of the shower, washing the sweat and dirt away. He closed his eyes and tried soothing his aching muscles and bones. Never before had he undergone such intense physical activity.

He came out of his meditation with the heavy pounding of Max on the shower door. 'Hurry up, J,' he shouted. 'Don't spend the whole day in there.'

Jerome sighed and raised his arm blindly, feeling for the tap. He tightened the valve and stepped out, wrapped in a towel.

'It's so nice to be clean,' he declared, walking by Max.

'You smell like a madam.'

Dinner was ready in the dinning room. There was a hatch through which the food was brought. They never met the people who delivered the food. Jerome waited for Max before he started to eat. They were both dressed in *yukata*.

'You liked today's training, didn't you?' Jerome asked during the meal.

'Yes I did,' Max replied with a mouth full of food. 'I love the acrobatic stuff and the fighting techniques. I think I'll make a good fighter.'

'I think you will,' Jerome agreed. 'You were punching and kicking the pads almost as powerfully as Henri did.

'Oh yeah, I'm the man!'

Jerome tried to smile but couldn't: the cruel competition Yves had set before them overshadowed any sense of pleasure.

Look at him smiling. He envied Max for the way he tended to forget about his unfortunate situation. Max didn't look bothered at all. Then Max spoke and his words came as a total shock.

'We will not let him get away with it,' he declared in a chilling voice, not specifying what he was referring to. Jerome stared wide-eyed at him, he had no doubt what the topic was. Max hadn't forgotten it after all.

'What do you suggest we do?' he asked.

'I say that if it ever comes down to it and Yves wipes one of us out then the other shall avenge him.'

Jerome swallowed hard. He was scared of what Max was suggesting.

'How?' he asked, exhaling through a tight chest.

'I propose that the one remaining kills the bastard. Make him pay with his life for the life he takes.'

5   Building the Foundations: Dai Ichi Kihon

Tanabe, Japan, 1891

'A FATHER CAN ONLY give his best efforts for the sake of his child.' Long ago, in his childhood, Yoroku Ueshiba had overheard these words at his father's house. As a young boy he had never understood the meaning of the words but now he looked at his son and knew their meaning, inside and out.

Young Morihei was the only male offspring in the Ueshiba family and the health of the boy's body and soul was a constant worry to the proud father. Yoroku was a wealthy, well-respected man in his village and had sat on the village council for many years. He had three daughters already and the birth of his son, Morihei, was supposed to complete his well-planned picture of happiness. He was happy, undoubtedly, but the happiness was soaked with worries, and plenty of them.

Morihei had only recently turned eight years old and he was small for his age and a little frail. Yoroku wanted his son to succeed in the newly modernised Japan and he knew that his son would need to be powerful if he was to excel. He had sent Morihei the year before to the shrine in Jizodera, forcing him to learn the holy scripts of the *Shingon* religion. The boy obediently followed his father's desires, to an extent that Yoroku had never expected. Deities were running in the boy's head during the day and leading his dreams while sleeping at night and Yoroku decided to teach Morihei swimming and *Sumo* wrestling, two earthly means of survival. Religious studies and physical activities were great tools to strengthen his son but they turned out to be his son's main obsession. Yoroku was worried yet had enough means to support his son into the future; he could allow him a bit of dreaming, something he himself was denied as a boy.

Sitting outside his house, he watched his son practising sword moves, the boy reciting battles he envisioned in his dreams.

'Morihei,' Yoroku called him a few times, the boy fighting demons in another world, the words taking time as they cut a path to his consciousness.

'Yes, Father,' he finally reacted and drew closer to him, replacing his wooden sword at his belt.

'Sit next to me, son. Relax with the morning's beauty.'

It was the end of the summer and soon the seasons were to change.

Yoroku was a farmer and knew his days according to the elements. He took in the surroundings, slowly turning his head to catch a panoramic view. It was an unusually bright day, following weeks of rain and dark clouds, exposing the shimmering countryside. Tanabe was stretched fairly flat to all sides, dotted with modest houses and lined with narrow dirt roads that divided the fields. It was bound by the ocean on one side and the mountains on the other, cutting the skyline high and bulky.

Yoroku had four acres of land and he loved to work his fields, enjoying being close to the cycles of nature: birth, growth, adulthood, old age and death.

'What will become of you, Morihei? What does the future hold?'

He was talking to himself more than asking, his left palm tenderly patting his son's head. Morihei was finding it hard to concentrate on his father's words, his mind drifting in and out of his fantasies. Yoroku smiled and sighed at his son's silence, knowing it is better to get busy than to talk.

'Come, let's go swimming,' he called and Morihei jumped to his feet, following Yoroku ecstatically, holding a wooden staff instead of the sword with which he had earlier been practising.

They reached the little stream and the boy ran around the rocky banks, banging his staff on the rocks and chanting to himself.

'And Kukai struck the ground and water gushed out as a river, obedient to the Daishi's will.'

He drifted inside the stories of Kobo Daishi, envisioning himself as the magical Buddhist priest, casting his spells on nature. Yoroku watched, his mixed emotions speaking through his body, changing from a stiff back and heavy frown to light hearted laughter that shook his shoulders. He wanted his son to be realistic but couldn't deny him the innocent joy of youth.

They finally had their morning swim and Yoroku lovingly helped Morihei improve his buoyancy technique, keeping his wide palms beneath his son's belly. The boy did well and Yoroku allowed him a momentary break as he sat drying in the sun. Morihei stretched up and stuck his palms down into the water, lifting his arms up and watching the water raining down from within his fingers.

'What is the meaning of that?' Father asked, as always intrigued by his son's inner world.

'It is the magic of Kukai, Father.' Morihei smiled shyly. 'He could make the rain come down by using the right Sutras.'

Yoroku returned the smile, his eyes at the same level of his son's, sharing the inflamed images. Yoroku knew of the stories of Kukai, the founder of the Shingon religion. *Shingon* plainly meant 'True Words' and indeed some of the Sutras used by Kukai were supposed to be very powerful indeed; the 'Lotus Sutra', to name one of many.

Yoroku played with Morihei a while, pretending to be the Emperor, begging the Kobo Daishi for rain. He watched Morihei performing the rituals he observed in the Shingon shrine and the worries penetrated his mind again.

When the game was over he led the boy back to the yard in front of their house, it was time for a wrestle. Yoroku was known to be a powerful man all around the region and he loved to exercise his body, advocating *Sumo* as the most important sports of all. For a few weeks now he had been teaching his son the basics of the fight, proudly observing the quick progress of his offspring.

'Are you ready?' he asked Morihei as soon as they finished stretching.

The boy nodded in enthusiasm and crouched low, one hand held high and the other touching the floor.

'*On a Yahashano*,' he chanted, pretending to hold the 'sword that cuts illusions' in his right hand and the Sutra of Wisdom, in his left.

Yoroku recognised the Mantra and its related deity, Bosatsu Monju. He burst out laughing and was caught unguarded, almost losing his footing on the wet ground. He overheard laughter coming from behind and he turned to face Yuki, his beloved wife. The boy used the break in concentration and charged again, this time toppling the big man down.

They rolled on the floor, encouraged by the cries of Yuki and the boy's imaginary world of gods and demons. Yoroku at long last got hold of Morihei and pinned him to the ground, tickling him in his soft armpits. The boy giggled and then hollered loudly, a ball of pleasure on the floor. Yuki called on him to stop and Yoroku pulled back, his son at his side.

'What will become of you, Morihei?' he asked yet again, flicking clumps of mud from his clothes. The boy looked back at his father, but his eyes were focused far and away.

'I want to be a priest, Father, just like the Kubo Daishi and I want to be as strong as a mighty deity, protecting this world from wrongs and helping the weak.'

Father nodded at the dreaming youth. 'I hope you'll be able to protect and help yourself first,' he mumbled, but the boy, who had already wriggled his way out, was not listening.

Quietly Yoroku sat there a little longer, suspecting that by trying to strengthen the boy he might have only planted new obsessions. Little did he know how right he was, that he had actually shown his son the life he would eventually choose.

6   Stomach Aches

Paris, 2172

No one could pinpoint the real cause of the transformation that transpired in Ueshiba *Sensei* but he was a different man when he came back from Mongolia. He had changed; anyone who had known him before would say so. For some unknown reason he was able to perform incredible deeds. He could make himself so heavy that no one could pick him up. He could make himself light, stepping over delicate china teacups that were filled to the brim, while spilling none of it. Ueshiba *Sensei* could roar like a lion and move in unexplained ways, sometimes disappearing altogether. He himself was baffled by these strange abilities but less than a year after his return from Mongolia he was enlightened and suddenly it all made sense.

Legend tells us that he was outside his house, standing by the well when the light struck him and he touched the *Skill*. At that moment he knew it for what it was and Aikido was born. Finally he could explain to himself the great feats that he was able to perform.

* * *

THE STOMACH ACHES started on the third day in the early hours of the morning and woke the boys. Max was the first to rush to the toilet, coming out sweating but not relieved. Jerome was standing outside, hopping from one leg to the other and clutching his abdomen.

'Hurry up,' he begged. 'I'm dying out here.' Max stepped out of the way, allowing him quick access to the toilet.

'Don't mind the smell,' he warned and returned to bed. It was four o'clock in the morning, an hour and a half before they were due to wake up. Jerome came back to bed, pale and shaken by the excruciating pain. He collapsed with a moan onto his bed.

'We probably ate something foul last night,' Max suggested.

'Probably so.' *Or was it last night's promise of vengeance?*

Jerome remembered how he had shivered soundlessly as Max proposed the killing of Sensei.
You will kill for me? Why?
'Are you listening to me, brother?'
Brother? Me? Could it be that you actually care about me?
'Jerome?'
'I agree,' Jerome whispered.
'What was that?'
'I agree! Yves will not get away with a killing. I will avenge it even if it's the last thing I do!'
Brother! Jerome now dared echoing the word inside his head. He had tears in his eyes, his stomach muscles twisted by the pain, *Brother of mine...*

They could sleep no more that night and at breakfast they hardly touched the food, afraid of losing control over their bowels. The pain, they soon realised, wasn't accompanied by diarrhoea or nausea although its acuteness forced them to be aware of it the whole day long.

At the usual time Henri escorted them to the Plain *Dojo* and took them through the same routines of the first day, working them tirelessly. They practised their breakfalls, strikes and turns. They didn't know how they managed that day, pained and lacking sleep, but they did.

At night Jerome reported to Yves about their condition. *Sensei* was instantly irritated with him, accusing him of trying to avoid training.

'A little pain won't kill you,' he concluded and sent Jerome away. Miserably he had to inform Max that there was no release from training due to their medical condition.

'The bastard!' Max shouted angrily and beat the mattress with his fists.

They went to sleep hoping that they would be rid of the pain in the morning. It didn't go as they hoped.

The next day they woke up the same way, with the pain in the early hours of the morning. It happened the day after that and in the days to follow. Gradually they developed tolerance to the pain, learned to accept its presence. They were aware of it at all times but it didn't feel as sharp as before. Yves was not worried about it. Pain was only harmful if it was a symptom of a disease. This wasn't the case and he knew it.

The Informer came to see him one night, two weeks after the boys had arrived. The Informer was the one who secretly observed the training. It was the best system of controlling what was really going on. It was one of the secrets of Yves' success in reviving the *Skill*. He kept his eyes on his students the whole time. Even if he didn't do it in person.

'How are things?' he asked, not lifting his eyes from his paperwork.

'Over all it's good, but Jerome hardly eats.'

Yves raised an eyebrow. 'That's not unusual; most of them tend to fast due to the pain.'

The Informer looked almost insulted. 'I know that,' he replied. 'But as far as I can see he is losing too much power, as though he is trying too hard.'

'What do you suggest?' Yves sighed and leaned backwards in his dark armchair. 'He will learn soon enough that the pain is not related to the food. Perhaps then he will start eating again.'

'You leave a lot to chance. I hope you know what you're doing.'

Yves smiled at the Informer. There was no need to be hard on him. He was young and not fully experienced in the process. 'Calm down,' he told him. 'I've done it a hundred times before. Each student behaves differently but ninety-five per cent of the time they have no real problem with the pain. I actually wish that it was the problem. At least then we would know how to control the process. You will see that the main difficulty will be to revive the *Skill* in him.'

The Informer didn't want to argue any more. There was nothing much to argue about. Yves was far more experienced than him. As he said, he had been through the process hundreds of times before. 'I find it amazing that all your experience and all your successful trials in reviving the *Skill* didn't teach you the precise mechanism of it.' He laughed briefly.

Yves was not smiling. He sneered angrily at the youngster. 'Don't forget your manners boy, especially in the presence of your betters!'

'Sorry, *Sensei*.' The Informer dropped his eyes to the floor. He was pressing the *sensei* on a painful truth that was shared by many Aikidoka worldwide. For years Yves had tried to identify the way the *Skill* was developed. He was very successful in producing *Skilled* Aikido practitioners, but he hadn't found anything new about the process. It was true that he had refined and improved it but he didn't really understand how it worked.

Yves was not a good or just man, never hesitating to lie if it got him what he wanted. One thing though – he was always honest with himself. He excused the Informer and sat hidden by the dimness of the office, slouching in the leather armchair, cursing himself and others and shaking his head from time to time. His dreams of exploration and fame had been shattered long ago, yet he didn't give up. A couple of years ago he had started looking for glory elsewhere; desperately he had moved on a dangerous course, renewing the search for Aikido's Holy Grail: *The Lost Book of the Skill*. It was the book the founder, Ueshiba *Sensei*, was thought to have written, yet no one had ever seen it or knew its whereabouts.

It was roughly two hundred years since the founder had died and there was very little evidence as to the book's existence. For years upon years *Aiki* crusaders had hunted for the book. Legend said that within the book lay the secret to the biggest question of all: the precise process for reviving 'The *Skill* of Diversity', the ultimate *Skill* of the founder.

Researchers believed that Ueshiba *Sensei* had hidden the book at the end of the Second World War, after the Americans had dropped the two nuclear bombs on Japan. Being a sensitive human being it had hurt him to learn how governments were using great inventions of the human mind to kill and harm others. He decided that he would have no part of it. He wouldn't let them get their hands on his invention.

He continued to demonstrate his abilities but taught only the basic level of his art. That is really what was left of his great expedition into the human soul: the martial art techniques, some vague philosophy about love and harmony, and many scattered clues to the *Skill*.

All of these clues had been gathered over a hundred years ago and were commonly used by the instructors of the *Skill*. Yves wanted more and he hoped to find the book, to go down in history as the one who established the correct system of acquiring The *Skill* of Diversity. He couldn't care less about the way the *Skill* would then be used.

There had been little gains he had made by himself during his twenty years of teaching the *Skill*, such as the stomach ache, brought about by a slight poisoning of the water, thereby giving the students the necessary awareness of their centre. Yves had statistically proven that it accelerated the process.

He shook his head and tidied his paperwork, looking at the message from Calvin. It filled him with an excitement mixed with worry. He had sent Calvin to find the book and Calvin was getting nearer. He hoped that it would be brought to him soon. The deal with Calvin had cost him dearly. What he had to give in return was too risky.

Yves sighed to himself. He knew that he had cut a deal with the devil.

In the *dojo* the boys were pushed through the pain, their instructor oblivious to their complaints and suffering. It was all part of a bigger plan, but they were not allowed in on the secret.

A month went by in which they exercised on a daily basis, hardly having enough time to rest. It left them bruised, tired and hungry, yet there was no escape from the daily stress. The bruises accompanied the occasional accidents. Fatigue resulted from intensive training and lack of sleep. Hunger was always present since they didn't eat much, the abdominal pains annihilating their desire for food.

Amazingly, and regardless of the hardship and exhaustion, they had made huge progress. Breakfalls, strikes and turns had improved beyond recognition. Max, with his natural abilities, was doing far better than Jerome; something that continually worried the latter. He couldn't forget Yves' words and knew how dangerous his position was. It didn't slow his efforts though. Jerome was not a quitter. He would give them his best, regardless of the results.

It was their first day of the second month in the School for Aikilibruim and it was time to progress to the next stage. So far, they had trained apart from each other, preparing their own bodies, gaining balance and strength. The only drills incorporating physical connection were the strikes, and even those were experienced against the punching or kicking pads.

Today, for the first time, they were to train with each other.

7 Locks and Throws: Dai Ichi Kihon

O Sensei was a methodical man and in no time at all the first book of the art was published. It was the book of the martial art techniques he composed for Aikido, that is known in modern days as basic Aikido or *Dai Ichi Kihon* – the first level of techniques. These techniques are the foundation of the art, serving as the bridge between the normal conception of life and the higher and much wider understanding of it.

All these techniques follow simple principles intentionally, allowing the students to concentrate on details usually missed by other martial arts. Basic Aikido is practised in almost laboratory conditions, on a flat surface, either in standing or sitting positions, without competition or fighting. To make matters simpler, each technique always starts with the assumption that the attack has already been identified. One of the hardest elements of combat is identifying the attack, its timing and direction. Basic Aikido doesn't deal with that major hurdle. It starts from the point where it is already known which attack is coming. It is a graceful place, the key to the magic of Aikido, the gateway for the higher arts.

* * *

HENRI *SENSEI* WALKED into the Plain *Dojo* where the two boys sat in *seiza*, the Japanese style of sitting on the knees, waiting for class to begin. It was part of the normal etiquette of any *dojo* and one of the many things that they had to learn. It might look silly and overly pompous but Yves *Sensei*, as it was with O Sensei the founder, knew the true benefit of it. It taught the students discipline and focus and increased their inner power. These were qualities too dear to be ignored.

Henri *Sensei* went straight to the centre of the *dojo* and sat in *seiza*. His back was turned to the boys.

'*Shomen ni rei!*' Jerome shouted the command and in response they all bowed to the front. On the wall was a miniature shrine sitting on top a shelf, the *Kami Dana*. Next to it and to either side, were little pots with branches of green leaves – the evergreen *Sakaki* to attract the spirits. One of the chores the boys had in the school was replacing the water in the pots daily and changing the branches themselves every three days. The boys were always observed and kept secure as they worked around the *dojo*, with no chance of escape.

Twice a day they had to clean, tidy and organise the school, a tradition that proved beneficial to the boys and as a bonus maintained the school in excellent condition. It was a common system in Japan, especially in the martial arts world. *Uchi Deshi*, devoted students who lived in the school, were expected to do all sorts of chores set for them by their masters and for their masters' benefit.

O Sensei used to demand that his students push him up the climb to a shrine in Iwama. Some students told how *Sensei* would lean on them with his full weight. It was good for them, so he said; it developed their instincts. Shioda *Sensei*, another one of the old masters, demanded that his students bathe him. He expected them to know the water temperature he desired and would change the desired temperature almost daily. Consequently he would end up throwing fits of anger at unsuccessful students. It was good for them, he argued; it developed their ability to read a situation in advance. There were numerous stories like that, all with the same conclusion: 'Whatever *Sensei* tells you to do is good for you.' It went well with the system, just like the cleaning of the school or tending to the *Sakaki* branches.

Under the shelf holding the little shrine was a picture of a man in *dogi*. It was a large picture with an impressive frame. The man in the picture was Jacques *Sensei*, the founder of the School of Aikilibrium.

Master Jacques was a legend, an explorer of the art and a leading figure at the time when the *Skill* re-emerged, fifty years after the death of the founder of Aikido. At first his skill was named '*Aiki Special Movements*', Aikilibrium was a name he thought up later on. Jacques *Sensei* was one of the original members of the International Aikido Board, formed to regulate and monitor the various *Skills*. Through the Board came international recognition of the Aikilibrium *Skill* and with Jacques' help Aikido won a respectable governing body. In short, Master Jacques earned his place in history and a place on the wall, under the shrine.

After they bowed to the shrine, Henri *Sensei* turned on his knees, still sitting, to face them.

'*Sensei ni rei*!' Jerome shouted and they bowed again, this time to show mutual respect between teacher and students. Max found all the formalities a little too tedious and rigid. He was often punished for not paying attention, or even worse, yawning during the formal procedures. After bowing they jumped to their feet, standing to attention, waiting for Henri's instructions.

'Today we will start the second stage of the first level of techniques. This means that from now on we will practise in pairs and not just shadow exercises. We will concentrate on locks and throws.'

Max looked excited and he winked at Jerome.

'Now, before we start practising I would like to explain the principles behind the techniques and what is to be achieved.'

There he goes again, thought Max. *Ranting and raving about stuff we already know.* He sighed quietly, bracing himself for a long speech.

The night before, they had been told to read the chapter about locks and throws and they had enjoyed reading it, anticipating training – not a speech …

'Hey!' Henri called. 'Are you paying attention?'

'*Osu Sensei*!' Max shouted. He looked sincere when he answered. He had learned how to conceal his true feelings.

Henri was smiling broadly. 'The main thing to understand is the nature of those techniques. Scholars believe that when Ushiba *Sensei* composed the techniques of basic Aikido he did it with a specific aim. He chose those as preparation to the higher arts and the proof for this assumption is the impractical nature of most of the techniques. Unlike other martial arts that relate their techniques to the fight itself, Aikido techniques, on the whole, cannot be used in real fight situations. Knowing the vast knowledge of O Sensei in practical techniques it is hard to conceive that he wouldn't know the techniques were not practical. Historians think that he did it on purpose, pointing out the way to the true achievement.'

He stopped and waited for questions to come. They didn't. A question would only prolong the agony. The boys' legs were aching, their spines painfully stretched.

Yves *Sensei* had taught them on the first week that the body was just a vessel, nothing more. 'You are the captain of this ship,' he said as they crouched in a low and awkward position; muscles burning in pain, particularly the ones around the thighs and the lower back. 'The pain will teach you not to give priority to the body. Surrender to the posture, until you are shaped as a sculpture. With time and practice you will need less attention to maintain the position and the mind will be free to explore. The body is only the mould of the soul, its jailer.'

It was the first week of training and they were pained and shocked beyond belief yet Yves looked at them, sweating over the drills, with indifference, turning his head away as their bodies blurred by spasms of pain.

'When you pass the point of uncontrollable body movement, as you experience now...' he stopped again and waited for them to reply with '*Osu Sensei*', dragging their suffering to greater heights. 'After that point you will find detachment. You will have no choice. Only then can you step aside and look at your body, indifferent to its petty calls.'

Jerome was in agony yet he sensed each and every word as if under a spell. He was aware of the stages Yves was talking about and he was aware of them as they were described by the *sensei*. He had passed that point and prevailed – a sense of euphoria descended upon him. He relaxed, enjoying the awkward position, pleased with his efforts. The pain was pulsating, but it came from a very far away place. It was a wonderful lesson that remained fresh in the boys' minds, yet it was easier to avoid the pain altogether. That is why the boys remained silent now – waiting for Henri to continue.

'Locks and throws follow the principle of momentum, stressing the need for flow. It is not easy to perform – you will need to cooperate with each other as in a role play, maintaining connection at all times. It is hard to do, yet on top of everything you are also required to deliver the moves from and to your centre.' Mentioning the centre aggravated the tenderness in their stomachs they hopelessly tried to ignore. Henri was a merciless teacher, smiling broadly at their efforts to conceal the pain.

'You are probably asking yourselves about the true fighting,' he continued a second later. 'I'm afraid you will have to wait for that, because real fighting will come much later, and only if we decide that you are ready and ripe.' A moment of silence. 'Let's get on with it,' he commanded, pumped by the power of self importance.

'About bloody time, Master Nothing!' Max growled, yet the sound of their feet sliding into Kamai, the fighting stance, muffled his words.

Jerome couldn't believe how quickly the day went on after that. The first technique was called *Ikkyo* in Japanese and they rehearsed it until lunch break. The tiring month of shadow training started to pay off; the turns presenting themselves as a sensible defence against full momentum attack although it was harder to perform with a partner.

'This is Aikido,' Henri reminded them as they struggled with each other. 'You have to work together in order to advance and understand the technique. *Uke*, the person the technique is initiated upon, should help the other and guide him in the appropriate direction.' At first Henri's words confused them; why should anyone help his assailant through the assault?

Ikkyo was an elementary technique of Aikido, concentrating on turning an opponent's bent elbow around the imaginary axis drawn between his palm and shoulder. A correct execution causes an opponent to lose his balance and collapse to the floor.

'Follow his lead, avoid resistance.' Henri instructed Jerome from the side as he took the part of the *uke*. Jerome tried to follow the instructions but his instincts would pull his body away from the direction of the technique as soon as he sensed that he was losing his balance.

'You are going to get hurt this way,' Henri barked. He came close and ordered Max to step aside. 'The only reason you didn't get hurt so far is because your partner doesn't know how to execute the technique properly.' He took Max's position in front of a confused

Jerome and bowed at him. Jerome returned the courtesy, giving a deeper bow to his superior. 'There are a few reasons why you should be a good *uke* and I will demonstrate them for you.' He took Jerome's arm in an *Ikkyo* hold and moved in a wide sweeping turn. Jerome, his instincts telling him to stay put, got splattered on the floor. He got up shaken to the waiting arms of Henri. 'Being a good *uke* means that you react with the *tori*, the one who takes you down. It's a basic Aikido principle; you use his energy and his destination to be ahead of him, to drain him of the harmful intention.'

Jerome started to understand. The *uke* didn't allow the *tori* the upper hand really. He was only moving with his momentum, stripping him from the capability of damage.

It was difficult to apply though, and Jerome's body resisted the move, no matter how hard he tried to fight against it.

'Get up and try again!'

'Osu Sensei!'

'Come on Jerome, you can do it.'

'Shut it Max, or you are next!'

On and on Henri kept going, executing the move again and again, and pushing Jerome to perform better. It didn't go very well; Jerome couldn't react as quickly as the *sensei* demanded.

'Get up, try again!'

'Osu Sensei!' Henri's face was red, his lips curled angrily down, assuming that Jerome's incompetence was intentional. He dropped him down mercilessly, thumping the student onto the floor. Jerome had no choice but to comply, to get up and be taken down again, knees banging heavily onto the *tatami*, focusing on connecting his other arm with the floor before his head would.

After an agonising fifteen minutes Henri let go of him. Jerome hadn't performed well but Henri gave up. He ordered Jerome to change roles, to become the *tori*. Jerome tried to take *Sensei* down and was met with the full resistance of Henri's body. He couldn't rotate Henri's arm or even move him an inch.

'This is the reason an *uke* actively participates in performing the technique; helping and sometimes guiding the *tori* in the right direction.' He ordered Jerome to execute again and this time he moved with him perfectly. Jerome couldn't believe the ease with which the technique flowed. 'When you allow the *tori* to lead you, you help him find the right path and you protect yourself as well. There is a third reason for following the *tori's* move and it serves as the base for the "*Skill* of the *Uke*".' He paused and motioned to Jerome to take him down once more, the latter grabbing hold of the *sensei's* arm, following the command.

Then something extraordinary happened, startling in its simplicity. Jerome sensed how Henri was losing balance and he started the turn on his elbow. But as he cut down the arm and turned, he realised that he himself was suddenly off balance. Henri had tricked him well, moving in perfect unison with Jerome's moves, adding a little energy to the turn. *Tori* had unknowingly become the *uke*, deceived. Once again Jerome found the floor, his nose slowing him into a halt.

'The *Skill* of the *Uke* uses the techniques similarly to the way I executed the last move on you. It relies on commitment, the commitment of the one who thinks he has the upper hand. In Aikilibrium we use the same sense of unbalance you had but in a controlled way. We allow ourselves to be off balance intentionally. It is one of our elements.' Jerome was shaken and beaten but he had an answer to his question. Max and Jerome resumed training together.

The first day was dedicated to the *Ikkyo* technique and they practised through the system called 'Monotonous Training'. The system was mentioned in their text books: 'The easiest way to achieve good technical ability in basic Aikido is by performing the techniques repeatedly. Repetition, the old masters advocated, was the key to registration.'

Jerome did his best but was finding it very difficult. Max as usual had no real problem with any of the techniques. He was a natural; it was obvious from the start. When the day was over they sat quietly together over dinner, clean, tired and very pleased. Finally Jerome, who had just finished his food, spoke.

'I think Henri has something against me. I think he doesn't like me very much.' Max pushed his plate away and looked at his friend.

'You are too sensitive, J. You take things too heavily. God knows how on earth you survived on the streets for so long.'

Jerome grimaced, Max wasn't sharing his worries. 'I don't think that it was my imagination. Feel how swollen my elbow is. I might be an idiot in Aikido but I know all about hostility, believe me.'

Max took the smile off his face. 'Let's see how it goes tomorrow. I personally think that it's all in your head. If there is someone he needs to hate it must be me. Just think about all the pranks I pull constantly.' He burst into a short laughter. 'No, J – it is definitely in your head.'

Jerome was annoyed, his words taken lightly, yet he couldn't blame Max for it. His friend was certainly not reading the situation they were in correctly. True, Max was doing all sorts of undisciplined mischief but Henri looked pleased with his performance and he emphasised performance more than the discipline.

Henri was for some unknown reason intimidated by Max and Jerome suspected it to be his friend's strength and determination, combined with his stubborn, explosive nature. Jerome decided to drop the conversation. He went to sleep almost as excited as Max, yet he was wary of what would come the next day.

8 A Bitter Day of Nikyo

Hisada Inn, Engaru, Hokkaido, Japan, 1915

A SNOW STORM was blowing outside, whistling through the cracks in the wooden structure and banging at its walls. Inside a fire was lit and a few lanterns illuminated the otherwise dim room. It was midday and it was winter, dark and cold. Sunset was early, sunrise late and the thin grey light that reigned in the in-between was a mere shadow by the time it reached inside.

Thirteen-year-old Norikai Inoue was sitting in *seiza*, eyes wide in awe. He was tucked tightly against the corner of the small hall, observing the living legend, Sokaku Takeda, giving a class. He had heard about him before; his fame as a warrior no less than his notoriety due to his obnoxious nature. Norikai could forgive and forget Sokaku's faults for now, as he observed the master in action.

He had arrived there the day before and participated in the welcome ceremony the locals threw for the hero. Norikai was the youngest of all attendants and he felt fortunate to be there, accompanying his eager uncle, Morihei Ueshiba.

The famous warrior, Sokaku Takeda, was short and skinny, dressed in a large overcoat that thickened his frame. He had a *hakama* covering his hips and legs, the belt securing two swords tightly to his centre. His lips curled down even as he laughed and his eyes were burning into the flesh of his opponents, murderously waiting for his prey.

Sokaku was of the old school, from a lost clan of proud warriors. His family were former *samurais* of the last Shogunate but now the Shogunate was over and Sokaku was left a *ronin*, a warrior without a master who was offering his blades and knowledge to the highest bidder.

Master Sokaku carried with him more than just the blood line of the clan because Sokaku was the only one remaining with the knowledge of *Daito Ryu Aikijujitsu* techniques.

Norikai had dreamt of this day for almost a week, relentlessly nudging his uncle to repeat the fantastic tales of the famous fighter. Now he watched the swords of Sokaku, imagining the battle he'd had with fifteen construction workers, him alone, that small old man.

'I don't know, Uncle.' Yesterday, after the meeting with the master, Norikai had confessed his doubts. 'Master Takeda looks so old and frail. I am kind of disappointed.'

Morihei laughed. 'He is indeed 56 years old but believe me, he is at his prime. I promise you, Norikai, this man is amazing. Just wait till tomorrow and you shall find out.'

Now Sokaku was smiling at the silent hall.

'Young Ueshiba wants to buy a technique!' he roared and gestured with his hand to Norikai's uncle. Morihei jumped to his feet, eager to please. He bowed deeply and reached to grab the collar of Takeda's coat, following the silent instruction. A cruel smile pulled at the lips of the 'Tengu of Aizu' and he connected with Ueshiba's arm, cutting it down sharply.

'*Itaii*!' Morihei screamed as he dropped, his arm held firmly by the master. They were as one, Ueshiba's arm serving as a lever through which Sokaku controlled his centre.

Norikai saw the ease with which the master moved. He was hardly exerting any power, although his body was standing frail compared with that of powerful young Ueshiba. Magic was the word to describe it; the minimal hold of Takeda twisting Ueshiba's body on the floor.

The scene brought to mind the tiring day's ride from Shirataki to Engaru. A memory of a doubtful tale that suddenly looked very reasonable.

'Assassins in the *onsen*, Uncle?'

'Yes, in the *onsen*, Norikai,' Morihei whispered. 'And these murderers came to surprise him at night, armed and ready for the kill.'

'But why in the *onsen*?' the inflamed youngster was cocking his head.

They were sitting on horseback, pushing through the snow that piled between the trees of the thick woods.

'Because the hot baths are the only place that Takeda goes

without his weapons.' The words were coming out in a mist of frost. It was a cold, bright day, and the sun was blinding as it hit the snow.

'So what did the master do?' Norikai was banging his gloves and wiping his nose, his eyes not leaving those of his uncle.

'Well ... There are small towels in the *sento*. And one of these in the hand of the master ...' To emphasise his words Ueshiba took a heavy piece of cloth and rolled it tightly. He then jumped off his horse, which was grateful for the short break, and rushed towards Norikai's side, flicking at him with the cloth.

It was not painful and the youngster laughed heartily, pointing at his excited uncle. 'And Takeda struck at his enemies, inflicting sharp wounds wherever the tip of the cloth ended. And then he chased them away!' Ueshiba's boots crunched on the snow, creating sounds that merged with the laughter.

It is strange to hear uncle speak of anyone with such admiration, Norikai thought as they continued riding. *Takeda has to be a special man!*

Norikai was quite an unruly boy at school and consequently his parents had sent him to stay at his uncle's house in the northern settlement, hoping that it would soothe his unstable character and teach him a lesson in life. He had laughed at that notion and agreed enthusiastically. Morihei was the one he loved and looked up to from childhood, a kind man to learn from, not like all those cruel teachers at school.

Now he watched his uncle try to recuperate on the floor while the master laughed at him. Norikai didn't like seeing his beloved uncle being battered and mocked. *It is not funny!*

'See how strong my *Nikajo* is?' Takeda bragged. 'See how it can topple a strong young man like Ueshiba.' He reached out and grabbed Morihei's wrist, who had just managed to get up, pulling the limb towards his chest.

'*Itai!*' Morihei screamed. This time the master maintained the grip on the wrist. He was nodding at the small crowd of students, who excitedly watched the victim twisting on the floor.

'Although I cut my enemy decisively, the *Nikajo* is far from finishing its job.' The master squeezed harder and Ueshiba banged continuously with his free hand on the floor, indicating that he was at his limit.

A show of strength can sometimes reveal more than what is intentionally on display and Norikai's attitude towards the master was changing by what he was witnessing. Suddenly the grace in which the deadly techniques were executed diminished and the mean character of Takeda shone through. Norikai watched his beloved uncle being hurt and ridiculed and he could see no sense in it besides sheer cruelty. He bit his lower lip, hurt and offended and he tried to stop the tears from coming.

But why is it suddenly so silent in here? He lifted his eyes and his head jerked back startled. Sokaku was standing in front of him, his face very close to that of Norikai.

'Little boy, would you like to train with me?' the master spoke softly, his hot breath on the boy.

'I don't want to train with an old man like you!' Norikai shrieked, his chin held high, defiance drying his tears.

There was silence in the room, everyone moving their eyes from the bold youngster to the master. Then Sokaku burst out laughing, exposing his toothless gums. The tension was broken and the master brushed at the youth's face and returned to Ueshiba.

'Sometimes it's difficult to apply *Nikajo* when the *uke's* centre is too strong,' Takeda punched at Ueshiba's face, too quick for the latter to react and block. It hit the nose and Ueshiba raised his hands instinctively, straight to the waiting hands of Takeda – who took him down again.

'Itai!' Ueshiba swayed off balance on the floor, still in the clutches of the master, his face contoured in pain and smeared in tears.

The spectators were laughing and marvelling at the hero but Norikai was sickened to his bones. *Evil old man! I feel sorry for any creature who ever crossed your path. And can only imagine the horror those fifteen construction worker must have felt when confronted by this mad man and his swords!'* Norikai shook his head in determination; *I would not be a student to such a man, teachers like him were the very reason for me leaving Tanabe in the first place*.

Later on, when there was a break in training, Norikai came to Ueshiba. 'Let's go home, Uncle,' he begged. 'Auntie must be struggling on her own and there is plenty to do at the settlement.' He saw how consumed his uncle was; sitting and rubbing oil on his aching wrists, looking eagerly towards the next session.

'What is it, Norikai?' Ueshiba turned to face the youth, sensing there was another reason behind the desire to return home. 'Only yesterday you couldn't wait to attend the ten-day training session. What has changed?' They both sat quietly for a strenuous moment, Norikai gaining courage to speak.

'I don't like him,' he finally blared out. 'I don't like what he represents!' The fire in Ueshiba's eyes dimmed for a second as he allowed the words to penetrate.

'But why? Aren't you impressed with his level of expertise? Look at my wrist and nose – the man has knowledge that I always dreamed of.' The fire returned to his eyes and Norikai saw that a distance was forming between them and it scared him more than the threat of ten *Nikajo* applied by the cruel hands of Master Takeda.

They stayed ten days at the Inn and Norikai refused to participate in any of the sessions, painfully sitting in *seiza* and watching his true hero tainted by the hands of the hard *sensei*. He would never understand his uncle's passion and desire for knowledge; a desire so strong that it would blind him from seeing Takeda's character. Ueshiba was a man of the living, a farmer, a man whose eyes shone lovingly as he cultivated and tended the crops. It pained Norikai to see him degraded in front of Takeda, who was contemptuous of life, and who was more than enjoying the terror he was imposing.

'He is asking for too much!' Norikai finally burst out. 'And Uncle, you give him more than he deserves.'

Ueshiba smiled. 'The desire for knowledge is the only true light in my life, Norikai. I will pay as much as the master asks of me and maybe more.' Uncle was talking about money but there were other prices to pay and Norikai was convinced that this time the price would be too high.

* * *

It was the first morning that stomach ache hadn't forced Jerome to wake up. The pain in his arm overwhelmed the usual pain in his abdomen and aroused him early from sleep. He was tired and exhausted. Not even once had he slept well at the school, unwillingly learning the secret of operating under minimal rest. Napoleon was famous for it and there were other people that used to do the same. It was a simple trick: all one had to do was stay tired the whole time.

It is so easy to slip into a comatose state and to function badly. So easy to do but I can't afford it! Jerome compensated for what he lacked in talent with hard training, pushing himself forward until he performed well.

'What are you thinking about?' Max called with a mouth full of food.

'Nothing much. Do you like the breakfast today? You seem to take your time.'

'It's all right I suppose. You can't go too wrong with sticky eggs or with toast, that by the way is hard as your head!'

'Thanks man.'

'No problem J.' Max giggled and flicked a piece toast at Jerome.

'Hey, come on man, stop it. You are making too much mess.'

'Shut up J,' Max laughed. 'You are just like a mother.'

'Henri will be here any minute and you know how he gets when the place is not spotless. Now help me out here'

'Relax mother, here I come to give you a hand.' They tidied the place up then sat back at the metal chairs.

'How's the arm J?'

'It's really sore. I hope Henri will take it easy today.'

'Don't be too hopeful, I doubt Henri will cut you any slack.'

'Thanks for the support, my friend.'

'Come on J, don't get angry. I am only trying to be honest with you.' Max was not the kind of person you could complain to. He could never really empathise with pains he did not share.

'There he is!' Max whispered, reacting to the familiar sound of Henri's footsteps approaching from the outer corridor. The door opened. 'Come on boys, it is time to go.' They stepped out and Henri waited for them to walk past, observing them as they entered the Plain *Dojo*. They sat in *seiza*, quietly waiting for the lesson to start. Henri slid the door shut and stepped onto the mats. They bowed ceremoniously and Henri stood up.

'Today we will learn our second basic technique, the name of which is second control or *Nikyo*. It's a technique derived from the one we did yesterday, the first control. All the controls we have in basic Aikido – and we have four of them – are stages of the first control.'

Henri showed the progression from first control to fourth control, explaining the logic behind the moves. The position of the arm from which the techniques were derived started with the palm facing down while the arm stretched parallel to the floor. *Ikkyo* occurred when the elbow was bent and rotated forward, dragging the rest of the body down. If the *Ikkyo* stopped halfway through the rotation, the arm ended up in the *Nikyo* lock. *Sankyo*, or third control, came about when the rotation of the arm was not sufficient, it twisted the wrist and caused the arm to rotate further.

Henri held Jerome's wrist while explaining the forth control. '*Yonkyo* rotates the elbow by applying concentrated force to a single pressure point on the wrist. The point you press is the point where you can sense each other's pulse.' He stopped talking and applied the pressure.

'Aaaaaagh!' The pain was unbeliveble, forcing Jerome legs to drive him forward in a mad chase. 'The pain is so severe it compels the *uke* to follow the rotation of his elbow in an effort to minimise the pain.'

There was one thing Jerome could not dispute at that moment: the fact that it was hurting in the most unbelievable way, sending currents of pain travelling from his wrist up to his temples.

Henri tightened his lips in an insane smile; his whole body consumed by ill energy. Finally he let go of Jerome's wrist and laughed heartily at the sight of the boy rubbing his arm.

'Feeble little baby,' Henri teased. He was laughing again.

Can't believe you brother, Jerome shivered at Max's laughter,

Can't believe you share anything with this fart Jerome looked away from the two, his throat and mouth drained of liquid, painfully dry; he was frightened of Henri beyond reason. It wasn't the first time Jerome confronted abusers but never before had he been in a situation where he had to face his tormentor on a daily basis. *That was why I had left home in the first place!* His arm throbbed with pain, it was surely damaged in some way and the day had only just begun.

'*Nikyo* attacks the arm in a specific place,' Henri continued, motioning Max to approach. He was holding him by the wrist, demonstrating as he spoke. 'You need the *uke's* little finger to face up and his elbow parallel to the floor and when you cut down on it you do so as with a sword.' He added his other hand to hold the arm under the wrist and then he cut down.

'Let go!' Max screamed, his face twisted in agony as his knees fell to the *tatami* floor.

Henri was laughing again but this time he laughed alone. *I am not taking part in this, you sadistic bastard.* Jerome knew the need Henri had for recognition and he was determined not to provide it. Henri stopped laughing as Jerome hoped he would but the look he received dried his mouth. The man had a vengeful nature and Jerome knew that he would pay.

For now he was safe though, as he and Max were practising with each other. Slowly Jerome forgot about his fears and concentrated on the technique. At first they hurt each other considerably but gradually they learned not to grind the wrists and their *uke* performance suffered less.

When Henri was happy with the direction of the locks they were conducting, he pushed them on to a higher level. 'Now I want to see you connecting the lock to your centre.' That was when the drill became harder. It wasn't easy to connect the centre to the move. Henri sat them down for the explanation.

'If there is a principle that you will need to know, it's the connection of your centre with everything you do. At the moment we practise basic Aikido and the connection between *tori* and *uke* can be broken occasionally, without losing the technique. When you reach the higher art, however, it is essential to master the connection and its relation to your core perfectly!'

He ordered Max to stand, demonstrating the technique and its application.

'Do you understand?'

'*Osu sensei!*' They resumed training, trying to master Henri's instructions. Then at one point he ordered them to be still.

'Here, let me adjust your hands for the lock. Yes just like that. Now keep your body very straight. That way you will sense your physical centre, its placement and direction. Max, drop your shoulders, that's right, allow the elbows to be suspended.'

'Like this, *Sensei*?'

'No, it is not good enough. Let me show you,' Henri indicated with his arm for Jerome to sit in *seiza* then used Max as *uke*, totally ignoring Jerome when demonstrating. *What are you scheming, bastard?*

The *Nikyo* that Henri *Sensei* applied was awesome: the movement of his centre dramatically illustrating the power of the body as a whole. Henri dropped his shoulders, his elbows hanging low and in slow motion lowered Max to the floor. He didn't need to generate much force from any specific muscle. It was an effortless synchronisation of the skeletal muscles, a lesson in human engineering.

'Now you try it,' Henri barked and training was resumed.

Jerome tried to focus on the task in hand and to ignore the hateful eyes of Henri. *I must fight the fear or it will consume me* Training went relatively well and incident free. At noon they were released for lunch.

'Are you alright, J?' Max asked as the door closed behind them.

'He is going to hurt me, Max, I know he will.'

'Come on man, not that again.'

'I know you don't believe me Max, you never do, but I saw it in his eyes.' Jerome's heaved with anxiety, but Max was looking sceptical.

'I still don't know why you say that, J. I am sure it's in your head.' Max put his arm around Jerome's neck, trying to lift his slumped head. 'I know that our situation is impossible and believe me, I will jump at the first chance of escape just like that!' and he snapped his fingers loudly above his head. 'But,' and here Max stopped and turned Jerome's head towards him, 'I don't believe that we are at risk at the moment; they need us, you see. It doesn't make any sense for them to harm us. Look at all the effort they take to teach us, it must cost them a fortune.'

These were sensible words but Jerome wasn't fully convinced. 'What if this guy Henri has something personal against me? Maybe I should report it to Yves *Sensei*.'

'That's a good idea. But wait till we finish the day, you might be wrong after all.'

'I hope so.'

When lunch break was over Henri came to collect them and led the way to the *dojo*. They bowed and once again he lectured. 'We are going to conclude the *Nikyo* lesson by learning how to connect to *uke's* centre. We already used our core to generate a movement of the whole body. In principle it's a reverse process, moving from the outer layer of the body to its core.'

Henri called on Max to approach. He put Max's arm in a position for *Nikyo* and started to cut down slowly. 'As you cut the movement down, your centre will squeeze *uke's* joints until *uke's* arm is locked, becoming a straight lever to the body.' He stopped at the position he was referring to and Jerome saw how Max's arm moved as one unit.

'The last thing left to do is to cut the *Nikyo* down in the direction of *uke's* centre, something you will need to practise and sense in order to achieve.'

Again Henri *Sensei* cut down the *Nikyo*, adding the conclusive element of the technique. First came the perfect movement of Henri's centre and then the connection to Max's midpoint. One moment he was standing, composing himself against Henri's cutting arms and in a bizarre motion, his knees buckled from underneath him. It didn't hurt Max and it didn't look painful to Jerome who watched Henri in admiration, allowing a little smile to twist his lips. Then he saw the cold dead eyes of the *sensei* and the smile disappeared. He had created an enemy in the one that was his teacher, the one responsible for his well-being.

They practised quietly a while, trying to follow the *Nikyo* direction as the *sensei* instructed, training for half an hour before Henri called the *Yame*. 'It's time for me to apply the technique upon you, so you will know which way to aim.'

Jerome's shoulders tightened and lifted to his ears, instinctively pulling his arms away. The whole day *Sensei* had avoided touching him, perhaps trying to postpone what was to come.

When Henri cut him with the first *Nikyo* Jerome exhaled in relief. Nothing happened or, more like it, a beautiful technique happened. It buckled Jerome's knees and guided him amazed to the floor. He didn't see the brutal look in Henri's eyes, dropping his guard way too soon. The next *Nikyo* was unbelievably painful, so severe and surprising that he screamed on the way down, yet it didn't end when he was down either.

'Sensei, stop please,' Jerome banged on the floor. 'You are breaking my arm!'

It is customary in the martial arts to demonstrate submission by tapping on the *tatami* floor or the *tori's* body. In this way the opponent knows he has won and can stop the assault.

Jerome's tapping, however, were to no avail and Henri kept crushing his wrist down, threatening to rip Jerome's tendons apart. There was nowhere for Jerome to go, squashed and twisted, eyes blurred by tears of pain. Finally Henri let go of him and urged him to get up.

'Left arm please.'

'*Osu sensei!*'

Henri gave the same treatment to Jerome's other arm, the one that was damaged from the day before. And he was much more successful in hurting Jerome.

'Don't just lie there boy – get up!'

'*Osu sensei!*' Jerome lifted as fast as he could. His face was covered in tears and his wrists were hanging numbly to the sides of his body. Behind Henri he saw the angry face of Max cursing silently, getting up to intervene. He shook his head at him. *Don't get involved partner – It is bad enough that I'm in trouble, and besides –*

if anyone deserves to punch him it must be me! Max was getting closer and Jerome instinctively reacted, swinging a 'hook' punch at Henri's face.

'Finally you show some courage!' Henri called as if waiting for the attack, easily diverting Jerome's strike and in an instant was standing behind him, his forearm across Jerome's neck. Henri held Jerome half choked in his arms, watching Max who was advancing.

'Good spirit, lads,' he whispered like a predator, 'but you are way out of your league. It will be some time before you are able to pull anything like that successfully.' He tightened his grip on Jerome's neck, squeezing a shriek. Max stopped approaching and stood staring at the two.

'You let go of him, you hear me!' he growled at the *sensei*, fists tightly swaying in front of his body.

'Sit down, puppy!' Henri ordered, focusing on Max until he obeyed. 'I can kill your friend easily and no one would know about it, no one would care.' He turned Jerome on the spot, quickly pinning his neck in a front choke. Henri looked straight at Jerome's face, his breath warm on him. 'Take it as a warning boys ... There will be no food for two days as a punishment for your attacks.' The discussion had ended. He let Jerome fall from his arms, looking at him as if about to retch. They resumed training but the atmosphere was grim.

After dinner time, in which they had nothing to eat, Jerome went to see Yves *Sensei* for the daily report. The headmaster was, as usual, busy with paperwork on his desk when Jerome entered. He lifted his eyes at the student for a second and returned to his papers, the heavy side door silently closing behind Jerome's back. Jerome stood waiting for the *sensei* to finish, rubbing his wrists that still throbbed with pain.

You are so vain Yves Sensei. Look at your office, so full with expensive ornaments and decorations – so full of yourself On one wall were oil paintings of all the headmasters of the school, most looking very impressive. *And you must be Master Jacques.* The picture of the Aikilibrium founder was especially imposing. He wore a long robe and had forceful eyes, standing straight and severe, a sword held in front of him, radiating blue. On another wall were shelves lined with dozens of trophies. Between the trophies were pictures taken from some colourful martial arts competition, which looked fierce and dangerous. *The trophies must belong to the school champions, for whatever competition it might have been.* Behind Yves were shelves of old wood containing books and a variety of pictures from around the globe. Everything seemed so well preserved and looked after.

'Are you entertained?' Yves *Sensei* raised his eyes in dismay. 'Perhaps you would like a drink or something to eat?' He looked at the boy as one would look upon the vilest of creatures and Jerome didn't miss his jailer's eyes. *I am looking for salvation in the wrong place.*

'Henri *Sensei* told me of your attack in class today.' Yves looked at Jerome, waiting for an explanation.

'I lost control. I am sorry, it won't happen again.'

Yves smiled wolfishly. 'So you promise, do you? And I can promise you that your behaviour only helps me decide who will excel in training and who will be dismissed forever!' He waited a second, still smiling coldly. 'You know what I'm talking about, don't you?' The floor was sinking fast under Jerome's feet. There was nowhere to find help; no escape from the threatening situation.

'I understand, *Sensei*, it won't happen again.' He waited to be excused, bowing politely as he left.

The door bolted automatically when he reached the bottom of the stairs; he walked with his head held low, peeping momentarily to the sitting room, spine arched and as rigid as a wooden sword. Max was there, reading the materials for the next morning but he didn't raise his head when Jerome walked by. Jerome went back to the bedroom and lay down on the thin mattress, clutching at his stomach and tightly shutting his eyes. Fear and despair joined the pain of hunger and poisoning stabbing at his core, threatening to cripple him. He cried and his body shook with the force of his weeping.

9 The Quest

Solon, Manchuria, April 1924

S PRING ARRIVED in Outer Mongolia to revive the battered land and its exposed inhabitants, portraying a blessed announcement from nature. Frosty ground bloomed with colourful patches of tiny flowers that pushed unified through cracks in the dry and harsh earth, fleetingly seducing the senses in beauty and fragrance – to disappear beneath a crusty layer of sand.

It was midday and the sun was in the south, shining low through the air and illusively interacting with clouds of dust, blinding the eyes of the spectators. Solon was a small town, its mud huts scattered without familiar arrangement or a known pattern, but it had an impressive square, the kind that allowed the crowds to gather round and observe the day's demonstration.

The great Wang Shou Kao, King of Protectors, was standing in the middle of the square, looking around and squinting his eyes, knowing that a blink might cause him to miss a potential foe.

Come on! he silently challenged. *Who is next?* It had been a long week of demonstration for him and his companions as they were in the process of recruiting an army and trying to convince the locals to join forces with them.

The Maitreya Incarnation Dalai Lama, the leader of the expedition, was gaining power and reputation throughout the region, something that was not missed by his rivals. He needed good strong men for his army if he was to continue on his quest to establish the New Jerusalem, and he hoped that Wang's demonstration would persuade the sceptical locals of their divine supremacy. Earlier on, the great Dalai Lama was showing his purification techniques and a long and successful session of healing; both very convincing for the throng, yet fighting men were expecting more than that ...

'That is why we need a King of Protectors, Master,' Lu, a local war lord and an ally explained to Deguchi when they first met.

Wang smiled. *It had been an eccentric trip right from the start,* a trip conducted by the great Onisaburo Deguchi! Deguchi and his band had met Lu as soon as they arrived from Japan. Lu wanted to control Mongolia and his ambition entwined with theirs. It was in his presence that all the Japanese were advised to take local names, so they would apply better to the locals. In no time at all Ueshiba was named Wang and Deguchi turned into the Dalai Lama; the master had never lacked imagination nor creativity.

'Very well then,' Ueshiba mumbled and watched the open area, waiting for the next challenger.

A huge Manchurian jumped from within the crowds and headed towards Wang, supported by the enthusiastic cries of the locals. Someone had to take out this weird-looking Japanese warrior who was hammering his opponents with ease, one after the other. The man approaching was the sixth challenger of the day, his steps cautious although he had a huge size advantage and was much younger than the 41-year-old Wang. His wariness was not out of fear but based on what he had seen earlier on, when the short and bald Japanese warrior took the centre of the square. He was surely no match for any of the local wrestlers, his bushy moustache bringing cries of laughter from the crowd. Manchurians, although poor, took great pride in their martial heritage that dates all the way back to the great Genghis Khan, and the sight of Wang stimulated them for the challenge.

The first contestant was disrespectful and cocky, and the great Wang enjoyed his defeat, damaging the man's pride, but not causing much harm to his body. He was there to recruit soldiers and to gain the trust of the people and being mean would only have the opposite effect.

Are you watching Master? He saw the eyes of the Dalai Lama concentrating on the new wrestler There was no real worry in that gaze, rather an academic interest at most. The Dalai Lama knew of Wang's fighting skills and he had no doubt that he would prevail.

The wrestler was almost at engagement distance when a small commotion to the left caught the trained eyes of Wang, momentarily taking his concentration away. The wrestler saw the opportunity and shot himself low and forward, aiming to take down the much smaller

Japanese man. '*Baka.*' Wang cursed at himself quietly but managed to stand his ground, the wrestler holding him in a bear hug at his waist. *Your grip is tight but you leave room for manoeuvres.* Wang smiled while dropping his centre of gravity and the wrestler lost his advantage. He could hear the crowds cheering their hero, thinking that he still had the upper hand, but there was no longer any justification for their joy.

Majestically, and with a broad and confident smile, Wang placed his palms on the man's shoulders and a wave of power rushed through his body, just as his feared *Daito Ryu* teacher, Master Sokaku Takeda, had taught him to do. The Manchurian groaned and crashed to the ground, his shoulders almost dislocated by the concentrated power of the great Wang. Angry shouts and cries of disappointment came from the surroundings and Wang pulled back, waiting for the local medicine man who rushed to the side of the beaten warrior. The cart was brought and the man was taken away.

'Anyone else? Anyone at all?' The crowds dispersed disappointedly, cheated of their champion.

Wang waited a while longer but there were no more adversaries left today. He swung around, allowing himself to look aside, to see what it was that so easily dragged his attention away. His eyes searched to the left until he saw the little park and a gathering of elderly people. They were indulging in some sort of a shadow dance, slowly mimicking the performance of their instructor.

But there are martial qualities to this dance – how dare he! Fury pumped his body with adrenalin, the blood thumping at his temples with each and every heart beat. He was the man of the day, there was no doubt about it in his mind, and the Shadow Dancing instructor should have watched and learned from Wang's demonstration.

Being victorious for so many days had dangerously elevated his ego and pride; he was arrogant but he didn't know it. Wang moved out, aggressively pushing his way through the people who crossed the emptying square, his eyes never leaving the park. He was absorbed and focused.

During the past few weeks he had tested his powers against the local heroes, hoping to be stimulated in a new and challenging way.

He was on a personal quest, a course set before him by his master, the Dalai Lama, a demand to establish a new form of martial application, something that the world had never seen before.

The Dalai Lama wanted Wang to combine the knowledge of the fight with the philosophical concept of the master himself and Wang listened attentively to his bidding – for four long frustrating years searching for a clue yet coming up with nothing, not even a sense of direction. Wang hoped that the trip to Mongolia would enlighten him on his quest because he could not find his inspiration in Japan.

He walked towards the park and detected his interpreter rushing to catch up with him, crossing the square from the other side, pushing at the stream of pedestrians. The Panchen Lama, the other companion of the Dalai Lama, stood in Wang's path.

'Well done, Master Ueshiba!' he congratulated Wang in Japanese. Wang gave him a courteous look and kept advancing to the common, his interpreter finally managing to squeeze by his side.

Two more steps and he jumped over the brick wall that surrounded the small recreational area. The instructor was walking in the opposite direction and Wang ran with the interpreter, in a couple of seconds both blocked the advance of the stunned man. The instructor was as tall as Wang but of a much frailer build. He was not Manchurian, perhaps Chinese.

'What is the meaning of this shadow training?' Wang demanded, waiting impatiently for the interpreter to deliver the man's reply.

'It is a Chinese art,' the interpreter presently replied with a hint of contempt. 'He says that it is very beneficial for the health of the elderly.' Wang looked at the instructor suspiciously, doubting that his words gave the comprehensive truth.

'Weren't there martial elements to those moves?' The interpreter nervously questioned the instructor who replied with a broad smile, causing Wang's face to contort further.

'It is based on martial elements,' the interpreter delivered, 'but it is done for the sake of health alone and, well ... forgive his disrespect, sir, but he asks if you would like to give it a try.'

Wang walked in disbelief towards the instructor, wanting to lift the insolent man in the air with his mighty arms. The instructor grinned softly, as if unaware of the immediate danger.

'Here Dancer, let me give it a try!' And Wang reached out and grabbed firmly ... but suddenly there was nothing there to grab.

'What the hell!' His expression changed to that of confusion and he almost lost his balance. Wang turned to face the smiling man who had somehow ended up behind him.

The instructor's eyes were friendly but intensely focused on Wang and he was explaining something to the interpreter, but Wang was too angry to wait.

'How dare you talk in the middle of a fight?' he bellowed in Japanese, insulted, not caring that the man couldn't understand a word he said. He grabbed him with his left, right hand lifting for the strike. He punched the instructor who then turned in unison with the attack, causing Wang to splatter on the dusty floor.

The uneven ground met his back, sharp stones digging painfully into his ribs and thighs, yet he barely winced, jumping up in haste and embarrassment. 'How did you do that?' He narrowed his eyes at his cheerful opponent, sucking in some air and twisting his head to one side. *Has anyone witnessed my awkwardness?* Wang quickly surveyed the surroundings but saw no one there.

'The man does not wish to fight you, Oh Great Protector,' the interpreter used the momentary break. He was standing between the two, his eyes sheepishly trying to pacify the fighter. 'He merely wanted to know if you would like to try some of the shadow movements.'

Wang heaved in relief then nodded in confirmation, signalling for the instructor to begin. Training was a dignified way out for him – he would never be considered defeated that way, and could justify it as a part of training.

Secretly, and beyond the blow he had just received to his ego, Wang was intrigued for the first time since he had arrived on the continent; the man had just beaten him and therefore must possess something worth learning. 'Let's do it!' Wang ordered and began to imitate the instructor's techniques. He was holding back to start with, uncomfortable with the movements which were almost feminine in nature and with the instructor, who was Chinese, a member of a conquered race ...

Then, after taking the first few steps, his resistance to the truth melted away ... *I hate to admit it to myself but this is exactly what I was looking for!* And fascinated Wang opened up to the new sensations, following the man obediently, becoming one with the shadow dance. The instructor stopped after an hour-long practice, facing Ueshiba and offering his arm.

'This is a drill called "Pushing Hands",' the interpreter explained from the side. 'He says that it will teach you how to divert resistance.'

Ueshiba raised his eyebrows in confusion yet followed the instructions, reaching out to the waiting arm of the man. The drill showered him with new and intense sensations, although some of the moves had a remarkable resemblance to the *Daito Ryu* techniques that he had mastered in the past. The main difference between the two arts was in the intention. The goal of *Daito Ryu* was victory in battle, composed of sharp and decisive moves to conquer the opponent; the new art on the other hand, aimed at pacifying the mind and healing the body – resistance dealt with and drained in a circular flow.

Visions from the past started to flash in front of Wang's eyes, mingling with his surroundings. He saw the image of the dancers following the music at the *Omoto Kyo* ceremonies, back in Ayabe, and he could suddenly sense the connection of the *Budo* to the dance. Unconsciously his spirit became aloft, his anger and heated temper subsided. Suddenly he was Wang no more but Morihei Ueshiba, not a king but a simple warrior on a quest, looking for his own Jerusalem.

Long hours of training passed yet Ueshiba was consumed by the new ideas presented in the drills, not noticing that the sun had sunk long ago in the west and that a cold wind was blowing softly, causing the bones of the poor interpreter to shudder. The circular motion introduced a sensitive and feminine component to the fighting techniques, allowing the connection to be more than physical alone. He could understand the joy that he saw in the instructor, identified with his softness and grace, the turns changing his mood and intention. For the first time he witnessed a victory that was brought about by bonding and pacifying rather than destroying the enemy. Ueshiba's thirst was frightening, trying to drink as much as he could of this strange art.

They went back to practise shadow movements before it turned completely dark, and Ueshiba deployed *Kotodama*, Words of Power, to the turning motions and they matched perfectly.

'Great!' he gasped, every move further elevating his creative pleasure. The instructor was drained of energy when Morihei finally pulled away and bowed politely. 'Thank you Sensei,' he whispered then moved from the hidden corner of the park at once. He had discovered the missing ingredient lacking in his art, and it was enough food for his thoughts and actions in the following months.

Although the lesson would be wiped out from his official personal history and from the history of the art – and it did not seem as though anyone had witnessed it – Ueshiba would never forget what had happened in that park. Still, he did suspect that his master had probably predicted its occurrence long before, maybe even observed it in one of his mysterious ways.

Ueshiba walked across the town square and suddenly saw the brim of a hat moving just ahead of him in the shadows. *No way! It is impossible!* He hastened his strides and quickly reached the sleeping quarters. *There you are.* The Dalai Lama, better known as Onisaburo Deguchi, was standing outside their mud hut, looking at the night skies.

'A fine evening for glorious discoveries,' he mumbled as Ueshiba walked by and the blood chilled in Morihei's veins, his face flushed with embarrassment. *What do you mean, Master?* He almost blurted out. *Could it be that you had witnessed the lesson?* He remained silent, knowing it would be futile to draw any sensible information from the illusive Deguchi. He bowed politely and walked inside, wanting to enjoy a warm cup of *cocha* and to contemplate on the circular movements he had just learned. A shudder went through his body when he saw the high brimmed hat that lay on the table and he nodded to himself and smiled, knowing that Master Deguchi had been at the park, ever present when something significant seemed to happen.

'Finally, Master …' it was Ueshiba's turn to mumble. 'Finally I will be able to provide what you have asked of me to create.' And after many months of gloominess Ueshiba was smiling.

* * *

That was the end of the chapter and Jerome closed the history book of Aikido and sat quietly, thinking about what he had just read. 'The circular connection is the key to the art.'

'Hmmm …'

It was funny how an art so majestic and beautiful was taught under such conditions, yet the founder hadn't exactly had it easy himself. Jerome turned the light off and went quietly to the bedroom. He could hear Max snoring in the next bed. He lay down and wondered how the next day would go. He didn't know how much longer he would be able to endure all the abuse. So far he was surviving. His left arm was almost completely numb, he couldn't move it much. There were only two things that kept him going. The first was Max and the second was the art. Even through the pain, fear and hunger he could sense the growing love he had for Aikido, regardless of the bad conditions which accompanied it.

* * *

Yves was excited. The Informer was paying him a visit and the *sensei* was looking forward to the report.

'How did it go today, young one? Henri called it a success but I can't rely on his words alone.'

The Informer snorted a laugh. 'I didn't think that Henri was capable of pulling off anything as smoothly as that, yet he did. You should have seen how frightened Jerome looked.' The Informer was enjoying the whole ordeal. His pleasure was more than the academic joy of a tutor.

Yves stopped smiling. 'Be careful not to overdo it. Failure

borders on success the whole time in this business.'

'Don't worry, *Sensei*, it's not my first time.'

'I know it's not, but still be very careful.'

'No problem, *Sensei*, your wish is my command.' He waited a minute, gaining courage. 'Any news from Calvin or Anton?'

Yves didn't look too eager to answer. 'Not yet. I will let you know if anything comes up.'

'*Osu, Sensei*,' said the Informer and moved back into the shadows. He wasn't pleased with his master's answer, feeling left out. *Yves Sensei should be careful with the way he handles business*, the Informer growled in frustration, *or else he would be creating enemies at home.*

The office went silent as the door clicked into position and the Informer was gone.

Yves sat biting at his nails, his left hand occasionally pulling at his earlobe. He was thinking of the book, the lost book of Ueshiba, and he was worried. He had received news this morning from Anton and Calvin. They were following a lead in the Ural Mountains in Russia but had found nothing.

At the bottom of their message was a suggestion of hope. They had a new lead, another one that would cost him more money from his dwindling resources yet promising enough to invest in. He forwarded more funding to Anton and widened the network for Calvin's crooked business. Yves *Sensei* had spent a fortune over the past three years with very little result. He was not deterred from his efforts, although he was on the brink of bankruptcy. Yves had good reason to be anxious but his hope for glory overshadowed his costly quest. 'Just find the bloody thing,' he wrote to the two, dreaming of their success, hoping they wouldn't betray him.

Yves didn't want the Informer to know everything; the only reason for it was the frustration he felt. He had to lie to the Informer, he had to – and he was certain the Informer knew that he did so …

10 The Day Before the Test: Dai Ichi Kihon

FOUR MONTHS of intense and brutal training went by, in which Henri terrorised Jerome at any given chance. Max was doing his best to attract some of the fire but the victim was already chosen.

Max's character was volatile and his focus lacked consistency, yet he managed to exceed Jerome's endeavours effortlessly; talented beyond reason. Max harboured no respect for authority, often looking down at Henri with contemptuous eyes, revealing disrespect in an icy blue silence.

Jerome, conversely, was doing his best to please the *sensei* and Henri was more than happy to react with displeasure. It was a relationship common in the martial arts world and in some sick way it resembled the dependency that abused children have towards their parents, and that of kidnap victims towards their captors. Jerome had such a relationship with his mother in the past, when her beatings inflicted bruises of guilt that throbbed more strongly than any physical pain. It was his fault when he was mistreated as a child and he was sure that it was his fault now; he must have been a bad *uke* for *Sensei!*

Bullying in Aikido was common no matter how hard the authorities tried to root it out. The fifty years between the death of the founder and the foundation of the International Aikido Board were tainted with pointless abuse. It was a confusing time for those who practised the art; the old masters were dying and there was no one able enough to give hope to the practitioners, to show the direction in which the art flowed.

In those days of uncertainty, Aikido practitioners considered the first level of techniques as the complete art of Aikido, unaware of the next two levels crucial for the bonding with the *Skill*. Seeking correlation between the incomplete art and reality, many of the confused pre-*Skill aikidoka* concentrated on the martial practicality of the art, researching its effectiveness 'on the street'.

Since there is no fighting involved in *Dai Ichi Kihon* techniques, only the relationship between partners, practicality was falsely judged as the strength in which techniques were executed. It was a fruitless direction yet it was decided on as the right course and no one knew any better or was brave enough to do otherwise.

Aiki dojo became the perfect ground for those scared of confrontation, allowing them to be technically efficient, to move up in the hierarchy of belts and become instructors. These pretend fighters would hide behind the mask of warriors, taking their frustration and fears out on the apprentices, using technical superiority and authority rather than fighting ability to gain the upper hand. Instructors would terrorise students in a variety of ways. They would hurt those who were afraid of pain rather than teach them how to handle it. They would smash students' heads into the mats in a sadistic and dangerous way, trying to show how strong they were. There was no doubt it was abuse; the proof was in the fact that students kept coming back for more.

Academic understanding towards abusive conduct was common at the time the *Skill* was found, since cruelty proved to be a vital component for the curriculum of the higher art. It worked successfully for almost a decade and then the rumours of the abuse came out and the public panicked, demanding exposure and restraint. The International Aikido Board was established before things got out of hand and its leaders governed the art, proving that their way of conduct was of no concern to the public. They carried out open demonstrations and spread the philosophical words of the founder about love and harmony – for the first time abuse in the *dojo* was legally condemned.

Most instructors felt under-equipped without the tool of abuse and for a few years the number of *Skilled aikidoka* dropped significantly, as all trails in reviving the *Skill* were futile. Eventually the Board allowed a certain degree of controlled cruelty back into the system yet the scale of such acts were open for interpretation and depended on the morality of the teachers themselves. So the mistreatment continued but in a more refined and secretive way.

* * *

There was nothing refined in the sadism of Henri and he didn't need to be secretive about it either. There were no external witnesses for his assaults, he was free to hurt them as he pleased, as long as it improved their performance. He pushed the boys to their limits and succeeded in the impossible, they gained the essence of basic Aikido, and became familiar with all the techniques that O Sensei introduced in his book *Budo*.

In less than five months they were ready for the black belt test, a test to judge their knowledge of the basic techniques. They hadn't mastered the techniques to perfection, hadn't had the time, yet *Dai Ni Kihon* techniques were to be taught soon after the test. The level of the students' *Dai Ichi Kihon* techniques was to develop over time and consequently to improve the art of the *Skilled aikidoka*, yet the perfection of the basics was not entirely necessary for touching the higher arts.

Henri was running the final few days of training at a tempo that was virtually impossible to follow. He came one morning and announced, 'In two weeks we will have our test on basic Aikido. You will have to pass this test. There is no way in hell that you will survive if you fail. We don't have time for failures, they cost too much.'

Jerome looked at Max and saw the frown and the eyes that were moving hectically; searching for a way out. Max had lost his cheerfulness lately; the place had finally started to get to him. They were exhausted and couldn't think of how hard Henri could push them further, how much more they would be able to take. Henri proved to them that they could be pushed further still, that what they considered a limit was only the halfway point.

They would train four hours in the morning and after lunch break they would continue for three hours more. In the evening they had to recite the Japanese names of the techniques and to read from the Aikido books, something they both loved to do. The stomach aches continued and Jerome had a constant hollow feeling in the pit of his belly but that was nothing new.

For three days they worked only on their 'shadow training',

shaping and reshaping their turns, breakfalls and movements of the body's centre. On the fourth day they started to work on their techniques.

Through their training they had learned a degree of sensitivity that allowed them to perform powerfully yet without harming each other much. By the time they had finished the two weeks of preparation for the test they realised how valuable a lesson it was; the amount of strenuous training repeatedly distracted them and they could get damaged easily. In these two weeks their ability to perform as a unit increased and they made a perfect fit, following each other's moves and knowing how to commit.

On the day before the test they went through 'Go' training – a quick teaching method designed for the registration of the techniques. One student would perform a technique again and again following the teacher's command of: *Hajime* or 'Go', trying to keep the tempo of the drill without losing strength or focus.

'Come on, get up and move!' They were forty minutes into the drill, their sweaty *dogi* hanging heavily on the taut bodies, the air hissing dry through their cracked lips. Jerome saw the heat steaming out of Max's head like an egg boiling on the stove. *You look silly partner – if only I had the power to laugh!* They had finished *Shihonage*, four direction throw, and were waiting in *kamai*, fighting stance, for Henri's instructions.

Max and Jerome were panting quietly, controlling their breath, hiding the movement of the trunk. It was the *Bushido* part of training, the way of the warrior. Henri eyed them heavily and then called the next technique, an *Iriminage*, a front throw – Jerome's favourite. A little smile pinched the boy's mouth, not noticeable except to the knowing eyes of Max. Until now he had battered Jerome with every throw and technique and he knew he deserved a taste of his own medicine.

First was Max's turn to perform and as Henri bellowed the *Hajime* command, Max did his best to pound Jerome to the ground. He was quick and strong, managing to hurt Jerome, but not too much. Henri shouted '*Yame*!' and then Max had to perform the same sequence on the left because every technique and every attack in

Aikido is carried out on both sides of the body, which is essential for the balance of the practitioner.

Max finished his last throw and the boys were back in *kamai;* it was Jerome's turn to perform – payback time!

There are no technical surprises when practising a basic Aikido technique. Both *tori* and *uke* know their roles exactly, which in turn makes the technique a lot harder to perform. A *tori* is limited to one technique while the *uke* can change direction in unlimited ways. It is similar to a magic trick that is known to the viewers and therefore difficult to perform.

On the first throw Jerome was testing the waters, judging Max's *uke,* noticing how his friend was shuffling from leg to leg, a quick move that aided him in controlling the fall. They had practised their *uke* technique as much as the initiating part of it. It taught them to be off balance in a controlled way and to follow the direction and power of the techniques. *Uke* was a commanding tool and a *Skill* in itself, yet Max could not use special abilities, it was way too soon in the training for that. He relied on his natural talent, which was enough to divert and hamper any Aikido technique – if the *tori* was unfocused and allowed it!

He tried to shift his balance from leg to leg on the next throw but Jerome was waiting – catching him off balance and in mid air. Max's eyes widened in anticipation, his body connected to Jerome's lever-like limbs that could roll him off them, in any way and as strongly as Jerome chose. It was an incredible sensation, one of control and power.

The hardest part to command, as *tori,* is the desire to exert full strength, the urge to smash the opponent to the ground. Max was not an opponent and he could take the fall, no matter how hard Jerome might thump him. He froze for a split second in the air and then came down, creating a tremor on impact. There was no control to the fall nor a proper breakfall. Max tucked his chin in to protect his neck – that was all he could do. He got up shaking his head and with a cry he punched at Jerome's centre, to Henri's shout of '*Hajime!*', ready to be taken down again.

Max, as Jerome expected, tried to change the *uke* direction again, dropping his hip slightly so that Jerome would lose some of the power for the throw. Jerome smiled to himself, forgetting the horrors and the mistreatment for a second. This was Aikido, it was working and it felt beautiful. In moments like this Jerome could forget all that was bad and concentrate on the two good things in life, Aikido and his friend, or victim at the moment. It wasn't really a mean game as they were very attentive to each other, stopping the pain before it went too far. Jerome followed that rule to its full extent and Max, who typically found it harder to control himself, was trying his best to do the same.

Max's next diversion was read and his new moves followed. He ended in a position worse than the one before.

'Good one J,' he moaned while getting into *kamai.*

'Shut it Max! Concentrate!' The boys were attached in a game of balance and Jerome was intoxicated by a sense of total control. His positioning was absolute, Max merely a bug resting against his centre. He fought the urge to smash Max, who momentarily lost all his human rights except the right to be Jerome's *uke.*

I think you've had enough, Jerome chuckled and dropped his friend down – but not too heavily this time.

'*Yame!*' Henri *Sensei* bellowed and approached Jerome. He walked around him like a sergeant in the army, close and intimidating. 'Are you showing mercy, trying to impress us with your good moral behaviour?'

The boys were now standing in *kamai,* facing each other, stretched and exposed: Aikido *kamai* is derived from the stretched fighting stance of the swordsman. It teaches students where their centre is placed and the line on which they need to move, yet it is a well-exposed position without the blade in hand, turning the body into a large target, making it easy to attack.

Henri was counting upon that trusty posture. He punched the fully stretched Jerome in the solar plexus, sending him to the ground in a curled ball of pain, clutching the *tatami* floor with his fingernails. The punch in the abdomen squeezed his intestinal fluids upwards and he gurgled in pain. Henri was not impressed.

'You think that you will gain mercy by showing some yourself, don't you? Well, my dear boy, once again you are mistaken.' To prove the point he kicked Jerome in the stomach and face. 'Get up, don't keep us waiting.' He smiled and spat at the twisting body on the floor.

Jerome dragged himself up a second later. Recomposing himself, he resumed the *kamai*. *'Hajime!'* Henri called out and the *Iriminage* sequence continued. *I will not play your games, bad breath bastard!* Jerome narrowed his eyes, *No matter what you do with me.* He preferred to be bullied than to hurt Max as was required of him. Henri knew of the boy's loyalty and he tried his best to provoke him into aggression towards his friend, sometimes shouting, 'Smash him down!' or 'Get him back!' But Jerome didn't change his ways, preferring instead to bear more bruises; already his left eye had started to swell.

Max shook his head at him yet didn't say a word. He had sensed, long ago, what Henri wanted to see, often begging Jerome to show more aggression. 'I can take it, J, you won't hurt me! Please, why don't you trust me?'

Jerome appreciated his friend's sacrifice, yet it only strengthened his determination not to budge in the face of his jailers. 'Don't you get it, Max? That's exactly what they are expecting us to do: lose our free will, follow our most basic instincts to hurt and destroy each other in the face of their threats. I am not going to let them have that satisfaction; they will not master my will!'

The conversation didn't end up too well. 'Are you suggesting that I am being controlled by them, judging yourself as my better?' He shook his head at Jerome and stood up. 'Are you that proud, J?'

Great! All I need now is a fight with the only friend I have! Jerome understood Max's argument but stubbornness and pride maintained the way he was acting. He avoided talking about it again, afraid of the confrontation.

They finished working on the basic techniques and broke for lunch; Jerome rushing to the medicine cabinet and placing a cool patch on his swollen eye. No words were exchanged during the meal; Jerome bending low over his plate and Max shaking his head continuously, twisting the corner of his lips.

After lunch they practised *jiyu waza,* free techniques, showing the true commitment and flow of their Aikido. The *sensei* commanded the attacks that the *uke* applied while the *tori* chose freely the techniques to use against it. The *uke* kept getting up and attacking while the *tori* used the assault against the attacker, against the *uke* himself. It was a hard and demanding exercise, requiring from the students the ability to react quickly, to sense each other's moves and to keep the flow, whatever the situation.

Max and Jerome started slowly yet they soon picked up the pace, moving harmoniously from one attack to another. It was flowing and it felt good. *This is great!* Jerome nodded to himself, forgetting about Henri and surrendering to the art. Life never felt more complete than when the technique was clicking, and the two knew each other just enough to fully trust and commit to it. Henri could not stop their momentum; treating the art with respect, just as a priest would treat a holy religious ceremony. They were only performing the *Dai Ichi Kihon* techniques, but it was an awesome sight, the *tori* leading the way in turns and twists, dynamically manoeuvring the *uke* to respond positively, instigating large circular motions.

Jerome attacked with a *Yokomen* side strike, raising his hand high, shouting as he inflicted the diagonal cut downwards. Max connected with the forearm and on impact turned to the rear, folding Jerome's wrist in a *Kotegaeshi* throw, compressing the body out of alignment in a circular fall. Jerome used the momentum to lift and turn for the next strike, Max synchronously moving in to meet the challenge, dropping slightly just before their bodies collided, fusing with the strike and cutting *uke's* arm down and around his own front foot. Jerome's hand was attached to his ankle, leaving no other option but to fall. The name of the technique was *Kokyunage,* or breath throw, and it splattered Jerome, head over heels on the floor.

'*Yame!*' Henri roared and they stood facing each other in *kamai,* panting and sweating profoundly, sticking their chests out, proud of their own efforts. Henri allowed them to go back to their room after that. 'Remember the test is tomorrow. If you do not perform to our satisfaction you will be eliminated. That's the rule.' He smiled cruelly at Jerome and winked. 'You can seek compassion and sympathy elsewhere.' And that was that.

They took showers and then ate quietly, their unknown fate looming over the evening. At long last Max broke the silence. 'We will not let them do this to us, will we?' he whispered and his eyes moved suspiciously around.

'I don't care what happens to me so don't expect anything.' The answer cut at Jerome's throat, the lie accelerating his heartbeat. He tried to sound depressed not frightened, yet Max pushed his plate away and slowly stood up.

'So you won't respect our agreement, J?' he bellowed at Jerome's cowed frame. 'Look at me when I am talking to you.' Jerome held his head low, not looking up. 'You coward!' Max growled and went to the bedroom.

Good, Jerome thought. *That way you won't put yourself at risk for me. I know you must be mad with me brother, but if losing your trust would help keep you away from harm then it's a price I am willing to pay.*

11 The Search for the Lost Book

THE INFORMER approached from the dark, startling Yves for a second.

'Can't you warn me that you are coming?' the headmaster asked, annoyed whenever taken by surprise, something the Informer loved to do.

'Sorry *Sensei*.'

'Never mind.' Yves sighed, his finger scratching under his chin. 'So how are we doing?' he enquired.

'I believe it'll be a good test tomorrow but we still have a problem with the aggression.'

Yves lifted his arm up and banged on the desk, his expression changed to that of fury. 'Do I have to do everything around here?' he roared. 'I don't have time to deal with these petty problems. Don't you know that the "senseless aggression" is a necessary step?'

'I know it's important and Henri tried to force it on him with every move in the text book but the bastard wouldn't lose control. I wanted you to know about it, I don't think Henri is capable of pulling it off.'

'That's not good,' Yves muttered and walked around his desk, taking a good look at the Informer who blended with the shadows of the room. 'You are getting bigger,' the *sensei* smiled and clasped his hands, yet a second later he was frowning. 'How are we going to revive the aggression in him?' he confronted the Informer. 'He is no good to us with these morals.'

'I have a solution,' the Informer smiled, 'one that Henri would object to, but still a valid one.'

'Speak up, my friend.'

The Informer was very inventive, not a part of his job description but a quality which had come in handy a couple of times in the past, when away from the school on secret missions. The Informer had other duties besides spying yet he maintained anonymity throughout. It aided him in performing all sorts of tasks for the master, some better left unknown ...

'Well, *Sensei*,' the Informer continued. 'Jerome tends to sacrifice himself for the sake of others and this can be used to trigger his aggression.' Yves narrowed his eyes and nodded, following the plot. 'We need to challenge Jerome's loyalty and friendship, *Sensei*, it would guarantee an aggressive reaction.'

A smile spread across Yves' face. 'But that would expose Henri for the attack, something he would be terrified of.' Yves liked the plan but needed full details to be convinced and the Informer stood silent a little longer, watching the master becoming intrigued.

'Of course he wouldn't like it if he knew, but he needs to know only what we tell him. Trust me; he is stupid enough to get Jerome going.'

Yves stopped smiling and grimaced. 'I hope that it works. I'm tired of finding new students and being disappointed. He'd better have it in him or we've wasted all this valuable time.'

The Informer looked out of the side window, enjoying the brief moment of fresh air and space. It was very claustrophobic to be confined to the school and not entirely healthy. 'It will happen. I don't have your experience, *Sensei,* but I think I judge him well. You will see him through to the next stage, trust me. No one can promise more than that.'

His words had an impact on the master who looked reassured, not expecting the following question.

'Any news from Anton or Calvin?'

The room went dead silent as tiny muscles of irritation twitched on Yves' face, not escaping the sharp eyes of the Informer. 'No,' he said finally. 'Nothing significant to report.' He was lying yet again and the Informer knew it.

Without further words the Informer bowed and left the room, cursing quietly on his way out, shaking his head from side to side like a wounded elephant. He had his interests to consider and he now saw them being stamped upon and ignored. He felt betrayed and angered, suffering from isolation and lack of trust in the master.

Yves stared at the closing door, wondering how far he could drag the Informer around in his schemes. *I can sense your growing resentment. Too bad. You are good at what you do but you are also* too involved. I'm afraid our path will have to part soon. Usually Yves used informers for a few years, but he knew that this informer would be finished soon., Yves had only himself to blame, having trusted the Informer and sent him on various unlawful deeds. The Informer had earned his right to be familiar with the details as well as a cut of the money, but Yves didn't like to admit it.

There was some news from the two men in charge of the chase but he wouldn't reveal the facts to the Informer.

Calvin, I hope you wont fail me. You owe me much!

Calvin, the ex-SAS soldier, used Yves' Aikido connection as a cover for his true dealings, which involved trading in anything profitable and illegal. In return he helped Yves in the search for the lost book of Master Ueshiba. It was a mad chase, even if the legend was true and there was a lost book, still crucial details regarding its location were absent. No one alive had seen the book, but Yves' money and passion justified the hunt.

Anton, his other accomplice was an *aikidoka*, a *Skilled* 'Seeker' in trade. The Seekers were a branch of the Aikido *Skill*, one that was best described as the *'Skill* of the Tracker', designed to find any person in the globe under specific conditions.

'Introduce me to the one you desire finding, tell me where he was last seen and I guarantee to find him' was Anton's motto and he was not bragging. The trade was indeed most effective if the Seeker knew whom to find and where that person was last seen. Yves hoped it would come in handy.

He reached inside his drawer and pulled out a booklet entitled *The Second Book of Ueshiba, Myth or Fact?* Yves opened it at a marked place, tracing the pages that recited the history of the lost book.

* * *

The first rumour of the 'Lost Book' emerged in the year 2030, more then ten years after the *Skill* was formally recognised by the international community. It was followed by numerous other stories and with each and every story the doubts grew. It seemed inconceivable that the book had travelled to all the places that the reports suggested. Serious researchers tried to separate the true stories from the false and even came up with a few interesting findings. Then in 2050 the first *Aiki* terror attacks started and the hunt was called off for nearly twenty years.

In the early seventies the search resumed, backed by the International Aikido Board. Much of the information and people involved were lost, yet the researchers came up with one lucky find. It was a statement, recorded by one of O Sensei's trusted students, pointing the way to a hiding place in the forests near Aoyama Shrine. A search party organised by the International Aikido Board secured the area and found the hiding place – but it was empty, someone had got there before.

Researchers traced the date in which the hideout was broken into as the third year of the new Millennium. Some of the forensic evidence gave clues to the identity of that person; a Japanese construction worker who had died a few years before. His daughter had recorded a statement to the request of the search party, openly sharing her knowledge of that account.

> My father was hiking one bright winter's day in the forests above the *Aiki* Shrine. It was cold and windy, ominous grey clouds forming far in the west. As he walked about, the wind pushed the clouds above and a soggy downpour started. He quickly ran down the hill, trying to find shelter among the denser bushes. Pushing into the depth of the forest, enjoying the beauty of the trees and fragrance of the wet moss, he soon forgot about the rain. Then Father's leg was caught in a little ditch, hollowed by years of rain and landslides. He sat down, cursing and rubbing his leg, when his fingers sprang back at the touch of a cold and metallic object. Shivering yet focused, he looked down at the ground, ignoring the itch of the water that travelled down his nose.
>
> He saw a metal box, secured by an old lock. His hands trembled and at first he wanted to break the lock on the box and look inside. His instincts told him otherwise and he dried the box and placed it under his shirt and ran home. He kept it safe for a few months, pulling it out from time to time to marvel at its hidden potential. The metal packaging was fascinating enough to keep his curiosity at bay, and as little as holding the box would cause his heart to race. It was

crafted from a dark metal with detailed engravings of dragons and beasts. On the back was the emblem of the house of Ueshiba, a symbol dear to my father who grew up on O Sensei legends as a young boy.

He called upon a locksmith friend to crack the lock and it took the man a few days to do so without damaging the beautiful box. Inside were found a few items of personal value to O Sensei, items that could be sold to a museum for a good sum of money. There was also a book inside that had its own catch and was too delicate to open. My father was afraid that messing about with the catch might damage the book, consequently dropping the value of the historical object. He sniffed around and realised that none of the authorities would pay much for any of his items. So he searched for private collectors, people that still had interest in the unpopular art of Aikido. His locksmith friend wanted a cut and threatened to expose my father's intentions to the authorities. The items were considered a national treasure and therefore illegal to sell outside Japan. My father panicked and sold the whole box to an antique collector from Russia.

That was the only true lead in the search for the book and the one that most search parties followed. Locating people was easy with the Seekers' help but the high expectations turned to heavy frustration when the collector was found to be an antique dealer, buying for sale rather than for keeping. The book was lost in a shambles of records at the late man's mansion, the three vague leads emerging from that house caused further complications to the plot.

What had started as a hopeful quest turned into a bitter disappointment. Slowly but surely the searchers lost funds and the institute's interest. The Board came to terms with the option that the stories of the book were fictional and therefore kept available funding, for the quest, at a minimum level. It left the real search in the hands of treasure hunters; usually millionaires who would look for the book the way they would look for the Fountain of Youth. It was out of official hands and that made keeping up to date with all the information virtually impossible. That is how it was for the past hundred years: speculations, high hopes and very little physical evidence to back up any leads or findings.

12 Senseless Aggression

THE SKILL received international recognition around the year 2020 although most scholars believe that it was present the whole time but on a very small and unsystematic scale. The main question, therefore, was why it underwent such a growth in the twenties when the only supposed written work on the *Skill* was the Ueshiba book that had never been found.

It is believed that a different book, one that was read passionately by many around the globe, was the main reason for the boom in *Skilled aikidoka*. That book was published in the year 2011 by a small-time Aikido instructor who studied the process of O Sensei's development and composed a theory based on these findings. He himself didn't get very far in the art and was subsequently ridiculed as a shameless impostor yet the ideas written in his book were seriously considered by many.

Eventually some young practitioners of the art, striving for truth and progress, took the book into practice and ... It worked! Somehow the book gave the biggest drive to the art – the first-ever substantial method to connect with the *Skill*.

Mr Hafez, the Saudi Arabian *aikidoka* who wrote the book, declared that a high level of *Skill* was obtained through Aikido training under specific conditions. Those conditions were experiences taken from O Sensei's life, especially from the time he spent in Ayabe and Manchuria.

Hafez recommended that those experiences be recreated in order to gain access to the next level of the art. Later scholars found that many steps suggested by Hafez were unhelpful and in some cases a liability. Even some of the experiences he assumed O Sensei had had were proven not to have occurred in actual historical records. Whether mocked by jealousy or by scepticism, the importance of the book could not be ignored or forgotten. It gave great *aikidoka*, such as Jacques *Sensei*, founder of the School of Aikilibrium, the clues needed to develop the *Skill* in themselves.

The adventures O Sensei had in Manchuria were not well documented, and subsequently some of his experiences recreated by instructors of the *Skill* were misinterpretations that continued to be practised despite having proved to be unhelpful. It was agreed that the process had everything to do with the desperate and cruel conditions of the founder in Manchuria but not many agreed with the application of those experiences in the *dojo*. Some of the experiences practised were challenged and subsequently declared cruel and illegal according to the Board's rules, yet were still practised in secret.

One of those cruel methods was called 'Senseless Aggression' and it was based on an unconfirmed story told by a jailer of Ueshiba and his companions. The story suggests an incident that occurred inside the jailhouse where Ueshiba was kept awaiting execution. Based on this story the whole scheme of Senseless Aggression was created, a scheme practised in all *dojo* of the *Skill*. No one knew how necessary it really was but it was part of the known process and no one dared remove or question any part of the equation. Not all *dojo* used the same method but all shared some form of the Senseless Aggression.

* * *

Tanglio, Outer Mongolia, 1924

The hissing of the wind was a blessed sound among the screams of terror coming from outside, bringing an interval to the killing. Master Deguchi observed from the bare window as a group of Chinese prisoners were dragged at gunpoint around the corner of their jail. One of the condemned men tried to escape, but only managed a couple of steps before becoming entangled with the chains on his ankles and dropping to the ground in a cloud of dust. A sentinel approached him and smashed the handle of his gun into the man's shoulder, causing him to holler in pain, to the laughter of the guards. It was a lesson in human cruelty as one by one Deguchi's local allies were taken outside and shot dead.

They had behaved arrogantly on their expedition, all of them, disrespectful of the local politics and power games, expecting to conquer and rule this land of wilderness. Master Deguchi must have known of his failure, although the illusive crocodile didn't look troubled at all, as if everything was going according to plan.

It was nearing sunset and the slaughter which started in the morning didn't seem to subside. Group after group of terrified men passed by the window of Deguchi and his five comrades, to walk around the bend and never to return. They heard the gun shots and the screams and after a while they could distinguish the cries of pain from those of terror, learning unwillingly the array of sounds of anguish.

Tanglio was a relatively large town, stretching wide into the wilderness, but the Japanese didn't see much of it as they were held within the city walls, looking outside to where the killing was taking place. All six Japanese were tied up together by a long rope, extending to a pole outside their window. This forced them to move as one unit, whenever they walked around. They were suffering from diarrhoea and could never rest, taking frequent visits to the hole serving as their toilet. They were handcuffed individually and shackled by the legs in pairs, which encouraged the rest of the dwellers of the cell, who were not bound at all, to feel they could safely taunt them.

At first the Japanese were hoping that Ueshiba, King of Protectors, would stand as their shield but quickly learned that it was not so. Ueshiba, for reasons unknown to them, was quiet and reserved, apart from the times when he saw the guards and would suddenly try to converse with them, even begging for mercy. It embarrassed his Japanese comrades, but not Shaman Deguchi who was ever so calm, composing *waka* after *waka* of their final stance in the world.

'When at long last they will come for us, they will find our spirits aloft and our bodies ready. Embrace me brothers, and together we shall leave this world as one.' Deguchi's words were like a sedative to his disciples, but not to Ueshiba who remained gloomy and defiant. He couldn't accept death the way his friends did because he had a job on his hands and a quest unfulfilled. The situation they were in was desperate, he had no doubt about it, but he wouldn't just await his death. He tried to communicate with the guards, degrading himself as the other inmates giggled and his friends watched in resentment. He didn't mind degrading himself if it would help to save his master, although the taunting of the other inmates almost caused him to lose control.

The ten or so other prisoners were criminals awaiting execution; they were Chinese and with a very different mentality from that of the proud and spiritual Japanese. They threw the occasional abuse at the Japanese and when they received no reaction they became braver and the abusive remarks were accompanied by a kick or a strike. The Japanese tried to stay out of their way but the cell was small and they were forced to move around a lot because of their excruciating stomach pain.

Ueshiba was busy trying to find a way out for his master and he did not care for the petty desires of his comrades for regaining their pride. He degraded himself so much that the guards finally listened to his cries and took his message to their superiors for inspection. It was a message addressed to the local Japanese army post, and although it was highly inconceivable that the message would ever be sent, let alone arrive in time if it ever did, it was an effort that he considered worth degrading himself for. The Japanese nation had a strong desire for colonialism on the continent and was looking for an excuse to conquer land. An execution of a supposedly important Japanese delegate, such as Ueshiba portrayed Deguchi to be, could have been the very excuse the Japanese army was looking for and that alone could deter their captors from executing them.

Now Ueshiba sat silently, attached to Deguchi by shackles on his legs but miles away in thought and senses. He was perhaps at the lowest point in his life, which was the total opposite to how he felt only a week before. Since the day that he confronted the Chinese instructor, things had been moving in a positive direction: he had found the missing fragment for his art and was in the process of combining it with the other components that were ripe, ready to be fertilised ...

The circular movements were a blessed discovery that at the same time aggravated his sensitivity; it was a pleasant sensation outside their jail yet in the current environment he had to assemble all the power he had left in order to maintain emotional control. He was unbalanced and confused, confronted by a sweeping avalanche of life-threatening events while desperately suppressing the volcano that pulsated from within, on the verge of explosion. He was gloomy and lonely, sitting as far as he could from his mates and subjected to the cruel behaviour of the other inmates.

They were rough, thieves and murderers but they were not different in essence from the Japanese who came to their land to steal it, possessing grace and style but thieves just the same. The Chinese felt the silent arrogance and they reacted, and since there was no response, they were turning into real bullies.

The evening curved into darkness as the slaughter subsided outside and Reverend Deghchi stood and started on the night prayer, his disciples crowding around him in despair. Ueshiba was forced to stay close, tied by a leash like a dog attached to his master. He kept to himself, sitting on a floor soaked with water and human waste, head between his knees. He was bruised from a few kicks he had received from the inmates, and something inside him was about to blow, but not just yet.

The prayer raised a frightening feedback from the Chinese inmates and the one who was the biggest of the lot called on the shaman, his voice shrieking through the air, promising trouble. He cursed and advanced towards Deguchi, his evil intent accompanied by a drool and a grin.

'Out of the way!' he spat and pulled on one of the Japanese who stood with his back to him, punching him powerfully in the face. The beaten man fell, toppling down with him some of his friends that got tangled by their shackles.

'There you are, Shaman.' The Chinese cried and licked his lips. It was the first time that Deguchi had stood exposed and vulnerable. He sighed while focusing his gaze on the assailant, trying to control him with his piercing eyes but the man was not deterred.

Raising his clenched fist he struck in the reverent direction, smiling, pleased, as if he had already succeeded. Something blocked the punch, connected with the elbow of the assailant and knocked him sprawling to the floor, not really hurt but mainly shocked. Now that it was night and there were no guards around, Ueshiba had nobody to hide his identity from and he stood grimly, to show that no one was permitted to hurt the master.

The assailant regained his balance and charged at Ueshiba, to be struck in the abdomen with an iron fist, his body folding in half.

'Come help me get him!' he roared. One of his friends came to his aid but he was knocked out senseless and his body hit the ground, showing the grotesque bloody mess that previously was his nose. The rest of the prisoners growled and cursed but none of them was brave enough to approach.

It would have been wiser if his attacker stayed down, to allow Ueshiba the time to regain his senses but the ruffian thought otherwise. He was the leader of the inmates and he was not about to lose face. He thought that Ueshiba wouldn't dare take the fight any further, remembering the cowardly manner in which he had behaved the whole day.

'Die!' he screamed and charged in without a second thought. He didn't understand the logic of the Japanese fighter and the stress that he was under or else he would have backed away. All day long Ueshiba maintained his degrading behaviour, trying to gain some sympathy from the guards but now that there were no guards around and no one to perform in front of, he had completely lost control! The cork was off the volcano head, allowing the hot and unforgiving lava to spring out in a vapour, bringing chaos to the surroundings.

He dropped on all fours on impact, pushing the side of his body forwards at the attacker's legs, causing him to crumple. He didn't wait for the man to get up but jumped on top of him, dragging the poor insentient Deguchi who was attached to his legs and was no match for Ueshiba's supernatural power. *'Sarah!'* Ueshiba's war cry echoed as he mounted the assailant, 'Is this is what you really want?' He roared at the terrified man and then pounded him with all his might, hitting so hard that each and every blow was accompanied by a sickening sound. Bones and soft tissue were giving way to the denting strikes, blood and fluids sprayed all over the floor but Ueshiba was not finished yet.

No one dared to try and stop him, no one called the guards; the cell was under a silent spell, the prisoners seized with terror, watching numbly from the side, witnesses to the unstylish and highly vicious attack. Ueshiba, the man of control, was towering over the whimpering man and was kicking and stomping until there was no more movement left to the body, not a twitch nor a sigh.

He finally stopped the thrashing and raised his head, fists drenched in blood and eyes like those of a guardian fiend. He scanned the people around the room, who were trying to hide in the shadows, then he sat back on the floor, rubbing his fists, his chest raising and falling from the struggle and the horror. Never in his life had he ever lost control or hurt a fellow human being out of rage; he couldn't believe himself, knowing that he could have subdued the man without the damage, that his victim would be lucky to stay alive.

Ueshiba's eyes caught a reflection of his face on the muddy floor and his head jerked back in horror for it wasn't his face that he saw in the filthy puddle but that of his previous mentor, that of the ruthless Sokaku Takeda. The murderous eyes that in the past he so longed to possess; the curled-down lips, filled with contempt for the feeble, stared back at him from the murky water. The realisation that his wish had finally come true was hard to endure, driving a chill down his spine, sending Ueshiba back to the dark mood that had engulfed him. He could sense an emptiness inside him and he went through the purifying techniques he learned as an *Omoto* religion practitioner, detaching himself from the world.

* * *

It was the morning of the day of the test. Jerome got up early as usual, tired and afraid, his sleep disturbed by the chronic dull pains in his stomach and the heavy ache in the arm that was not yet fully recovered. He was afraid of the test itself, uncertain whether he would be able to perform properly, dreading what Henri might do to him if he failed. The months he had spent at the school had taught him to fear the teacher for so many reasons.

He looked at Max as he got up and walked to the toilet and he shook his head.

'You'd better not be late today!' he warmly called.

'And why is that?' Max stopped but didn't turn to face him.

'The test remember?'

'Oh yeah – the test.' A moment of strenuous silence went by.

'Max?'

'Yes?'

'Are you all right, man?'

'Yes I'm fine.' Max turned his head and smiled gently, 'But I am not going to rush for anything but the toilets. Yves, Henri and the rest of the world can wait! Now if you excuse me.' Jerome smiled and watched Max disappearing out the room.

I envy you, Max, Jerome sighed. *You fear and respect none of these bastards while I am petrified by their authority alone! I have to conquer my fears, or else I am doomed.* Jerome sighed again then got dressed and walked to the bathroom, brushing by Max.

'Hi, J.' He clapped Jerome on the back and peered at him with sorrowful eyes. It seemed as if Max had forgiven him for the conversation of the night before.

Maybe you do understand, maybe you know that I am not a coward after all.

In no time the door was open and Henri ordered them to move. Jerome walked in front, not missing the wounded look in Max's eyes. He might have forgiven Jerome but he certainly hadn't forgotten.

They reached the Plain *Dojo* and walked in. Inside there was nothing to suggest the occasion, no spectators, as was the custom in most martial arts tests. Students of the *Skill* were sheltered and kept out of the public eye at all times. They sat in *seiza* waiting for the test to start and Henri took a position in front of the two. Jerome and Max exchanged looks; Henri had never sat so close to them before.

Five minutes later the door slid open and Yves *Sensei* stepped in. He walked to the centre of the *dojo*, tall and confident, and sat in front of the picture of Master Jacques. Henri called the bows and then Yves got up and walked quietly to the edge of the mat. Majestically he lowered himself into sitting position and gave a sign with his hand.

Henri shouted, '*Osu!*' and dashed to the front. He ordered the boys to stand up; they bowed and assumed the *kamai* position, facing the *sensei*. Henri called the first technical command and they started with the shadow movements, going through basic Aikido elements and demonstrating the placement of their centres. There were many turning moves, most of which were done in *Suri Ashi*, moving by sliding rather than stepping, an essential ingredient for the connection to the floor. The boys were sliding left and right, turning and spinning around to Henri's commands.

Yves raised his arm and Henri gave the order to change techniques. Now they were demonstrating the same moves but as partners, operating as one, an awesome display of connection and fluidity.

Jerome loved Aikido for precisely that reason. The moments when he was engulfed by the art were the best moments of his captivity and perhaps the best moments of his life. Everything went perfectly well, there was no resistance in the movements as they flowed together, a pure joy to the eye.

'*Yame!*' Henri bellowed, following the silent gesture from his master. Jerome and Max pulled away and stood in *kamai* facing each other. Their chests were heaving quietly but they remained composed, disciplined and focused. Henri waited a tense moment and then took them through a variety of locks and throws. They knew all the techniques and performed them beautifully, flowing harmoniously with each other. Everything they did was powerful and dramatic, but no one got hurt. Once again Henri called them to pull away and by this stage Jerome had started to sway a little.

He tried to stay straight and collected, but his body shook in response to his efforts. From the corner of his eye he saw Henri watching him angrily and he tried to maintain his composure, knowing how badly Henri was trying to impress his mentor with the results of his teaching. He fought his body to relax and was caught off guard as the free techniques started.

Max attacked with *Shomen Uchi*, a swordlike cut from above, which landed straight on Jerome's forehead. His head bounced back but he managed to turn and initiate a feeble *Kokyunage*, breath throw, aided by Max's *uke*. He knew that it wouldn't escape the trained eyes of Henri and Yves but it was the best he could do.

Max continued the attack until Henri gave the command to change roles.

I am so exhausted brother, Jerome panted while staring at his friend. *I can barely stand!*

'*Hajime!*' Henri ordered and Jerome cried in frustration and moved in. He did the best he could to get up and re-attack Max yet the more he was launched onto the mats the harder it became.

'Come on!' he encouraged himself, the words cutting at his dry mouth. His legs shook madly, his whole body out of control and eventually he had to crawl to the attack. Max looked empathically at him, he was not as exhausted as Jerome was, his high level of expertise allowing him to use far less energy.

'*Yame!*' Henri finally roared and the boys faced each other in *kamai*. To the appropriate commands they tidied up, bowed to each other and then to the *sensei*. Yves left the room soundlessly and Jerome remained half dazed, sitting on the mat in *seiza*.

Henri only waited for the door to close before he charged at Jerome and kicked him in the face. 'I warned you, didn't I? I told you what would happen if you shamed me. Now you will pay.' Without further words he kicked Jerome in the ribs as he lay on the floor, holding his bleeding face. Jerome felt his heart pumping fast in reaction to the pain and stress.

I know you are out to kill me! Jerome curled into a ball, face covered in blood and his arms shielding his head, more an instinct than a conscious act.

'Stop it, you'll kill him!' He faintly heard Max's voice in the background and suddenly the beating stopped, Henri was shifting his ill intentions elsewhere.

'You!' he spat at Max. 'You dare try to confront me, you little shit!' He sounded angrier than he ever had before.

Jerome lifted his head and through the blur of tears he saw the broken nose of Henri. 'Idiot!' he cursed quietly, blaming himself for the clear danger Max was in. It was his fault; Max was only standing up to protect him.

'I wanted to be rid of this useless chicken,' Henri growled and pointed at Jerome. 'But it looks like I will have another chicken after all.' And he launched at Max, face contoured in hate, smeared with blood and tears.

'Come on, grandpa, show me what you've got!' Max teased the *sensei*, diverting his blows with ease and relative success.

Don't get cocky Max – you are not that good. Max look out! A punch from the left caught Max dead on the temple and it sank him to the floor.

Henri laughed loudly. 'Oh, what's wrong, pussy cat? Can't take the beating? Is my fist too strong for you? How about a kick then?'

Desperately, Jerome realised that Max was about to be killed; watching Henri kicking him mercilessly, all because he had come to protect him.

'No! You let go of him!' A sudden surge of energy drove Jerome up and he charged at the brutal instructor. First the fears vanished then the terrifying thought of what he must do. 'Arrrgh!' he screamed, and landed the first punch, then he didn't think any more. Henri's surprised face was turning to confront him, his mouth bellowing commands Jerome couldn't make out. The world around Jerome was silent, his vision filtered through the colour red.

Young fists pounded through the *sensei's* defence, hitting anything in the way. Henri had exhausted himself assaulting the two boys and he was panting heavily, his shoulders sore from the effort of lifting his arms to protect. Jerome cracked through the weak defence and struck the *sensei* on the inside. 'No!' he kept crying while hitting ruthlessly at the hated *sensei*. The dissociation was pushing him in a wild and senseless attack, an assault driven by primitive reflexes. Jerome was not aware of his actions, operating without a thought or conscience and Max watched him quietly from the side, not daring to intervene. The primeval pleasure of crushing his instructor took over Jerome. He broke some of the bones in his fists as he was hitting Henri and when he could hit no more with them he used his elbows and knees. 'No!' he cried and screamed, striking wildly at Henri, long after the *sensei* stopped giving resistance.

Eventually Max pulled him off and pushed him to the wall in a bear hug. He clenched Jerome strongly, the muscles in his arms and shoulders tightening as hard as rock. 'Shhh … Stop brother,' he whispered to Jerome who was trying to charge back at the bloody pulp on the *tatami* floor. All those months of self-control and focus were gone in a mad frenzy, liberating and confusing.

Jerome started to unwind slowly, to connect with his surroundings. He looked at Henri and he looked at his bloodied hands and blood-splattered shirt, acknowledging that most of it was not his own. Recognition sank in, slouching his whole body down. He was a victim of Senseless Aggression. Now he would have to live with it.

13 Second-Level Techniques: Dai Ni Kihon

The spiritual world of Aikido is based on the mysticism of sound and vibrations, *Kotodama* in Japanese. Ueshiba was adept in its practicality, often boasting that he was the only one who still practised true *Kotodama* in Japan. For years the purpose of the art was lost as many *aikidoka* failed to take Ueshiba's words seriously and when the true nature of the *Skill* finally emerged much of the information connecting first- and second-level techniques was gone forever.

The second level of techniques use the physical fundamentals of Aikido as a vehicle to allow the spirit to flourish. The founder emphasised spirituality as the main objective of the art and both privately and publicly engaged in sacred practices throughout his life. Aikido was an obstacle course for the founder, taking almost forty years to complete, but he was well rewarded, finding the right path to his *kami*.

Ueshiba was a secretive man, privately conducting the spiritual ceremonies, and with them the right combination of *Kotodama* sounds. He preferred not to donate too much information to others, a lesson he had learned thoroughly during the Second World War. He was avoiding glory well deserved and concealing his true powers.

Fifty years after he had passed away a new generation of *aikidoka* were painstakingly processing a pattern that would pave the way back to the *Skill*. It was crude and not very effective, overloaded with the founder's life experiences gathered through studies involving trial and error. That was the reason everyone longed for the book of the *Skill*, although it didn't stop the researchers from exploring and improving the known patterns. Some of the researchers were experimenting with the chronological order of events in Ueshiba's life and eventually changed the order in which those experiences were practised, simply because it proved to hasten the process. One of those irregularities was the timing in which the spiritual studies took place.

Ueshiba practised mysticism hand in hand with his martial art training and that joint fascination paved his way to the *Skill*. It might have been the way in which the art was formed, yet the 'chronological researchers' proved that the employment of spiritual studies after the completion of the first level of techniques was far more beneficial. It produced the quickest and most efficient results yet. The physical training serves as a perfect mould for the primal experience of the divine, which is at its most pure and potent when experienced for the first time.

'*Kotodama* practice is at the heart of the art,' Ueshiba *Sensei* once declared, 'because true Aikido is performed in the twilight zone of creation, at the *Kotodama Su*.' The spiritual practices include *Misogi* – purification of the body and mind; *Chinkon Kishin* – calming of the spirit and the return to the source; *Kokyu* – breathing and the understanding of *Ki* – energy. Most of these rituals incorporated Aikido body movements or used weaponry techniques. Aikido and weapon practice were not the only applications for these *Shinto* religion-based practices but they were the ones that O Sensei used and therefore the preferred methods for reviving the *Skill*.

With all this rough science around, all that remained for the *Skill* revivers was to put the ingredients together and hope for magic to appear.

* * *

Outer Mongolia, winter, 1924

The master was drained of power yet there were plenty more patients to attend to, the line stretching far beyond the flapping entrance of the tent. It was another cold, dusty day, most of the patients swaying in the wind, eyes squinted and supported by hopeful friends or relatives.

Lu, the Chinese warlord, had ordered the day's activities, and had as usual acted with senseless excess. He sat outside the tent on his beautiful white horse, shouting commands for law and order to be maintained, loudly praising the great Onisaburo Deguchi.

Ueshiba watched the master treating a young girl that lay on the mattress; her pale face followed every move of Deguchi, fingers clutching weakly at the hard straw mat. He reached out and rubbed Deguchi's back, fearing for his fragile health, knowing how much the healing was taking of the Reverend's resources. They were outside Solon, yet again demonstrating the Japanese Shaman's powers, gaining support from the locals for the realisation of his dreams ...

The girl coughed on the dirty mat and Deguchi wiped her face, chanting while holding her thin wrist. The colour was returning to the sallow cheeks, she was feeling much better, blessing and thanking the master in an unfamiliar dialect and language. Her mother was called into the tent and she carried her daughter while bowing to the miracle man, who looked paler than her daughter.

Ueshiba called the interpreter. 'Go and tell Lu to send some of these patients away – there are too many!'

'But sir,' the man begged, 'Lu is not a man to change his decisions.'

'Get going!' Ueshiba barked, gesturing forcefully with his arm to emphasise his words.

'Yes sir,' the man called then ran outside. He had to obey the mighty Wang, challenging the warrior's authority once was more then enough.

And here is the next patient – Ueshiba sighed as another sickly-looking person was helped into the tent. Deguchi sighed heavily and coughed productively into a filthy piece of cloth.

'Morihei, you will have to replace me!' he ordered and rolled off the healer's spot, lifting his upper body momentarily, to collapse on the mat behind his warrior. Ueshiba mumbled uncertainly as he helped the wide-eyed patient lie down, glancing at his master worriedly.

'I will be fine Morihei, don't worry. I just need a break, honestly, that's all!'

The master was truthful, his eyes shining powerfully from within the tired face. A new worry confronted Morihei and he questioned his ability to perform the task in hand. It wasn't the first time he had practised 'hands on' healing techniques yet he had never treated the truly sick. That was Deguchi's speciality, which was what he was famous for – not Ueshiba though, who was a troubled man of war. He looked out of the door flaps and saw Lu shouting orders around, his soldiers dispersing the less ill patients. Ueshiba exhaled loudly, mildly relieved although there were plenty more patients to attend to. Lu wouldn't let them off the hook completely.

'*Sensei*,' he started to complain, sitting down in front of the bluish old man, twisting uncomfortably inside the thick coat. Deguchi leaned towards him, supported on an unstable elbow.

'Don't worry, I said I am right here to help you.' Ueshiba bowed severely, the only sign for his growing distress being the raised shoulders. He sat in front of the patient, confused, not knowing where to start.

'This one is simple,' Deguchi remarked and fused back with the mattress. 'You won't need any help with him.'

'*Osu!*' Morihei replied, sweat appearing on his forehead despite the bitterly cold air. He sat cross-legged and closed his eyes, trying to relax, remembering the words of the master, long ago, when he had taught him how to heal.

'You are no good to anyone if you can't relax yourself before the treatment. The depth of your *Chinkon Kishin* will determine the results of the procedure.'

He nodded to himself and joined the breathing cycle, circling his shoulders, the tension easing away. *Ah ... that's better.* His fingers rubbed his face gently, sensing how the hard lines were softening to the touch. Ueshiba opened his eyes and placed his hands on the man's abdomen. He felt for the man's cycle and he joined him with his own, sensitive to the movements of the trunk.

'Your hands need to connect further to his body and the breathing muscles. Concentrate!' Deguchi called, 'For you must seek the inner secrets of the soul.'

The words reminded Ueshiba of what to do, the presence of the master behind him serving as a soothing backbone against failure. It also made him weary of mistakes, feeling shadowed by the Reverend.

Following the rehearsed pattern he eased the intense tightness of the man's chest, compelling the tears to dry out and the pain to disappear. The patient was taken outside, the session declared successful and Morihei motioned for the guard to send the next patient in, more confident than before. The next two patients needed simple tending for facial wounds and the Reverend watched briefly then ordered Morihei how to clean and dress the wounds; a down-to-earth kind of healing. The fourth patient was a repetition of the first, a simple stimulation of the breathing cycle and the problem was over. It was superficial, yet it worked, and Ueshiba's confidence was established.

'Not all patients are that easy.' Deguchi suddenly whispered.

'I know Master – yet I hope today they will be.'

'You hope so,' Deguchi giggled, the words ending in a heavy productive cough and a much damper handkerchief.

The tent door flipped open and an out-of-breath woman was carried in, leaning heavily on two large Manchurians. Ueshiba motioned them to lay her in front of him yet she refused to recline, sitting with her arms stretched to the ground, supporting the upper body and a chest that inefficiently pumped the air in and out. Veins were bulging at her neck, eyes terminally focusing forwards, pleading for salvation without a sound. He tried to connect to her, placing his hand on her centre to calm her down, yet she was oblivious to his wishes, and was fighting for her life.

Panic overtook the fragile confidence of Ueshiba, his incompetence from bitter memories of the past suddenly returning to haunt him. *This is way beyond my capabilities!* Ueshiba looked in despair at the master who lay quietly with a knowing smile.

'You have to intervene, Morihei. This is no time for your fears to commence. Place your hand once again on her centre and I will help you treat the flesh.'

Morihei obeyed and closed his eyes, connecting to the patient with his hands, the master supporting his lower back. The woman was showing growing signs of stress, her breathing louder than before.

'Feel her pulse, Morihei. Close your eyes and listen to the sounds.'

Drenched in sweat and uncomfortably warm, Morihei reached and held the woman's wrist, searching for palpitations with his coarse fingers. The pulse was weak and fast, he could sense that much, yet he didn't know what it meant, couldn't comprehend the hidden cause. He closed his eyes just to open them once more, startled, suddenly very aware of the master's hand.

'Close your eyes again, Morihei, be part of the process!' Deguchi demanded. 'I am using you to channel back and forth to the patient. It won't hurt, yet it will drain you from some energy.'

'What Master?' Ueshiba asked confused.

'Shhh Morihei, stay alert; trust me – it will be an important lesson today.'

His words sounded focused and strong, the way he would sound when teaching a complicated lesson. Morihei was tempted to take a careful look at the master, to judge whether he was truly exhausted or simply luring him into a trap, one of his many deceptive teaching methods.

'The patient is waiting,' Deguchi reminded him, sounding faint and unwell again, coughing and spitting into the cloth.

There was no time to waste and Morihei closed his eyes and concentrated, surrendering to the warm and soft palm at his back, giving himself to the master.

He held the agitated patient's wrist and felt much calmer than before, Deguchi's arm moving in synchronisation with his relaxed breathing pattern. The connection between the patient and Deguchi was established and Ueshiba waited for the process to begin, remembering to stay erect and strong – a beam of energy for the use of the master.

This is unbelievable! Knowledge was pouring from the patient's body and ebbing towards the master's arm; it rewarded Ueshiba with its truth and meaning, blazing through his body and projecting to his mind. Vividly he sensed the irritated heart muscle, felt the organ's electricity disrupted in an unsynchronised flow.

It is so feeble. Blood was pumped insufficiently to the demand of the fragile body, the condition further aggravated by the patient's fear and stress.

I must remain strong! Ueshiba reminded himself as knowledge robbed him out of vital energy. *Don't worry, Master, you can trust me. I would hold on for as long as necessary.*

'Move your palm to her upper abdomen,' Deguchi suddenly whispered. 'Quickly now, her heart is running out of power!'

Ueshiba obeyed, face contoured in concentration, recognising the signs of distress in the patient. His hands rested on the woman's middle, on the lower ridge of her ribs. Deguchi's hand pulsated behind him, each and every stroke stimulating Ueshiba, tearing energy from his core. *I can sense the flow of your power, Master!* Ueshiba was bewildered, guided by currents that shot down his arm. The patient reacted to the stimulation; her stomach muscles spasmodically compressing and then relaxing, influencing in turn the diaphragm to jerk between loose and tense. Ueshiba wanted to pull his hand from the patient's aggressive body movement, fearful of causing her harm.

'Don't you dare move your arm,' he heard the master demanding, as usual sensing Ueshiba's every intention, stopping him before the connection was lost.

'*Osu* Master.' He held his spot, keeping his palm calm and supportive, firmly attached to the combative woman. Deguchi finally stopped the strenuous stimulation and the patient collapsed backwards, her chest heaving with strain. Ueshiba opened his eyes and pulled his lip backwards, inhaling in a soft whistle and then loudly exhaling.

'Focus on relaxing her breathing, Morihei, the woman is now out of danger. You really don't need my help any more with this one; I think that for now I am done!'

Shaken, though determined, Ueshiba held the woman as was ordered, the master's hand removed from his back. She reacted positively to his soothing touch, her breathing calming down, a grateful look in her eyes. Beyond the gratitude Morihei felt the calmed pulse, slower and fuller, the medical emergency solved. That was the extent of the information that he could retrieve by himself, the deeper more detailed sensation removed with the master's hand.

Deguchi ordered a course of herbs to be taken by the patient and the woman was dragged outside.

'This is so difficult!' Morihei complained then dropped down to the mat. He stretched out, his spine cracking with the release of tension. He glanced at the master who lay on his back next to him, staring motionless at the pointed ceiling, a mischievous expression on his face.

'Are you all right, Morihei?' he asked without moving a muscle, his lips barely pushing the words out.

'Yes, *Sensei*,' Morihei grunted and sat up in time to welcome the bowing man who stood at the entrance, a new condition to combat.

Ueshiba took another glimpse at Deguchi, wondering what the old crocodile was plotting now. As if to raise further suspicion the master chuckled to himself, then coughed and spat once again.

You are so deceiving Master! Morihei sighed and placed his hands on the patient's abdomen with a sad smile: there was plenty of work to do and the day had only just begun.

14 Recollection

Every person is an island, a body that gives rise to the soul, a deserted place vacant for only one. Some enjoy their little island while others ignore it, terrified to be alone on the shores of their own true reality.

Human beings are constantly bombarded by external information which causes them to forget how alone they truly are. It provides a blessed escape route for the torments of the soul but also forces the spirit to recollect socially or environmentally, to leave the centre of the island unguarded.

External recollection is the phone call people make to their friends after a fight with the boss, to tell them of their troubles and to hear that they are all right, that their place in society is secure. It can be the house, the room, the village or the town, wherever it feels right and safe. Ultimately, external recollection stimulates the core, the private shores of the individuals but the connection is indirect and therefore feeble.

Recollection needs more than a simple phone call, yet most people would never experience their real 'collection point' as life rarely presents such an opportunity and not coincidentally so. For touching the source is the hardest task of all, one that requires a look on the inside, to find where the self truly hides.

JEROME PUT the book down with shaking arms, the movement accompanied by sharp rays of pain that travelled from the swollen knuckles to his neck and head. It has been a week since their test and the healing process was slow. Quietly he lifted up and walked towards the sink, washing his hands carefully and watching the battered face that was reflected from the little mirror above the tap. The left side of his face was covered with black and blue marks, swollen lips and a bloodshot eye. Hastily he shifted his gaze from the sight, from the bitter reminder of his actions and their consequences. *I miss you, Max – hope you are well.* He started to sink into the dark and deserted corner of his soul, when the door opened and George entered. He looked at Jerome and gave him a warm smile.

'I see that you have finally woken up,' he said and pointed with his hand to the door. He waited for Jerome to follow his gesture and the latter obeyed without a sound.

The past few days had been a real torment for Jerome, and none of the rest, food and lack of stomach aches could have pacified the pain he felt on the inside. He had lost control in a way that shook him to his core, to the foundation of his judgment of good and evil. His morals and perspective of himself were shattered where previously they had been the only stable things in his life. He had no one he could trust as he and Max were separated after the test, each taken to different quarters. At first Jerome thought that he was being taken to be killed but gradually he reasoned to himself that the place must be some sort of recovery room. It was located in the same building as before but he was staying to the right side of their previous quarters while Max was taken to the left.

It wasn't easy to break the two friends' grip after the test without hurting them, and four strong *aikidoka* had to be fetched for the task. Jerome remembered the last words of Max before they were finally separated. 'Don't let them kill me, J! You are the only one here for me.' Then he was gone and Jerome felt lost and lonely.

He was confined to solitude, recovering from his injuries and catching up with some sleep. Then, two days ago, the door opened and George arrived, gradually resuming Jerome's training. It was nowhere as intense as the way he had been practising before.

George was very patient and lighter in his attitude compared to Henri although he did maintained formality and discipline. Jerome didn't mind being back at training. He had grown to love and respect the art with all his heart – and exercising Aikido with George was relaxed and fun.

'Slept well?'

'Yes I have, thank you *Sensei.*'

'Very well then – are you ready for training?' Jerome nodded and walked towards the softly smiling teacher.

George, you are treating me very kindly but I suspected that it's only a trick intended to lower my guard. Sorry Sensei but I can't trust you! Jerome eyes were narrowed as he approached the door but if George sensed any of his distrust he failed to show it. He led Jerome through the corridor with the doors to the training halls on both sides. He passed by the Plain *Dojo* and stopped in front of a door slightly ahead and in the opposite wall from his previous training hall. Jerome stood behind George obediently, waiting for the *sensei*'s move.

'This door leads to the meditation room, a place we use to learn and perform spiritual practices. It is equipped with the most advanced technological devices to help you with the study.' He looked at his student to see if he understood, then opened the door and let him step inside. Jerome was excited as he entered, for it was the first time he had seen a different hall – a hall that was not plain at all!

The floor was coated in thousands of white pebbles, unified in size and tightly packed. They behaved as a giant canvas, brushes occasionally rearranging the positions of the tiny stones, portraying imaginative designs of Zen Buddhism that twirled in wavy patterns on the floor. Dark rocks broke the even surface, penetrating through the waves, looking like huge islands, their shores washed calmly by an even sea of stones. The walls were made of fine oaken wood, their soft, rich brown colour trickling to the whiteness of the floor, mingling with the room's peaceful atmosphere. The odd spectacle of the ground had a soothing effect on Jerome, consuming some of the stress that his body maintained.

The hall was much larger than the Plain *Dojo*, with a vast empty space in the middle of the gravel sea. George smiled at Jerome and gestured with his hand to the middle of the circle. Jerome walked in front.

'Sit down in *seiza*,' George ordered and then sat next to Jerome. 'I will try and teach your first meditation technique. I believe it will help you deal with some of the experiences you've had in your life.'

'Do you mean stuff like being kidnapped and threatened with death?' The bitterness did not escape George's sensitive ears.

'I am not your enemy, Jerome, but on the contrary, I am here to make your stay appealing, productive and satisfying.'

'But you won't be able to stop all the madness that is going on here and it won't change the fact that either myself or Max will be sacrificed, will it?'

George grimaced and gave a little sigh before answering in a very final fashion. 'Everyone dies, my dear boy. That is the price all of us pay for being alive. Yet there is no guilt if you live a short and fulfilling life, believe me, as it is ten times better than a long and sheltered one.'

Jerome instinctively gave a resentful laugh. 'How can being confined to a prison, be it an Aikido prison or any other jail, can ever be described as fulfilling?'

George contemplated the question for a moment. He knew the answer but calculated his words before responding. 'Try and think about it,' he finally said. 'Theoretically speaking fulfilment has nothing to do with the place that you are at, the people that you see or even the danger you are under. It is the attitude you have towards your situation, as hard as it might be, that counts. Wouldn't you consider the ability of tackling your present condition as the greatest gift of all, situations that in a way reflect the impossibility of life itself?'

Jerome found it hard to accept George's words although they made perfect sense. 'You might be right on this issue, although the impossibility of life at the moment is directly connected to this place.' He held his chin high and George allowed him to blow off steam; something Henri would never let them do.

'Many of the great spiritual leaders confined themselves to isolation and imprisonment in order to reach higher understanding. I could argue your position as the best possible condition for such studies.' George was making sense and infuriating Jerome further.

'I guess I'm as lucky as can be,' he said sarcastically but George ignored him this time.

'There exists external and internal spirituality. Each is located in a different place of the human consciousness and each is extremely important. Yet it is the inner world that is emphasised in this part of the training, the one that is the base for both states.' It all sounded very obscure to Jerome but he stayed silent and attentive.

George shook his head and gave a little smile, sensing his

student's doubts and confusion. He ordered Jerome to close his eyes. 'Avoid the temptation to have a look as it will break the flow of your practice.' He spoke softly, his words pronounced, elongated in their ending. 'Now concentrate on your breathing: slowly allow its cycle to take over your control; let it become your inner drive of movement.' Jerome followed George fully, his forehead in folds of concentration.

'Focus on your abdomen and put both hands on it gently; feel its warmth.' Jerome couldn't tell where George was leading but he tried to let him be the guide, to let him control the inner workings of his body.

'Imagine the air is coloured white and of pure and tender composition ... Gently flare your nostrils, tempting the air to move in ... Inhale, sense the way in which the stomach muscles expand and interact with your palms, pushing them away from the centre ... Hold the air a comforting second before the release ... Exhale, allow pain and discomfort to travel away from your body and soul, the palms moving gently towards your core.'

Fractions of George's words made a strong impression on Jerome but his natural instinct was to resist and his body refused to cooperate. George sensed his inhibition and he stopped the drill, ordering Jerome to stretch his legs. *Seiza* sitting position was not the most natural or pain-free posture but it kept the body centred.

'We have to try something more basic to begin with; your breathing cycle is not well established.'

Jerome chuckled involuntary but his eyes showed the confusion; he was not sure whether the *sensei* was joking. 'I don't understand,' he said. 'I am breathing well enough by myself and I don't feel any difficulty in the process. Well, not unless I am pushed to do *Ukemi* for half an hour.' His words were gaining passion; he was being pulled back to the memories of the test, getting angry ... there was no resistance to the speech and he quickly returned to the original conversation. 'So why do you think I can't breathe?'

George looked at him with amusement, as if he were a silly child.

'I never said you couldn't breathe; I only stated that your cycle is not well established.' He stopped smiling, his hand gently resting on his thigh. 'Under normal circumstances the body's demand for oxygen is far lower than the amount the lungs can provide. That is the reason healthy individuals in the world breathe effortlessly. It is also the reason for tightness, pain and imbalance in the body, caused by laziness driven by abundance. If you have too much of something you lose your respect of its true value. There are plenty of numb or overly tense muscles surrounding the trunk because of this laziness, and it breaks the flow of the body and disturbs the mind. I will stimulate these numb muscles in you, ease the tension until you reach your natural cycle.'

Jerome's eyes were squinted, concentrating on every word, finding it hard to understand. 'So what's next?'

'The first step for you to master is coordination, to force the breathing muscles to work in synchronisation, just as you learned to do with the skeletal muscles in *Dai Ichi Kihon Waza*.' Jerome raised his shoulders and George smiled again. 'Don't you worry, true appreciation of my words will soon come with practice.' He closed his eyes, stretched and centred his body, palms still resting on the thighs. He waited one second in total silence and then opened his eyes, smiling caringly at his student.

'We will start with stomach breathing so please sit in *seiza* once more and place your left hand on the abdomen.'

'Like so?'

'That's fine. Now I want you to pay attention to the pit of your stomach, the most creative place in the body. Try and let the stomach muscles relax as you inhale, pushing the abdomen out. When you exhale reverse the process, flexing your stomach muscles.' Jerome raised his eyebrows looking more confused than ever, but he followed George's instructions. There wasn't any real difficulty in performing the exercise and Jerome was in no time sensing and joining the natural cycle of his breathing.

'Keep your eyes closed and stretch the spine; the hips connecting to the earth, the head reaching for the heavens.' The words were operating the student, turning the slouch into a straight and centred posture.

'Try and maintain your concentration on your breathing and

posture alone. Get into the process until you become the process itself.' It baffled Jerome to hear such sensual descriptions, not entirely sure whether to allow them to take their effect. His thoughts were shifting and drifting in all directions but they gradually faded away, permitting an unbelievable stillness to descend upon him. The little hairs on the back of his neck stood erect from the current that rushed down his spine; never before had he felt so comfortable and easy, a sensation he had longed for all his life. He was like a turtle, snug and comfortable in his own shell. George waited quietly a few moments and then he gently ordered Jerome to open his eyes. He obeyed and swayed on his knees, light-headed, intoxicated as if drunk.

'Get out of the *seiza* position and stretch your legs.' George patiently waited for Jerome to comply, rubbing his palms together, looking pleased and undisturbed.

'I feel so relaxed.'

'Nice one, I guess you sensed a bit of what I was talking about. Now I want you to try another exercise, concentrating on your chest breathing.'

'*Osu sensei*!' The doubts Jerome had before the last drill were all gone now, if anything he was deeply intrigued by the sensations he had experienced.

George ordered him to resume *seiza*. 'Place your left palm on the centre of your chest, close your eyes and start breathing.' Jerome listened and tried to follow but this time the exercise was much harder to perform. Technically the drill made sense but it presented Jerome with unexpected difficulties; the harder he tried to perform the harder it became.

George was aware of the complications and he soon tried another way. 'Keep your eyes closed, slowly recline backwards until you are lying down fully stretched.' He supported Jerome's back, helping him to follow his words. 'Now I am going to place my hands over your centre ... Try and follow my palms with your concentration and move the place I touch with your breathing muscles alone.'

'*Osu sensei,*' Jerome whispered and followed the George's warm and soft palms. His tight chest was hurting from the movement within, a pain that was surfacing, reacting to the tempting touch.

George was attentive to Jerome's reaction, sensing him through his hands, watching the muscles of his face twitch. 'Don't panic, young Jerome, the pain you are experiencing is the pain of your soul ... Resist it and it will get worse ... Let go...Concentrate on my palms and your breathing; let me worry about the pain.'

Normally Jerome would show strong resistance to anyone trying to penetrate the shield he had built around his core but somehow he allowed George access; perhaps too intoxicated by the cleansing act of the air to object.

George worked gently with his hands, brushing at boy's chest until he finally reacted. *Ahhh ... it feels so good!* Jerome's chest was spreading wider with each and every gulp of air, the movement almost reaching to his shoulders. Then as his usual flow of thoughts was clearing away the vacancy remaining allowed a deeper voice to surface. Suddenly he was fading away from the process, wandering adrift. He was not in charge any more, George's hands stimulating him further. Then George touched the place where the chest was fused with resistance and Jerome stopped reacting, his conscious lost and his body in deep sleep. George didn't wake him right away but waited a few minutes, allowing his student to regroup and calm his heart rate.

A gentle hand was at Jerome's shoulder and George's words reached the boy through his deep slumber. 'Wake up, young Jerome, but take your time; there is no rush.' Too late! The boy jumped up to his feet, shaken by the experience. George looked at him and nodded in approval, calming his student with the sincerity in his eyes.

'What happened?' Jerome demanded his mouth dry and his eyes moving in all directions.

'Nothing unusual, I promise you, a reaction that is totally normal. You are not used to people prodding at your core and as you are starting to find out, breathing is not just the action of inhaling and exhaling; it is the seam between your mind and body, a remnant of the divine.'

'OK,' said Jerome not very convinced or understanding. 'Now I am really at a loss.' George sighed and scratched his head. It was not going to be an easy lesson.

'It might be some time before you grasp the full implications of my words yet they are not fiction. Breathing, you see, is the inner mechanism of the body and soul.'

'The inner mechanism?'

'Oh yes. The abdomen, for example, is considered to be the source for the power of creation while the chest is the kingdom of the emotional plane. The harsher the conditions the more rigid and protective the chest wall becomes. Feel your own – it is as hard as a rock!'

He took Jerome's hand and placed it on his chest. 'Feel the movement of my chest and try to memorise the way it feels.' The muscles in his face relaxed and he started to breathe. Jerome closed his eyes, his palm on the *sensei's* chest. It was quite a display of emotional control; George demonstrated a variety of breathing patterns, comfortably explaining, as if unaffected by the sensual wealth.

'First the depressed person's breathing,' he announced and his lower jaw dropped in a miserable expression, chest sunken and breathing shallow, exhaling in a sigh. 'Depressed breathing is superficial and stuck in the throat area, which is the cause of the noise. Now angry breathing.' His nostrils flared, upper lip exposing teeth and gums and his breathing became powerful, the energy trying to burst the cover of his emotional shield. 'Angry breathing is characterised by the air entering through the nostrils and the chest expanding to its fullest.' George's breathing sounded like that of a raging bull and he looked comically scary.

'What are you laughing at?'

'Well,' Jerome chuckled, Your face!' George went through a few more demonstrations then Jerome resumed exercising, lying down with George's hands to guide him.

'Relax my boy.'

'I will do my best *Sensei*.' He tried to immerse himself in the breathing cycle but would either fall asleep or open his eyes as soon as the breathing became too deep or too sensitive. George had plenty of patience, calmly reassuring and guiding his student back to the drill.

'Close your eyes and follow the touch of my hands,' he repeated yet again. 'Breathe to where they are placed.' George was moving harmoniously with Jerome's chest, avoiding resistance, gently stroking around it, peacefully dispersing the tension from the painful trunk.

Jerome tried very hard to keep with George's hands and his mind didn't drift away this time, the breathing becoming smoother, reaching deeper than at the last attempt. Then George lightly touched the sternum and Jerome's body started to shake. They weren't the spasmodic shakes that he had when practising a demanding physical exercise but rather the uncontrolled chest movements that are commonly released when a person cries.

'Slow down, slow down,' George whispered softly as he rolled the boy to the side, positioning the body like that of a baby in the womb. Jerome was suspended in a semi-dream, a shadow world that allowed him to breathe. His chest was moving powerfully in and out, connecting inhalation and exhalation, aware but out of control. Pain, great pain was escaping from within, squeezing and choking the tight throat, pushing at the mirror of the soul and flowing from his mind in a wet stream of tears. There were no thoughts in him or awareness of what he was doing and in a state of hypnosis he continued breathing heavily until he fell asleep.

George sat next to him, his palm connected to Jerome's abdomen, shifting the boy's attention from the chest.

'Jerome, can you hear me?' Consciousness took Jerome by surprise, appearing too quick and abrupt, sucking him back into reality. He jumped startled to his feet, looking accusingly at George.

'What have you done to me?' he frowned.

'I merely showed your spirit the way to its core, to the soft part of your soul. It is not a bad thing and you shall soon learn the benefits.' Jerome was sceptical but remained quiet. George could sense the doubts but decided not to push the argument further 'It's enough training for one day,' he said and looked at his student reassuringly, capturing his eyes with his trusting manner.

'You will go back to your room now and read the chapter about

Misogi and tomorrow we will start exercising it's applications.' George stood slowly, waiting for the boy to follow as he led him back to the room.

'Enjoy the reading – I will see you in the morning.'

'*Osu Sensei!*'

Jerome sat quietly for a while, contemplating the day's events. He felt violated by the prodding of the *sensei* but could not deny the benefits of those actions. There was a sense of vacancy in his chest cavity, a space that was unnatural to the emotionally oppressive trunk. *As if a large boulder had been lifted off my chest.* Breathing came easier and he could sense the ease with which the chest moved. He went to the sink and washed his face, avoiding the mirror as he dried his hands. Sighing, he walked to the reading room and opened the book.

15 Misogi

Misogi literarily means 'ritual cleansing of the body with water' and is a traditional Japanese custom, introduced by the Shinto religion long ago. The custom emerged from a tale of the divine Izanagi, one of the creator gods of Japan.

'Izanagi was longing for his other half, Izanami, who was in the underworld among the dead. Driven by love and despair he pursued her, tainted and taunted by the dead. Bitterly he learned that she refused to leave the underworld and he remerged. Emotionally distorted and stinking of death, he decided to decontaminate himself in the river called Tachibana No Odo, to purify his body and soul.'

This traditional cleansing could be carried out in various ways, ranging from sitting under a waterfall in nature to bathing oneself with buckets of water at home. It is not a physical act alone, as one would do in the shower, but a spiritual concept, demanding a deeper understanding.

Master Ueshiba practised *Misogi* as a daily routine and would often emphasise its importance to his students. Although traditionally *Misogi* refers to the use of water, it is a part of other customs based on the same idea. Cleansing one's house and environment was a demand of O Sensei and it was legendary how unbelievably clean and tidy was the road that led from his house to the *dojo*. Indeed he himself advocated the importance of keeping the six senses (ears, nose, tongue, eyes, body and mind) clean and fresh in order to truly connect and interact with the world.

There were other types of Japanese cleansing rituals that Master Ueshiba adopted. Fasting and a proper diet were employed, purifying and minimising the body's intake. Breathing exercises were a daily routine, cleaning one's heart and mind of dirty thoughts and deeds. O Sensei rigorously practised *Misogi* and he often referred to Aikido as an art of purification.

Although not fully based on the past, there is strong evidence to suggest the connection of Ueshiba's *Budo* practice and *Misogi* rituals. One of those martial applications was the *Misogi No Jo* that he created and deployed later in his Aikido practice. Here is the tale of how he made the first connection between his martial art techniques and *Misogi*, a painful memory cherished by the master throughout his life.

* * *

Tanabe, Japan, 1920

A refreshing January wind was blowing softly at his face, warm compared to the freezing cold of Hokkaido, his island for the past seven years. A keen 37-year-old Ueshiba scanned the streets of his home town Tanabe, as he stood at the station and placed the few belongings on his back, his heart pounding with excitement. 'Ahhh ... Finally home!' Rushing off the platform towards his parents' house, he clumsily dropped a bag to the dusty floor, and bent down to lift it, irritated by the undesired stop. *Come on, not now!* He was in a hurry, a few days behind schedule, knowing he could have been there long before. He had sent his family from Shirataki, the northern town he had helped to establish, as soon as he heard of his father's poor health. 'I will leave here the moment I am done,' he had promised his wife. Concluding all his affairs he followed hastily in their footsteps, giving the house and a few belongings left in Shirataki to his *Daito Ryu* master, Sokaku Takeda.

He was on his way down from Hokkaido to Tanabe, like a good son should, when the old obsession of his soul compelled him to make a detour. *Father, I know you will understand ... I just couldn't resist ...* His disciplined spiritual hunger was suddenly tempted and he followed the pacifying course. He ended up in Ayabe, the *Omoto Kyo* religion's base, near Kyoto city, where he was exposed to the living legend Onisaburo Deguchi and his unique spiritual methods.

A dog barked in the distance and Ueshiba turned his head to the left, momentarily exposed to the surroundings, but only momentarily. *Now what was I thinking about?* He walked enthusiastically, juvenilely reciting truths he had learned in Ayabe, wanting to preserve the fresh and vivid knowledge. Most of the things he had observed were too complicated and detailed to remember yet he took part in the ceremonies which sparked in him ideas, delivering what he was forever searching for. It was quite ironic on his part: he knew it but did not care.

Morihei had witnessed ceremonial dances before he ever heard of the *Omoto Kyo* and Deguchi. From the mid-nineteenth century there existed numerous countryside religions combining traditional *Shinto* rituals with ecstatic dances. Nao Deguchi, the founder of the *Omoto Kyo*, practised similar religious methods as a child and when she developed the *Omoto* religion she was ordered by her guiding *kami* to dance the traditional *Shimai*. She couldn't dance yet she understood the message and it was the main reason for the *Omoto Kyo's* strong reliance on the practice of other arts such as painting and music.

Morihei remembered the amused passenger on the train to Ayabe, who obviously wasn't a follower of the *Omoto Kyo*.

'Why would you bother to come here and take part in the religion of the farmers? Surely there are countryside religions in Tanabe.'

Ueshiba smiled to himself, too vain to answer.

The *Omoto Kyo* found a way to popularity by changing its social and political structure, thereby avoiding two key problems that beset most of the shamanistic religions at the time. The first problem was that all the contemporary leaders were female and the second was that many participants were uneducated, unsophisticated, non-urban and fanatical. Master Deguchi changed all of that, and did so with grace and beauty. He was an educated man, able to communicate both with country people and the cultured elite of society. With him as director, ceremonial practice combining dance, movement and religious practice became very appealing to a wide range of society.

Deguchi used methods familiar to the *Shingon*-educated Ueshiba but the difference lay in the ceremonies: the graceful dances that represented serious spiritual content. One of the dances that intrigued Morihei the most was the *Misogi* dance, an application of the purifying practice. In no time at all he began to envision a similar use for his martial art – not the empty-handed techniques, as those for the time being were far from connecting with the circular movements of the dance, but rather the weaponry practice that was completely applicable.

Morihei's hand clutched the staff, eager to begin his trial of the *Misogi No Jo*. He was ignited by the example he saw in Ayabe, wanting to fuse the two opposing worlds of spirituality and war.

I am almost there! He smiled and turned at the street corner and then his jaw suddenly dropped, his eyes widening in dread, 'What is going on?'

He saw the dark curtains on the windows and the gloomy-looking people coming out of his parents house and he gasped, the air trapped inside him, colder than the icy wind of Shirataki. *But it can't be true ...Didn't Deguchi promised that everything will be well?* His mother came out to greet him and his heart missed a beat, the recognition of the loss starting to sink in. 'Oh no, father no!' He was too late: his detour to Ayabe had proved very costly, infecting his sorrow with guilt. 'But I need to speak to you ... there is so much to say!'

Confused and pained he stayed with the family and paid the necessary ceremonial respects. Then, one night, he took off for the mountains.

For three months he roamed the hills, swinging his staff around like a crazed man, fighting fiends from within and without and scaring his whole family with his bizarre behaviour. It was not madness; on the contrary, it was a time of purification, when the swinging of his *jo* would heal and clear his heart from dirt and pain. The dance routines that he observed in Ayabe introduced sensitive aspects that he incorporated into his techniques, using them to drain the tears and sorrow. Ueshiba had lost his father and would never be able to redeem himself, yet, as at so many other times in his life, sorrow would be the very tool to draw greatness out of him.

* * *

The next few days were all about *Misogi* rituals. George practised and recited some basic Aikido techniques but special attention was given to purification techniques. Each morning started with the cleaning procedures of Jerome's living quarters and would progress from there on. George gave a new touch to the cleansing techniques on a daily basis, adding different flavours and purpose that challenged Jerome.

'Anyone can hold a broomstick and sweep the floor,' George told him. 'It is not what you do but rather how you do it.' His words made perfect sense as he demonstrated the necessary posture and attitude; his breathing sequence monitored, shoulders loose and elbows tucked in. 'You must clean the place in a state of meditation, otherwise you are no different from a regular cleaner!' It was an important lesson, giving meaning to the little things in life that are so often ignored.

At breakfast George paced the speed and rhythm in which Jerome consumed his food, annoying him with the restrictions. 'Food is not to be taken lightly,' he explained. 'Think about it. You take external objects and insert them into your body without too much consideration. Yet food is much more than mere matter or energy and the proof lies in the way it can make you ill when dirty, and unbalanced when consumed in excess.'

Jerome looked at him and burst into laughter, something he wouldn't dream of doing in front of Henri. George smiled back at him and nodded his head. 'You probably think that I'm making it up, but I stand by my words and can convince you of their truth.' One meal abundant in sugar was enough to prove George's words; every muscle and nerve in Jerome's body was pumped with the tense energy. He did not argue with George again.

After breakfast George would take him to the meditation room and there they would start with breathing training before getting under the waterfall!

The first time Jerome saw the waterfall he was shocked. He had entered the meditation room, heard the rushing sounds of water and looked at George, raising his eyebrows.

'There is no need for explanations,' the *sensei* told him. 'Just get in and have a look for yourself.' Jerome murmured something indistinguishable and entered the hall weary and excited. He found the back wall of the meditation room gone, exposing a garden of sweet water vegetation surrounding a small pool. A bulk of rocks climbed out of the pool and up to the ceiling where a waterfall sprang out of the top, gushing down to the pond. Jerome turned his head to George, eyes and mouth wide open, bewildered and excited.

'This is amazing!' he declared and walked towards the waterfall.

'It is beautiful but it's here for practical reasons,' George explained. 'Here you will learn how to perform *Misogi*, just like they used to do in the old days.'

'I don't mind that,' Jerome declared. 'I quite like being clean.' George snorted a little laugh and asked him to touch the water. He obeyed the *sensei*, brushing the surface with the tips of his fingers and instinctively pulling them back. 'It's freezing cold!' he stuttered and looked at George with a miserable face.

'Indeed it is. The temperature is close to freezing, as cold as O Sensei had his water in *Misogi* meditation.'

George undressed carefully, folding his clothes and placing them neatly on the pebbled floor. Jerome copied his moves, removing most of his garments as well, until both stood in their loincloths.

'Now is the time to judge how well you have learned your breathing techniques as they are the only means to conquer the cold.' He ordered Jerome to join him and the latter complied unwillingly, slowly dipping into the water, shoulders raised to the ears.

'You have to trust your inner engine, your breathing, to keep you warm. Try and connect to the pit of your stomach, transfer the energy needed for combating the cold from there.'

George shuffled deeper into the freezing water, Jerome tiptoeing behind. The *sensei* sat under the downpour and gestured for Jerome to sit at his left. *I am going to die here!* Even at ankle depth the water was bitterly cold, freezing Jerome to the core. His instincts told him to back away from this madness but his resolve was much stronger, forcing him to comply. George was already deep in meditation, his eyes closed and his breathing pattern regular but Jerome reacted otherwise, his body flinching from the sting of the water and he started to shiver.

'Close your eyes.' He heard George's words coming as if from far away, beyond a wall of ice that was his body. 'There is warmth inside you and the deep breathing techniques are the key to connect to that force. Reach it, allow it to surface and there will be no more cold or stress.' He placed his palm on Jerome's back, between the shoulder blades. His touch was amazingly warm and soothing. It gave Jerome time to recuperate, to calm the panic and to regulate his breath.

'Maintain your spine erect and fix your eyes forwards; keep them shut yet not tightly so. Let the eyelids rest, the skin adjoining the orbits soft and warm. Forget yourself because now there is Jerome no more but a pure energy vessel, lingering on the primal source of creation, on the sound of the *Su*.'

Logically George's words were absurd but practically they were effective. Jerome followed the instructions and soon the icy water turned bearable. Breathing was regular and relaxed; he was sitting erect, aware only of his centre and the air moving in and out of the lungs.

'Imagine that the air is colouring your body white, and allow it to travel up and down your spine.' With that he let go of Jerome's back and the cold and panic challenged the space he left, seeking a way in. Jerome managed to retain his concentration and the negative feeling was gone.

He sat next to George, engrossed in the process of breathing and the movement of the white colour inside. No thought entered his mind to break the meditation; he was clear and pure as the water, his essence acted as a giant heating device. Then, without warning, a thought penetrated his mind, a word that shook and shattered his composed constitution. Jerome's body slouched and his breathing became irregular and shallow. Spasmodic quakes ran through him and he started turning blue. Heavily he sensed how his body was being pulled out of the water, watched George's lips moving through a screen of ice. None of it came through; the only word flashing in the closing darkness was the same one that had broken his concentration before. He had reached into his soul and found another person within.

'Max!' the thought screamed like a mantra, pulling him further into a comatose state. 'Max!'

16 Misogi No Jo

WHEN HE WOKE UP he found George's compassionate face staring directly at him. He looked around, still dazed and confused, and realised that he was in the meditation room. He tried to sit up but couldn't, then looked in alarm at George, who shushed him gently, signalling him to stay down.

'You let something break your concentration and you nearly died. It took me a while to warm you up. What happened in there?'

Jerome did not answer instantly but waited for his senses to recollect. He was wrapped in a blanket on the floor, not completely warm. He noticed that George was still in his underwear, sitting tall and indifferent, as if he had never been under the same freezing cold water. The thought was brushed away without a warning, replaced by that which had nearly killed him in the waterfall, by an image of a frightened boy.

'What is happening to Max?' Jerome demanded. 'Is he OK?'

George was taken aback by the question. 'Max?' he replied. 'Do you mean to tell me that it was him you saw in your meditation?' Jerome sat up slowly, not knowing what the *sensei* found so bizarre.

'Max is my friend!' he proclaimed. 'And I want to know if all is well with him.' The words were driven out of him by a nameless sense of guilt.

'Forgive me,' George said with a glint of bewilderment in his eyes, 'but it is such an unusual thing to say at this point.' The *sensei* could see the furrows starting to appear on Jerome's forehead and hurriedly added, 'I can assure you that your friend is in the other classroom and that he is also undergoing the same kind of training as you. I realise that you are concerned about him and so I must remind you how talented he is. In this part of the training you are required to remain separated, that's all.' The sound of George's voice and the sincerity of his explanation soothed Jerome; he squeezed the trapped and painful air in his chest, exhaling forcefully, as if shooting a cannon ball with his mouth.

'It is highly unusual,' George explained after a while, when he was certain that Jerome had calmed down.

'What is unusual?' Jerome frowned, not understanding.

'When you performed the *Misogi* you were quite deep in meditation. That was why I let you slip out of my grip for a while, thinking that you had reached your core.'

'I am sorry about that,' Jerome said, not wanting to disappoint George.

'There is nothing to be sorry about,' George cut him short. 'You have done what was required of you and reached the core. My problem is with what you have found there, not with what you did.' He paused and sighed. 'The place is taken by somebody else. Instead of finding yourself you have found Max.'

'I can't help thinking of him *sensei*. I feel guilty, you see, since we were separated because of me.'

'Why would you say that?'

'Because I attacked Henri.'

'Nonsense!' George shook his head.

'But.'

'Come on Jerome, be sensible. You are worried for the wrong guy – you should be thinking of yourself. I don't want to have to remind you what Yves has promised both of you if failed.' George was nodding in concern. 'Make sure that you are doing your best.' He tapped Jerome on the shoulder and motioned for him to follow. Jerome lifted himself up and although dazed he followed his *sensei*.

First they went back to the living quarters and got changed to their *dogi*. Then George led him to the Plain *Dojo* and sat next to Jerome in front of the *Kami Dana*. They bowed and after a short warm up George went and got each of them a *jo* that was lying next to the entrance. He handed one majestically to Jerome.

'We will practise something special today,' he told Jerome. 'A meditation technique that the founder developed. It helped him to purify his body and soul, helped him get through some of the worse times in his life. He named this exercise *Misogi No Jo* – the purification of the fighting staff.'

Jerome gazed back in confusion. 'How can it be,' he asked the teacher, 'that a fighting staff could purify anything? It is only a weapon.'

George scratched his head, searching for the right words. 'That was the popular opinion in the times before the introduction of the *Skill*, but even then many *aikidoka* benefited from these rituals.' George saw that Jerome was at a loss, so he ordered the pupil to sit as he continued the explanation. 'Aikido was described by the founder as an art of purification, a kind of *Misogi*. This revelation came to him as he was swinging his *jo* in the mountains above his home town of Tanabe, using it to mourn for his father who had passed away.'

'I still can't see how swinging fighting staffs cleanses the body and soul,' Jerome said, sticking his chin stubbornly up. George nodded and smiled in understanding.

'You need a full explanation in order to perform, don't you?' he laughed. 'Very well then, just stop me if it gets too boring. In order to understand the genius behind the *Misogi No Jo*, you must understand the conflict of the human condition – the duality of existence.

'We human beings are composed of two main characters that usually oppose each other. The first is the physical constitution we use for survival in the material world. It is a harsh world and the body is designed to confront its conditions, facilitated by millions of impulses that advocate greed, promote the ego and selfishness, towing the individual behind sexual urges, forcing him to kill in order to survive. The other human character is spiritual and soft, floating over the world of the flesh, immortal and creative, confronting the body and controlling its urges and faults. Both characters are present at all times inside us all yet they usually oppose each other, rarely do they combine in harmony to satisfy both worlds. Most people live in compromise, jumping from one world to another, until the conflict inside is well concealed. Ueshiba did not hide, he confronted the condition head on, stimulated by that challenge.

'The founder of Aikido, like all men, was torn in two, yet the dualities of life inside him were uncompromised. On one side he had his obsession with *Budo*, which represented his masculinity, his strong bond to the physical world and on the other side stood his spirituality, desperately trying to connect with his feminine side, relentlessly searching for that softness through vigorous religious practices. It was only when he met Onisaburo Deguchi that he learned how to combine the two. Deguchi, who became his master, emphasised art in his spiritual practices, taking great pride in the ceremonial dances he composed. This inspired Ueshiba who found it easier to be calm through dynamic art rather than tranquil meditation. The *Misogi No Jo* was the first connection Ueshiba created between the two human constitutions. It was a work of genius and even without the *Skill*, it's a wonderful technique for relaxation.'

'What is so feminine about the staff?' Jerome kept pressing. 'What makes it spiritual?'

'The feminine part is in the staff and the turns. The staff is made of wood, a living element and the turns, the water element, nourish it, giving it a feminine aspect. It allows the individual to blend with his emotions, to release them in a physical form.' George stopped talking, smiling at the confused and twisted face of his student and motioned Jerome to take his place on the mat. 'Enough of this nonsense talk. Now you should try it and feel for yourself!'

They bowed and George started to teach the moves of the *Misogi No Jo*. There were a few elements in the dance that were copied directly from the practice of the founder, such as swinging in the four directions of the wind. Some other elements were picked through the painstaking research of the new masters of the arts and added to the old pattern.

To begin with Jerome had to concentrate very hard in order to follow George's moves, yet after a short period the repetition became familiar. He could sense the soothing effect of the movements and in no time he was one with the staff, making it an extension of his soul. On and on they went through the moves, his staff swishing through the air in mad circles, liberating his mind and blending with his breath.

'Coordinate and tune your muscles, allow the *Kata*, the training pattern, to flow through you.'

Jerome sensed the words rather than understanding their meaning.

He was consumed by his efforts, not realising the amount of time and energy that they had spent. After a long and tiring session, George suddenly ordered him to stop and they dropped down to their knees, sitting in *seiza* and facing each other. George called the *Rei* command and they bowed.

'Your body was stimulated by the *jo*. Now try and assess the effect!' George's words were emphasised by an elongated whistle. 'Close your eyes and inhale deeply, expand your chest wide. Keep your back erect and try to reach the core once more, try and find yourself within.' Jerome closed his eyes and followed the instruction yet very quickly his body started to tremor. He was hyperventilating, inner pain released with each and every quiver.

'Allow your body to shake. It will liberate the stress consuming your mind. There is no need to worry about the kind of pain you are releasing; emotional stress has no words but rather a disabling physical effect. It is a good release, the effect transforming your body and soul, purifying and cleansing your vessel for the art.' Tears were rolling down Jerome's cheeks and he did feel drained from pain, but only for a moment.

Suddenly, just as it had happened before, the nagging thoughts about Max crept up on him. However, it didn't disturb Jerome's emotions as it had before, proving the truth of the *sensei's* teaching, that emotional release has nothing to do with words and discussions. There was no stress in Jerome yet he could not find his own self within: no matter how hard he searched in his core he found only Max there and the guilt was mounting. *I can feel something is missing, something crucial.* He was right but would not learn about that component yet, not before he learnt how to perform *Misogi No Jo* properly, along with a few other elements required by the school's curriculum.

It is getting harder to perform with every passing day Jerome thought. The unresolved sensitivity gradually became a liability, causing him further imbalance and distress. Purification was not a pleasant feeling but rather the pain of toying with an infected tooth. Max's image was always there to confront him.

17 The Search for the Lost Book: Part 2

THE INFORMER had been sent elsewhere, his spying routines not needed for the time being. He was now on a train to Switzerland, to meet up with Yves' conspirators and he was pleased with himself, smiling as he remembered the conversation he'd had with *Sensei* prior to his departure.

'I know that you need a break, a breather. Don't think that I've forgotten about your needs.' Yves looked into the Informer's enraged eyes. 'Quieten down. Why are you so uptight?' The teacher knew exactly why, but wanted the Informer to get it out of his system.

'Calm down?!' the Informer bellowed at the *sensei*. 'What do you mean by that? I've been stuck in here for almost half a year, not seeing the sunlight, being kept uninformed, completely in the dark. You want me to be part of your scheming but you offer very little in return.'

Yves needed the Informer for the completion of the boys' education; losing his trust at this stage could be catastrophic. He had to soothe him for now and get rid of him once the training was complete. Not yet though, at the moment he would need to produce a bone for this dog to chew. Yves sighed, lifting a piece of paper from his desk. He was certain that this would do the trick.

'Here.' He handed it to the Informer. 'I only received the message this morning, we are closer than ever. We know where the book is! Calvin and Anton are preparing to move in as we speak.' The Informer nodded and looked at the writing. The office was dark, yet Yves saw the sparkles appear in the Informer's eyes.

'This is unbelievable,' he announced and looked at the master. Yves smiled gently back at him, knowing the youngster had swallowed the bait.

'You are stressed, could use some fresh air; I thought that Switzerland be a good choice. What do you think?'

'I think Switzerland is an excellent choice.' The Informer tried as hard as he could to conceal his emotions but knew that he had already given too much away.

'Fine,' Yves smiled. 'I am glad this is settled.'

'Thank you *Sensei.*' The Informer bowed and was about to take his leave when he heard the *sensei* calling.

'Don't carry it back with you, I don't trust our friends that much; greed seems to be their best motive and you will find them impossible to hide from – Anton is a well-established Seeker.'

The Informer tightened his lips, controlling the smile that wanted them parted. *Their main motive is greed.* He raised an eyebrow. *And what about you, Sensei?*

He did not however share the irony with Yves, instead asking, 'So how do you want the book to get here?'

Sensei's instructions were sensible: the Informer had no desire to become the biggest target in the world.

'Use our secret network,' Yves replied, 'and delay the postage, let's say on the week of the demonstration. Let them choose randomly the exact date and hour. I don't want you to know too much, it's too risky, in case you get caught by those who desire the book.'

The Informer nodded slowly. *Thought you were worried about me for a second*, he mused. 'No problem,' he said. 'I shall do as you ask.'

'Oh … and come back as soon as you are done. We have plenty of work to complete here.'

'As soon as I am done,' the Informer repeated and left the office to get ready for the trip.

* * *

'Tickets, please,' the conductor called, shaking the Informer out of his daydreaming. He smiled at the sweaty overweight man and handed him the ticket, the look of a saint on his face. The conductor left and the Informer relaxed into his first-class seat.

There were a few more hours to kill before the train reached Zurich Central and the Informer reviewed the information leading the search party to Switzerland.

Calvin and Anton's failure in Russia raised the concern that perhaps the box with the supposedly lost book was gone forever. It was especially disappointing to learn that one of the leads which Calvin was pursuing proved to be a decoy. But then if somebody was taking the time to conceal the path to the book then perhaps it was out there after all, waiting to be found.

The only clues remaining had led them to a small cabin outside Oslo. Anton, who was a member of the International Aikido Board, had unlawfully looked at official documents in the city hall; seeking for the owner of the property, abusing his respectable position on the way. Luckily he found the owner's name, a wealthy Swiss businessman who lived in Zurich and who used the small dwelling on occasional business trips to Norway.

Anton immediately informed Calvin of his discovery and together they left for Switzerland. They raided the premises of the late Swiss owner and found his great-grandson living at the same address. They tied him up and searched through the documents of his ancestors which happened to be filed with great efficiency and detail. There they found the connection they were looking for, a transaction with the Russian antique collector that didn't balance out with the old piece of furniture it represented.

That late Swiss businessman had been one of the chief advocates against the power and influence of the Aikido Board. Opposition was still a trend in the present day, feeding on the ignorance of the masses who feared the abnormal qualities of the *Skill*.

With hands stained by the blood of the Swiss owner, who denied possessing any knowledge of the lost book, Anton wrote his plans to Yves *Sensei*, notifying him that the owner was more than likely lying and that he would soon lead them to the parcel. The Informer was amazed how easily Anton had found the location of the parcel. Those who opposed the Board tended to be blind to its powers, handling the *Skill* with disrespect. The owner was released and they followed him from afar, using Anton's Seeking *Skill*. A couple of days later the final message from Calvin arrived; the parcel was to be found in a little village above the town of Interlaken, high in the Alps. Anton must have been pleased – mission well accomplished!

The *Skill* of the Seeker is based on *zanshin*, a connection maintained without physical touch. In basic Aikido it is described as the perseverance of the *tori's* concentration whilst throwing the *uke* to the ground; his whole body extends in the direction of the *uke*, as if a hidden thread attaches the two. In basic Aikido the accuracy and power of this connection is emphasised, the *tori* determines through it where his *uke* will land; shaping the space between the two into a palpable matter.

Skilled Seekers use the same principle of *zanshin*, yet in the most extended way possible, to connect to their subjects from afar. In order to perform, a Seeker needs certain details of the sought-after person, preferably a previous personal contact with him or her, although a name or a picture would work just as well. It was also vital to know where that person was last seen. The more personal the familiarity of the Seeker with the target and the closer to the point of origin he was, the easier it became to reach a quick and decisive conclusion to the search. This *zanshin* connection allowed the *Skilled* Seeker to locate anyone, anywhere in the world; a quality Anton used in order to find the hidden place in the mountains of Interlaken.

Anton wanted to move in, to take the parcel, but Yves' orders were to wait for the Informer, and Anton had to obey since Yves sponsored the whole operation. Anton was a member of the Board and he was a great Seeker but as far as business went he was useless. Any extra cash that he ever had he would lose gambling; he owed more than he could ever repay. It was not surprising that Yves sent the Informer there and ordered Anton to wait; it was a sensible measure of security for his investment. The Belgian was somewhat disturbed by the lack of trust yet he knew himself well enough; he wouldn't trust his own kind.

The Informer shook these thoughts out of his mind upon hearing the announcement for the train's final destination. Anton and Calvin were to meet him at Zurich Central Station. He had met them before, learned to respect their abilities and to keep his guard up.

The Informer stood as the train came to a halt and stretched his back, his face contorted from the popping sound coming from his shoulder. *Bloody hell!* It was an old training injury that refused to heal, highly unusual at such a young age. Picking up his few belongings he walked down the platform, enjoying the icy wind that stood in contrast to the artificial air of the train. People rushed around, trying to catch the afternoon trains that left the city. They were mainly tourists, carrying backpacks and suitcases.

He came out of the station and saw Calvin's balding head next to a big car. He paced towards him, shaking his hand curtly.

'How are you Master Calvin?'

'Not bad, thank you. And yourself?'

'I am well!' The patronising look on the ex-soldier's face did not escape the Informer's eyes. *Fool!* he snorted a laugh *Your pride distorts your judgment!* the Informer was one of the greatest Aikilibrium *aikidoka* in the world and his size was deceptive, hiding his true level of expertise. He was small, young, yet very strong, and could easily have competed with any adult fighter. His *Skill*, however, was concealed from the eyes of the beholder, even from those who knew of his abilities. It served him well, appearing only at the point of action – only when it was too late ...

He got into the car, where the smiling face of Anton awaited him.

'*Mon ami!*' the Belgian exclaimed and hugged him, slimy as always. The Informer smiled back at the Belgian, playing his part in the game. He didn't like Anton's attitude towards him but he was the youngest and therefore expected to be treated as such, no matter how annoyed he felt about it. Yves had taught him emotional control and it was a useful discipline at the moment, keeping his head clear for business. 'Time enough to get even later on, when you've really got the upper hand' was one of Yves' most valuable lessons.

'How are you, Master Anton?' he beamed. 'I see that you are in good shape.'

'Rubbish!' the Belgian laughed. 'You learned how to be political from your master; I'll be worried about the competition when you grow up.' They were sweet-talking each other, keeping the atmosphere civilised.

'Put your seat belts on, gentlemen,' Calvin announced from the driver's seat. 'We have a two-hour drive that I'll try and cut short to one. We don't want to spend too much time in this freezing hellhole.'

It was indeed quite cold and it was only late afternoon – the end of summer could be surprisingly chilly.

They started out towards Interlaken with Calvin driving as if his life depended on it. They left the city behind and drove upwards, using the expressways to cut their path to the mountains. The transition in scenery was gradual, dense forest rolling next to the road which climbed higher and higher, shadowed by the hills and the large pine trees. Nature was displayed wild and fresh, intoxicating compared with the urban scenery that the Informer was used to. They drove behind a bend and the sharp peaks of the mountains were suddenly above the tree line; an icy crown for the mighty forest.

Calvin drove fast but the traffic was heavy and it took one and a half hours to reach the lake. 'Look at that!' The mountains spilled to the banks of the water, covered with open grass patches, lush with life and vitality. The Informer was marvelling at the beautiful landscape, politely answering Anton's questions.

'Hello there!' he heard Anton calling and saw Calvin peering in the car mirror laughing. 'You would think that he'd never been out in his life.' The Informer smiled politely yet could not take his eyes off the window.

Interlaken was set at the end of a long drive around the lake, gently reflecting in the water. They drove through it, crossing the relatively empty streets, the road leading swiftly to a small bridge that marked the edge of town. From that point on the road was sheltered by trees that hid the mountains. They drove by a sign reading Habkern and the car turned to the right. The road suddenly changed, becoming dangerously narrow and twirling up in a sharp climb. Whoever built it must have been a genius in engineering, conquering the sloping curves of the mountains, forcing nature to obey his will.

The Informer marvelled at the view, watching the trees that grew between the wet stretches of the tarmac road. He noticed the irrigation holes that pumped water down the road, keeping the walls of the mountain intact. A little slit of the window was open and he stuck his nose out, inhaling the fresh mountain air. *You disgusting pigs – how can you breath?* The car was full of smoke, the two adults huffing and puffing their nicotine clouds. They wouldn't allow him to open the window further, complaining of the cold and the Informer had to settle for this little breathing hole.

Suddenly the car jerked into the open and to the round hills of the summit that was Habkern. In the winter the area was used by tourists on skiing holidays but in the summer it was mainly deserted. The road coiled further up and the Informer caught the last glimpse of the beautiful green mountains, before darkness took over, painting the world in black and grey. He loved the lush, fertile land; it was comforting and peaceful, in contrast to the acts they were about to commit.

'We will stay in the car until we decide to move in; we don't want to be seen in the area,' Calvin said as he brought the car to a halt.

'No doubt,' Anton agreed.

Calvin was methodical and organised, one of the main reasons that Yves liked his work. The car was parked in the middle of a small field, beyond the village borders. The door opened and the Informer stepped out and stretched while Calvin moved to the wide back seat, spreading a map on top of his knees.

'This forest extends to the back of Habkern, only ten minutes walk from here.' His finger followed the road as it crossed the small village and travelled into the dense and dark forest. The road ended at what looked like a huge and ugly structure. 'It is far uglier in the light.' Calvin giggled, seeing the Informer taken aback by the monstrosity of the building. He couldn't visualise how a thing like that would fit in such a stunning piece of God's creation.

'They are a proud and senseless lot, the Straubergs,' Anton explained, speaking of the owners of the place. 'Their family fortune stretches back to the middle of the eighteenth century and for a long time they were considered honourable members of society. Then something went terribly wrong and consequently they became hostile, particularly against the members of the Aikido Board. I couldn't find any real reason as to why the hatred for the board has dragged on for so many generations.'

'That's what we're here for!' declared the Informer, sounding a little more cheerful than he intended. 'To stop this hostility once and for all.'

'You are game for the hunt,' Calvin said and offered the Informer a handgun. 'Check this one out; it will fit you perfectly.'

The Informer backed away from the weapon, his face twisted in contempt. Calvin observed him, amused and then turned to Anton. 'He won't take the weapons. Don't tell me he's an idealist, that he follows the rules.'

The Informer was truly disgusted by the ex-soldier; he was insulting his art and trade. He looked at Anton, hoping the more experienced *aikidoka* would stand for his defence. To his horror he saw Anton fiddling with a gun of his own.

The Belgian lifted his eyes at the youngster and smiled. 'You don't have to use a gun, my dear, yet your chances of survival will improve with it and besides ...' Here he stopped talking, suspiciously looking around, as if to detect anyone who might be eavesdropping, 'I promise I won't tell anyone, if you don't,' he whispered secretly and Calvin burst into sardonic laughter.

'I'm sorry, monsieur,' Anton giggled. 'You do what you think is best but I won't tell a soul if you use a gun, honestly.'

The Informer shook his head and backed off. 'I don't need any guns; I can handle danger without it.'

Calvin looked at him, this time more annoyed than entertained. Guns were forbidden to *Skilled aikidoka*, under the treaty signed by the Aikido Board at the time of its creation, a time when excitement and admiration were mixed with hostility among the public. Reason for the hostility could be seen in the situation presented, fear of unlawful use of the *Skill. You are a disgrace, Anton,* the Informer wanted to scream, *I could have chocked you with my bare hands right now!* Informer was a proud youngster, holding the *Skill* as a sacred tool, the way a *samurai* might. He swallowed hard and maintained his composure. They were, after all, his allies.

'How easy was it to follow the man?' he asked, hoping to change the subject. Anton enjoyed telling stories of his accomplishments, and there was a certain jest in his eyes as he spoke.

'Our Swiss friend might be rich and hostile but he has no idea who he is messing with.' The Belgian raised his voice slightly, pumped by self-admiration. 'We released him three days ago and he must have travelled all over Zurich trying to shake us off his tail, changing cars and places. We were almost tempted to chase him, seeing how nervous he was without knowing where we were.' Calvin was giggling in the background, remembering their joint venture. 'I kept my connection with him but maintained it as fine as possible, in such a way that he could never detect our presence.'

'What presence?' Calvin exclaimed. 'We were nowhere near him at any given second since we let him go.' *Skilled* Seekers such as Anton were masters of the non-physical connection, sensing the core of their prey from afar, waiting for the right time and place to lay their trap.

'The instant I sensed he was settled we started to head in his general direction. Believe me, he doesn't know we're here.'

The Informer found it hard to believe, couldn't comprehend why a sworn enemy of the Aikido Board wouldn't suspect the presence of a Seeker. It did not matter to him, he was there on a mission which he intended to fulfil to its completion, to his own satisfaction.

'But how did you know that the book would be here?' he asked curiously.

'Well,' Calvin smiled, 'we had an intense conversation with one of the servants the other day.'

'An intense conversation indeed,' Anton agreed. 'One from which he will never recover.' The Informer joined the renewed laughter, his eyes studying the map of the house.

'It is an ugly structure but has a wonderful defensive advantage, situated well, hidden obstacles and booby-traps,' he marvelled with a smile, his head shaking in appreciation.

'You sound pleased with the way they are protected,' Anton spat, stung by his partner's words. 'Have you any idea how to enter the place?'

The Informer raised his shoulders involuntarily, silently bouncing the question back. He looked annoyed at the map and the seemingly impenetrable building. Many things were annoying him lately and he found it increasingly difficult to control his temper.

'We've got you, haven't we, Mr *Skill*?' Calvin winked and pointed at the Informer, who started to understand.

'The designer of the place covered it with spikes and other protruding sharp objects for protection but he also created a wonderful playground for the one who controls the Aikilibrium *Skill*.' Calvin had never been impressed by the fighting qualities of *aikidoka*, perhaps because he never truly witnessed one in combat yet he was most certainly amazed by Anton's tracking abilities and with Yves' super acrobatic skills.

'Are you as good as Yves claims you are?' Calvin asked and measured the Informer up, as if checking an accessory. The latter straightened up, inhaling through his inflated nostrils; he didn't want to be judged but forced himself to wait patiently, his teeth clenched tightly behind his semi relaxed lips. Calvin watched him a second longer and pulled on his shoulders. 'Here goes,' he said and drew the plan before them, going through it twice and then questioning them on the details, stopping only when he was satisfied with their familiarity of the plan. They had one hour to kill before they would be on their way.

The Informer walked out of the car, escaping the smoke and the scrutinising eyes. Outside the night had taken over and the clouds were scattered wide, attached by the abundant clusters of shiny stars. A couple of hay bales were resting against one of the wooden houses, looking like giant mountain trolls.

He stood and prepared for what was to come, the excitement building up. He could not have asked for a better assignment, to collect the most sought after relic in the world, the book of the founder Ueshiba.

His moment had nearly arrived.

18   An Assault by Night

THE INFORMER appreciated the value of the sacred information the book held, an appreciation he was certain his other two comrades did not share. Calvin was a soldier and Anton was smoking and using guns! They were lower than low in his eyes, he would rather have shared none of his time with them, yet the discipline pushed his trivial wishes away, focusing on the true task ahead.

Yves had been clever in choosing to send him there; not trusting these two hyenas – but then again, was it wise of Yves to choose him? The Informer was no longer sure where his loyalty lay, whether his *sensei's* good faith was important to him any more. *Sensei* was not fulfilling his end of the bargain and he knew what happened to those Yves labelled as unnecessary. The Informer had to protect himself and his interests; that's how he saw it!

In his reports to Yves he had already left out the blood oath Jerome and Max had made, he did it regardless of the fatal trouble he would be in if Yves ever found out. It was his insurance policy, so to speak, against Yves. *Sensei* would never anticipate one of the students attacking him and the Informer knew what a powerful tool surprise could be. Yves could not be trusted; he had no fidelity to his disciples.

The door of the car opened and the Informer heard Anton through the smoke.

'Are you coming, *mon ami?* It is time to go.' He tried to push a gun in the Informer's direction one last time and the Informer declined, this time much more restrained and polite.

They swiftly walked away from the car, following the sure strides of the Seeker. Anton was annoying in every aspect of his being but he was also a true professional. It upset the Informer to see a man with such low personal qualities possess such a high level of *Skill*. It was annoying but it was true, character was never an issue in developing power and *Skill*; those who believed these romantic ideas were fools who confused moral issues with the work of nature.

They pushed into the darkness of the green; the grass opening to their sides, wet by the dampness of the early night. A chilled wind blew from the mountains across, the air trying and penetrate the Informer's shirt. He was beyond disturbance now, his focus completely on the task ahead. They pulled off the path and further to the right, avoiding the main road, walking parallel to it. Lightning brightened the horizon followed by the muffled crash of thunder; it sounded far yet there was no mistaking the approaching rain. Calvin cursed and followed Anton with renewed energy, eager to fulfil the task before the weather hit them.

The Seeker stopped and motioned them to stride in a low crouching position, climbing down a ravine that crossed a little stream. On the other side they found the forest and the giant trees, blocking any light that tried to penetrate the thickness. They stopped walking, Anton tying them with a rope, keeping a short distance between each end. Calvin was about to protest but Anton silenced him.

'It is the quickest way,' he promised and started to walk. They followed blindly, trusting the Seeker's senses and his *Skill*. Not all of Anton's moves were related to superhuman abilities. A *Skilled* Seeker had to have the base knowledge of the common tracker, just as the Informer was a talented acrobat, the base for a *Skilled* Aikilibrium *aikidoka*.

'Dark bloody Hellhole,' Calvin spat. The Informer could see nothing but his feet detected the texture of the forest bed and he was somehow more orientated than the irritated soldier. After ten minutes of careful walking they stopped and Anton whispered to the Informer, 'This is it. The walls are two metres ahead. Go on, see if you can get to the top.'

The Informer stepped to the place indicated as the wall. He could perceive the difference in the air density and his eyes could see what was immediately in front of his nose. He felt with his feet for a clear space in the wall and thumped it gently, sensing the vibration spreading throughout the wall. He continued checking the surface and texture of the partition until he could visualise it enough to practise his art. He smiled, inhaling heavily through his nostrils and then, without warning, his body coiled in, the vitality draining from his extremities.

A split second later he shot through the air, limbs swinging madly, four tentacles around the trunk. His relaxed feet hit the surface of the wall exactly where he planned; the accuracy of the *Skill* was frightening. Aikilibrium used windows of opportunity as they presented themselves in nature. It was a power in tune with the environment, driven from the core of the *Skilled* artist. With another swing of his body the Informer was at the top of the wall, keeping low, not wanting to be exposed.

Looks quiet and safe! He observed for a while and then dangled the rope down, securing it to one of the many protruding objects. *Shameless!* He grimaced at the sight of the night vision equipment the two were using and he was pumped with renewed contempt. *These guys have no pride in their trade.* He wondered if he was too young and uncompromising, if life would turn him into something similar. He shrank from the thought silently, *I'd rather die than sink that low!*

He jumped to the other side of the wall and waited for the two to follow. They were quick with that one, silently appearing at his sides. Anton took the lead and in twenty quick strides they were in front of the building.

It was built as a castle, the walls thick, high and with sharp pins that made the climb impossible. The Informer was inspecting the structure, searching the options for his art, when a side door opened and a man stepped out with a gun in his hand. His mouth was opening to shout but the only sound to escape his lips was a gurgle. A knife jutted from his neck and Calvin's teeth shone in the darkness, exposing a smile as he pulled the knife out of the guard's flesh, lowering him gently to the ground.

Now they had access to the house and they didn't hesitate to use it. Calvin led the way, more familiar with the interior of the house than the other two. They rushed up the stairs, knowing where to find the owner, the one who could supply them with the goods.

A door swung open to their right and a woman with a knife ran towards them, cursing loudly in her flight. Anton moved to her side, quick and deceptive, his outstretched arm smashing the gun into her face, the metal meeting the tender tissue with a sharp crunch of cartilage and flesh. She landed on the ground silent and Anton shrugged his shoulders and followed Calvin, not seeing the resentment on the Informer's face. It did not matter any more; if they got caught now the offence of carrying guns would be minor compared to the crime they were committing. It didn't make it feel right though. *Let's get it over with, I need to get away from these guys.*

They reached the top of the staircase and Calvin rushed them over to a bolted door. He kicked it in and ducked down instinctively, sensing a bullet flying next to his cheek. There was an exchange of shots from both sides of the door and they were unable to move in any further. The Informer saw Calvin reaching for his hand-grenade and stopped him.

'Don't!' he ordered him softly. 'Let me try and get in first; the grenade might destroy the book.' With that he coiled and jumped through the air, using the momentary break in gunfire. Anton cursed but listened attentively, trying to assess the situation through the renewed gunshots.

Inside, the Informer rolled on the floor and coiled to the air yet again, before the bullets could get him. He reached behind a small cupboard and sensed the darkness, memorising where the gunshots came from. *Hello!* His patience paid off soon enough; the silhouette of the person inside the room appeared to his left. He judged the distance and with the first window of opportunity emerging before him, he snapped through the air. His body spun, a mere blur in the dark, for the body was never between places when it jumped but here one moment and there the next. His legs propelled dangerously in the air, until they landed with full impact in the shooter's face. 'Arghhh,' he cried and the gunshots stopped. *Anyone else?* The Informer scanned the room a moment longer, looking for other assailants.

'Come in!' he called to his mates, 'and don't shoot.' The two came in, their eyes covered by the night vision equipment. Calvin reached out and flicked a switch on the wall, filling the room with bright yellow light. 'Idiot!' The Informer cursed quietly at the arrogance of the soldier, the carelessness of his behaviour.

'Where is it?' Calvin asked while moving things around, looking for the book. His hands rubbed against the wall, searching for a hidden hinge, a safe. 'There we go.' He beamed a couple of seconds later when his trained fingers found the hidden door. On the floor the shooter was coming back to his senses, screaming in terror when he saw the face of Anton. Outside the room there were sounds of commotion as guards rushed to the aid of their master.

'Call them off,' Anton told the man and waved a short, pointed dagger at his face. The man cowed away in fright; he knew of Anton and of what the mad Belgian was capable of. He screamed in German and the footsteps stopped outside. Then someone talked to Strauberg and the later answered.

'Were you given permission to speak?' Anton smiled and snapped with the sharp blade, causing a little gash to appear on the man's face and a scream of pain to accompany it.

'What is the combination, brother?' Anton asked softly, holding the man's mouth to muffle the screams. He waited until the man calmed down and gave out the numbers. 'Got it?'

'Yep!' Calvin opened the safe and the Informer stood on tiptoe behind him, trying to get the best view of the inside.

'Is it inside?' Anton asked, annoyed with the silence. The man beneath him gave a groan and Anton kicked him in the head until he stopped moving and groaning. 'Noisy bastard,' he spat at the man and lifted his head up.

'Found it!' Calvin called and moved away from the wall, in his hands he was holding a metal box, the metal box. Anton and the Informer got closer, both staring in awe at the relic. Calvin stared back at them and smiled. 'It's all here, boys, but there is no time to enjoy it now.' He shoved it into a large pouch attached to his middle.

'Come on, follow me.' He threw a hand-grenade out of the room and waited for it to blow. As the thunder of the grenade was heard Calvin and Anton blasted their way out shooting, hitting anything that was in their way. A few terminal screams and a couple more hand-grenades saw Calvin leading them out of the front door.

Back in the forest it was Anton's turn to pilot the group. He led them as quickly as they could follow, Calvin collapsing twice and cursing plenty. In half an hour they were back at the car, observing the Informer wrapping the box for the delivery. The Informer was to handle it from now on, tempted beyond reason to open the beautiful metal box.

'Seal it well!'

'He will,' Calvin promised, 'Now back away.'

'Sure,' Anton nodded but remained at his side. He was supervising how it's done, concerned that anyone should have a glimpse before him. 'We will open it the week after the annual demonstration,' he said, 'I will be there with you guys. Yves has promised me!'

The Informer nodded, not wanting to challenge the greed he saw in Anton's eyes, knowing that he was safe as long as Calvin was around. The Seeker would not hesitate to kill him and take the book. As for Calvin, he didn't care for the book or Aikido or whether there was a book inside the box and if indeed there ever was a book at all. His interest was elsewhere, in the *Aiki* network, through which he spread and dominated his businesses. Calvin sensed the hostility intensifying, reading the greedy determination in the Informer's and Anton's eyes. A fight between the two would be entertaining but there was no time for that. He hurriedly started the car, taking the dangerous slopes of Habkern at heart-stopping speed.

When they reached the bottom of the hill Calvin stopped the car and ordered Anton to drive.

'But why?'

'Because I had had enough of the tension between you two. It is not professional.'

'So?'

'So you'd better drive now.'

'But I don't want to!'

'Drive and cool off!'

'Very well then.' He drove fast and in deadly silence, in an hour the car surrounded by the orange urban glow.

'Stop the car!' Informer barked when they were a couple of blocks away from the secret delivery station. 'I shall see you later,' he said and jumped out.

'See you soon, *mon ami*,' Calvin called. 'Goodbye.'

The Informer walked off, his back rigid, anticipating the worse.

'Let's get it from him!' Anton whispered in the car.

'Man,' Calvin barked, 'Now don't be an idiot.'

'But.'

'No Anton, no way! Now shut up and get us out of here. We need to get rid of this car.'

'What a shame,' Anton sighed and drove off.

It was clever to secure the delivery of the book and the Informer appreciated it as he was sending the parcel. It was hard to separate from such a marvel of Aikido but he had other things to worry about at that moment. He sent the parcel to Paris on a delayed postage yet he knew exactly on which day it was to arrive, promising himself to be there on that day and hour, to collect it himself. He reserved the right to hold a winning card in case something went wrong. There was always danger involved in his trade and it was better to be prepared.

The book was his, he trusted Yves no more.

19 String Theory

WHO WOULDN'T WANT to discover the theory that governs all things, demonstrating that the science of physics is indeed controlled by identical rules?

At the beginning of the twentieth century scientists introduced two theories to elucidate the laws of nature. Relativity Theory was one, explaining the behaviour of 'large objects' in the universe, while the other theory, known as Quantum Theory, explained the behaviour of 'small objects'. Both theories answered major questions successfully in their own fields of expertise and were practical as well, laying the groundwork for technological developments in the centuries to come. And that is where the problem lay, because if both theories were correct in their analyses, why couldn't they be combined? And why did data, placed in quantum mathematical equations, produce different readings when placed in the equations of the Theory of Relativity? Physics is physics and the laws of physics should apply to all natural phenomena, big and small.

String Theory claimed to successfully combine the quantum and relativity theories, proving that all things in nature were indeed governed by the same set of rules. It was a major breakthrough, although it didn't convince the minds of conservative scientists of its era. Not that they objected to a universal rule for nature; they simply found it difficult to believe in a hypothesis that could not be proven by proper scientific means. String Theory was mockingly considered a nice mixture of words and equations with no root in reality, based on claims that were impossible to test. The theory suggested, for example, that the universe had ten dimensions, an idea which left scientists baffled; another problem was the difficulty of observation, hence proving or disproving the behaviour of small particles.

Accurate or not, the String Theory provided logical explanations to nagging questions in the field of physics, demonstrating how certain particles can disappear and reappear in a different time and space, and revealing the reason for the diversity of universal substance.

The theory was based around an idea of a common building block for all things in nature, its unique character the answer to questions unsolved. That unit was primal, beyond matter or energy – rather both things and neither of them at the same time. It was best described as a string or a rubber band, charged with energy and radiating sound – pulsating in a tempo of lights. The string unit vibrated at a specific frequency and as it changed resonance it transformed the character of the string, creating a new unit of sound and form. These tunes and their combinations ultimately composed the largest symphony of all – the universe!

It was an exciting theory, yet without validation it remained an intellectual speculation, a dormant theory without the experiment to support it, waiting patiently to be proven right. As it turned out, the theory didn't need to wait long to be established, although the proof came from an unexpected source.

In the early thirties of the new millennium the *Aiki* Research Centre was erected as scientists strove to understand the strange behaviour of the *Skill*. It was sponsored by the International Aikido Board and aided by its growing connection to *dojo* of the *Skill* worldwide.

First to be analysed was the philosophical background of Aikido, seeing that the founder believed it to be the key to his art. Aikido derived its philosophical principles from that of the *Omoto Kyo* religion, based on the belief in *Kotodama* – creative sounds from which the entire universe emerged. The most sacred and basic *Kotodama* of all, according to that philosophy, was the sound of the *Su*.

In the words of the *Aiki* Research Centre, 'The *Su* is the word of creation, delicate, susceptible to change. It spirals around the cosmos, transforming into new sounds and vibrations, like the *Yu* and the *Mu*, that when put together dissolve into *Umu* – the ancient word for birth in the Japanese language. These sounds are further evolving, interacting with each other and ultimately composing the whole universe.'

Now the attention turned toward the field researchers. Interviews of *aikidoka* differing in style, *dojo* and geography were conducted and analysed until a correlation between the evidence was found. There was much dissimilarity between the testimonies yet one important aspect was shared by all: the connection to the vacancy of the *Su* within the self and the employment of a variety of *Kotodama* sounds and vibrations within that space.

After collecting the evidence there was a tense period of time during which the researchers looked for the scientific base of the art. They were at a loss, just as the supporters of String Theory were, until a coincidental meeting brought the two camps together and they carried each other perfectly!

Both theories had the same principle building block that was charged with frequency and was susceptible to change. More important than the common theoretical background were the abilities of the *Skilled aikidoka* to perform feats available to the primal unit alone, moving between ten plains, appearing and reappearing in time and space and so on. It put to rest the minds of those who looked for scientific proof for the *Skill* but it also led them to a new question, of how a whole human body, composed of billions upon billions of these building blocks, could perform as one single string.

Perhaps the recorded evidence of a *Skilled aikidoka* of the era explains the phenomenon: 'My *Skill* operates with the application of *Kotodama*. First I connect to my centre, touching my creativity, touching the *Su*. Then I allow sounds to spring out of the core and to resonate through my body. It stimulates the rubbery building blocks from within, changing their character by vibration, forcing them to operate as one. I can sustain myself united in order to perform but only for a short period of time, the body has the tendency to resume its diversity, returning to be human once more.' It was a common piece of evidence heard by the academics, although it differed slightly according to the varied *Skills*.

The final verification was a testimony shared by all:

'And what does this primal unit look like? Can you describe it in words?'

'Mmm ... It is like a string, elastic and active; sometimes whole – vibrant and interacting, sometimes open, especially when shifting between planes ... The string is visual; sound compels it to change colours and intensity. It is extremely beautiful!'

There it was, the theories were united – a human proof for the ultimate question of physics.

Now the research shifted its aim once more, looking to explain the process in which the strings were activated. The scientists learned that the main objective was to reach the point of the *Su*, a primal necessity in deploying the other, more refined *Kotodama*.

A person who wished to reach the *Su* had to do so by removing himself from his own core and allowing the *Su* to emerge instead. It was almost impossible to do voluntarily and consequently this was the reason for the cruelty exercised by *dojo* of the *Skill*. They did their best to take the students out of the centre of their lives, keeping them suicidal, depressed and desperate. This practice worked on most students but there were a few that proved harder to teach.

Those were the ones who sacrificed themselves for the sake of others. They were never at home, never claiming the place of their own *Su* and instead had others sitting at their core, more important than their own lives. Like a parent who protects a child they guarded that individual and would die for him, the value of their own life secondary. Such a strong bond between a guardian and his master demanded huge amounts of energy to break, and, just like a nuclear bomb, the energy released was ten times stronger than any other broken bond. Difficult or not, without clearing the individual's core from physical attachment there was no room for experiencing the *Su* – no place for the *Skill* to emerge.

Although the sound of *Kotodama* could be sung externally with practical results it was almost impossible to perform. It could only be employed that way by those who learned to sing from infancy; those whose vocal cords were shaped by the art. Others, who learned to sing at a later stage, could never match their abilities. There was a large community teaching children *Kotodama* singing in the mountains of Spain, but they kept themselves from the rest of the *Aiki* world. Hidden in the clouds …

Historically, *Kotodama* practice was an art long forgotten and there were very few people who knew the most potent combinations of this skill. Master Deguchi, the director of the *Omoto Kyo*, revived the old art and its practicality and Master Ueshiba learned it thoroughly, adding it to his own knowledge of the ancient art.

There were plenty of methods and theories that he learned but ... Ueshiba finally, and by his own accord, managed to touch the *Su* in a new way, allowing it to take a physical application. He was proud of his success and declared numerous times that he was practising Aikido at the point of the *Su*.

His encounter with the *Su*, however, came during the worst time of his life as a parent and as a son. It was before he developed Aikido, before he acquired the *Skill* – a time when external events forced upon him internal discoveries.

* * *

Japan, 1920

Ayabe was a hot soba soup in September, infested with shimmering heat and humidity. It was a harsh climate to endure; the elements of nature constantly demonstrating their uncompromising strength. No one could escape that weather as there was nowhere to hide, the high temperatures boiling the heavy rain; disease and landslides threatening the poor and unfortunate.

Thirty-seven-year-old Ueshiba was no stranger to inhospitable weather. If anyone could be regarded as experienced under harsh cold conditions it was him, the man who had lived out in the icy island of Hokkaido for the past few years. This however was a different kind of exertion, a new challenge for body and soul. 'Here I am,' he exhaled and walked into his modest family home, carrying the two huge buckets of water, so big that no other man in Ayabe could carry them – no one but Ueshiba.

He heard the baby cry and the tenderness of that sound, that innocent cry of pain, burnt him to the flesh. There was nothing more inspiring than children, the purest form of creation, spawning out of the womb, transpiring the love of their parents, just as Izanami and Izanagi imagined the world with their lovemaking. Ueshiba had learned great new things about himself in the past few months, the main one being the value of the family. His father's death in January had left him miserably depressed and only recently could he breathe properly, the weight shifting off his chest, yet only briefly as there were new tragedies ahead. Now the pressure on his chest had returned, intensified, threatening to destroy him completely. He had good reason for that. The death of his first-born child and the worries for his second and only remaining son ...

The scale of infant mortality in Japan was seriously high at the time and reaching adulthood was considered almost a miracle. In memory of the tragic past the Japanese people kept certain traditions, which remain to this day, such as the attendances of young women to the shrines, thanking the gods for allowing them to reach their twentieth birthday.

Ueshiba fixed the water to boil over the small fire and then rushed to his wife's side, longing to tend to Kuniharu, his one-year-old son.

'How is he?'

'Burning again.' Ueshiba bit his lower lip and sat by him, cooling his forehead with a wet towel, mumbling prayers to the gods.

That morning his wife saw the physician and the latter gave her some herbs for the child's fever, telling her that he wasn't safe as yet. Now she smiled at her beloved husband, hiding the pain, loving him for what he was and not out of the duty required by traditional laws. She was lucky to have such love and she knew it; her heart aching from the pain he might experience if something indeed happened to their one-year-old Kuniharu, afraid that Morihei might lose his mind completely. Loss was the name of the game in the Ueshiba family of late and it was something none of them could ever get used to.

'Shhh ... Rest Kuniharu ... Good boy.' The baby finally fell asleep and the couple sat quietly in the kitchen, having a cup of cold tea. The wife waited obediently for him to strike a conversation, reserved as ever, exercising good manners. They hadn't spoken much during the past few weeks, especially since Takemori, their three-year-old son, had died of the disease, the same disease that was threatening the life of the baby.

Ueshiba's emotions were bolted within, his face a mask of calm, desperately trying to keep composed, watching his son fighting for his life. There was not much he could do but pray, his mother and wife nursing the baby, doing their best to keep him alive. Despite the situation, Morihei got up early every day and helped in cultivating the farm, ordered to do so by the great Onisaburu Deguchi. 'It will keep your mind off the mental anguish,' the master explained. Again Ueshiba was advised that there was nothing he could really do to help, but this time he took Deguchi's advice with a heavy heart, remembering the last advice he'd followed in December, the one that caused him to miss his father's passing away, filling him with guilt forever.

Father's death was tragic for Morihei but it made sense as far as nature goes. Losing a child, on the other hand, was a whole new kind of challenge. It might have been commonplace in Japan but that statistic didn't make it any easier to bear.

'Sit down.' His mother ordered him as his daughter started crying in the other room. She rushed to her side, fearing that the girl might become sick as well, keeping her away.

Involuntary he shook his head and the wife sighed in concern, aware of Ueshiba's sensitive nature, dreading the price he would have to pay for keeping all this pain inside. Everything in life was costly. A debt would never cease to be without the necessary payment – especially emotional debt. It was better to be rid of it early on, before it accumulated interest on top of the stress.

The baby moaned and Morihei jumped and rushed to his side.

'No Morihei, let me have him,' his wife whispered and stepped in front of him, taking the baby in her arms. Kuniharu was burning yet again and his breath sounded shallow, too tired to ventilate himself. The weather aggravated his condition, the heat and humidity serving as a conspiracy of nature against the baby. Kuniharu tried to cry but only feeble sounds were heard. Worried, his wife turned to face Ueshiba who was looking in despair, knowing all too well the signs – the same ones that took his eldest son's life.

'Get the physician,' she ordered and it took him a minute to react. He didn't want to leave, afraid he might miss the last precious moments of his son's in the world. 'Go now!' she ordered again, this time a little more determined. He rushed out, looking for the man.

The physician entered the house a few moments later, panting behind Ueshiba who pushed the door wide open. The baby child was convulsing from the fever, the disease possessing him whole.

'No Kuniharu, no,' the wife was crying, shaking and rocking the small boy. She was trying to revive him, her eyes full of tears. The physician took the baby and stripped it of the cloth that wrapped him. He inspected him with a heavy heart and then looked firmly at Morihei.

'He is not going to last long,' he said in a dour voice. 'It will be over soon.' He ordered cold compresses to be applied, moaning about the cruelty of life and with a compassionate smile he left.

Morihei looked at his wife, rocking with the baby, savouring the few moments she would have with her last living son. The baby stopped convulsing and they both watched him sink into a renewed coma. Ueshiba didn't know what to do or say, looking at the son that would never grow, the man that would never be, his male offspring. They cooled and tended the little thing, keeping desperately to their parental duties until he passed away.

'Kuniharu,' the wife cried and hid her face in Morihei's shoulders. He didn't hug her or said a word. He was numb, like a knight with a dented shield, none of the blows reaching inside. His face stayed expressionless throughout the funeral ceremonies and the burning altar of the tiny baby. Expressionless, maybe the lips curling down lower than before and the eyes darker and distant. *I have nothing left in me no more!* He waited patiently for it all to be over and then he took to the mountains, a sword at his belt and the staff tied to his back, once again charging at his soul.

'Master,' he told Deguchi as he left, 'I am sorry but I have to go.'
'Where to Morihei? Where will you go?'
'To the mountains, Master, to be alone. It was the only thing to help me when my father was gone.'
'I see.'
'Goodbye Master.'
'Goodbye Morihei and don't you worry, we will look after your family like it was our own.'
'Thank you master.'

'And Morihei,' he called as the student was about to leave.

'Yes Master?'

'Be careful! You are far more sensitive now, the studies stimulated in you the water element – the Yin.'

'Yes Master.'

'And don't forget your meditation and *Kotodama* training.'

'Yes Master.'

'And one last thing to remember.'

'What is that Master?'

'Your task to establish a new art!'

'I won't forget, Master, I promise.' It wasn't the first time Deguchi demanded Ueshiba to establish a new kind of *Budo*, a new kind of art.

The usual meditation and *Chinkon Kishin* didn't apply as much to a man of the martial ways, not without some physical manifestation, and Deguchi acknowledged it. Morihei was frustrated that his fighting abilities were not connected with the beauty of the arts, that the only tool to bring him calmness, in his trade, was the staff and the sword. He handled the *jo* in a new way, the way of *Misogi*, inspired by the sadness of recent months. This was undoubtedly the worst year in his life and at the same time the one with the most amazing revelations. He couldn't honestly feel what Deguchi was preaching about, not the *Su* and definitely not its enlightened applications, but he could sense that he was close, wishing that life would give him the necessary time to learn rather than mourn.

'Reach out for *Satori* (enlightenment),' his inner voice chanted.

'No, not yet,' another voice confronted the first and he obeyed, concentrating on the walk, for now holding back.

After his father's death, almost nine months ago, he was pulled away from his selfish core, for the first time lost and absent from the centre. The *Su* emerged from within, yet it was as unstable as he was, lacking the sophisticated revelations that he acquired in Ayabe. Morihei was ashamed to think about *Satori* rather than his tragedy, but he recognised it as the only way to keep sane in this mad reality.

He climbed up the mountain; his body more tuned than ever, a perfect shrine for the artist of the soul. The climb was strenuous but he did not stop for a rest, putting agony on his lungs as his pulse raced higher. He hadn't eaten for a couple of days yet the dull emptiness that was echoing in his middle, deeper than any abyss, mocked the hunger away. Morihei stopped and moved his head around, scanning the magnificent scenery of Ayabe.

'Enchanted place. Glorified nature!' He was sweating, chest heaving and throat dry. The brief rest stimulating painful emotions to surface, to be liberated from the cage of his chest. He lifted his head up, wiping his dripping forehead on a sleeve.

'A little higher still!' he spoke loudly, to no one but himself.

In one hour he reached the summit and the clearing he knew from before. Morihei sat down for a moment, closing his eyes, trying to calm the spirit and return to the divine, the *Chinkon Kishin* techniques. He went as far as he could go and then stood up, taking the *jo* in both hands and swinging at the four directions of the wind, synchronising his respiration with the motion. The hollow he felt at the pit of the stomach broke away, yet he was distant from touching its numbness, like something was blocking his way. The hollow wasn't denying him the absolution, he realised, because the true obstacle was the tightness in his chest. The wood became alive in his hands, a part of his constitution. Wood was an excellent material for the task of purification, an element of life itself.

The *jo* rotated large and circular in his hands, employing all the chest muscles in perfect unison with the rest of the body. When he felt warm and tuned he started to deploy *Kotodama*, humming the sound of the *O*, vibrating it at his chest. He repeated the powerful sequence a few times, gaining necessary strength, and then he allowed the sound to naturally lift his spirit with the transition to the *U. I am breaking away* The tightness in the chest was crumpling, it frightened him yet he kept going.

'Oh no Kuniharu, Tekemori!' he cried, 'where are you? How could I have failed you both?' It was like opening Pandora's Box, allowing disease to be unleashed from his soul.

With his mood inflamed he swung the *jo* like never before, exhaling air with the painful song of his loss. Tears rolled down his cheeks, dampening his skin and his collar. His chest vibrated with his cries, his hands swinging the *jo* at the gods and at the cruelty of his condition. 'Why? What for?' he hollered, the lifeless faces of Takemori and Kuniharu blurring through his tears, seeking the strong father who was unable of scaring death away. Ueshiba cried and his body shook with the staff, wave after wave of strikes and emotions until he screamed, the mountain echoing his roars, sharing the burden of his pain.

Haah, finally the void ... He was moving with his eyes closed now, grief subsiding and only the emptiness remained. The perfect movement of the body and the effortless respiration turned him into an instrument of the divine. The flow was within and without the empty core, the throne cheated by those who had passed away, his family, his sons.

Without warning, eyes still closed, he was suddenly confronted by the *Su*, sensing it floating in his mind, vibrating at his soul. It was as he remembered it from the mountains of Tanabe, where he had spent a great deal of time after his father had passed away. *It is different somehow, as if more controlled and stable.* He could sense all that Deguchi had taught him, he was in the *Kotodama* dimension.

Ueshiba stopped moving and dropped to his knees, exhausted, face cracking from the dried tears and the eyes remaining shut. He sat as the Buddha for a long time, marvelling at the new find of the *Su*. He realised that it wasn't a mere sound but an image as well, a coiled coloured rubbery band that twirled and pumped energy at an inner tempo. He inhaled and the colour of the string intensified, collecting depth and strength from the environment, and when he exhaled the colour weakened, the *Su* expanding to the horizons. There was unexplained calmness in that state, a wholeness he had never known. The *Su* was sung by Morihei in a world where the miseries of life had no footing, the before and after nowhere to be found.

It was the ultimate present and Ueshiba savoured it for as long as he could. Until he was confronted by the *Ki* ...

20 The Song of Creation

TIME WAS FLOWING BY unwasted, days upon days in which Jerome practised relentlessly, mastering the spiritual doctrines that he was taught. The *Misogi No Jo* was particularly progressing, the staff swinging naturally in his grip, an extension of his being. George pushed him beyond his physical and mental boundaries, tackling his student's weaknesses until he prevailed. Proudly he would watch Jerome meditating under the gushing freezing water, chin held high, a little smile curling his young lips, finally appreciating the purifying effect of the cold.

It was not his only achievement. He could breathe easier while practising the *Chinkon Kishin*, the air healing his emotions. He was connected, yet not fully, never reaching the inside, an invisible barrier denying him the essence. George sat him down for a conversation one day, to discuss his progress.

'Is Max still attached to your core?' he asked bluntly.

Jerome looked over his shoulder and tightened his lips, afraid to disappoint the *sensei*. His life had been a succession of unhealthy relationships, short in duration and flittingly unstable. He could never rely on anyone, weary of disappointment and danger, until he met George.

George was like a father to him; quickly gaining his trust and establishing his self-importance. Jerome was liked and accepted, a sensation both new and enjoyable.

'Speak up,' George demanded after a long delay.

'I guess that I am still worried about him and his well-being.'

'It is more than that, don't you understand? Worry is an internal force that pushes you away from yourself! Here. Have a look.' He took his finger and drew on the pebbled floor, exposing thin paths between the little rocks. They were sitting in the meditation room, after another unsuccessful and tiring trial of *Chinkon Kishin*. George pointed at the diagram he had created, a circle with a prominent dot in its centre.

'The dot is your core, the dwelling of the *Su* and the space between the dot and the outer circle is everything else that you are, everything that is inside you.' He glanced at Jerome, studying his eyes for a glint of understanding. The boy nodded and the *sensei* continued his explanations.

'It is this dot in your centre that worries me; this is the point that is taken up by Max. You are hanging out here,' and he pointed at the space outside the boundary of the circle. Jerome's eyes were big and wide, there was a tightness at the back of his neck; looking at George like a puppy would look at a scorning owner. His worries were gone in an instant, seeing the pained expression on George's face, as he softly touched Jerome's shoulder with his hand. Compassion was a frightening emotion, its warmth blinding and compelling the boy.

'This is what we call detachment,' George explained. 'A detachment from your core.'

'What can I do to fix this?'

George smiled at him, the lines of his face relaxing. 'It's not a bad thing really, not when employed positively. It's one of the ultimate goals of the art, very effective if controlled and stable,' and he pointed at the dot in the centre of his drawing. 'True detachment leaves the dot vacant, without Max at its midst.'

Suddenly George went dead quiet, twisting his nose, poking his tongue out and then bursting out into hearty laughter, rolling on the pebbled floor. Jerome joined in, unable to resist. He was laughing with all his body, his stomach spasmodically pushing the air out of his lungs. The sensation was pleasant to begin with but quickly turned sour. The laughter was stimulating his middle, pulling demons from the core. Sweat was flashing at his face and he felt helpless, struggling to control his own body. 'Stop! Please!' He finally managed to stop the laughter yet guilt had already settled in, consuming him with worries for Max.

'Let me tell you something that might change your perspective on things, I have mentioned it more than once, yet you choose to ignore it.' He gave Jerome a meaningful look and continued. 'You can't help Max, you see, but through your failure and knowing Max's abilities I would say that your chances are quite high at that. And besides ...' and here he got close to Jerome, whispering the last few words. 'I might be able to sneak you out of here in the coming days, before anything seriously bad happens to either of you.'

The statement thundered in Jerome's ears although George was whispering it.

'To get out, to be free?' He looked around shaken, instinctively wary that it might be one of the cruel institutional tricks. His eyes shifted to the gentle expression on George's face, the sincerity contradicting any ill intended thoughts. Jerome maintained his confused silence, his fingers rubbing slowly on his lap.

'I know that you won't and can't believe my words but they are true. I can help you get out of here.'

'Why?' Jerome asked bluntly and immediately regretted it, afraid he might cause friction with the *sensei*.

'Because I want you to live and because I like you. Helping you out of here won't be the end of the world to me.' Jerome eyed him with slight suspicion, something didn't feel right.

'Won't you get into trouble?'

'Don't worry about me, I will be fine. They would never know what happened to you and the worst they could do is kick me out.' The *sensei* sounded genuine, his offer ringing true in Jerome's ears. A second later the usual worry crept in. 'You are wondering what will be with Max, aren't you?' George said with a smile. 'Max will probably advance to the next stage since he has all the talent to succeed but I am not so sure about you. Like I said to you before, Max is fine and there is nothing that you can do for him, or more like it, there is nothing that he can do for you.' George's words were overwhelming, the warmth of his manners compelling Jerome to trust. No one had ever cared about him before and the thought almost brought tears to his eyes.

'We will discuss the plan in due time but for now you must continue with your training, it is a vital part and I want you to study it thoroughly; we don't want to raise any suspicion.' He looked at Jerome who nodded in confirmation. 'Have you read the part in your book about the String Theory and *Kotodama*?' Jerome smiled happily, intrigued by the practice to come.

'I read it but I can't say that I fully understood a thing.'

'That's all right. Our kind of study was never about understanding. The input, the accumulation of details is what we seek. Memorising the meanings of *Kotodama* sounds is far less important than remembering how to combine them to the *Aiki* applications because *Kotodama* is beyond any articulate language, a spell that triggers reaction.' He motioned Jerome to sit in *seiza*. 'The sound has to grow inside you, to vibrate your body from within. Shall we begin?'

And they started to chant, first with the sounds of the *A, O, U, E, I*, which form the basis of the Japanese language and from there they closed into the core sounds, to the *Umu* – birth and the *Yu* and *Mu* – the nothing and something, until they finally reached the *Su*. Each and every sound had to be vibrated in a specific way in order to get the best results. The *Su* made the biggest impression on Jerome, its power transpiring more strongly than all the other sounds. George detected his student's enthusiasm.

'We hold the *Su* as the predominant sound because of its strong impact on breathing, the human bridge to the higher arts. In other traditions it is the *A* sound, yet in Aikido the *A* has a different role.' Jerome couldn't understand the lesson just as George had promised him, but he tried his hardest to imitate the sounds required. There was no stagnation for body and soul at that given moment and the air flowed freely in and out of his lungs. George's words rang magically in his ears, exorcising emotional waste, lifting choking memories.

'Ultimately, when you reach the *Su*, you will see it as a rubbery ring, shining, agile, and unbelievably tempting!'

Kotodama practice resumed after a short lunch break. 'Come on, tidy up – lets go!' George led the way to the Plain *Dojo*, where he put sounds to the basic moves of Aikido, teaching Jerome how to vibrate the right *Kotodama* through the techniques.

'Let it sing inside you, enthusiastically vibrating to your core, to the *Su*.' Jerome was doing well, his chest expanding unchallenged.

How could I have been such a fool, to think that Max was in any danger? The only danger around here is Max's success, and that is my biggest threat. It was a calming thought and the lines of his face softened the flesh, finally free of commitment and guilt.

For three more days they practised the combination of *Kotodama* with basic Aikido and Jerome was performing well. He could fit all the techniques to their relevant sounds, not understanding or feeling their true promised value, yet satisfying George with his efforts. On the fourth day they were back at the waterfall, back in the freezing water.

'What does it mean?' Jerome asked once they had finished practising a chant carried out under the waterfall.

'It's a prayer for the Dragon God, the holy saint of Aikido,' he laughed warmly at the baffled look on Jerome's face. 'The Master of Aikido, Morihei Ueshiba, was the reincarnation of the Dragon God, or so he and his followers believed. This chant is to call upon the grace of this deity; the sounds stimulate it to act.' The explanation sent a shiver down Jerome's spine, the hairs at the back of his neck erect.

They sat under the waterfall, calmness and grace fizzing with the rush of the water, the chant wet and tempting and the piercing cold refreshing every breath. There was something amiss though, the *Su,* the primal sound to activate the rest was never detected, not as vividly as George suggested it could be.

'It is very strange, *Sensei,*' he told George one night, 'but I actually feel good. My breathing is stress free and for the first time in my life I am truly happy.'

George looked at him questionably. 'What's so strange about that?' he asked. 'What is wrong with being happy?'

'Being happy is fine, but I feel like I am failing because of it.' Jerome was looking at the *sensei's* feet. 'I can't sense the *su sensei,* I do feel good but I know I must be missing the point.'

George thought for a minute and then smiled. 'It could be a good sign. It might be that Max is finally being pulled out of your centre and that you simply can't cope with the change or realise it.'

'But it feels odd.' They were sitting in Jerome's living quarters having tea together. George poured some of the hot liquid to his empty cup and said. 'It feels odd because no one desires change, that's human nature. In order to change one must be forced into it. For it is the natural tendency of our race, to get lazy and comfortable.

That's why most people are forever stuck in their ways, even if it hurts them or worse, costs them their lives.'

Jerome thought that he understood. 'So what I regard as happening is simply a blessed change that I should cope with?'

'More than that, what is happening here is the removal of Max and the penetration of the self. You are coming back to your centre.'

'But I thought that it's detachment that we seek.'

'Indeed we do, but the right kind of detachment, not the one that replaces one with another.' George waited patiently for Jerome to contemplate his words, enjoying his hot cup of *Ocha*. 'We seek a detachment that removes the self from the core,' he said quietly. 'It's the only kind that is beneficial to the art.'

Jerome's eyes were wide open, obediently concentrating on the master. 'So what should be left there, nothing?'

'Nothing and something are not the terms I would use. It's more like a place between the two, where both reside and none at all, the point of the *Su*.' He smiled at the student, seeing him scratching his head. 'Don't worry, Jerome, as you progress the detachment will become yours to command. I promise you.'

'But I have less control than ever,' Jerome stated, his face twisted in confusion.

'You can't do anything about it for now because it takes an external stimulation to create detachment. I will make it happen for you, but let me surprise you with the timing.'

'So all this training was for nothing? I would never be able to touch the *Su* by myself! Will I always be dependent on others to activate it?'

'You've got me wrong again, twisting the meaning of my words. The training is not for nothing. It is done as preparation for the detachment. First reach the *Su*, then learn how to control it, that's how it goes.'

With nothing else to ask they called it a day. Jerome continued the *Kotodama* training and the other spiritual practices that he had learned in the past few weeks. His *jo* technique improved significantly and so did his meditation abilities. All practices were enjoyable in George's presence yet basic Aikido was what Jerome felt most comfortable with, its application intriguing him the most. The *Su* remained a misery and a mystery for the time being, a truth to be explored at a later date.

21 Ki: Katana Blue

Ayabe, late September, 1920

THE MOUNTAINS were calling him at nights; he was compelled to obey, creeping away from home, trying hard not to wake up his poor wife. She was shaken by the recent loss they had experienced and to see him roaming the mountains like a madman again could have brought her to breaking point. He couldn't explain to her that those nightly trips were actually healing his broken heart, that they were taking his mind away from the pain. It was detachment on a scale he had never experienced before, although the strength of the ordeal was wearing off as time went by. Detachment, Ueshiba realised, was a key factor to control, the most vital component for touching creation and the point of the *Su*.

He was possessed by the detachment, passionate for the beyond, yet found it very hard to stay detached, a contradiction he could not understand. How did the endless effort, the desire to succeed, push away the achievement? It was an important question to answer and he was starting to feel at a loss once more, sensing the pain healing in his core and with that relief the weakening of his ability to detach, to experience his internal void. He wasn't consciously controlling the opening for the detachment, it was done through his experience with loss, the mental anguish serving as the main drive for the connection to the *Su*. In despair he sought that pain once more, hoping for the tragic memories to become vivid again, to throw him out of his foundation.

Temperatures were mild for the first time in months; the wind blowing softly at the mountain top, conducting sounds and sensations, reviving the world. The ancient musty smell of the woods was intoxicated by the changes of season, magical fragrances created by a blend of old and new.

He reached the mountain clearing and sat in preparation for *Chinkon Kishin* meditation, the thoughts challenging the peace of the dark. *Chinkon Kishin* was a very wide concept that governed all that was calming and bringing about connection to the divine.

He started with breathing exercises, coordinating the movements of the chest and stomach muscles and gradually allowed spiritual qualities to join in. *Let the air flow within my body, to the fingers, the head and toes.* He took his time, knowing by now how imperative it was to keep all the senses sharp and ready, to clean the mind and to synchronise the way in which the body moved. He breathed in, inhaling and expanding to the four corners of the universe, savouring his surroundings, and when he exhaled the universe was sucked in, collapsing onto Ueshiba's nucleus, into the *Su*.

He had made huge progress in the field of meditation with the help of his mentor, Master Deguchi and it significantly cut the time taken to reach the point of purity. Ueshiba pulled the *jo* out of its leather sheath and stood up, cutting at the air with the *Misogi No Jo* he had developed, internally singing the songs of *Kotodama*, a melody for the other worlds.

Clean and tuned he finally stopped cutting, holding the *jo* in the *Jodan* stance momentarily, to place it back into its sheath. He exhaled effortlessly and sat down in *seiza*, the erect position on the knees, chanting *Kotodama* of the 'High Heavenly Plain'.

'*Ta Ka A Ma Ha Ra* ...' The chant vibrated inside his body and he waited patiently, knowing the pattern and what to expect.

Two minutes later and he was inside, floating along a corridor, in a world between worlds. A thought threatened to cross his mind and he brushed it softly aside, harmonising with its direction, blending and moving it away. Emotionally he was far from balanced, yet he was drained for the moment, the *Misogi No Jo* cleaning away the ill feelings, delaying confrontation with what was burning on the inside.

His upper body rocked steadily, the *seiza* creating a wide and supportive base for that move. Ueshiba's eyes were shut, enjoying the familiar and soothing silence of the *Su*. Absently his left thumb pushed on the guard of his sword, separating it from its scabbard. The metal touched the air and his thumb rested against the cold spine of the *katana*.

Suddenly a pulsation was felt inside. *What is going on?* He was shocked, almost losing his focus for a second. The pulsating sound was coming from within, from the point of the *Su*, born at the core yet fed on an unknown source of power. *Where is it coming from?* Ueshiba was intrigued, eager as a child to explore this new discovery. His thumb pushed down on the guard, returning the blade to the scabbard and the sensation disappeared immediately. *I see!* He pulled it out again, resting his thumb on the spine of the sword and the sensation returned. *The metal is acting as a booster for the drive inside me, amplifying its strength and resonance.*

He stood up and withdrew the sword sharply, eyes shut and posture erect. The familiar world of the *Su*, usually dominated by shadows and sounds, was radiating phosphoric blue, illuminated by the blade. It pulsated with Ueshiba's breath, becoming one with his body and soul, like the magical sword of Bosatsu Monju. He moved the sword around, cutting through the world of shadows and shifting plains. He didn't know why it was tainted in colour and why blue, yet that is how it was presented and there was nothing to judge.

For hours upon hours he stayed on the mountain top, savouring the fresh air of the night, cutting through the shadows a new song of power, the song of the pure energy of *Ki*. He knew it derived from his essence, from his little part in the eternal existence of the *Su*. It was primal and fascinating to explore; a search for the right *Kotodama* and their applications.

Later he would contemplate on the differences between the *jo* and *katana*, realising that their disparity was predominated by the different elements they represented. While the wood, the *jo*, was directly related to living elements, the *katana* the metal element, represented materialistic unity and the pure energy that composed it.

The closing gap in his soul would ultimately push away the detachment, leaving Ueshiba to struggle a few more years in search of another opening. The *Su* and *Ki* were not to be controlled voluntarily, yet he had touched them both and was one step closer to the heart of creation. That night he had made a giant leap in his studies and it was more than enough for a while.

* * *

Ki is the moving force of the universe, in all its forms, strength and velocity. It represents the spark of life, the tendency of constant motion and change. In the universe it appears pure for a fleeting instant before being consumed by the variation of resonance. It plays on the Strings of the *Su*, singing with the building blocks of creation, rewarding each unit with a unique sound and character. *Ki* is then used to connect between the units, its energy the glue – to compose universal substance.

The founder of Aikido, Morihei Ueshiba, often spoke of *Ki* and its two main depictions. The first was the crudest form of energy, such as food and fire; palpable and easy to control yet low in strength and capacity. The other form of energy was pure and direct, appearing at the essence of things and difficult to manipulate when released, such as an atomic blast. All materials in the world are charged with eternal power, all have the potential to be absolute energy, to be part of that pure *Ki*.

In Aikido it is vital to know and control the *Ki* – without it the *Skill* would be wasted, the *Su* an image of beauty with only one sound. *Ki* has no preference or moral direction, only the power to move and alternate. Good energy and bad energy are terms to signify the use of *Ki*, yet these characterisations are set long after the *Su* and the *Ki* lose their pure essence ...

(from *Introduction to the Skill*)

Jerome closed the book and sighed, reclining backwards and turning the night light off. It was very late at night and he had to get some sleep or be completely exhausted the next day. This part of the training was interesting and pleasant; he actually chose to stay up late. *Max* he smiled guiltlessly, a little chuckle escaping his lips; *You are in no real danger, would excel where I would fail.*

Placing his palms on his stomach he exhaled in relief, but then he thought of George and his heart missed a beat. *George would release me from detention any day now.* Jerome's desire to will his own destiny was bordering on anxiety. *But what will be with all the things I have studied? Will they be wasted away?* There was an impulse that fought him to stay in the school; a deep acknowledgment of his personal gains, an urge to complete what was so hard for him to achieve.

Familiar pain forced him to open his eyes, to wince and rub his battered hands. Softly he stroked the tender flesh, a disturbing reminder of the cruel nature of the place. He was blessed to have George as an instructor, yet it was a temporary thing, a lucky strike that he couldn't rely on for long. Jerome was torn between his survival instincts and the thirst for the knowledge of the *Skill*.

'Don't worry so much about it,' George had tried to pacify him a few days before. 'Outside you will be able to join one of the free schools and study in a less demanding atmosphere, not all the *dojo* of the art are run this way, you know.'

Jerome listened attentively to George, trusting his words; after all the *sensei* proved to be a very competent individual.

Jerome contemplated his present condition, remembering conversations he'd had with *Sensei* about recollection and of finding the spot of the self. The more he thought about recollection the more he realised that he was there, finally standing at his core. He knew that ultimately the goal was detachment, but first the ego had to be established and the recollection point stable.

'Once you detach from your centre, the *Su* gets on its way and it is a condition both dangerous and unstable. A *Skilled aikidoka* wisely knows how to swiftly recollect or risk madness or even death. Our art, Aikilibrium, is shifting constantly from detachment to recollection in an acrobatic way; controlling these two elements is essential for minimising the risk of injury.'

Jerome understood George's words but couldn't sense their spiritual truth; a barrier forbade his consciousness from penetrating the centre. The only comfort in his incompetence was his honest efforts.

'There is nothing wrong with your performance.' George smiled softly, answering Jerome who complained about the numbness that he sensed. 'It is only the background work for the real development to come, a teaching technique we use in this *dojo*. First you learn and practise the physical base of the art and when everything is ready we add the last ingredient that sparks the commanding change. I dare say that you are close to realisation; unfortunately, we will have to get you out of here before that happens.' The last words he whispered while scanning the hall.

'Why is that?' Jerome asked, whispering as well.

'Because once you have mastered this part of the studies I will leave. My job here is to teach you the spiritual elements of Aikido. When I am done a new instructor will come.' It was Jerome's last chance for survival.

The conversation had taken place at the Plain *Dojo* the previous week, after completing an enjoyable afternoon session of basic Aikido.

'What a master!' Jerome remembered with a smile.

George was not only a great spiritual teacher but his knowledge of the soul took a practical application while practising basic Aikido; the connection created by him more than physical alone. It was an hour-long session, George going through some of the most complex movements of the art, adding the appropriate sounds to accompany them.

'When you apply *Kotodama* to basic Aikido, you must do it internally, so your *uke* doesn't guess the resonance you are creating. Aikido is a martial art and although the *uke* is not an enemy your intention should not be revealed.'

They practised on and on, George attacking and Jerome trying to harmonise with the attacks, trying to choose the right *Kotodama* for the moves. Analytically he was making all the right choices yet he could only sense the very superficial meaning of the 'sound and movement' combination.

'Your frustration is natural yet pointless; the connection will materialise once the last ingredient is added.' George sighed. 'Follow me,' he said and got up. They walked to the side of the *dojo* where a little heap on the floor was covered in a cloth. George knelt down and ordered Jerome to do the same. With an air of holiness, like handling a relic of divinity, he unwrapped the cloth, revealing two swords sheathed in their scabbards. Jerome's mouth hung open, breathlessly watching in reverence. The dark cloth mingled with the black wooden handles and scabbards. The sword's pommels were made of shiny silver yet their glow was swollen by the dominant shade.

George reached out and grabbed one of the swords with both hands, handing it to Jerome with the convex side towards him. Jerome took it and bowed, patiently waiting for the *sensei* to continue. George took the other sword in his left and pushed it into his belt, motioning to Jerome to do the same.

'You are not going to chop my head off are you?' he asked with a little smile, slightly easing the tension.

That was one of the things that was great about George. Any task, no matter how hard, looked far easier when he was around.

'The sword was always considered a spiritual tool in Japan; the *samurai* believed that their soul was forged with the blade, that it was a part of their constitution. Words and explanations aside, the sword or the *katana*, as it is called in Japanese, is one of the best tools to teach about *Ki*, the eternal force. Somehow the metal and the way it's forged makes it an amplifier of energy, a strong manifestation for *Ki*. We will first learn how to handle and use it and then we will apply the right *Kotodama* on top. Master Ueshiba cherished the qualities of unity and concentration gained through sword techniques and he merged them into the art of Aikido. Ueshiba would also refer to the forearm as the *Tegatana*, meaning the blade of the arm.'

George smiled at him, 'I think that's enough said for a while. Let's train.' And then they practised, going through each and every ceremonial step in handling the *katana*.

'Your connection with the blade is critical; treat it with respect, as a pure substance, as a part of your soul.'

They repeated the tiring procedures a few more times and then George demonstrated how to cut with the sword.

'When you cut with the sword you concentrate on its tip; the last 20 centimetres of its razor sharp crest.'

He cut a few times in the air, quick and sharp, the sound reaching the ears an instant after the blade stopped moving. Jerome's body was fixed and relaxed, his mouth filled with juices, *Come on! Let me have a go!*. To his surprise it was not easy to cut precisely with the sharp edge and in no time his shoulders and arms started to ache.

'You are using the wrong muscles for the movement. Look at the way I am using my elbows; listen to the sound of the blade cutting through the air, it is your best guide.'
Jerome listened and copied to the best of his ability.

* * *

It took Jerome a week to learn the *kata* and then, one morning, they added *Kotodama*.
'We are letting the blade sing,' George explained.
Most of the sounds were high pitch, sharply resonating as the sword cut down, powerful and focused. Jerome was tuned to the art, sensing the *Kotodama* vibrating, imagining it colouring every cell of George's body.
He was standing at attention, the sword resting by his left hip, eyes following the *sensei*. The walls of the Plain *Dojo* echoed in answer to every strike, the air sliced and battered by the razor sharp blade. George was demonstrating a certain combination of movements and sounds; a magnificent performance, connecting with the blade in an outlandish bond. He finished the demonstration and gestured to Jerome to try and copy. Jerome grimaced but sang through the pattern, following each and every move the *sensei* performed before him. He didn't miss any of the pattern, yet was again denied of the drill's full realisation.
'You are very close. Don't lose heart, keep trying. Sense the unity of the metal, its flexibility, the way it is radiating power and strength. You have admitted being far more focused in basic Aikido since we started practising with the *katana*. This is the first sign of the development of the connection. The *Ki* is there and it is radiating blue, waiting for you.'
Frustrated Jerome was denied access to the deeper connection, failing with each and every attempt.
'You are floating on the surface of comprehension, unable to dive in. Your head is held breathlessly inside the water, doomed to watch yet not swim among the beauty of the underworld.'
He got closer to Jerome who stood in *Kamai*, the tip of the sword

held high.

'Close your eyes and try again,' George whispered. 'Do it well, we don't have much time. You will have to leave soon.'

Jerome's eyes widened and he inhaled loudly through his nostrils, opening his mouth to speak.

'Shhh. Close your eyes. Don't say a word.'

He obeyed automatically, regaining his self-control after the initial shock.

'It will take place next Friday evening, a week from now.' He walked quietly around Jerome, as he usually did when teaching.

'Now, compose yourself. When I call the command to begin, try and follow the moves one more time.' The last words were said loudly, leaving Jerome to fight the passionate thoughts in his head.

His heart was twisted with mixed emotions, wishing to escape and wanting to grasp the truth of the art at the same time; so close to both contradicting desires.

'*Hajime!*' George called the command and Jerome extended the blade forward, sensing its weight and purpose.

He tried his best to stay focused, not to lose his orientation with the eyes closed; flowing with the pattern, his sword slicing through the air. From time to time he felt a sort of numbness on the inside, followed by an unexpected surge of energy. Those fleeting seconds connected Jerome to his core, allowing him to touch the source.

Jerome opened his eyes and they shone from the inside.

'I saw the blue glow,' he cried. 'There were a few times that I cut down and could actually see what *Sensei* was talking about.' George smiled at him.

'Did anything significant or different happen to your body while you experienced the glow?'

'I was distant from myself, present and absent at the same time.'

George sat down and ordered Jerome to do the same. He sat quietly awhile, inhaling deeply and exhaling long and slow.

'You have finally touched the detachment. An opening to the core was made. For a few seconds you were allowed to sense the *Ki* and to peer into the realm of the *Skill*.'

'Could you see me "seeing" the glow?' Jerome asked confused.

'Of course I could. All *Skilled aikidoka* can see *Kotodama* deployment in others. What I couldn't tell until now was what would trigger you to do it, but now I know.' He sighed as if remembering something and stared severely at Jerome.

'You must know, since you brought up the question, that it is very hard to conceal the *Skill*. Hiding the *Skill* is indeed an art to itself.'

It was a lesson worth knowing, George as always touching the flaws and obstacles of the art, bravely and honestly stripping it to the foundations.

He led Jerome back to the living quarters when the lesson was over and, opening the door, silently motioned Jerome to follow him in. He stopped and got close to Jerome, placing a warm hand on his shoulder.

'Next Friday evening after training we will leave the school through a secret exit. I will be coming with you, to make sure that all goes well.' He pointed at a large metal door that was always locked. 'This door will be open that evening around eight o'clock. I will be waiting for you on the other side.'

Tears collected in Jerome's eyes, the *sensei's* compassionate voice stimulating a volcanic emotion. They bid good night and Jerome sat alone in the dark, thinking of his situation. He knew that he would miss Max and the training but leaving was his only means of survival. His heart felt heavy with the thought that he might never be able to grasp the hidden meaning of the *Aiki*; that all the work had been done for nothing. He realised that a passion for life was ebbing inside him, his own well-being becoming a consideration that had never bothered him before. He shook his head, trying to be rid of the colliding thoughts. The passion for the art had given him a purpose, a fountain of enthusiasm that he would surely miss. His mind drifted to the brief encounter he'd had with the *Ki* and he was flushed with excitement.

He had one more week and he was determined to try and touch more of the hidden art before leaving, *I must learn as much as I can! I am to leave school - my achievements can never be a threat for Max well being – even if I excel and touch the Skill....*

22 Shaking Up the Su

'Shaking up the *Su*' refers to the aggressive creation of an opening in the self, causing temporary detachment. Master Ueshiba was stimulated by such vigorous means numerous times yet he had no pattern to follow; he was an explorer, going through many processes of trial and error, and challenged by uncontrolled detachment every step of the way.

The schools of the *Skill* managed to minimise these events into two episodes in total, with quick and decisive results. Needless to say questions regarding physical and mental health issues were left unasked and unanswered. It was taboo, a subject better left untouched, for fear it might hamper the developments of the *Skill*.

In most *dojo,* the timing for the first shake-up was at the conclusion of the spiritual studies. Students learnt the necessary spiritual elements, following their master's instructions senselessly and only at the very end would the shake-up take place, thereby creating the strongest input possible. After this shake-up there would be another gap of time before the final and conclusive shake-up occurred.

In the past, some *sensei* tried to hasten the process even further and ended up with very grievous consequences. The known pattern was the quickest way to go about it, the only way that didn't cause permanent physical and mental instability.

(from the book *Moral Issues in Modern Aikido* by Stockwell and Jones)

* * *

A MEETING WAS HELD in Yves' office, a meeting before the main meeting.

'So how was Switzerland?' Yves asked, his eyes revelling his hunger for answers.

'It was fantastic *sensei*. Thank you.'

'And the mission?'

'Went better than we had expected.'

'Perfect!' Yves cried and licked his lips, 'Come on lad, tell me some more!'

Look at you sensei, the Informer fought the urge to smile. *As enthusiastic as a schoolboy.* He was enjoying his moment of patronising power, for once taking the role of the master.

'Speak up boy!'

'What do you want to know, *sensei*?' Painfully and slowly the Informer answered Yves' questions, leaving out the punchline, the secret he had saved for himself.

'Calvin was very impressed with your performance; he said that you took him completely by surprise.'

Took his ass out of trouble more like it, the Informer recalled and smiled softly. *But you don't need to know about that, now do you, sensei?*

In the assault on the house in Switzerland, one of the security guards had rushed at Calvin with a bayonet, aiming straight at his chest. Frozen for a split second, Calvin recognised his inevitable fate when unexpectedly the Informer pushed him out of the way to take his place on the same spot. Calvin's eyes had widened as he watched, amazed and trying to regain balance; the Informer, instead of moving out of the way, drained into himself, as if being sucked into an internal vacuum.

'Look out!' Calvin cried. The tip of the bayonet ripped through the shirt, about to penetrate the delicate flesh. Still the Informer remained motionless.

'Move away you fool!' Calvin tried again, the steel almost touching the body.

Then, soundlessly and unexpectedly the Informer shot into the air, pushing through an invisible window of opportunity. His trained arms connected with the assailant's wrist and the bayonet was torn away from the man's grasp, following the Informer's flight.

'Arrghh!' the guard cried before crashing unconscious to the floor, his arm dangling limp and broken.

'Good man, old Calvin,' the Informer told Yves. 'Very reliable.'

'I wouldn't trust him that much if I were you,' the *sensei* advised but the advice was not needed. The Informer was unlikely to trust anybody; he was a student of Yves after all.

He opened his mouth to make a wise remark when the door slid open and George entered the office. Yves looked at the Informer and the latter nodded in confirmation – he was no fool! George wasn't taking part in the search for the book; it was safer that way.

'George, come in please,' Yves called, politely pointing to a chair in front of the desk. George walked in smiling and sat down, nodding to the Informer who remained standing straight.

'Is he ready?' Yves asked and the Informer looked at George, waiting for his reply.

'He is ready, although very different from all the students I have seen before.'

'What is that supposed to mean?' The *sensei* frowned, as if challenged by the lesser teacher.

'As you are well aware most students are recollected from the start. The teaching's aim is to force them to realise it, to prepare them for the detachment to come. With Jerome we have a very different story.' He sighed and Yves looked annoyed, waiting for the speech to finish. Informer listened, confused – he couldn't sense any real stress between the two teachers.

'Most of my time was spent in detaching Max from within Jerome,' George continued, 'only then I was able teach him how to recollect. The intensity of his devotion is too fierce, you see. I hope the usual drills will be sufficient.' There was a tense second and then George snorted a laugh. 'Are you worried?' he teased the confused Informer and after a few seconds of silence both adults burst out laughing.

The Informer stood politely quiet, not really understanding their private joke or humour, a different generation altogether. He didn't know that George always pointed out the obstacles he judged they might face in completing the process and that Yves always teased him about it in return.

'Are you ready?' George asked the Informer when the laughter finally died down.

'I am back,' the Informer replied and winked at him, proudly sharing the space with the adults, a place he felt he justly deserved.

Yves rubbed his palms together and smiled viciously. 'Let's get him!' he said.

23 The Mirror of Amaterasu

AMATERASU, THE GODDESS of the sun hides in a cave, shading her light from the world, punishing it for the way she is tormented by her brother, Susano-O, the god of storm. It had all started in a rather silly way, with lots of good intentions but, as the saying goes, 'The road to hell is paved with good intentions.' In this story it was very true.

Susano-O was missing their mother, Isanami, who was in the world of the dead and he decides to pay her a visit. On his way he stops by his sister, Amaterasu, to bathe himself in her glow and warmth. She accepts him and takes his sword, a symbol of strength and domination and she chews on it, the crisp blade turns soft and supple. From her mouth materialises in a mist, three female deities, the symbol of beauty and tenderness.

She thanks the bewildered Susano-O for his kindness and he asks for Amaterasu's five diamonds in return, the symbol of purity and beauty. She gladly submits the diamonds to her brother who chews on them. Beauty is ground into a paste of strength and out of his mouth charges five powerful warrior deities. Susano-O boasts about his creation and Amaterasu, in her vanity, reminds him that it was not done by his effort alone, that they were her diamonds that he had used.

Insulted, Susano-O furiously storms around Amaterasu's house, stomping on her rice field, throwing faeces into the temple and blocking the irrigation around her house. He is the god of storm after all, creator of commotion and change. She begs him to stop but he refuses, throwing a carcass of a horse to her sewing room, killing one of her sewing maids, some say even injuring Amaterasu herself.

With her elevated ego hurting beyond comprehension she runs away and hides in a cave, sliding a huge rock across the entrance.

Darkness falls on the land and the 800 deities of the world come near the cave.

'Come out,' they beg her. 'We can't see a thing!'

She declines, stubbornly keeping to the shadows.

'I know what to do,' Ame no Uzume, the goddess of laughter declares. 'I can lure her out.' She goes off and soon returns, wearing only leaves and bamboo shoots, dragging behind her a bathtub, holding a mirror in her other hand.

'What is going on?' Everyone asks but she smiles at their bewildered faces and remain silent. Without a single word of explanation she turns the bath upside down, then jumps on top.

'Here we go,' she declares then passionately starts singing and dancing, stomping her feet as loud as she can. The dance progresses and her clothes drop away and everyone cries, 'Look at Ame no Uzume, she is completely naked.' The performance is not intoxicating, but rather funny, and the gods join the party outside the cave, burning the ears of Amaterasu with their joyful cries and laughter. The goddess, tempted by the cheerful noises, comes closer to the entrance of the cave, where a huge rock shades her away from the world.

'What is all that commotion?' she asks, jealous of their joy, hoping they would suffer without her.

'It's just that we've got a new sun goddess, no offence,' replies the cheeky Uzume, chuckling quietly.

Amaterasu is intrigued and starts rolling the rock away from the entrance, wanting to observe the rival to her throne. While she rolls back the rock, Ame No Uzume quickly places the mirror in front of the entrance and the deity of strength waits to pull Amaterasu out, as soon as she peers outside.

Amaterasu, the elder daughter of Izanami, looks into the mirror and the glare of her reflection burns in her further shame. Thinking she is confronted by the competition, she charges out of the cave, forever to shine in the world's sky.

Many conclusions and opinions are drawn from this story coming from the old scriptures of the *Kojiki* but perhaps the one adopted by the *Skill dojo* is the one intended; because it represents the practical adaptation of the story which is used in attaining the *Skill*.

The sun goddess was glaring naturally, purely and simply, detached like a baby in the skies. When confronted by her brother, as one would be confronted by the anguish and passion of life,

Amaterasu reacts and creates with him, choosing to hide in the dark, to lose her detachment. Hiding in the cave of her soul, as all people do, she experiences her world from within those walls. An external force is required to release her from her self-imprisonment, and Uzume does just that, tempting Amaterasu where she is easily seduced.

As Amaterasu is lured out of the darkness she is confronted by her own image, by the reflection of her soul. Detachment becomes the only choice, preferable to dealing with demons. Away from trivial worries Amaterasu shines again in the shrine of her world, colouring the skies with the glow of her nature.

This was the principle the *dojo* of the *Skill* followed, mirroring students their self demons and achieving detachment through it.

Master Ueshiba emphasised the importance of the mirror and often proclaimed that 'True victory is a self victory.' He himself was confronted by a few strong episodes of self-realisation by which he achieved detachment even before he was aware of the *Skill*. Students of the *Skill*, on the other hand, are mirrored only when ready for the application of the *Dai Ni Kihon* techniques; when prepared to reach the *Su* and the *Ki*.

Objectively, the lesson is to realise the options of recollection and detachment – the two basic concepts of the higher arts.

The story of the mirror is part of Japanese heritage, a sacred concept by some.

The mirror of Amaterasu is kept in the Temple of Ise to this present day.

* * *

Tanabe, Japan, Winter 1920

His hands dipped into the water shaking, the thoughts going wild in the head, assessing what had gone wrong, what he had missed. It wasn't supposed to go that way, it wasn't fair – hadn't Deguchi himself told him that his father was fine, that there was nothing he could do to help him?

The Shrine of Kumano was built in the mountains above Tanabe, Morihei's birth place. It was an enchanted place, believed to hold the gateway to the divine.

Ueshiba raised his head and looked at the holy structure, so familiar to him from childhood. The scenery around was frosty, the trees looking pathetically fragile, almost breaking in the soft wind. Today there was no beauty to admire, the lonely cold realisation of his father's death turning his attention inwards, staring at places in his soul that he had never dared look at before. He tried to look inside his mind and a thought materialised in his head, a thought that inflamed him. It was blame and guilt that struck at him and he was facing them head on, justifying his chain of actions.

'I left Shirataki as soon as I heard of my father's poor health, I did what was necessary yet failed to arrive in time for his passing away. What more could a man do?'

He was arguing bitterly with himself, not noticing a worshipper that passed him by; looking very bewildered at Ueshiba's behaviour. He was closed to his surroundings, shut within himself, a rock blocking the entrance. Two questions came to mind, two questions he could not face before and now could not ignore.

If it was for father's fragile health that I left Shirataki, then why did I sell everything I had over there, determined never to return? And if father's health was so dear to me then why did I make a detour and stay in Ayabe for so long? Forever too long ...

He remembered the message his father left behind and it only pained him further.

'To live free of inhibition,' his wife recited the message. 'To do all that you desire in life ...'

'What did you mean by that, Father?' he mumbled quietly. 'Haven't I done that all my life? Chasing my own dreams, living by the financial support of my father, ignoring what was real?'

Ueshiba could no longer hide from the harshness of life, now that he had lost his backbone to the world, his father ...

He felt the weaknesses inside like a hollow in his stomach and he hated himself for it. *I'd had the time to get to father's side if I really* wanted to, plenty of time to get there but I chose to be elsewhere.

Morihei looked at the water and reached out; wanting to wash his face from the sweat that formed on his forehead despite the sharpness of the cold weather around. His reflection caught his eye and he shrugged back in horror, the twisted expression staring back at him, trying to conceal what lurked beneath the surface. Ueshiba's knees buckled and his throat suddenly felt very sandy and dry. He knelt on the floor, in front of the water and balanced himself against a pillar.

What have I done? Unexpectedly all the painful truths burst out of his chained chest, out of the safety of his murky depths. *I had left Shirataki for other reasons than father's illness and even used Father as an excuse for the run, to escape Sokaku.* The *Dayto Ryu* master, his teacher, was a man of death and cruelty and that was precisely where the attraction had lain for Morihei to begin with. It was a kind of a boost to his ego, to be associated with such a feared fighter as Sokaku Takeda. *And I had brought you into my house!* Sokaku had accepted Morihei's invitation to teach in Shirataki yet he was very demanding and the price of this association was more than financial alone. *Sokaku, you had choked the happiness and balance of my family. I wanted to be rid of you long ago and Father's illness presented itself as the best excuse ...* Morihei would never have admitted that his motives were so low, yet now, as he was faced with the consequences of his actions, he had no other choice.

This act of running away or avoidance, he could have concealed and reasoned to himself, had he gone straight to Father's side and fulfilled his own excuses, yet he didn't. He stopped at Ayabe, to see the great Onisaburo Deguchi and spent a considerable amount of time there. The shaman had, it was true, said that there was nothing Morihei could do for Father, but Morihei was the one who decided to interpret the master's words as a hint that Father was well and waiting. *It was my decision to stay longer in Ayabe, me and no other!*

Morihei could hide in his cave no more, the truth's reflecting from the water of the shrine's basin like the mirror of the gods. He had left Shirataki out of fear and had gone to Ayabe out of his own selfish desire for the divine.

Ueshiba watched his face in the water, tears dropping from his eyes like a gloomy day's rain. His palm clutched at the floor, crunching dried leaves and earth and then beating them at his face.

'Father, what have I done? What have I done?' He was crying, mumbling, senselessly shrinking from the pain. After a while he managed to compose himself and he stood up. *I need to find somewhere private.* Still shaken, he dragged himself away from the shrine, heading for the mountains.

His body was limp and he needed all his concentration to climb to a small clearing, sheltered from curious eyes. He leaned on his staff, the *jo*, and sat in *seiza* with his eyes closed. The image of his face reflecting from the water was glowing vividly in his mind and he watched it from afar, completely dissociated. The weaknesses and sins were mirrored to him through his own expressions and for the first time in his life he was confronted with what he really was. He got up and started to swing the staff around, using it to sort his personal affairs and dig deeper into his soul. He had experienced detachment and he had no way of knowing it, although he did possess some tools to activate the vacancy of the self. He knew of the void of the *Kotodama U* from childhood and of the creativity of the *Su* which he had learned from the great Onisaburo Deguchi himself.

Morihei spiralled the *jo* over his head as he chanted, trying to find the connection to the *Su*. Detachment came as a surprise, created by the crash of the selfish mind and the truth reflected by the water. With the chanting he fell to the world of the void and heard the call of the *Su*. The song joined his breath and together in an unstable fashion they moved in and out of his core.

Never again would Ueshiba ignore his true mind; the mirror becoming a symbol of his life and art.

Only after long days of thought, exercise and purification techniques did he managed to set his personal issues aside – to pacify the demons of his soul. That is when he could finally mourn his father's death in peace.

* * *

A week went by and some of the physical discomforts of the first few months in the *dojo* returned, namely the stomach ache and with it the sleepless nights. Over all Jerome was relaxed, the only interruption to his inner peace was the healthy excitement at the prospect of escape. He trained constantly, enjoying the spiritual rituals, marvelling at the perfect unison in which he communicated with George while practising basic Aikido.

Satisfied and recollected he sat after the *Misogi* rituals in the afternoon, when George walked by.

'Tonight at eleven o'clock I will be waiting for you on the other side of that door. Be punctual!'

The words were whispered, barely moving the air, yet they thundered inside Jerome's body. Tonight he would be free of the threat looming over his life; to continue his studies elsewhere, away from the beastly conditions of the school. As for Max, the thought repeated itself, well ... George probably knew that Max was the chosen one and George was the only one in the world he could trust.

The afternoon continued in a normal fashion, training as on any other training day. George emphasised the spiritual rituals and the world of *Kotodama*, the essence of vibration. For Jerome it presented the biggest frustration of all.

'Everything is in tune and in perfect synchronisation, *Sensei*. The movements and the sounds flow inside my body in undisturbed resonance but,' and Jerome took a big gulp of air before continuing, his eyes looking down at the floor, 'I don't sense any of it at my core, or at the *Su*, as you would call it, *Sensei*.'

George waited until Jerome raised his head again. 'You've got to be patient, my dear. The time will come and you will find this combination of movements and resonance very useful. You have to trust me on this one.'

'When?' Jerome asked eager to the point of despair. George looked at him with his soft eyes.

'Don't worry about it now. Let's get to the Plain *Dojo* instead and run some *Jiyu Waza*. It will clear your mind of the cluttered thoughts.'

Jerome was excited, at once forgetting about spirituality and achievement; basic Aikido presented the perfect *Misogi* for him.

The evening hit him before he was ready and after the shower he stood still, staring at the clock on the wall, waiting for the right timing. *Come on, hurry up!* After a while he sat down in *seiza*, his few belongings tied up to the *jo* by his side, and practised *Chinkon Kishin*, trying to bring some peace to his racing heart. *I must stay!* To his horror an inner voice was demanding, *I shouldn't leave!* Angrily he tried to brush these thoughts away, his forehead squeezing into a frown. He wasn't sure why he felt that way; whether he had become comfortable in his jail or whether the good old guilt was up to its tricks. *I must dissociate myself from these thoughts, I can't handle them at the moment.* Life was taking him on a new course and he had to follow, rationally supporting the way it went.

Jerome looked at the clock and swallowed hard, in five minutes he would walk out of that door. He quit trying to meditate, the excitement overwhelming any attempt at relaxation.

The clock struck eleven and Jerome held his palm on the door handle, taking a final look at what had been his home and jail for the good part of a year. He had arrived here just before he'd turned sixteen and soon he would be seventeen; that is if he escaped the promise of death that awaited him at the school.

He sighed and pressed down on the handle, for a second his breath getting caught in his throat when the handle didn't give way. He placed more body weight on it and the unused hinge was finally conquered. With a chilling screech the handle pressed down and the lock unbolted. The door had a heavy frame and he had to push with all his might to get it going. *Come on!* The stubborn hinges suddenly weakened their resistance, taking him by surprise, flying full momentum into the other side of the door.

He fell to his knees and immediately jumped back up, his eyes focusing forwards. Someone stared right back at him and Jerome's head jerked back in terror.

24 Reflection

HIS HANDS instinctively reached for the staff, fearing the attack of the passionate image in front of him. *It is only me!* Jerome realised yet his weariness was mounting. A mirror, not too big, was hanging on the wall opposite the door, creating a strong effect in the brightly exposed room.

'Finally you showed up.' He heard a chillingly cheerful voice, the wrong voice, shocking like a blow to the nose. Jerome turned his head slowly, to meet the contemptuous face of Yves.

'Oh, I am so sorry, expecting somebody else?' The cruel joy in the *sensei's* voice sent a shiver down Jerome's spine and a cold explosion of thoughts crunched inside his head, as if the thoughts were made of snow, sluggishly slowing his efforts to fight and justify. He didn't have to say a thing, Yves so it seemed, was taking great pleasure in inflicting the blows of truth.

'You must be looking for your friend George. Well, don't! George has been dealt with; never again will he interfere with my pupils.'

'What have you done to him?' Jerome's voice trembled, his knees threatening to buckle at any moment.

Yves smiled broadly, shaking his head. 'Remarkable. The man got you into a pile of trouble and you are still worried about him.'

'He is my teacher and he cares about me,' Jerome spat, trying to ignore the sarcastic remarks. Yves continued smiling and threw something in front of Jerome's feet.

'Have a look and see what kind of an ally you've got. Learn how much he really cares about you.'

What is it? Confused yet hardly intrigued he obeyed the *sensei* quietly, the only option he had was to buy himself some time and assess the situation. He had a look at the folder that was lying in his trembling arms and opened it, letting his eyes read some of the contents. It described a deal where Jerome was the object of purchase. *Yeah right!*

'What is this all about? Where is George?' He stood and threw the folder down.

'You don't get it, do you, my dear? George was about to deliver you to another *dojo*, to use you in a school that he was about to open.'

The forms matched the *sensei's* accusation.

'I don't believe you,' Jerome cried. 'He wouldn't do that to me.'

'I don't care what you believe, I only state the truth and its consequences. From now on you will be instructed directly by me, the only other instructors you shall interact with will be there to make sure you study properly. You are my most precious investment at the moment. It is obvious that you don't care much for your friend, as you were planning to run away and leave him behind, yet he is not doing very well with the spiritual studies; it is his good fortune that I caught you before you escaped.'

'No! Oh, no.'

Yves studied Jerome's face and the smile on his face widened further. Jerome was shaking on his feet, like a marionette attached by cords to the *sensei's* words and gestures.

'You didn't know that, did you?' Yves asked and started to laugh loudly, the words hurting like a whip, tearing at Jerome's nerve endings. 'Isn't that something? I have to admire George's cunningness. No, Jerome, the answer to your unasked question is no, your friend is not doing very well and in fact from now on the only thing to keep him alive is your progress in the art.'

'Oh, no!'

'How fortunate Max is! We found you before you escaped and left him to die.'

'You bastard!' Jerome shouted, the anger blinding him to a rage, his fist clutching the staff.

'You will stay here for a while, waiting for your friend to catch up, and you shall practise all the applications you went through with good old George. I shall be watching you all the time, making sure that you don't slack off and allow your friend to die.'

Jerome was barely breathing, a red impulse pushing through his tears of despair. *If I only had the courage to strike at your evil smirking face.*

'I can see your anger but don't blame it on me,' the soft voice slithered onwards. 'Perhaps you are angry for believing that George cared about you, or maybe you hate your desire for human warmth, a desire so petty that it would force you to do anything at the slightest sign of compassion.' He stopped talking and laughed briefly yet when he continued there was no smile on his face and the words came out sharp and clear.

'Perhaps you are angry for believing in George's promises, quickly abandoning your friend to my mercy. You wanted George's approval and leaving the school was the easy way out of harm. You choose to look after your own ass and forget about Max. It is your fault, George has nothing to do with that.' And the laughter resumed, stinging the ears of the student, blurring the air around the room. The staff fell out of Jerome's grip, his body spiralling around. The anger faded away, replaced by a desperate sadness.

'Look in the mirror and see your true mind,' Yves continued in a chilling tone. 'You shall have no sleep or food until further notice.'

He left the room and the door shut slowly on Jerome's new jail. 'You!' Jerome cried as his demons smiled and spat at him from the spotless glass, 'I hate you!' Yves was right, his desire for love and compassion had played straight into George's hands. *George had lied to me, saying that there was nothing I could do for Max.* Jerome kicked his feet and cursed loudly, yet remembered that it was he who had decided to interpret the *sensei's* words as a positive sign. *George never really said that Max was doing better, not directly so. It was easy to follow the sensei's plan, to forget about my friend.* Jerome hated himself for so conveniently falling into the trap of his recollection.

He screamed at his reflection and then collapsed entirely, shocked by the sudden detachment. A few weeks of recollection had placed him snugly at his core. He was soft and unprotected; no barrier to block the devastating blows. The guilt and self-realisation threw him out of his centre and it was vacant, for Max as well was absent from the spot. Without control he began reciting some of the *Kotodama* he had learned and in an instant he was in a world of shadows and sounds. The 'Shaking of the *Su*' had been completed successfully.

25 Third Level of Techniques: Dai San Kihon

In the town of Iwama stands a *dojo* and a shrine. The place is enchanted and vast, giving a hint for the future and a glimpse of the past. Around the *dojo* a garden is stretched, where the *Aiki* master lovingly cultivated and tended to the land. Inside that garden oval prayer stones are hidden, embedded in the earth; O Sensei used to sit near them daily, to meditate and pray. The *dojo* itself is fairly small and simple, made out of dark planks of wood. It smells old and damp yet somehow cosy and warm. The *tatami* floor slightly illuminates the *dojo* in a creamy colour, it used to be white before but time and training dulled its shiny glow.

For years upon years historians and worshipers came and roamed that special place; there is much to look at and admire yet most come only for one thing. For if you stand inside that *dojo* don't look around or down, right up on the ceiling is all you need to find. It is a single footmark, small and faded by the years, the place where the master's body hit while performing a feat of *Skill*. For if it was not by the *Skill* alone, then how did Master Ueshiba end upside down above a crowd of striking foes; smiling confidently at their bewildered faces, to reappear behind their back and to drop them in a roar.

(from the book *Introduction to the Skill*)

THE THIRD LEVEL of techniques presents the applications of the *Skill*, the ways in which it diverts. All *dojo* followed a similar pattern for teaching the first and second level of techniques; dissimilarity apparent only at the third level, where a specific *Skill* was to develop.

The diversity of Aikido *Skills* could only suggest what a truly great art it was, inspired and abundant in options. There was the 'Seeker *Skill*' – the *Skill* of the tracker, the '*Aiki* Healer *Skill*' – who could expose physical frailty by a mere touch. There was the *Skill* of the '*Aiki* Grappler' – the deadliest in a close-range fight and there was Aikilibrium, the art of the performer, developed by a stunt man. These were only examples from a far wider range of abilities;

representing two hundred years of trial and error.

Although differing in the *Skill* they developed, the *dojo* used a similar pattern by which the *Skill* was embodied in the students; deploying a second detachment as the final act of the third level of techniques. During that second detachment the *Skill* was poured and sealed in the vacancy of the students' core: a new entity to sit at the point of the self and to activate the *Su*.

Each single Aikido *Skill* was highly sophisticated, reaching a degree of expertise far greater than any single *Skill* the founder ever possessed; O Sensei would have needed ten lifetimes in order to accomplish all of these achievements.

There was one quality, however, that no other *aikidoka* but the founder accomplished, and that was the ultimate '*Skill* of Diversity'; a *Skill* representing the ability to change, to know a few if not all the *Skills*. Some *aikidoka* had variations of this *Skill* but it was a variant based on the *Skill* they possessed in the first place.

The '*Skill* of Diversity' demanded that the opening at the core of the student, created by the second detachment, was to be sustained, forever allowing knowledge to penetrate. Yet numerous attempts to try and keep that opening sustained ended with tragic consequences. This unaccomplished *Skill* was the main drive for those seeking the Lost Book of Ueshiba, hoping to find the ingredients for the '*Skill* of Diversity'. It was the highest capability available to the human body and soul; a possibility of achievement, a dream that only one man so far had explored.

26 The Spark

> Balance is as you perceive it,
> Gravity is only a mask,
> By learning all the powers surrounding,
> You'll blow the fog out of your path.
>
> (Jacques *Sensei* – Founder of The School of Aikilibrium)

IN THE YEAR 2015 Aikido's popularity was reduced to nearly nothing. It was a dying art, undesired, practised for the sake of tradition and preservation. Those who persisted and studied the art were challenged by frustration and financial hardship; their arms were stretched out like those of the blind man, trying to find their way in the dark; palms facing hungrily up as those of the beggar's since the food of knowledge was expensive and scarce.

Jacques Patye shared the gloomy mood of the era, his despair no exception to the rule. In 2013 he was 33 years old and a fifth dan Aikido instructor. Proudly he tried to make a living out of his art yet failed miserably, fighting constantly to make ends meet. By 2015 he was forced to seek finance elsewhere and he went back to work as a stunt man. It had been his trade initially, before he quit everything and flown to Japan, before the Aikido bug had captured his heart wholly.

Jacques *Sensei* was introduced to Aikido while working as a stunt man, wanting to learn breakfalls and their application, in order to expand his knowledge in the art of falling. It could be argued that Jacques was a brilliant *uke* even before he studied Aikido, just as a stunt man alone, yet Aikido gave him extra tools to use, more options and qualifications.

Jacques was a phenomenal *aikidoka* and he wanted more than what the art offered; working hard as a stunt man and at the same time trying to develop beyond the contemporary boundaries of Aikido, to find the gateway to the higher arts.

The long-awaited breakthrough came with a copy of Mr Hafez's book, presenting a system for acquiring the so-called *Skill* – exactly the information that Jacques and so many others needed. He was hooked; his journey to the world of the *Skill* began.

Those were glorious days, the golden age of the art; times of explorers in search of the land of the soul, filled with passion and longing for the beyond.

Master Jacques, used his influence in the Aikido world to organise a group of young yet highly capable *aikidoka*, and together they structured the first European curriculum for the *Skill*. They spent days upon days reading books and analysing video tapes featuring Ueshiba *Sensei*; going through similar experiences to those of the founder, just as Mr Hafez suggested in his book. Together they searched and reached the conclusion for the second level of Aikido techniques, its peak the confrontation with the self, with the mirror of Amaterasu.

Their revelations were shocking and so were the results. Out of the twenty *aikidoka* to start the journey only five actually managed to grasp the *Su*. Eight others were left frustrated and angry, never to return to Aikido, passionately preaching against the art, particularly against the study of the *Skill*. They had strong arguments to support their claims as seven of the group's members lost their minds, three eventually committing suicide. Luckily Jacques outranked the accusers of the group and his excellent reputation silenced their arguments for a while.

All five *aikidoka* to reach the higher arts stayed together and documented their path to the *Skill*. They took into consideration errors and lessons learned, designing a formula for a lawful practice, aimed at achievement and at the same time protecting future students from the way of harm.

It was an important decision, sensitive to the basic fears of the human race. Societies were forever wary of exceptional individuals, fearing their abilities and finding reasons to put an end to the unfamiliar. Master Jacques anticipated the legal problems before they even started, eventually becoming a major part of the solution in the years to come.

Despite the good results Jacques had to disbanded the group

shortly after it was gathered; worries for the health of his wife forcing him to return to France. He needed money for the expensive medical procedures Marie was going through; unwillingly back at work from his studies, pulled away from the realisation of his find.

As a stuntman, Jacques specialised in string work – 'pulleys' as they were nicknamed in the industry. Practically speaking it meant being pulled by a taut cord that jerked the body in the direction the performance demanded. It was a pretty basic operation, a powerful yet small engine, cables, scaffolding, precision of planning and guts, mainly guts.

His mind was still absorbed by the *Su* and the *Ki* as he returned to work; a blend of chance and bitter reality that offered a spark for success.

The first job he secured was for an advertisement, promoting some giant communications company. It was a fairly simple procedure, 'to travel backwards eight metres, in the process swooping upwards in an arc which, at its peak, was four metres high'. The stunt took place in the back lot of one of Paris's movie studios on an unusually chilly summer's day. Jacques was standing in the middle of a yard, a cord, barely visible, stretching from his back to a pole. From the pole it angled down to a little engine where a short man stood, staring at his wristwatch.

'Bloody hell!' The man cursed as he looked up, shaking his head at the skies. The sun was blocked by a dense wall of cloud, radiating golden through the seams of the bulky white masses, beautiful but allowing very little light.

'Alan, can you please come and check these straps at the back of the suit. It's pinching my skin.'

Alan, the short man, rushed to obey; fiddling about with the cable attached to the hidden jacket beneath Jacques suit.

'How does it feel now?'

Jacques turned his shoulders and exhaled heavily, causing Alan to smile.

'You are looking stressed, *Sensei*!'

'It has been a while,' Jacques apologised and smiled back at his student, hiding the painful truth of the detachment that still haunted him; clenching his jaw against the desire to shout about his discovery. He held himself back, not ready to talk of what he himself could not comprehend.

Waiting for the cord to spring him backwards, he closed his eyes and tried to relax; shaking his tall and skinny body in order to disperse the tension. Gradually he stopped moving, his intention shifting internally, concentrating on breathing. He slumped his head and shoulders forwards, his thick dark hair dangling behind, the string attached at his lower back supporting his weight, allowing him to lean further forward and down.

Stuntwork had an element of dependency, of being out of control. A performer had to put his fate in the hands of the act, the engine and the cord. Jacques frequently prepared the stunt himself, knowing more than most in the field how to calculate the vectors necessary for the pull, looking for that small, forgotten detail that might swing the cables in an undesired and perilous course. It was a dangerous business as it was and there was no need to take further chances.

Jacques leaned forward heavily; draining the energy out of his limbs, the only thing to keep him balanced was the metal cord. Absently he chanted away, stimulating the *Su* and *Ki* to show their presence. It was an impulse he had developed since the detachment had confronted him two weeks ago; the sensation was present, it was calling and he had to obey. *There you are*, he thought in delight as the detachment took over. In an instant he forgot about the work, shutting down all internal sounds, only concentrating on maintaining the delicate spell of the Strings. The *Su* coiled inside him, its stringy composition pulsating softly at his core. Being suspended in complete dependency strengthened the sensations inside; thumping his whole body in the unpredictable movements of the *Su*, compressing Jacques into the vacuum at his middle.

'Are you ready?' Alan asked, his left hand on the lever that would pull the *sensei* away.

Jacques nodded yet didn't hear the question, absorbed and enchanted by the shadow world of the *Su*. Then, suddenly, the winch pulled at his centre, pushing the air out of his lungs. The Strings expanded outwards in a tune, reacting to the intention of the cord, fusing with the cable, as it raced towards the pole. It was a strong and vigorous movement and at the same time focused and controlled.

Ahhh, Jacques smiled when it was over, *I almost forgot how good it feels!*

'Don't move,' he heard the voices and was suddenly aware of their meaning, 'Stay where you are!' Confused Jacques opened his eyes and instinctively his leg reached out, searching for the mat that was placed beneath the pole. 'What the—' He was surprised, swaying on his feet, hearing gasps of relief as he regained his footing. Disorientated Jacques looked around in disbelief; what had sensed right and controlled in the world of the *Su* had taken him to an inconceivable place; physically impossible.

'Is everything all right, *sensei*?' he heard the question and he looked down, standing erect on top of the pole, the cord dangling limply beneath his feet.

Jacques did not answer but instead jumped down and rolled forward on the crash mat, he was deep in thought.

'How did you do that?' Alan questioned while wiping his sweaty bald head with a towel. He was glaring at the *sensei* and walking beside him out of breath.

Jacques scratched his trimmed beard, a movement that always caused Marie to tease him, to call him the 'Statue of the Thinking Bushman', untidy as he was.

'There must have been a mistake in calculation, probably overstretching the cord.'

There was no way in hell the cable could have landed him perfectly on top of the pole, he knew it was impossible yet it was the only rational explanation.

'Impossible,' Alan protested. 'The cable arrived after you did, slacking behind, unused and useless.'

Jacques shook his head, pushing the fog from his mind, concentrating on the puzzle he faced. There was a connection, a fraction of a second before the winch pulled; he had sensed a suggestion of movement, a window of opportunity. He turned his head to the confused Alan, frowning and glaring through him for a short while.

'What did you see?' he asked quietly, as if dreading the answer.

'I don't really know what to say,' Alan replied, relieved that the *sensei* had finally spoken. 'It is more what I didn't see than what I did. One moment you were coiling like a ball, almost freezing in mid-air and the next you were spiralling away.'

Jacques' eyebrows formed a solid bridge, supported by a thick column of creased skin; he was not pleased with the vague answer.

'But how the hell did I get there?' He pointed at the high attachment point of the cable.

'I couldn't see how you got there, *Sensei*,' Alan said inflamed, eyes blazing and sweat pouring down his red cheeks. 'You were standing there, on the floor and then suddenly you were gone, materialising on the pole.'

Are you sincere with your observations? Jacques wondered while studying the face of his student in concentration, to see if he was not blinded by his high expectations from his master. Alan was forever behaving like a worshipper when it came to Jacques, despite the numerous times that Jacques had demonstrated his humble humanity in front of him. Aikido students frequently behaved like religious fanatics, only seeing what would fit their passionate beliefs.

He looks inflamed yet his eyes are shining true and honest. Jacques judged in confusion, *But how can he be right? Didn't he just stated that there had been no continuous movement to my flight? It is an impossible observation Alan, for I know with conviction that I experienced the stunt all the way, that I had been there the whole time ...*

27 A World of Shadows and Sounds

JEROME WAS NO MORE for a while. A composition of sounds and movements taking his consciousness to another world, another dimension. It spiralled him tirelessly into the void, uncontrollably dependent, until the emptiness stopped the rotation and an internal vacancy forced a sudden drop. His core became a vacuum, the awareness sucked in, silencing all commotion and then exploding in all directions of the wind. Jerome was lost in what appeared to be nothing and everything at the same time and the sensation was intense, his orientation shattered.

A thought dared to cross the void and shake it, yet it floated away without resistance, leaving the emptiness stable and detached. An independent engine worked inside the body, dismantling pain and discomfort, losing nameless guilt and faceless fears, clearing the mind of ill feelings.

He hovered in the void peacefully, drained of desire and intention, the calmness George so often spoke of finally turning into experience. It lingered on, an eternity of the moment, unbroken, real and consuming, there was nothing else.

Silence! Slow thumping heartbeats, breathing in and out, the body lying still, awareness gently coming about. A vivid depiction penetrated the darkness – an image of a rubbery string, glowing thickly by an eternal spark and moving lithely as a dancer. It twirled in space, changing size to large and small, projecting beauty in all directions ...

It was the *su* and Jerome was the *su* himself, his insides coiling and expanding, spiralling and floating. He stayed there for a period without beginning or end; sensing the now as a gentle breeze, pushing softly at the bubbly surroundings. Then the String gained new character, detailed patterns that surged from the *Su*.

Jerome nodded in the world of shadows, realising that the giant String was actually composed of billions upon billions of little Strings, individually holding the same elements as those of the complete ring. Colours poured into the image and the billion Strings suddenly differentiating in colour and intensity, their resonance humming softly yet seeming to have the strongest impact on their behaviour.

Time passed by, allowing new details to emerge and to alarm Jerome. He was suddenly aware of his perpetual chanting and how the chant itself, with its pure application, was running through his body and changing the resonance and character of the Strings. Some *Kotodama* stimulated a certain kind of String while others stimulated all of them at the same time; compelling them to act as a single String.

Gradually the shock of the initial detachment subsided, allowing a fraction of recollection to penetrate Jerome and to orientate him in the present. He was lying face down, in the same room Yves *Sensei* had left him and he was running his arm along the floor. Something was amiss, perhaps only a sensation, yet Jerome's hand continued to search blindly, slowly and patiently feeling its way until he touched the staff, the *jo* he had dropped earlier with the rest of his belongings. Jerome was drawn to the *jo* as if it were a magnet, an inner spell forcing him to comply. The pressure inside him needed to be released and the training he had undertaken during the past few months naturally guided him to the *jo* and its cleansing qualities.

Through the shadows and sounds he rose, the *jo* held high in hand, and he started to cut in the *Misogi No Jo* routines; using the wooden staff as an extension of the self. The defilement, which he mirrored and had so blessedly forgotten in the world of the shadows, reflected again at him; impossible to ignore with the *jo* in hand. He spiralled and turned the staff, stimulating the feminine water element of the individual, allowing sensitivity to enter.

The wooden staff struck at the inner demons, slicing the agony away with each and every blow. Jerome didn't use his eyes and didn't need to, the combination of sounds and movements giving him enough information of reality and of the world around. He moved and chanted, stimulating the tears to flow, allowing the pain of shame and the flaws of character to surface from the abyss of his soul, to confront him once more.

He felt wretched at the weaknesses that he saw inside, painfully realising that he would have to live with his flaws forever, that they were part of what he was. The best he could do was to learn how to use them to his own advantage, and how to ignore their corrosive nature.

The locks over his darkest secrets were unbolted, unleashing inflamed memories for confrontation; circling around him like serpents with poisonous fangs, gaining courage before charging in. He did not panic – in the world of resonance they were easy to subdue, the ill sensation cheerfully sung away without proper words or meanings. He kept swinging and singing until the *jo* dropped from his grip and he stood clean and aloft, complete like never before.

Jerome swayed gently on his feet, his heart rate slowing down, returning to the dreamlike pattern of this extreme meditation. Breathing was sensed strangely creative, the intensity of the *su* changed as the air travelled in and out of the lungs; influencing the colours of the Strings. The space between inhalation and exhalation perpetuating itself as especially vital; he was tempted to try and toy with it yet he could not judge how he was supposed to tackle it and what were its uses.

He leaned backwards to stretch his back and immediately jumped forward, startled by a cold object that pulsated and stung his flesh. Through his recollected thoughts he realised it was the blade of a sword lying naked and parallel to the floor, attached by its tip and handle to a weapon rack. It was unusual to hang a sword without the sheath but Jerome was beyond such earthly thoughts to notice. It was there and it was part of his tools of perception and the long hours of training guided him without a thought.

He reached for the sword yet his hand jerked back at him once more, this time by the sheer power of the pulsation. The metal was alive and glowing blue; he lucidly connected to it, the handle clenched tightly in his fist as the dance of the *Ki* began, energetic and pure.

He cut, he sang and cried until he could do no more; until the sounds and vibration faded away and he was left alone with the shadows, deep in a dreamless slumber of exhaustion …

Out of a timeless span, days and hours unknown, a voice cut

through the void, a worried hand touching a friendly shoulder.

'J!' came the anxious call. 'J, are you all right?' The voice broke the strong bond to the detachment, releasing Jerome to the contemporary world.

It was Max, he was back.

28 The Eight Powers

France, 2016

JACQUES WAS STUDYING the founder's old charts, bearing among others the symbols of the Eight Powers. Yawning, he placed his elbows on the kitchen table, huge palms supporting a bearded chin. He tightened his lips and returned to the open pages of the book; forehead pulling on heavy lids, skin folding up in lines, assisting the eyes to remain open. Weeks had passed since the extraordinary performance of the stunt and he was starting to appreciate the process in which it worked; practising and analysing days and nights, pushed by desire and desperation. Marie's health was deteriorating fast and tending to her needs took a lot of his resources. Time, oh precious time – the less he had the more he valued it.

Jacques was associated with tens of *aikidoka* who tried to conquer *Dai Ni Kihon* techniques and searched for the applications of the art themselves. Enthusiastically he contacted them, hoping to share information, yet found that most were unsuccessful in their progress while others, on the brink of separate discovery, were too absorbed by their own applications of the *Skill*. He had no other way but to continue by himself, motivated by the will to succeed.

Careful analysis of his stunt pointed to the two elements responsible for his unearthly display. The first was the internal work of the self and the second was the interaction with the environment. His eyes focused on the book, on the chart to represent the Eight Powers, the secret for the internal work of the self. He read them out loud.

'Movement and Stillness, Expansion and Contraction, Extension and Retraction, Division and Unification.' His head bobbed excitedly, feeling he was close, very close …

'Jacques,' came a feeble call from the other room and his mind was immediately shut off to art and personal discovery.

'What is it, Marie?' he asked and in an instant was next to his wife, taking her pale hand in his strong palm.

'Oh, it's nothing, dear,' Marie coughed, the words leaving her throat painfully, draining her of vital energy. 'I had that dreadful dream about you again, so I called.'

'Not the same old dream, Marie? I told you, I will be fine.' Pained he held her hand, the optimism gone, replaced by the constant sadness. Marie, a woman so full of vitality and life, had suddenly been stripped of her vigour and pride. The sickness was biting into her mercilessly; faster than it took the doctors to diagnose her disease.

'I will be fine, Marie, don't worry. Please, just rest!' Marie was always thinking of his well-being. Even in her most desperate hours the main topic of her dreams was Jacques and what would become of him when she ultimately passed away.

Jacques ran his fingers through her hair, caressing her shoulders gently, singing a soft tune in her ears. He dipped a piece of clean cloth into a small bowl of water and ran it over her dry and broken lips. The pain in his heart compressed his chest and radiated down his arm; a lump was at his throat whenever he swallowed. He sat by Marie and watched her fall asleep, tending to her needs until the pained and worried expression turned to that of peace and relaxation. Poor Marie, who was so proud of her natural attitude to medicine, never taking any chemical therapies in her life, strongly advocating against their uses ... Now she was bloated by hated substances that battled the disease and at the same time disfigured her body and soul.

He got up and kissed Marie's forehead, quietly leaving the room. Never had he kissed her like this before, on the forehead and not on the lips, as if declaring the change in their relationship, from passionately loving to compassionately caring.

He sat in the kitchen once again, frowning at Ueshiba's chart, hoping inspiration would come. All the information was there in front of him yet he couldn't comprehend how to retrieve and connect it.

'What is it that I miss? How can I stimulate the Eight Powers?'

A thought crossed his mind and he took a pen and a piece of paper. With shaking hands he started to draw. Art was a blessed escape from the harshness of life and sometimes it also brought about the spark needed for discovery.

'How about a device to stimulate the Eight Powers?' he asked himself loudly and his hand drew with renewed enthusiasm. He was close, really close. In a few minutes Jacques finished drawing and put the pen aside, observing the new device he had ingeniously imagined. It was based on his knowledge of the pulleys; a special suit attached by strings to the walls and suspended above the floor, allowing it to pull the person attached in a wide range of directions. A regular pulley's action was not sufficient, in fact it was rather limited in its options for movement. The new device would allow him to move in all desired directions, and on paper it looked very promising. He smiled to himself, his trained eyes spotting the unmistakable option for success in the diagram.

'Absolute genius!'

His gaze shifted back to Master Ueshiba's drawing and he sensed the connection at his core. Slowly and patiently Jacques wrote the first four drills for his new machine, four exercises to stimulate the four pairs of opposing powers.

For Jacques it was a discovery, a new and uncharted territory to map, but for future generations it would be known as part of the curriculum for the new art of Aikilibrium. A stepping stone on a triumphant yet steep climb.

* * *

'Morning lads!' Yves shouted and a smile spread across his face, opening the door to the training hall. Jerome's chin lifted in resentment yet he followed obediently behind the *sensei*. Max hurriedly tightened his belt and closed the heavy door, his left hand brushing at some remaining breadcrumbs.

For five days they had been together and Jerome's anxiety was steadily building, stimulated by the open wound of detachment that pulled him in and out of reality. It was hard to communicate and concentrate on conversations. He loved Max yet it was easier to confront the personal changes on his own.

Yves walked tall and proud in front, his back a reminder of the conversation they'd had the night before at the office.

'Tomorrow you will start training on the third level of techniques, the concluding chapter of your studies. I brought you here to make you aware of your position, so there will be no surprises later on.'

The training was resumed two days before with repetition on the first and second level of techniques. Jerome enjoyed the basic Aikido tremendously but the spiritual drills caused him considerable emotional aggravation, repeatedly mirroring his faults and guilt.

'Are you listening to me?' Yves frowned and raised his voice, bringing the student back to reality; daydreaming was a by-product of detachment, very hard to control. Jerome shook his head and tried to focus on the *sensei*.

'Good! Keep looking at me and listen. Your achievements in the second level of the art were remarkable. In fact your progress was so quick that it basically shadowed any chance Max ever had in picking up the pace.'

Jerome, who stood to attention facing the hated *sensei*, instinctively reached out to grab at the large wooden desk, to balance himself against the urge to collapse. Yves smiled and rubbed his palms, enjoying the suffering of the student.

'There is a way out for him,' he stated compassionately, his eyes widening with care. 'But it all depends on your efforts.'

'What do you mean by that?' Jerome spat bluntly, lips curled down, not impressed by the *sensei's* suggestion of care.

'It means that he's got a chance of survival. I promise to spare his life on one condition; that you shall perform to my satisfaction.' There was no need to explain any further, Jerome knew the facts and didn't wish to hear Yves' words. Now he followed and watched the *sensei's* back. Every step they took served as a grim reminder. Yves passed by the Plain *Dojo* and stopped in front of a door opposite the Meditation Hall.

'This room holds the secret to our art; the machine that teaches the amazing capabilities of Aikilibrium movements. Jacques *Sensei*, the founder of Aikilibrium, designed it in a moment of inspiration and to the present day we are still using the same kind of machine.

Some improvements were implemented during the years, based on technological advances, but overall it's the same old device.'

The boys looked at him indifferently, knowing the theoretical background; they had read about it in their books the previous night, just as Yves had ordered.

'It's remarkable how Jacques *Sensei* managed to make the connection between the Eight Powers and the option of movements; relying solely on movies showing demonstrations by O Sensei, and by studying ideas the great master wrote, painted and lectured. Ueshiba *Sensei* presented all the elements of Aikilibrium in his techniques yet couldn't get to the same level of expertise of Master Jacques since he lacked the right tools to develop any further. Jacques' machines are the key to Aikilibrium, expanding the possibilities of balance and motion and amplifying their manifestation.'

Yves stopped talking and the fire in his eyes died out; back to his cold and passionless mood. *Finally!* Jerome thought as he bounced from leg to leg, *Now let's get in and see that great invention of the twenty-first century.*

'Do you need to pee?' Max pointed at the groin of his bouncy friend but a scornful look from Yves shut him up.

Patiently the master observed the expression on the boys' faces, demanding their full attention. He nodded in satisfaction and turned sharply to face the door. His hand reached out and he slid the door aside to reveal a padded wall. Yves turned his head and smiled at them.

'It is padded to keep noise at a minimum; we don't wish to disturb other *aikidoka* training in the nearby halls,' and he stepped inside, motioning the boys to follow.

The wall was just in front of the sliding doors and they had to turn left and enter through a heavy, soundproof door. It shut behind them and they found themselves in a very small passage with another door at its end. Jerome and Max exchanged glances, appreciating the care taken to keep the place silent.

The next door was open, revealing the largest and most lavishly equipped hall in the school. Hi-tech devices were everywhere, computers, levers and colourful lights. It was a training hall fit for astronauts.

The boys saw a network of cables extending out from small protrusions on the walls and attached at their other ends to two suits hanging on a pole right at the centre of the hall. The small protruding platforms on the walls had the ability to change position, giving new attachment points for the cables. Yves allowed his students to marvel at the pride of the school, pausing a couple of minutes without a word before addressing the kids again.

'Boys, I give to you the "Marie7", a state of the art device, an essential tool to master in the art of Aikilibrium. You will use this machine frequently in the near future, at least until I decide that you are ready to move on.'

They listened and their eyes scanned the room and its options; seeing all the equipment yet not visualising the way it was used. Yves walked straight to the middle of the hall, placing his hand on the pole.

'Come and get your suits on boys, we haven't got all day!'

'Let's do it baby,' Max mumbled with a determined frown and walked towards the *sensei*, keen to get started. He reached the pole and his arms stretched out to grab a suit.

'Wait one moment before you put it on.' Yves cooled him down. 'First listen to the instructions.' Max reluctantly pulled his hand back, Jerome standing to his left.

'This room is sterile, free of diverting powers, allowing fixed options of movements from each and every platform that the cables are attached to. See that the walls are full of small holes? These apertures determine the options for movements by controlling the air flow in the hall. In this place you will set about your training of the Eight Powers, studying them in pairs, starting with Extension and Retraction.'

Max raised his eyebrows and repeated the *sensei's* words. 'Extension and Retraction, whatever you say, *Sensei*, let's just get on with it.' Yves ignored him completely, as if he wasn't there, as if he didn't matter.

'Extension and Retraction is what you saw me doing the day we met at the bakery, remember?'

'How can we possibly forget, *Sensei*?' Jerome answered, the sarcasm loud and clear in his voice.

Yves was beyond all petty comments, ignoring them all together. 'I will demonstrate the use of these two opposed powers; notice how vivid my movements are to your perception, palpable compared to the time when you first observed me in the bakery. The spiritual training you've undertaken during the past few months should enable you to see the *su* in action.'

Jerome waited for further explanation but none was necessary. Yves knew exactly how to emphasise his point. One moment he stood erect as a dancer, smiling to himself, his chin held high, and then his body went limp, silent and collected. Life was drawn out of the limbs, vitality returning to the source of the *Su*. Jerome was dazed, his senses amplified, the movement stimulating his core and shaking his legs.

Yves' centre retracted deep inside the frame of the body and it forced Jerome to join in. The sensation held for a second and then the compression inwards was reversed, the *sensei* extending into the air, his body a resonance of smudged movements. There were two images of Yves to see, the first a human form, legs propelling madly in the air, directed by the hips. The second image was that of a pure movement as was portrayed in the world of the *Su*.

I can see it! Jerome thought as he followed the *sensei* flight, his eyes were shining brightly, his body shaking like a leave. Yves ended on one of the wall and the magic was over. He was standing on a protruding platforms, balanced on one foot and smiling at the boys. Jerome heaved, the display of the *Skill* opening the wound of his detachment further, compelling him to see the application of the Strings.

'Here we gooooo ...' shouted the *sensei* and coiled in, emphasising the *O* on his last word, singing it in the world of the *Kotodama*. Yves thundered out and down, Jerome sharing the drop like a forced rider on a musical roller-coaster. He heard the sounds composed by the *sensei's* flight, saw them playing on the Strings. The sound altered the Strings' colour and shape, turning Extension and Retraction into a fully sensual experience.

The demonstration continued and, having got used to the movements, Jerome could relax and analyse the display. *The Retraction is carried out in the opposite direction to where you moved, sensei,* he reasoned, *your body tensing on an unseen cord that stretch between the starting point and the place on which you've landed.* Jerome smiled and nodded his head, like a person who has just spotted the way a magician performed his trick. He heard the giggles and was pulled away from his intense observation, looking straight into the smiling face of Max.

'Oh, you are back again,' Max said and burst out laughing, Yves cheerfully joining in.

'It's not easy to grasp and perform according to the Eight Powers, it takes a bit of practice to master. You saw the Strings operate within me as I moved, yet it is easier to see the *su* in action than to stimulate them to perform. Master Jacques understood the importance of accessories; of their capacity to elevate the art further, and he built this device.'

Yves watched their faces, seeing their silent understanding before resuming the explanations. 'The suits you will be wearing are attached to dozens of thin and very strong cables. The cables works in correlation with the wind patterns in the hall; you must be very attentive to the tiniest of changes in air density. When your body is in tune with an option for a movement a cable will jerk you in that direction. The purpose of this practice is to sense the options for the moves and to use these options before the cable does the work for you. It won't be easy to do, despite the advantage of supportive environmental factors that are strictly straightforward and unchanging.'

Yves stopped talking and helped them into the suits, tightening the strips and binding the boys securely.

'Don't want to harm our little investment,' he said and winked at them. 'Now hang loose inside the suits, suspended at the edge of your balance and seek the *su* and its options.'

Jerome pulled at his shoulder and his eyes opened wide in confusion. *Don't know what you're on about, sensei,* he thought, yet undeterred conviction guided him to follow the *sensei's* words. He closed his eyes and imitated the posture Yves took before each and every one of his Extension flights.

'Good boys, very good. This position protects your neck from whiplash injury: the pulling powers of the cables are surprisingly strong and jerky. Now be attentive, because the first few flights will probably shake and disorientate you completely.' He raised his eyebrows and looked at them both. 'Here we go boys, compose yourselves for the flight and remember, movement without the cables is your ultimate goal!'

He turned around to face the control panel and reached for one of the many colourful levers. Yves pulled on it and an electrical current hummed through the dozens of cables attached to the suits.

Jerome hung slack on his feet, trying to reach for the sensation inside. There were remnants of the *Su* in him – the detachment a recent event. He tried to coil in like the *sensei* had but couldn't find what to look for. Through confused thoughts he suddenly remembered the cables and sensed a tightness at his core. Startled, he opened his eyes wide and then he shot through the air, dragged by one of the cables. *Bloody hell!* The air was trapped in his lungs, arms reaching as tentacles in all directions. It was a desperate attempt to protect the body as it inevitably crashed to the wall. Jerome breathed out in relief, the wall had a padded surface.

'Not a bad effort.' Yves nodded, looking at the two boys dangling unbalanced from different parts of the wall. 'But try and find the connection to your destination first, you need to retract against something.'

On the second attempt Jerome detected a hint to the direction of the pull, a split second before it actually happened; although it didn't stop him from splattering on the wall.

'I know it's hard perform, too quick to grasp all that is taking place.' Yves smiled curtly. 'We must have forgotten an important ingredient.' And he started reciting the sounds to accompany the flights; the resonance needed on the inside. It made an immediate difference.

'Nice of him to share this piece of information,' Max mumbled angrily. 'Like, he couldn't tell us about it before.'

Now, with *Kotodama* deployment the whole ordeal made much more sense as both managed to land on the platforms rather than crash senselessly into the walls. Max had far more difficulty in operating through the *Skill* yet he compensated for it with his acrobatic abilities. Acrobatic training, the kind they had both undergone in basic Aikido helped and supported the art of Aikilibrium. *But for how long would you be able to cover your lack of Skill with acrobatic manoeuvres?* Jerome wondered, a pained expression on his face. 'Keep them fooled. Do your best!' he wanted to tell his friend.

By the end of the day Jerome was part of the whole process, experiencing it in the world of the shadows and sounds. He couldn't create the motion from within though, the way Yves *Sensei* did.

After dinner they stretched on the floor of their quarters, using the stools in the dinning room to pull against.

'Did you see me in action?' Max asked as he pushed on Jerome's back, trying to force the chest to the floor.

'Yes, you did quite well,' came the muffled answer.

Quite well? I was superb!' Jerome turned his head sharply in reaction to Max's words, forgetting his friend was leaning on his back.

'Yes, you were wonderful,' he sighed. 'Superb.'

'That's what I like to hear,' Max said and waved his arms in the air, forgetting about the stretch.

Later on, Jerome lay in his bed, eyes open and staring hazily at the ceiling. He heard the snoring sounds coming from Max's bed and remembered the arrogance with which Max mirrored himself. *Perhaps that is what's lacking in your performance, my friend. Perhaps that is why you have suddenly become expendable.* There was nothing in Max's behaviour to suggest that he knew of Yves' intentions though, and Jerome wasn't planning on telling him about it. It was bitterly funny how the perception of his reality had changed. *Bloody hilarious!* Jerome thought and bit his lower lip.

Suddenly he was the one to excel, the one responsible for his friend's well-being. *It must be another one of your cruel games of deception. sensei,* Jerome wondered to himself. *But is it a double game that you play? Is Max a player too?* He dismissed that thought immediately; knowing Max would report to him if he had a conversation such as he'd had with Yves. *It is inconceivable to think that Yves uses the same tactics on you, my friend, but perhaps he is playing you differently ...*

29 Division and Unification

'THIS IS IMPOSSIBLE, *Sensei*,' Jerome protested and shook his head. 'I can't do it.'

'Quiet! It is easier than it looks.' Yves spoke softly yet there was determination in his voice. 'I promise you, it is risk free!'

Jerome turned his head in a judging angle, obeying the command of silence, yet his eyes squinted in distrust. They were practising the opposing powers of Division and Unification, and the idea of Unification petrified the boys.

Division was the ordinary condition of life, the way in which the *Su*, the basic building block of creation, was spread around the body, diverse in resonance and complexity. Each and every living body was an orchestra playing upon billions of Strings, differing in character and sound yet together devising a well-synchronised symphony. Unification, on the other hand, meant to behave as one unit, where all the building blocks of the body resounded as one big String, as the primal *Su*. The chapter the boys had read in the book about Aikilibrium explained the options presented by Unification:

> It is possible to achieve Unification for a fraction of a second; long enough to perform greatness but not too long as to lose self identity. The bond of Division represents the complexity in which the self exists. Altering this bond in a controlled and unified fashion represents the key to all the movements of Aikilibrium, the key to all the Eight Powers.

Jerome read it yet remained sceptical.

'How can it be the base for all the Eight Powers? We already practised a few.' Yves laughed at his words.

'And how successful were you in performing according to those few? Admittedly you failed in most attempts, both of you. You couldn't find the connection to the *Su*, couldn't compensate for your lack of *Skill* with acrobatic manoeuvres either.' He eyed Max severely on that last sentence. 'Not everything you study here is taught in the order you wish to learn it, Jerome. I don't care if it doesn't make sense to you. I am interested in results and that's the way you study.'

'So how can Unification be the base for the art, *Sensei*?' Jerome asked sharply, not impressed by the master's tutorial skills, wishing to get an answer.

'Because Unification is the glue for all our movements, providing the ability to shift as one unit between the universal plains and the opposing powers. We tackle the powers from so many angles yet they are all derived from the one, from the *Su*.'

Jerome was about to ask another question but Yves raised his arm to silence him.

'Come on, let's get started, we haven't got all day. On the next exercise, as with the one we practised before, you are free from starting the motion – the cables will do that for you; the only thing you must do is remember the right *Kotodama* and their timing.'

The boys practised the sounds required for the drill and Jerome sensed the *Kotodama* echoing inside his body, at the seams of his breath. The short interval between inhalation and exhalation was presented as the perfect place in which he could sense the Unification. It was driven by the fire and water interactions, at the heart of the *Aiki*.

Jerome stood in the middle of the training hall, attached by cables to the Marie7. In front of him was a barrier that blocked most of his options of movement, apart from a small gap to the left. The cable was to pull him sharply towards the barrier and he had to change the direction in which he moved; to guide the Unified self to the gap and thereby avoid crashing into the barrier.

'Even sharply directed movement leaves a gap for manipulation. Modifying the position of the limbs or head can spring a motion away from the centre and so can vigorous movements of the trunk. Your triumph rests in the ability to connect the centre with the environment, to collect the energy necessary for the internal song of *Kotodama* that can bring about the change. Unification is possible with the tools you possess, mainly the detachment you've recently gained. It is a powerful tool but it won't last forever so I suggest that you get on with the drill, don't lose precious time. You have only a few weeks remaining before the detachment fades away.'

Jerome knew all too well what the *sensei* meant, sensing the detachment losing its grip, the vacancy at his centre steadily being replaced by Max. Max had a stronger grip on him; the guilt amplifying the effect. *I can still sense the void though,* Jerome nodded to himself. *It is not stable any more, but it's there!* Closing his eyes he relaxed his breathing pattern, slowing the speed and increasing the depth, connecting with the *Su* and the *Ki*. He hummed a couple of times, judging his internal resonance, and then he opened his eyes and nodded to *Sensei*, focused and determined. Yves smiled, pulling a slender palm on a lever, releasing the cord.

Jerome was prepared; the sensation of the cable pulling at his hips familiar by now. He was relaxed and collected inside, waiting for the power to be unleashed. When the pull came he did not panic, judging for the right timing, maintaining the Division for a while. His eyes were shut yet he sensed the barrier and the gap blindly, aware of his options and concentrating on the limbs. Yves had taught them that the shift in direction relies on the limbs that propel around the body. He reminded them again and again that the aim was to stimulate the Unification through the limb that is the nearest to the gap.

'You can't tell in advance which limb is going to be available at any given moment; it is much too much to ask.'

The cable tore Jerome from his spot and he shot through the air, collecting momentum towards sure collision with the barrier. Desperately he tried to search for the options yet too many thoughts played at his mind and the timing was gone. The only option left was the barrier itself and he looked for a soft spot on its surface, trying to save himself. He quickly sang the resonance of Expansion that they had practised the week before and managed to decelerate the velocity of the flight. It took some of the impact away but it didn't stop the pain of the crash. He got up from the floor, shaken and dazed, to the laughter of Yves and Max.

'Don't look so accusingly at me,' said Yves. 'I saw your hesitation and how it cost you the timing for the detour.' He motioned Max to get ready. 'Let's see what you are capable of doing, genius.'

Max got up and walked to the space in front of the barrier, clearly unhappy about it. He gave the sign for Yves to release the cable and an instant later he was in the air. Jerome watched him cringing, seeing the wall getting ever so close. At the last moment, and in perfect timing, Max suddenly composed himself and spiralled outwards, a display fit for acrobats. He calculated his move well and managed to pass through the gap – completely unhurt – landing gracefully on the other side. He turned his head, grinning, but Jerome was looking at Yves instead, *You saw it too sensei, didn't you?*

Jerome was now able to sense *Skilled* movements in the world of the Strings and knew that Max's display was wholly earthly in nature, beautifully performed yet without any connection to the *Su*. Yves turned his head and with a cold smile winked at him, showing that nothing escaped his observation. The only one, so it seemed, who didn't know about it was Max himself. He walked back towards them, holding his chin arrogantly high and, just as Jerome expected, Yves told him nothing of his incompetence.

'Very well, good show,' he said and clapped his hands together, tapping Max's shoulder warmly and smiling icily at Jerome. The barrier training was cleverly designed, leaving room for callisthenics gained by a good sense of balance and natural acrobatic skills, qualities that Max possessed.

'But, Max ...' Jerome started.

'What is it, J?'

Jerome bit his lip. 'Nothing,' he answered defiantly. *Perhaps it is better that you don't know how off the mark you are, Max. Sensei, you are such a sadistic bastard!* He watched Yves as he was nodding maliciously behind Max's back, enjoying his friend's disillusion, a bitter reminder of Jerome's heavy responsibility.

'Are you ready for the next attempt?' Yves asked, his hand on the lever, ready to pull.

Jerome took his eyes off the teacher, shaking his arms and legs. 'I am ready,' he said and slouched down.

The cable jerked him back without warning, but Jerome was ready, meditating in a chant. A world of shadows and sounds opened before him, moving in a timeless span, seconds sensed as minutes, allowing awareness of his every move. *It feels so good!* The body, an endless combination of resonating Strings, was propelling through the air, directed by the cable attachment of the suit. The air was full of particles, of many other Strings, and Jerome cut his way through them, causing a momentary shift in the composition of the air. He saw the approaching barrier as a massive block of intervening Strings, the gap to the left he sensed as a vacuum, full of air and motion.

An inner song revealed the timing for the shift and Jerome's right leg reacted, using the opportunity to its fullest and he changed the *Kotodama* resonating at his core. The sound and the focus on the limb was enough to swing him in the right direction, blurring sharply through the air – in an unearthly display. He succeeded in avoiding the barrier yet found it hard to regain control over the senses after the Unified experience; he landed on the other side of the barrier and his knees buckled down, a liquefied hinge, upper body sailing above.

'Bravo!' Max laughed. 'What a final!'

'A Prima Ballerina no doubt.' Yves added.

You can laugh all you want assholes, Jerome grinned at the pair, *Because I don't care!* He knew with conviction that he had made it and that was a comforting thought in a day full of failure.

'Nice walking style, Wobble,' Yves teased and wriggled his fingers. 'It happens sometimes when the body becomes Unified.'

'So I've noticed, *Sensei*,' Jerome replied coldly.

'Very well then. Now shall we go again?'

They were tired by the end of the day, drained physically and mentally, yet Max found the energy to ask a question.

'You would like to ask a question?' Yves raised an eyebrows in wonderment.

'Yes I do, *sensei*. What is wrong with that?'

'It is not wrong but surprising,' Yves snorted a laugh. 'You never really asked anything before.'

'Well I want to now,' Max growled stubbornly.

'Very well lad. So what is it? Come on, spill it out!' He was looking at Max in amusement as the later took his time in calculating his words.

'How come we learned all the powers besides the first most elementary ones,' he finally asked, 'How come we ignored Stillness and Movement?'

Yves pulled on his nose. 'You have already learned them in basic Aikido training, the *Dai Ichi Kihon*. You mastered it and you didn't even know it. I've told you before, without basic Aikido you will have none of the *Skill*. If you ever stop practising the basics you will surely lose some of your *Skill* abilities. Basic Aikido is exactly what its name insinuates, the base, the primal elements of the art, containing a bit of everything, just like the two basic powers of Movement and Stillness.'

They went to bed exhausted, for once forgetting to eat or even talk. Jerome was dazed, reclining to the comfort of his slumber, yet he heard Max mumbling and the words squeezed at his consciousness, waking him in fright.

'You are my only friend, Jerome, so don't worry if you do badly; this time I shall protect you from these brutes, whatever the cost.'

Jerome wheezed the pained air trapped at his chest because he knew exactly what the cost would be.

30   Windows of Opportunity

France, 2016

MASTER UESHIBA stood in the middle of the *dojo*, surrounded by sword-wielding students. The tips of the sharp instruments were focused at the master's middle, getting ready to inflict a devastating blow. O Sensei's expression was one of calm, with almost jest in the corner of the eyes, confident, reading the human environment and connecting to the elements. He sensed the power and the intention behind the blades, his mouth tasting the atmosphere, nostrils flaring as he inhaled, fingers rubbing gently against one another. He was the master of the ultimate '*Skill of Diversity*' and the drill was not a real challenge to his well-being. Every fraction of a second he was the duality of creation, one moment in the world of the living and the next surrounded by the Strings, simmering quietly on the song of the *Su*.

The body of the master spiralled ceaselessly, the water element blending with the blades and their deadly intensions. He reached out and rested one of his palms on the spine of a sword, the metal making an immediate connection to the heart of the *Ki*. The timing was right as a 'window of opportunity' appeared to his right. He smiled and the students pushed in, a mysterious spell forcing them to attack as a unit, relying on their combined numbers and force. O Sensei was there and suddenly he appeared behind them smiling, away from the danger and the foes.

The picture froze as the large thumb pressed the rewind button, taking the movie back to the instant before the master disappeared from the circle of steel. Jacques wrinkled his forehead and put the old movie on play again, this time in extreme slow motion, not wanting to miss a thing.

He could sense Ueshiba's moves by merely observing the old movies. Jacques eyes squinted as he watched the master squeezing through the gap he had found, the Strings stretching and leading him through the opening. Jacques knew about the Eight Powers already as it had been the main topic of his studies for the past few weeks. He was analysing the movies for a different reason, mainly to investigate the interaction between the *Skill* and environmental factors. The machine he had designed was a work of genius, no doubt, but it was operating in a sterile environment, and just like any other stunt was performing under strict settings. It was as good as training in laboratory conditions but reality had far more complex options than rehearsed drills. Jacques was a practical man and he wanted to widen the options of his art.

Marie was not getting any better although the doctors had finally come up with the cause of her condition. She was apparently suffering from a rare auto-immune system disease, the kind that was widespread in the world after the cellular revolution of the mobile phone. Her body was digesting her own muscle tissue and the grim future that the good doctor drew before the couple kept him in a very battered spirit. There was a cure, an experimental medicine that had just come out on the market. It was not part of the free health insurance medication, they had to buy it privately. The doctor's words filled the couple with hope, until they learned the cost of the medicine and their hearts sank lower than before.

There was only one thing Jacques could do to raise the money; endangering himself for the pleasure of the crowds, a course stimulated by sorrow and despair. He started to perform stunts, crazy stunts, based on his new discoveries and abilities. It attracted the interest of some rich sponsors and soon Jacques became hopeful once more, in a matter of weeks acquiring half the funds needed for his wife's remedies.

That was not the only benefit of the danger he put himself in – his *Skill* grew as well, gaining aim and shape – finally he knew exactly what he was looking for …

Jacques watched the movie dissociated from the surroundings, his facial muscles contoured in concentration. In his mind he broke the master's moves into short intervals, determining how Ueshiba found the gap through which he travelled, how he channelled himself through the windows of opportunity.

A 'window of opportunity' was a term used to describe the option of movement the environment presented to the *Skilled* ones; a kind of tunnel created by the interaction of the surrounding forces.

For a week he had searched for a system to connect with these windows. He was unsuccessful yet didn't lose his passion. Today he was trying a new approach, planning to divide the environment into the powers composing it and to study each and every one of them thoroughly and intimately.

He took out a sheet of paper and wrote down ideas on how to interact with the powers he identified. He wrote faster with each and every passing second, as if the ideas were a meal that he had cooked in his brain all week long and now he was merely dishing out the results. There he laid down procedures that are studied to the current day. The key to using the environment, the secret of how to sense the windows of opportunity. Jacques stopped writing and pulled his head up, smiling satisfied at what he had just composed on the paper.

Marie coughed and moaned softly in the other room and he froze and dropped the pen. 'Coming my love,' he called and rushed to her side, the tears reforming just by thinking of her. *Dai Ni Kihon* gave him wonderful sensitivity and with it an emotional depth that he sometimes found hard to control. 'What is it Mari?' he asked and sat by her side, although she was sleeping. 'Fight on my love,' he whispered, 'There is still hope.' Crying, he pressed his head against the agonised flesh of his wife and held her tightly, forgetting the studies and listening attentively to the weak beating of her heart.

* * *

'Take a couple of minutes to look around you, boys, I am sure that you will find it very interesting.'

They were standing in a hall they had never been in before, full of hi-tech gadgets as was the hall of the Marie7. It was, as Yves put it, a hall to teach a very delicate part of their studies, the recognition of windows of opportunity.

The ground of the hall was mainly bare, although seams running across it suggested that the floor could adjust differently. Cables hung from the ceiling and the blue gloomy walls looked monotonously threatening. It was equipped with high-quality lighting, a surround-sound system and a couple of giant projectors on opposing walls; combining to create the perfect illusion.

'Here you will learn about the environmental factors which ultimately guide you to the windows of opportunity.' Yves elegantly gestured with his hand to the middle of the hall, waiting quietly for them to approach.

'Master Jacques, our graceful founder, divided the environmental factors into major categories and designed special exercises for each factor alone. The goal is to increase the sensitivity required for the craft of Aikilibrium. Today we shall concentrate on the first factor, on the "texture" of things.'

He surveyed the boys smiling, enjoying their lack of understanding.

'I know you have read about it in your books but it's not an easy concept to grasp.' As he spoke Yves' hands busily fiddled with some levers located on a control box near the centre of the hall. The floor suddenly illuminated phosphoric light blue and a yellow pathway appeared in front of Yves, directing him to one of the hall's corners.

'Another path will appear in the opposite direction when both of you perform the drill.' He became silent, watching the floor. 'Be quiet for a moment boys. I will demonstrate what should be done.'

The lights on the path stopped shining and all that remained was the general direction the path had indicated before. It did not matter to Yves, his eyes were closed to start with. He placed one foot on the path and carefully transferred his weight upon it. His other foot scanned the floor, hovering over it, until he found a new place where he stopped moving and once again placed his weight on top. In this bizarre way he progressed slowly until he reached the designated finishing point. He sighed and opened his eyes, the lights on the path shining once more.

'That is how you complete this drill. Slow and sluggish to the eye but believe it or not, I hold the world record for completing the path in the fastest time.'

The boys fought to control their facial muscles, tightening their shoulders against the urge to smile. Yves didn't look deterred by their obvious distrust.

'Not too impressed are you? You'd better try it yourselves. Put the strap suits on.'

Jerome reached for his suit.

'I don't need the Pinocchio string suit,' Max whispered yet his voice was amplified by the vacant hall.

'Oh! You will need these straps, my little champion, you are not that skilful.'

Yves waited until they were suited up to his satisfaction.

'OK, boys, the drill will start in one second; try and sense the floor for the footing, feel where it is right to walk.'

Jerome nodded and started to prepare, synchronising his breathing, about to close his eyes when a sharp movement to his right caught his attention. Max, who could not wait any longer, ran quickly forward, his strides wide and powerful. Yves and Jerome froze and looked bewildered as Max managed a couple of steps that took him to the middle of the path. On the third step the floor caved in and Max sprawled down on his face, the straps pulling him back to the starting point.

'Don't say a word!' he warned Jerome, trying to avoid his friend's eyes; Yves cleared his throat behind them.

'Your suits stay on until you both have completed the task. Good luck, boys.' And with that remark he left the centre of the hall.

The boys looked at each other, for the first time left without any close supervision. They followed the *sensei* with their eyes until he stopped and stood near the entrance. They both sighed. Looking confused at each other.

'Shall we start?' Jerome gestured with his hand.

'After you, my friend.' They had no system or pattern to follow and in the first three attempts they quickly lost their footing and were pulled back by the straps to the starting point.

I must search for the void, Jerome thought, feeling inspired; he closed his eyes, concentrating on his feet, a chant building on the inside. The daily routine of basic Aikido and chanting tuned his body to the *Skill*; he relaxed and merged into the sounds and movements, without a thought creating the right resonance. Breathing out slowly he lifted one foot up; hovering it over the floor, touching it and not touching at the same time. His foot captured the sensations beneath, and a variety of heat patterns and textures started to emerge. He followed the patterns, ignoring Max who nagged him with questions, until he was able to distinguish between all the different sensations emanating from the floor. The next thing he did was to identify which surface was safe to tread upon and which wasn't.

'I've got it!' he finally exclaimed and looked at Max with a broad smile. The latter turned to face him, losing his footing straight away.

'You've got what?' he asked angrily. 'I haven't seen you moving an inch yet.'

Jerome nodded in excitement. 'I can sense the different patterns of the floor. I know how to finish the drill.' He looked towards the entrance but couldn't see the *sensei* any more.

'He's gone, Max,' he said and they both scanned the room suspiciously.

'He must be around somewhere, perhaps near the entrance.' Max frowned. 'I'm going to find out where he is hiding.' He pulled on the suit but found it impossible to peel off.

'I see,' he grimaced. 'Guess that's why there is no one inside to watch over us. We can't go anywhere anyway.'

'It's not so bad,' Jerome tried to pacify him. 'I know how we can finish the task.' And he started to explain his system to Max who didn't seem very eager to listen.

'I will follow your footsteps,' he told Jerome. 'There is no one around to see what's going on.'

Jerome pulled on his shoulders yet nodded to confirm; he didn't want to argue. Max stood behind him and they started to walk, slowly marching towards Jerome's corner. 'Now I see why *sensei* was jumping like a duck!' The floor was very illusive, the texture differing slightly in temperature or coarseness. Jerome led the way, slowly and surely until they finally reached the end. Jerome's path immediately lit up, yet Max's path remained dark. They both looked at Max's path, 'I guess there are no short cuts today.'

'Bloody typical.'

They went back and walked Max path, this time a little quicker. Both were sweating profoundly by the time the walk was over. Max's path lit up and the locks on the suits opened. A green light appeared on all the walls and the entrance opened to reveal Yves. The *sensei* offered no words as he quietly led the boys back to their living quarters, to clean themselves up and prepare for the evening training.

* * *

'I hope you had a good rest and that you didn't eat too much.' Yves smiled annoyingly at them. 'The next exercise might prove a bit upsetting on a full stomach.'

They were back at the special training hall, following Yves' finger as he pointed at the floor. There were two pathways on it and each of the boys was ordered to stand on the starting position, which was illuminated in blue. They were strapped in their suits and Yves approached to check each suit personally, making sure that they were safely locked. He then handed them half-open helmets and ordered them to be put on. They were soft and comfortable, fitting neatly, covering the head for protection and locking beneath the chin. When the helmets were secured a screen declined from the top to rest in front of their eyes.

'This device transmits sounds and sights. It is a unique gadget, equipped with a powerful sound system and numerous colourful screens that change voluntarily in front of the eyes, allowing the wearer to see patterns projected on the walls.'

Jerome rubbed his chin and looked at his path. It was winding in all directions and was fifteen metres long; his path was coloured green while Max's radiated yellow.

'This exercise is basic, an introduction to the diversity of plains and dimensions, disorientating the senses by a mixture of sounds and lighting. It's called the "Illusionary Path" and you must walk it back and forth twenty times in order to complete the assignment. Each time you fail you will start from the beginning.'

'No problem,' Max confidently assured the master, and Yves

raised an eyebrow and snorted a laugh.

'It is an important drill for your studies, amplifying and guiding the way to the use of the powers surrounding.' He finished talking, bowed with a smile and left the hall.

The boys looked at each other through the glass of their helmets and then to their paths. This time the task was completely personal; there was nothing they could do to help each other at the moment.

'Shall we?'

'Yeah, why not.' They started to walk, and on the first go nothing happened, just a walk over the flat floor. 'Hey this is easy!' Max exclaimed.

'So far so good.' As they turned to walk back, however, the path suddenly emerged from the floor, protruding a metre high and 30 centimetres wide, resembling an artificial hedge. Jerome immediately lost his balance and hung off the path, supported by the cables; Max was quick enough to maintain his ground, completing the second round as Jerome was hauled back to the starting point.

He adjusted his footing on the declining path and lifted his head, startled by the sound of Max's shouts. Something had shaken his friend, something Jerome couldn't hear or see. Max regained his balance and kept walking, tapping the helmet with his fists. 'What's going on?' Jerome enquired.

'Oh you will soon find out,' Max giggled, 'Have no doubt of that!'

'Thanks for nothing mate,' Jerome sighed and warily he turned on his feet when completing the second round. The helmet, that was so light and airy up until now, suddenly blared loud and confusing sounds, some of them very disturbing.

On the fourth round the path became extremely tricky, the walls producing shifting images that confused the eye and blended disharmoniously with the sounds; Max fell down cursing, Jerome managed to complete the walk yet lost his own balance on the fifth round, when the path fluidly twisted in wavy patterns. There was no point of reference, disorientation complete, and Jerome was at the starting point once more.

The sounds and vision drained from the screen and he stood

panting, watching Max who successfully progressed through the paths. It went from hard to impossible and Max raged and raved, struggling with the winding pathway. He must have been on the ninth round, for the path was now performing insane manoeuvres.

I must focus! Jerome decided and returned his attention to his own path, trying to ignore the distracting shouts of Max. *I can't rely on the eyes or ears for orientation. I need to seek the void and the Su.* It took a while but he found it and at once was tuned to the other world, a world of shifting dimensions, creative and optional. He sensed the path beneath him and the Strings that composed it, his feet fused to the surface.

Taking a deep breath he started to walk and suddenly the path could shake him off no more. Dimly he recognised that the surfaces and structures around were constantly changing. He was very relaxed, knowing of the unity of the surroundings, operating on a different dimension. Jerome cut through plains of existence yet it was the most stable path of all, the most reliable option. He didn't count the rounds that he walked and was startled when the path dropped level with the floor and the insane soundtrack and the visions on the walls were gone. He stood motionless, immersed in a blessed silence. 'Ahhh … finally!' The helmet and the suit unlocked and he reacted, taking both off and rubbing his face, watching Max in his desperate efforts. He opened his mouth to offer a word of advice, but the door suddenly opened and Yves stepped in.

'Come on, get out of here, you can't help him. Don't waste your time.'

He was escorted back to their quarters.

A couple of hours later Max entered the dormitory, sweaty and annoyed.

'Did Yves say anything about me?' he asked, a suspicious look on his face.

Jerome was wrapped in a towel, stepping out of the shower.

'He didn't say a thing about you,' Jerome replied and walked by Max, avoiding the burning eyes.

'I couldn't complete the task,' Max whimpered with his head bowed down. 'Yves came in the end and released me.'

'It's OK, Max,' Jerome whispered, rubbing the back of his shaken friend. 'There are numerous other drills that you perform much better than me!' He knew that wasn't true but he dared not say so.

Max stopped shaking but there was no comfort to the worried creases on his face.

'Don't let him kill me, J, please don't let them do that!'

'I won't,' Jerome promised and caught Max who collapsed crying into his arms.

Jerome was silent; lost for words of comfort. There was nothing he could say to ease his friend's pain. Max was confronted by a horrid realisation, finally understanding that he was to be the victim.

31 The Thirst for Detachment

JEROME RUBBED his scorched hands and spread on some of the soothing cream. He looked to where Max was seated and offered him some.

'Thanks, J.' Max bowed, applying the cool paste to his bare chest and stomach. They were both suffering from numerous first-degree burns after toying with the flames. Windows of opportunity were still the main objective of their studies and they were on their final part of that lesson, which was the 'forces'. Yves had given the topic a very short introduction.

'You've learned how to recognise texture and how to avoid misleading environmental factors. Now is the time to explore the true forces which create the windows for the Aikilibrium moves.'

They began practising the powers, commencing with electricity and magnetism, finishing with the basic elements themselves, such as wind and water.

The 'Heat Hovering' drill, carried out in order to experience the fire element, must have been the most dangerous exercise they had performed so far. Jerome had literally been fighting for his life and Max did just as badly, despite the downgraded risk level that Yves placed before him. It was an insane exercise, dangerous for the most *Skilled* of people.

'We did it, J!' Max cheerfully called and straightened up, cleaning the cream from his palms with a paper towel. He tapped Jerome on the shoulder and the latter reacted with a cry, the flesh ever so tender.

'Sorry, J, didn't mean to hurt you but you can't believe how happy I am that we made it through today.'

'We certainly did make it,' Jerome confirmed with a smile yet the smile didn't reach his eyes. *You are right, Max,* he thought bitterly, *we did survived the day but it was only by sheer luck.* The drill, on the whole, served as an enlightening shock for Jerome as he was suddenly faced with the peril that his waning abilities placed him under. He had never seen it coming.

The introduction to the fire element was very deceiving, exploding with sensuality, tempting and comforting. One evening Yves came and took them to the meditation room and when they entered they found a bonfire blazing in the centre of the hall. Following Yves' instructions they sat near the fire and looked around.

It was a beautiful spectacle, the fire illuminating the hall in a new and enchanted way, giving it a different feel altogether. Flames performed a shadowy dance on the rocks, and the waterfall was dotted with sparks, flickering from drops that escaped the main downpour of the small surge. For a moment Jerome felt as if he were outside in nature, where the elements are strongly sensed.

'As much as I would like you to enjoy an evening outside, to sit around the campfire and to roast some chestnuts, it is not going to happen. We are here to study, to learn the secrets of fire. It will be beneficial later on, might even save your lives.' The boys were semi listening, too taken by the strange scenery.

'Now concentrate please; sit cross-legged and maintain your spine erect. Get into the rhythm of your stomach-breathing and relax; you have to be aware of the interval between inhalation and exhalation and to connect to the *Su*.' And he paused to teach them a new form of *Kotodama*, specifically for fire.

'Fire is a masculine element and as such should be the easiest for you to comprehend. Don't take it lightly though, it is the most perilous element of all, the one with the most traitorous character.' He paused one more time and positioned their hands in front of the flames, at a relatively safe distance, allowing a tolerated amount of heat to be sensed.

'Now start to chant the *Kotodama*, and don't worry about their meaning. Connect your palms to the flames and direct it to the core.' And he left them at that, watching them sitting and becoming familiar with the new sensation.

At first Jerome could only detect the heat, but as the sounds started to mingle with his breath he slowly began to sense the connection. Both him and the fire were feeding on the oxygen and both had a breathing pattern, a unique cycle for the usage of the valuable air. But that was only a superficial observation, one that created a logical explanation to the shapes and meanings of the Strings. He reached further and further into the flames, the energy passing through him in a controlled and safe fashion. He was part of the flames, and like the flames he could not be hurt by their deadly intentions. It might have looked similar to what Max was doing but it was a different kind of control altogether. Max meditated on the flames, modifying the position of his palms according to the intensity of the heat. Consequently he managed to place his palm relatively close to the flames, but it was the wrong kind of connection, dissociated from the source.

The boys sustained the heat and stayed virtually unharmed; it was a pleasurable experience, hastening the passage of time. 'I love the fire drill, *Sensei*,' Max announced when it was over, 'it is so calming!'

'See what you think about it tomorrow then,' Yves laughed and escorted them back to their room. In the morning he came to fetch them, leading the way back to the meditation hall. The bonfire was gone from the centre of the hall, replaced by an orange path of burning coals.

'I will go first!' Max declared sternly, frowning head first as he approached the scorching surface.

He only managed to walk fifteen metres before jumping off in pain. Yves was laughing and banging his thighs while Max sat and cursed on the floor. Jerome ignored them both, standing and staring at the burning path.

'Listen to the coals,' Yves whispered in his ear. 'They try to tell you something.'

Jerome twisted his lips on one side, resenting the *sensei* yet obeying all the same, focusing on the internal world of the *Su*. He watched the coals, listened to them whistling in red; meditating until he finally reached the point of connection. Jerome cleared his throat and placed a foot on the burning surface, detecting the energy and intent of the flames, joining their breathing cycle.

'Come on, get on with it, "scaredy",' Max teased as he sat and rubbed his crimson feet. Yves gave him a warning look that silenced him.

Jerome kept his position fixed, singing with the flames until he could disperse their overwhelming force between the *Kotodama* plains. From there on it was simpler. He walked the flames for as long as he was told to, although he did get a little burned. Connecting to the *Su* became harder with every passing day, and he sometimes found the detachment impossible.

That exercise had looked excessive on the first day but when they reached the third day they realised it was an innocent drill compared with what they now faced – namely the 'Heat Hovering' exercise.

They were harnessed by flexible metal cords over a huge oven. The oven had an open top from which blazing flames randomly escaped. They had to balance themselves or get burned, using their detachment and *Skill*. The oven had a levelled aura that could be detected fairly easily through the *Skill*. The hard and dangerous part was to sense the surprising eruptions of sparks and flames. Max as usual volunteered to go first, twisting comically over the flames; his acrobatic manoeuvres helping him escape most of the burning dangers. Max's display was accompanied by numerous screams of pain and desperation; he was frequently hurt and came out bright red, eyebrows half-burned to the flesh yet surprisingly without any serious damage. Jerome ignored Max's screams, meditating until Yves ordered him to stand.

'It is your turn, Master Jerome.' He winked at the frightened boy.

Jerome was strapped over the oven, trying to get involved inside the *Su. Please don't forsake me now!* he silently begged, *I must connect!* There was no answer to his longings as the *Su* illusively escaped him again, forsaking Jerome in the face of danger. 'Arrgh!' he screamed in pain as a powerful jet of flames caught him on the face. Yves had to stop the drill and pull him out of there, and not a moment too soon by the look of it.

The time that had passed since his self-confrontation with the mirror had weakened the connection to the *Su* considerably. It was the detachment that was missing from the equation, a sense that was slowly fading away. Max was gaining residence at his nucleus yet again and Jerome felt utterly hopeless in blocking his way. He was cheated from the only tool that could help him save Max – pushed away from the only goal that was left in his life. Jerome felt hopeless, unable to perform properly without the necessary detachment. He looked down at his hands and grimaced in pain, seeing how the connection he had sensed was gradually dwindling away, abandoning him in a very precarious situation over the flames.

He sat quietly in the study after Max has gone to sleep and searched in the books, looking for some clues from the past, some pieces of information to shine over his ever-darkening reality.

* * *

France, 2016

Master Jacques was becoming frantic, seeing the only love of his life, his wife Marie, dying a little with each and every passing day. He was frustrated as well, sensing her only hope for deliverance, which was his detachment, treacherously slipping away. It wasn't fair! He did not deserve it!

Life, however, was never about what was fair. 'You take what you get, my dear, and say thank you, look after yourself and hope that health will sustain for as long as it possibly can.' It was one of Marie's favourite sayings and now she was confronted by the cruel truth of her own words.

He knew that in the end death catches up with everyone. That there was nowhere to hide as it jumps out of some dark corner, gleefully affirming while dishing out the final cut: 'Ready or not here I come!' Jacques *Sensei*, as it stood, was not ready to quit his fight against death just yet; on the contrary, he was about to take it a step further.

That's how he ended up on the high platform, staring at the beast of a stunt that he had devised for himself. He was not going to make it without the help of the mechanical cords or the safety of the protective gear – he didn't even dare try it!

Master Jacques had reached the borders of his limitations to find that he was perhaps over-enthusiastic and aiming too high and too far. He didn't want to accept that he had failed, didn't want to admit that all these years of high philosophy and belief in the beyond were a simple waste of time.

Standing on the high platform he watched the course of the stunt that he had created and swallowed hard, *It is impossible,* he knowingly nodded to himself. *Far beyond my capabilities.* The stunt was designed as an obstacle course, with twelve different stations to go through, all in succession, without a pause. It started from where he stood, a platform 30 metres high in the air, based on a metal pole. For the moment the platform was secured and stable but on the day of the stunt it was to crash in a dramatic explosion, leaving no alternative but to jump away. The only salvation from crashing to the distant floor below would be the shifting platforms.

The first shifting platform was levelled with the starting point and he had to progress from there to the next platform in a specific fashion and timing, once again precision turning into a matter of life and death. These platforms were placed one after the other at different heights and angles, moving on the circumference of giant wheels, powerful enough to crush him flat if he missed the timing, or lost his aim. After the shifting platforms came the rotating pins, grinding at each other, forcing him to squeeze through the narrowest of gaps or be pounded to death. That was only the beginning of the course, and there were quite a few other acrobatic manoeuvres that were impossible to do without the presence of the *Skill.*

The waning of his detachment frightened him the most. Losing it at this moment would cost him more than reputation alone. He cursed himself quietly for ever taking this risk but at the same time knew that there were good arguments to support his actions. First there was his poor Marie, dying in bed just because he couldn't get his hand on the funding needed for her medication. The money he would receive at the end of the stunt guaranteed to cover the cost of her medication and much more – that in itself was enough reason to go ahead with the plan. Then there were the other, more personal reasons that pushed him to face the extreme. He was taking ever-increasing risks because he realised that the high level of threat helped him sustain some of the detachment that was slipping away. He felt like a junky craving for drugs but unlike the junky he was lost, not knowing where and how he was going to find his next fix. The extra danger did help him raise money, as people were ready to pay well for high risk stunts, but it didn't stop the gradual evaporation of the *Skill;* it only slowed it down.

He laughed bitterly when he thought of the promises he had given his sponsors, and of the money they had invested in the building of this amazing stunt. They would surely tear him into tiny little pieces in the court room should he lose heart and fail to deliver the goods. He could already visualise the newspaper headlines and his face flushed an embarrassing red – Jacques the small-time impostor! Jacques didn't think of himself as a con artist, knowing that the only reason he had gone this far was the desperate situation of Marie and the fact that every time he pushed at his limits, the *Skill* would express itself the most.

He remembered a book he'd read in the past, *The Magician of Lublin* by Isaac Bashevis Singer, telling the story of a magician who was setting up a stunt that he was not going to be able to perform, although he believed himself to be favoured by the divine. In the book the magician realised his limits as a man and quit his stunt, swallowing his pride and learning the lesson of humility, and Jacques was afraid that was the course he might have to choose, to give up the fight and surrender.

Jacques stretched up on the high pole, at the starting line of his stunt, attached from above by the blessed cables. He watched the device and shook his head. *Without the Skill I am disabled,* he sighed. *I do not have the environmental sensitivity to deploy the creative energy of the Su. My normal acrobatic skill would never suffice, no matter how hard I tried!* Detachment and *Skill* were wearing away quickly while the goals he had set for himself were aiming for a level of performance that he had never achieved.

Marie was replacing the detachment at his core and he could do nothing to stop it. It was like a vicious cycle, the more he needed the *Skill* in order to save Marie's life the less attainable it became. He wondered if O Sensei had ever been in such a desperate situation and a humble smile spread across his face. Even in his grim condition he knew that the Aikido founder had gone beyond any borders of reasoning in search of the same stimuli. *My efforts are pathetically safe in comparison to yours, Sensei.*

Jacques raised his head and composed himself, shaking the weakening thoughts away. There was no time and there was still a lot of work to do if he was ever to make it. Determined, he resumed training, keeping the founder's thirst for the art as a drive of his own...

* * *

Mongolia, 1924

The road to Tongliao proved to be a road to hell, but by the time they realised it they were as useless as captives, drawn by the mad ambition of their comrade, the Chinese warlord Lu Zhankui. Lu still believed that he would prevail with his plan to conquer Mongolia even as they ran for their lives and to certain peril by the look of it. Ueshiba knew their situation to be desperate; discussing openly the course that would be the wisest to take but his advice was being ignored. He looked at the Reverend Deguchi, his master, and knew that even he was now a mere doll in the hands of the sightless Lu.

They had left Japan in late February and now it was early June, days of warm air and blinding clouds of dust. They would have been better off elsewhere but Lu had insisted that they should travel to Tongliao, using the presence of Deguchi as an insurance policy against their pursuers.

'I am protected by the elements and their earthly representative – the great Onisaburo Deguchi!'

Deguchi blinded Lu with his abilities, allowing the latter to develop a larger than life image of the *Omoto Kyo* master. Now Lu was so convinced by Deguchi's enchanting words that he believed nothing could stop them from achieving their goal, not listening to Deguchi himself who tried to sway the warlord from his decision to travel to Tongliao.

'It is a bad omen! I read it in the stars.'

'Human foes are no match for the divine supremacy.' Lu smiled confidently at Deguchi. 'It is only your humbleness that stops you from crushing them all. You could always use your powers to control the elements if the worst comes about, maybe even drown our enemies with a heavy downpour or a flood.' At these words the reverend grimaced but remained silent.

Deguchi would never admit his own shortcomings and, who knows, at this stage it was possibly the wisest choice not to contradict Lu. Even if Deguchi had admitted his lack of capacity it would not deter the warlord from going to Tongliao. The Japanese were the prisoners of Lu's passionate ambitions and behaving with dignity was all that was left for them to do. There were at least four more days of riding before they would reach their destination. They were pressed for time and Lu informed them that they might have to ride the whole night.

'Long days and long nights.' Ueshiba yawned and looked around.

It was nearing sunset and their shadows lengthened as the sun started to tip down in the west. The dusty landscape created a permanent cloud beneath the horse's hooves and sitting on horseback gave Ueshiba the illusion that they were riding in the skies.

Ueshiba's reasons for participating in the trip had nothing to do with Deguchi's ambition, and Deguchi knew of his student's personal quest, promising Ueshiba that he would find what he sought here on the continent. For four long years Ueshiba had searched in Japan for the detachment he had experienced when his father had passed away. He had tried numerous measures to find the detachment on his own yet failed to come up with the results.

'Detachment is like an opening blocked by a heavy door,' Deguchi explained while discussing Ueshiba's inability to detach. 'Learn what forced the detachment on you in the past, what experience swung that door open. Recapturing that experience might be the very key you are seeking, the one that matches the lock on your door.'

Those were wise words of guidance yet Ueshiba failed just the same. His craving for detachment was tearing him apart, affecting his family life for the worse. Perhaps he should have listened to all his mentor had to say in that long ago conversation.

'Detachment is very hard to achieve with an inner drive alone, there is always a need for an external stimuli.' The words of the reverend at the time had been meaningless to him.

Ueshiba rode behind Deguchi, staring at the master's back and bowing involuntarily; he acknowledged that the trip had presented him with one surprising gift already, the circular motion for the fight, the blending. It was a valuable piece of information, giving him one of the missing components for his art, the feminine aspect of the water element. The master's promises were proving accurate yet Ueshiba was worried that he might not be able to realise his findings. Death was closing in fast in all directions – they had been ambushed twice in the past week. He didn't know it as yet but those desperate incidences had loosened the resistance of the self, the honest risk stimulating the detachment to surface.

Suddenly gunshots were heard and a rider in front of Ueshiba collapsed screaming.

'A trap!' someone cried. 'Off the horses!'

They were riding through a narrow ravine, shadowed by a large land fold – a perfect place for an ambush. All jumped off their horses but it took Ueshiba a fraction of a second longer to react. For a moment he stood frozen in the stirrups, glaring at the place where the dead body lay, his eyes shining wide. *But why did you fail to see the bullet coming?* he wondered in confusion. *It was travelling so incredibly slowly ...*

As if in a dream Ueshiba came off the horse and looked around at the battle scene. Bullets were flying left and right, some finding their targets while other whistled away in the darkening evening. Ueshiba shook his head, remembering his duty and seeking Deguchi in the unfolding madness. He saw the reverend and ran to his side, hovering over him, sheltering him from the bullets with his own body, searching for a secure spot for his master.

'Over here, Master,' he cried and dragged Deguchi behind a carcass of a horse. Deguchi was safe and Ueshiba raised his head and drank in the sounds and sights that stimulated him madly. 'Ahhh,' he exhaled in relief, 'finally you have decided to come!' Detachment was back, not fully, but in a way that he hadn't experienced for four long years. It could have been a jab of heroin to his veins, he looked that intoxicated.

Darkness was almost complete, the source of the attack now revealed to everyone by flares of light. It directed Lu's band, who fought back the assailants.

'Come on!' the warlord screamed at his men, 'Shoot them!' Bullets flew in all directions and sometimes found a living target, their aim undetected to all but Morihei Ueshiba. *I can hear them singing through the air*, he nodded silently, *looking so beautifully bright and colourful.* For him the bullets were presented as flashes of light that cut the night sky and penetrated bodies; disturbing the delicate harmony of the human Strings. The thought of the joy he was experiencing crossed his mind and he wanted to denounce it as immoral; it simply frightened him to admit that he was enjoying the proximity of death and the mayhem around.

Sounds of the battle were playing a new harmony around Ueshiba and were accompanied by an exhibition of lights. He felt safe and in total control, walking around head held high and dodging bullets that dared to try and strike him. Finally the craving for detachment was somewhat relieved, yet it was merely an appetiser – for he was still hungry.

32 The Ring Fighter

IN THE YEARS preceding the end of the second millennium a new kind of competition was gaining hysterical popularity. This competition was known as 'Pride' and took place in Japan, the birth place of Jujitsu. Top fighters from all over the world and from a variety of disciplines, came to compete against each other, trying to get their hands on the highly prized winning trophy. The competition continued into the third millennium and during the years in which the *Skill* became known, the Pride fighters were faced with a new kind of challenge. One fighter, a *Skilled aikidoka* entered the ring and in a sweeping victory took the championship title and trophy. A few more competitions went by and the non-*Skilled* fighters, who stood little chance against the new challenge, requested a new law to be written and enforced.

Meetings were held with delegates from the International Aikido Board present, and it was decided to separate the non-*Skilled* from the *Skilled*, to keep the competition balanced. And so the '*Aiki* Tournament' was born, where the world could witness the marvels of the *Skilled*, and pump the fighters and the board with reputation and money.

From time to time a non-*Skilled* challenger would surface and risk the ring, trying to beat the *Skilled*; these were brave efforts yet no one had been successful so far. Due to money and prestige, many *dojo* tried to find the *Skilled* students who could face the ring, those who were cut out for the fight.

Not all martial artists possessed the fighting urge and masters had no choice but to force a challenge on each and every student of the *Skill*, to see if they could handle the ring. It was similar to the way a bull was judged before a fight, when it had to show two main qualities in order to participate. The first was the desire for the fight and most bulls, unlike people, were naturally aggressive. The second quality, which was harder to evaluate, was the ability to conform to the rules. Just before performing in the ring, the bull would be introduced and his instincts would be judged. If the bull was to charge or move unexpectedly, such as cutting corners or swinging sideway with its horns, it was considered too dangerous and not allowed to fight. There were other issues to judge as well, such as the reaction of the bull to the crowds, as some might experience anxiety attacks in crowded places.

Similar evaluations were carried out on *Skilled* fighters, as incidences in the past taught instructors to check their fighters thoroughly before sending them to compete. A strong fighter could encircle the *dojo* he represented in finance and reputation, yet could also be a disastrous embarrassment if he behaved unethically. No serious master of the *Skill* would allow it to happen if he could help it. There had been an incident in the past where a fighter destroyed the reputation of a whole school by showing bad manners.

* * *

He was nicknamed 'Vulcan' and no one remembered his real name. Vulcan was a retired champion of the *Aiki* Tournaments and earned his living as an 'evaluator'. He worked freelance and was called upon by different schools of the *Skill* to assess the chances young students had in becoming professional fighters.

Vulcan was a *Skilled aikidoka*, originally trained in the *Skill* of the *'Aiki* Grappler', notoriously deadly in technique, even without the touch of the *Skill*. Grappling was not a new art in essence but the *Skill* itself was what made it so unusual. A good *Aiki* Grappler was a master of the close-range fight and an unfortunate opponent to get clenched in their tight grip would need a miracle to set himself free.

Vulcan was 54 years old, a pleasant and well-mannered gentleman on most occasions, although a few outbursts of temper in the past had rewarded him with a doubtful reputation. He was born in a small village near the Amazon, suffering poverty and a rough childhood. One day, like so many other children of the time, he was taken against his will to a school for the *Aiki Skill*. He had spent a few good years at the *dojo* and from there he emerged as ferocious as a storm, taking the *Aiki* Tournament championship three consecutive years. He kept fighting after that, but never regained the successes of his past. Forced to quit at the age of 37, he became an evaluator of *Skilled* student's potential and he was known to be very good!

Vulcan was not a big man, weighing around 190 pounds and five foot nine in height. He had a dark complexion and a low forehead that made him look like a caveman. His black eyes shone forcefully, the concentration beaming forwards, undeterred.

Yves *Sensei* treated him with great respect, something he didn't do for everyone.

'So, tell me more about this student of yours,' Vulcan asked as they entered Yves' office, holding a glass of wine. They'd had an hour-long casual talk in the school dining room, accompanied by a full course dinner.

'He is a young lad, not seventeen as yet but quickly gaining the necessary strength and stamina for the fight.'

Vulcan tightened his lips but remained silent, hiding his displeasure on the tip of his wine glass. He knew his business and went through the required social codes in order to cut a deal, but here he was sitting after a long hour and all he was being given were diplomatic answers. Vulcan, however, had no choice but to endure the painful chit chat; Yves was very successful at reviving the *Skill* and as such was a stable source of income.

'Is he cut out for the fight? Have you seen him operate under violent circumstances?'

Yves nodded and took a sip of his drink.

'I have seen him operate on one of my staff and he nearly killed the chap. He can be aggressive enough, I have no doubt about it, but as for his self-control—' He stopped and scratched his head, searching for the best description. 'Let's just say that he might be a bit unstable.' He concluded with a satisfied smile and Vulcan raised an eyebrow at the last remark.

The evaluator was not concerned but rather intrigued by the challenge presented, hoping to come across some new stimulation in his known routine. 'In what way would you say he is unstable?' he prodded deeper.

'It's like he won't really fight in order to protect himself but would do it happily for the sake of others,' Yves replied. 'And when he finally does fight he can be extremely dangerous.'

Vulcan laughed, unconsciously sticking his chin out and inflating his already large chest. 'Provide me with the facts and let me worry about the danger.'

The smile didn't leave Yves' face but his nostrils widened slightly and his fist tightened under the table, irritated by the arrogance of the former champion. 'Very well then,' he said formally. 'What would you like to know?'

'First, tell me about his "triggers".' Triggers referred to sensitive points in a student's constitution that could stimulate aggressive behaviour.

'What would you like to know first?' Yves asked.

'The name of the instructor who introduced him to the mirror stage.'

'Straight to the point are we?'

Vulcan smirked in reply. He tended to use this taunted memory against the students, as it caused quite a reaction in most.

'His name is George, and the student was very fond of him.' They both burst out laughing, knowing how deceptive the spiritual training was.

'Any signs of the *Skill* yet?'

'The usual abilities that students illustrate at this stage, maybe slightly lower than average standards.'

'OK then,' Vulcan said and shifted in his seat, anxious to leave. 'Will he be ready for, let's say, next Wednesday?'

'I think that Wednesday would be perfect.' They shook hands on it. 'See you next week, Vulcan; my secretary will transfer all the necessary funding to you.'

Vulcan bowed and walked away, satisfied with the deal. He didn't like Yves much, never had, but Yves paid well and called upon him often. Vulcan interlocked his fingers and cracked the joints, relieved, and put business behind him. He was on his way to town to do some shopping; it wasn't every day that he found himself in a metropolis such as Paris.

* * *

There was something different in the air that morning, a sense that it was going to be a dissimilar kind of day. After the morning routine Yves led them towards the main exit, the door that was across from their quarters. They walked through the corridor, passing by the doors to the training halls. Yves turned right at the end of the corridor and led them to a great oak door, which he unlocked. He let the boys step inside and quickly followed behind. They entered and stood quietly, enjoying the incredible vastness of the hall, the biggest space they had been to since they started training.

'Boys,' Yves called. 'This is our training hall for the *Aiki* Tournaments, and this arena has almost the same structure that the main arena in Japan has. Look around and memorise it well, it is vital to know as much as possible about the surface that you fight upon.'

The boys nodded, knowing very well of the *Aiki* Tournaments from their books and the trophies in Yves' office. They looked around, mesmerised by the space and its gadgets.

'What the hell was that?' Max asked, startled by a sudden vibration beneath his feet.

Yves sighed and pointed at the ground. 'Just don't fall between the cracks.' He twisted his face at Max.

The floor in the hall was composed of some elastic material. It had hidden levers and hinges beneath, allowing it to reshape the surface randomly, to create new manoeuvring options for the fighter. That was only the floor, one element out of many that the three-dimensional arena presented. The walls had daises protruding in all sizes and forms and floating platforms hovered freely around the room, humming at the height of the boys' heads.

'Be aware of those,' Yves warned. 'They can take your head off if you are not careful.' Both boys nodded silently, their eyes moving hectically from side to side. 'The hall is designed to balance the advantages that any single *Skill* might have in any particular surface and space. It also requires the fighters to think more strategically.'

Yves had his palms on his hips, a proud smile across his face; the richness of the place reflected on him as a sign of success.

'Impressive isn't it?' he asked and Max opened his mouth in a cynical expression. Yves didn't wait for an answer. He clapped his hands and the hall went dark, bolting the words in Max's mouth. A thick beam of light drew a circle on one of the walls and then started to rotate round and round. Jerome and Max blinked, dazed by the sudden change.

'It is worse when the shouts of the crowd are added – not the best of places for shy and reserved individuals.' Yves led them around the hall for almost an hour, showing them the apparatus in the room, demonstrating and explaining their uses and meanings.

'*Skill* and fighting abilities are not sufficient to survive this ring; spirit and strategy ultimately determine the outcome of a bout.' Briefly he went through the rules of the fight, not wanting to waste too much time and energy before he knew of Vulcan's evaluation.

'That's about it for now. Take the next half an hour to wander around and explore for yourselves. Take your time and learn as much as you can about your options. You will need this information sooner than you realise.'

They didn't take his words lightly, suspecting and anticipating the worse and they spread out, exploring each on his own. Jerome walked to his left, drawn by the floating platform, scanning the hall for a way up. He detected windows of opportunity all around him, sensing their intense options, smiling when a soft rumble was preceded by a strong gush of wind. The air flow was under tight control, just like the hall of the Marie-7. He waited until another burst of concentrated air whooshed into the hall, sensing and learning its innovative options. For a *Skilled aikidoka*, such options of relocation were more than enough, but Jerome wasn't qualified yet, his abilities premature. His main difficulty lay in initiating movements; sensing the Strings compressing within as he coiled in, yet could never find the necessary energy to begin the reposition. The only way for Jerome to participate in a *Skilled* move was by using an external stimuli or a non *Skilled* jump-start, such as running or falling. Once his body was set in motion he could apply certain *Skilled* manoeuvres, as if the non-*Skilled* moves gave him the required energy to kick out.

'Now how am I going to get up there?' Jerome asked himself, his index finger resting under his chin. Attentively he stood and watched the floating platforms, judging distance and timing and then breaking into a sprint, jumping high as he got near the wall. His feet connected with the perpendicular surface to ricochet in a large arc backwards, landing balanced and standing on top of one of the floating podiums. It wasn't a fully *Skilled* journey but it got him there and he was pleased, searching the hall for further possibilities. The platform was advancing very slowly yet its surface didn't stay parallel to the floor for very long, suddenly flipping, almost spilling Jerome off it. He overheard the *sensei's* giggles but he ignored the tease, blending in the momentary loss of balance to cut a new spin in the air. He ended up on one of the many protrusions on the wall.

'Bravo!' Yves shouted mockingly and got closer, his hands clapping loudly. 'You must know that all the platforms will stay parallel to the floor for only thirty seconds once you step on top of them.' He motioned with his hands for the boys to commence. 'We will have a short recess before starting with the real training.'

Jerome jumped off the wall and sat heavily in the centre of the hall, observing Max finishing his exploration. Max was finding his footing easily; even without the presence of the *Skill* he performed almost as well as Jerome did.

'Show off!' Jerome called as Max somersaulted down from a dais, to land and roll dramatically on the floor. He winked and sat cross-legged next to Jerome.

Twenty minutes later Vulcan entered the hall. He stopped near the entrance and exchanged a few words with Yves but the boys couldn't hear what they were saying.

'Sit in *seiza,* boys,' Yves ordered as he approached the centre, Vulcan pacing behind him and to the left. The boys sat and stretched their backs, studying the newcomer, their faces showing no emotion. 'I would like to introduce to you the honourable instructor of the day.' Yves gestured politely with his hand to the old champion. 'I give you Mr Vulcan!'

Max chuckled at the mention of the name and Jerome looked at Vulcan, to see his reaction. Vulcan's face was unreadable, looking at

Max portentously calm and distant.

'Mr Vulcan was a champion of the *Aiki* Tournaments and has quite a reputation as a warrior. He is here to evaluate your chances of becoming professional fighters.' Yves smiled coldly and turned his head to Vulcan. 'They are all yours,' he said and backed away, observing indifferently from the side.

33 The Evaluation

THERE WAS a moment of silence as Vulcan watched them intently and then he motioned Max to get up, to be ready.

'Stop me if you can!' he called and charged forward, dropping on his front knee just before impact, rising up with Max held tightly in his arms. Max was expecting an attack but he didn't expect anything as strong or ferocious as that. His legs lost contact with the floor and the more Vulcan rose up the higher Max was in the air. He had no chance of resisting the perfect timing of the collision, or the sweeping drive that followed. It slammed them both to the ground with a huge thump, Vulcan's body ending up on top of Max. Max screamed all through the flight and Jerome grimaced instinctively, imagining the pain that the crash must have caused.

Max tried to revive himself, shaking his head as Vulcan shifted his attention to Jerome, motioning him to rise, to prepare for the assault. The attack was similar, sprawling Jerome backwards, his head bouncing on the floor, Vulcan almost ending up on top again. Somehow Jerome had managed to use the momentum to coil and change direction, rolling over the powerful back of Vulcan. He could have struck at the instructor but chose not to, a fact that did not escape the old veteran.

Max in the meantime, had regained his composure and advanced towards Vulcan, slightly cautious.

'Let's get the son of a bitch,' he called. 'What do you say, J?' He was almost caught off guard as Vulcan charged at him.

Max, however, did not panic. He quickly turned and swept the fighter with a *Kokyunage*, breath throw, or so he believed. Vulcan at the moment of contact clenched himself tightly to Max and together they fell to the ground.

'Get him off me, J!' Max cried, while Jerome leaped around them, looking for an opening to hit the instructor. In a way he liked the lesson, regardless of the brutality and the lack of style, just because it was honest. Vulcan ended up on his back, holding Max as a shield against Jerome's attacks, choking the boy with his forearms.

Max passed out and Vulcan rolled backwards and quickly stood up, facing Jerome. Thoughts were running anxiously through Jerome's head, the events unfolding much too fast for him to comprehend. Max was down and the best Jerome could think of was to pull the fight away from his friend. He didn't really need to, though; Vulcan suddenly raised his arm and motioned Yves to step forwards. The master passed by Max who was sitting on the ground, coughing and rubbing his neck.

'Take him back to his quarters; he is not going to make a ring fighter.' Max started to protest but Yves didn't want to listen, quickly guiding the frustrated youth outside. Vulcan turned to face Jerome, smiling with bad intent.

'Are you ready for some more?' he teased and circled the youngster. Jerome remained quiet, calmer now that Max was gone. He backed away towards the walls, hoping to change the battleground, but the floor decided otherwise. Suddenly he felt a drop and the place where he had stood caved in.

Vulcan used the opportunity and he slipped intentionally forwards, grabbing the confused youth. Jerome wriggled in Vulcan's mighty arms but his efforts were rather clumsy. He had lost his main drive for the fight, there was no one to protect. Vulcan snorted in contempt, sensing the sudden lack of resistance, angrily smacking the boy above the earlobe, causing Jerome's head to ring from the inside like a tower bell.

'Do you think the fight is over?' Vulcan asked as he backed off, eyes intensely on Jerome. 'George told me what a silly ass you are, the protector of friends. Give me a bloody break!' He laughed and motioned with his hand. 'Get up, puppy; if you won't fight you risk your friend's life further. Isn't that so, Master?' The last question was directed at Yves who had just returned to the hall to observe.

'It's very true,' he confirmed with a warm smile.

Jerome looked from one to the other, angered and lost; the two adults were toying with his defenceless constitution like children playing with a doll. He had no choice but to comply, and he charged in, punching at the fighter's face. Vulcan blocked easily and threw the boy to the ground with a sharp *Iriminage*. Jerome got up dazed but attacked once more, knowing that Yves would not be satisfied if he gave less than a hundred per cent of his effort. He ended on the floor once more.

The same ordeal was repeated a few times and then Vulcan called '*Yame!*' and backed towards Yves. Jerome was trying to recuperate, folded in two, panting heavily whilst holding his sides.

'He is going to knock himself out with these blind launches,' Vulcan whispered to Yves. 'I see the *Skill* in him, and I can see the passion and the fight. He has got it all yet refuses to let himself go, reserved in his efforts.'

'Let's increase the pressure,' Yves suggested and Vulcan went back to the centre of the ring while Yves addressed Jerome. 'I want to see you fighting vigorously and trying to win. Don't run forwards like a fool. Think of what you are doing and of your options. I am watching the whole time. Do it properly if you care for your friend's well-being.'

Jerome narrowed his eyes. *Very well you bastard!* he nodded to himself, giving a murderous look to the hated *sensei*. He had to do as he was told, had to play their game. He shook his head and bit his lips; undesirably committed to what might be his forced future. Jerome took a quick run and bounced himself off the wall, onto one of the platforms.

'That's better.' Vulcan smiled and hurried towards a ladder attached to one of the walls. He climbed up and jumped onto Jerome's platform. The moment Vulcan's foot touched the hovering surface Jerome charged with a series of strikes, trying to hit Vulcan before he would regain his balance.

The experienced fighter instinctively collapsed and rolled forwards, connecting with Jerome's legs to spring explosively up, catching and clinching the boy in a deadly hug. Vulcan squeezed his way up Jerome's body, going for the choke. The platform twisted sharply to the left and they dropped off. The momentum of the fall played in Jerome's favour, offering an opportunity he could not resist. Out of nowhere the correct enchanting *Kotodama* sprang to life and the Strings reacted as one unit. When he hit the floor he was free of the deadly grip.

'Not bad,' Vulcan said panting. 'Not bad at all!'

Forward he launched, double striking at Jerome's face. He used the distraction for a surprise drop onto his knees and his hands reached for the take-down. This time he had a perfect hold and down Jerome went, his chest cavity crushing under the full weight of the grappler.

Aiki Grapplers had a *Skill* that set them apart from regular grapplers; they could connect to their opponent's aura and use its radiance to soar over them, to keep them pinned and controlled. Numbly Jerome sensed how Vulcan was hovering around him, using the energy that Jerome's body produced for his movements. Jerome panicked and twisted inside Vulcan's grip, pathetically useless.

Suddenly the connection was broken and Vulcan rolled over him, walking towards Yves, ignoring Jerome who sat on the floor, recovering his breath and rubbing at his ribs.

'He's not bad at all, maybe even excellent once the *Skill* is fully established,' Vulcan whispered. 'Now I will assess his attitude towards honour and his self-control. I will give him an opening for the strike, to see how he reacts. Get him off me if he gets too worked up. I will give you a sign.'

'No problem,' Yves assured him and Vulcan went back to face Jerome.

'Let's fight some more but this time you must be very attentive; remember to stop fighting when you hear the *Yame* command, never mind what you're doing at that moment.'

Jerome nodded, watching Vulcan with a frown, bouncing from leg to leg.

'Don't blow it; your friend's well-being relies on your performance.'

You had to mention it again, didn't you? Jerome smiled bitterly at him, teeth clenched tight, murder in the eyes.

Vulcan stood legs apart and bowed to Jerome and the latter returned the courtesy, dropping his guard for a second and immediately receiving a strike to his sore ribs. Vulcan laughed heartily and stretched out his arm to Jerome who was sprawled on the ground in pain.

'Never let your guard down in the ring,' he said as Jerome was lifting up, using the outstretched arm of Vulcan for the pull. He was halfway up when Vulcan, with a friendly expression, thumped at Jerome's nose, hard enough to hurt but not to break the delicate cartilage.

Jerome found himself on the ground once more, blinded by tears of pain and anger. He heard the renewed laughter and the blood in his vein boiled. He jumped back to the attack and as he advanced he heard the command, '*Yame*!' He backed away growling, his tongue licking the dry lips while circling Vulcan.

'Don't be such a sore-headed bear,' he heard Yves calling. 'Everything he did is within the rules.'

'This one isn't,' Vulcan said, side-striking at Jerome's temple and as the strike was blocked he kicked hard at Jerome's groin. *You bloody wanker, you!* Jerome gagged and fell, his eyes bloodshot, the hands grasping between the legs. His muscles were tight when he got up, the eyes squinted in evil intent as he charged forwards.

'*Yame*!' Yves cried smiling and Jerome moved away snarling in frustration.

The same kind of torment continued for a while and Jerome's face was flushed red, his self-control stretched to the limit. He tried to retaliate but whenever he would gain an advantage the cursed *Yame* command would be called, forcing him to back away.

Vulcan nodded to Yves; it was time to give an opening. He charged and semi-slipped, ending up underneath Jerome who was trying to sprawl away. Blindly Jerome sensed the option and dropped his knee down on Vulcan, lips tightening with pleasure as he hit the target. *Have some, you old bastard!* It was a release, the stress dispersing with the strikes. He didn't stop hitting, couldn't resist the opportunity to avenge.

Vulcan realised that the student was out for the kill and he motioned with his arm for Yves to call *Yame*, receiving two kicks to the face as his arm lifted. Jerome held him from above, chest heavy on Vulcan's upper back, clenching the shoulders beneath the armpits, launching his knees down with an explosive force.

'Back off, you crazy bastard,' Yves called as he dragged Jerome away. The boy was not listening; his mind clouded by vague sounds and smudged red colours.

Vulcan rolled up, his nose bleeding and a bruise quickly forming at his temple.

Jerome looked at him panting, wriggling in Yves' arms, wanting to attack. Vulcan was not combative any more, his eyes pacifying and calm. He got close to Jerome and whispered softly, 'It is over, young man, your evaluation is over.' They remained there until Jerome regained control and was taken back to his room.

'What do you think, Vulcan?' Yves asked when they were alone.

'I think that next time I won't rely on you to save my ass. What the hell was that supposed to be?'

'I know that it took a bit longer than usual to control him. but you got him really worked up. I warned you that he's not stable.' He waited for Vulcan, to hear the man's reply but the fighter became reserved, knowing that the money was dearer to him than his broken nose – that part of him would heal soon!

'What's the verdict?' Yves finally asked.

'I think you know what the answer is; he could have been a good ring fighter but as you yourself observed, he is not stable.'

'Just as I thought,' Yves agreed. 'Well, he will still make a very good fighter.'

'No doubt about that,' Vulcan summarised the conversation.

They talked a little longer, but Vulcan's mind was elsewhere, politeness pushing him to fulfil his social obligations. He took his money and went away as soon as he could, exhaling with relief as he stood outside the Aikilibrium centre. Vulcan considered Yves a sadistic bastard who pushed his students way too hard, threatening their physical and mental stability for the sake of his reputation, to show that his *dojo* produced more *Skilled aikidoka* than any other *dojo* in the world.

He might be successful at reviving the Skill, Vulcan thought as he turned his back on the building, *but he only produces a big bunch of nutters.* And that was all there was to it as far as he was concerned.

Vulcan was well travelled, his profession taking him to dozens of *dojo* around the globe. He knew that all the *Skill dojo* had a certain degree of cruelty to them yet they greatly differed in the severity of the abuse. Vulcan considered Yves as one of the worst headmasters he had ever met but Vulcan was insignificant in the global games of politics. He walked away quietly from the place and when he was a block away he sighed and rubbed his palms. The shiny banner of a wine bar was tempting him, pushing the dark thoughts away. He nodded in silent agreement and walked towards it, ready to trade money well earned with the memory wasting liquids.

* * *

'*Sensei*?' Jerome asked that night, just before leaving Yves' office after the daily report.

'Yes?' Yves said, lifting his eyes off the desk to look at his student.

'Did I pass the test of the ring fighters?' he asked shyly of his jailer. Yves looked frozen momentarily and then threw his head back in delight, snorting a laugh.

'You don't remember a thing, do you?' he chuckled.

'Remember what, *Sensei*?'

'The *Yame* that I called? I think there were twenty of them altogether.' He was laughing again, seeing the confused frown on Jerome's face. 'You were out of control, boy, had to pull you off him. You can't fight in the ring, no one wants another Arturo.'

'Arturo?' Jerome raised his eyebrows and shook his head.

'Never mind about that, let's just say that you failed because you were out of control.' He smiled at Jerome. 'It's time for you to go now,' and he followed Jerome with his eyes until he left the office.

Jerome walked downstairs slowly, his mind deep in morbid thoughts, feeling lost and lonely. As he approached the living room he saw Max sitting and holding his head, eyes damp and red, wet teary paths on his face. Jerome composed himself and sat next to his friend.

'What's going on?' he asked. They hadn't conversed with each other since Max had been sent away by Vulcan.

'What's going on?' Max returned accusingly. 'Didn't you see

how they kicked me out right at the beginning of the drill, like I was not worthy? They are going to kill me, J. I think it's pretty much determined by these guys,' and he broke down, falling into Jerome's arms with a hysterical cry.

Jerome sat and hugged Max without a word, his friend's pain shaking his very foundations.

34 The Second Shaking of the Su

The Second Shaking of the *Su* was the final super stimulus, a step taken before sealing the process complete. Through years of practice this procedure was reinvented and enhanced, gaining precision and accuracy as a highly developed science. There was no room for mistakes at this stage!

Dojo of the *Skill* differ in their approach to the Second Shaking of the *Su*, each following the footsteps of their own founder yet overall these were minor differences. The essence of the procedure remained the same, namely the use of the fear of death and the sense of loss.

Once again life in peril proved to be a moving force and a drive for human development; inspiration captured on the feeble bridge between life and death ...

(An Introduction to the Skill)

Tongliao, Mongolia, mid June 1924

THE MARCH progressed hazily, wind spiralling the dust around the ankles, blinding the eyes and blocking the nostrils. Overhead thick clouds loomed ominously, rumbling across the angry skies, threatening to realise Reverend Onisaburo Deguchi's prayers for a flood. Slowly the condemned Japanese men shuffled on the path, their chained ankles rattling as they advanced. The malicious tempo of the machine guns was approaching and the dead lay everywhere, mutilated by bullets, their faces a fixed expression of emptiness.

One of the band lost control over his sphincter and urinated as they walked, causing the armed Chinese guards to burst out laughing. The urine mingled with the stench and dampness that was embedded in them all and they just kept walking. The Japanese were stripped to their underwear, mocked and led to be executed by the firing squad. The group walked around the corner of a building and were stopped in their tracks, forced by the armed soldiers to sit and watch.

A brightly coloured wall of an old building was used as the setting for the execution, and ten of Deguchi's Mongolian comrades were lined before it, pleading loudly. Ueshiba's pupils were dilated and he shook his head in terror and disbelief, observing the numbness of the executioners as they pulled the triggers, to the further laughter of the guards. Some of the Mongolians tried to leap to escape but the machine gun caught them in mid air, twisting them agile and full of vitality in a hailstorm of bullets. They thumped heavily to the gory muddy ground.

It was brutal, senseless and without any warning it brought about the detachment that Ueshiba was longing for. It seeped in slowly, fed by the horrors he observed outside yet it was active within as well, using his resources to their full capacity. Ueshiba watched the bullets in their flight, cutting the air and creating small fuzzy flashes of light. He wasn't threatened by them, knew with conviction that he could have dodged them easily, had he not been chained to the rest of his Japanese allies. He heard the endless calm chant of the reverend and he refused to join in, knowing that it might bring about the full detachment. Ueshiba didn't want to self-indulge at the moment, frantically trying to assess a way out for his master.

'Please have mercy on the master, the Great Master!' he called to the guards, but no one was listening to his cries.

The dead bodies were dragged away from the wall and the Japanese were ordered to stand up and march forwards, taking position for their final stance. Onisaburo Deguchi walked tall and proud, his hair messy and wild, and Ueshiba followed behind him, not willing to be subdued. It was bitterly funny how in moments like that, when hope had very little time to materialise, that greatness appeared. They were lined up in front of the wall, now forced with the threat of the bayonets as some foolishly tried to escape. There was nowhere to go, their bound legs made any attempt to escape a mockery. Ueshiba stood next to his mentor, his back almost touching the gore that was splattered on the wall. He wanted to fight his way out, not wanting to accept the inventible fate, his loyalty to the master not letting go.

'Morihei.' He heard the soft and pacifying voice and his heart missed a beat, dropping slowly in tempo. He lifted his agonised eyes to meet those of the reverend and in an instant he was consumed.

'Morihei,' repeated the master. 'Don't let petty thoughts enter your mind; use the situation to better yourself; marvel at what the world has to offer you and join me as we chant; it is your Jerusalem, you have found it!'

The master kept his grip on Morihei's eyes and the familiar chant started. Ueshiba joined in and the words immediately vibrated at his core, elevating his body and spirit. He could hear the machine guns cocking ready to shoot and the mad vision of the last few months in the continent flashed in front of his mind. He was saddened by the uselessness of his findings and how death would wipe all his significant achievements away. The sounds of the chanted words, so monotonous and powerful, consumed the morbid thoughts, allowing a strange, comforting peace to settle. He saw the executioners gripping the triggers and his knees suddenly buckled and he dropped to the ground. The guards laughed harder but Ueshiba ignored their sounds and continued to chant, suddenly aloft from the situation. He was detached once again, like never before, and a world of shadows and sounds blurred his perception and shook his foundation absolute.

Master Deguchi kept his eyes on Ueshiba, his lips calmly chanting, a little smile at the corner of his mouth. He knew that his prophecy was being fulfilled, the task nearly completed. There was no fear or worry in the master's expression, his eyes lifting now to the horizon searching for further clues ...

It was time and the officer gave the command, the Japanese chanted louder and embraced themselves for that final act. All except Ueshiba, who was moving between the plains, far into the world of the Strings.

* * *

'The demonstration will take place in five weeks from now, on May the fifteenth, and each of you will have a different role to play, exhibiting a separate aspect of the art. From today you shall spend all the routines and training separately, each according to his own demonstration.'

Yves spoke as they were getting ready for lunch, after finishing a session in the 'Marie7' hall.

'What do you mean, a demonstration, *Sensei*?' Max asked, tidying his *dogi*.

'Every year we celebrate the founding of Aikilibrium by Jacques *Sensei*, 150 years ago; it is part of our tradition, a way to show the public the colourful display of the *Skill*.' Jerome raised his shoulders in indifference, knowing of Yves' flashy style and his desire for fame and glory; he didn't need any further explanation.

'Why on that specific date, *Sensei*?' Max kept asking.

'On May the fifteenth 2016, Master Jacques, the founder, performed his stunt of the *Skill* and on that day Aikilibrium was invented.'

'OK,' Max nodded, his lower lip sticking out. 'So, what do we have to do?'

Yves smiled and pointed at Jerome. 'Jerome will demonstrate Master Jacques' stunt, as it will combine all the training of the art that you've been going through. And as for you—' his attention shifted back to Max '—you will demonstrate *Kobudo* with me, you have proved to be a great *uke* in weaponry.'

Max continued to chat enthusiastically with the *sensei* but Jerome was deep in thought, a lump forming at his throat. *What are you planning, sensei?* he wondered anxiously. *What is the motive for this decision?* Demonstrating weaponry with Yves was very dangerous for the most skilled. Jerome had once witnessed Yves fighting Henri with the *naginata*, an oar-like weapon and the *sensei* had nearly taken Henri's head off with one of his strikes. *I know that you love the fight, Max, and that you are an excellent uke, but I really don't like to see Yves blades flying next to your throat.*

After lunch the *sensei* took them to the demonstration hall. They had to go through the reception but not before Yves made sure that the entrance was securely locked. He led them towards the exit and stopped just in front. There were giant doors to each side of the hall, guarded by a severe-looking *aikidoka*.

'The door to my left is the *dojo*, where normal students of the art are training, and to the right is the demonstration hall, where we hold our annual ceremonies.' He turned to the right and the giant *aikidoka* at the entrance grabbed the silvery handle and opened the large door, the resisting weight of the wood bulging his muscles.

It was dark inside and Yves clapped his hands twice. The place illuminating in response to the sound, hundreds of spotlights embedded in the walls shining all at once.

It was a huge hall, with space to hold at least 2000 spectators, designed as a semi-amphitheatre and, like the Coliseum in Rome, was high and circular. The centre stage, which was down beneath them, had enough room to accommodate an army of performers. A large part of the stage was taken up by a complex of levers, bridges, shifting platforms and ropes. Master Yves watched Jerome's eyes widen at the sight of the giant device.

'You are looking at the equipment Master Jacques used for his stunt,' he whispered in a sticky voice, almost seductively. 'It's the machine that forced him to greatness.'

'What do you mean by that, *Sensei*?' Jerome mumbled, his eyes on the stage.

'Let me show you.' Yves patted his back, eyes shining, as he led their way down to the arena. He walked to the edge of the stage and stopped in front of a tall ladder. 'This is where the stunt begins, an obstacle course from the word go. The ladder is the first hazard of the stunt, designed to collapse and disappear, leaving the performer on top with no way to turn back.'

He pointed upwards with his arm. 'Once the top platform is trodden upon, it triggers a small explosive device beneath. This explodes and drops the platform one minute later. Jacques forced himself to perform; doomed to choose between death by shame or death by trying to carry out the stunt.'

'Why would he do a thing like that, *Sensei*?' Jerome asked, his face twisted in confusion. 'Why would anybody drive himself to such extreme risk?'

'He had no choice; he was driven by his love and ambition. The woman he loved was in need of expensive medical attention and he was trying to raise money by executing this stunt.'

'But why would he risk himself so much? What was the point in raising all these extra obstacles?'

Yves leaned back on the ladder and sighed, his face lit with a sort of romantic air. 'Master Jacques needed money quickly as the chances of survival for his beloved Marie were diminishing significantly by the passing minutes. In his desperation he designed a stunt so daring that the promise of substantial payment on its completion was absolute.

'But there was one obstacle, a major impediment in his ability to perform the *Skill*. It was his receding detachment, a force paramount for performing the stunt.'

Yves stopped talking, his eyes focused on a far away place. 'Master Jacques practised this stunt daily, suspended by cables and aided by his loyal assistant Alan. He was not going to make the stunt without the cables, but he was obligated just the same, knowing that the insurance company would give Marie enough money in the event of his death. He didn't think he would make it, but rather thought of it as a *Kamikaze* mission, crashing to death in the name of eternal love.'

'So how come he managed to do it in the end, *Sensei*?'

'Who knows? Some say that it was the risk that gave the conclusive ingredient, while others advocate that the love the master had for his wife was the cause of his development. There are so many ways to look at it but I prefer the romantic version of the story.'

Both boys appreciated the story and remained silent all through lunch. Jerome wondered about the version that Yves had told them, as always not trusting the words of the master. He suspected that there was something important that the *sensei* was leaving out. He didn't know how right he was ...

35 The Stunt

Paris, France, May 2016

'Jacques! Jacques!' the crowds chanted frantically, surrounding the space around the Eiffel Tower, waiting for him to begin. He was nervous enough as it was, did not want any further distraction, although he already had a crisis on his hands.

'Alan!' he called angrily for his assistant, his cries muffled by the crowds. 'Where the hell are you?' He was in a tent used as a dressing room, and he needed Alan there now as the show was about to commence.

He wondered whether Alan would come at all, remembering the way the concerned assistant had pleaded with him not to carry out the stunt.

'It is madness, Master, impossible to perform! I beg of you, *Sensei*, please don't do it, you are going to get yourself killed!' Alan was shouting passionately at Jacques, tears blurring his sight and obscuring his words. Alan loved and worshipped Jacques beyond reason and doubt and would never bring himself to confront the *sensei* on any issue at all yet for the past few weeks he had stressfully watched Jacques' determination and devotion pushing him to the ultimate risk. Jacques remembered how he tried to pacify the highly emotional Alan and how he was enraged when his student became overly personal and accused Jacques of performing out of pride. The anger forced the truth out of Jacques.

'I am not doing it out of vanity!' he bellowed at Alan, for the first time in years raising his voice at the delicate assistant. 'I am doing it for Marie.'

'How can you say that you are doing it for Marie if all that will happen for sure is your death? The sponsors would never pay any compensation. No one would benefit from it. Please, *Sensei*, call it off!'

Jacques had just finished another unsuccessful attempt at the stunt, the cables yet again saving him from a sure crash. He unhooked himself and walked towards his student, nostrils flaring like a raging bull. Alan cowed back, holding his breath, burned by the flames he saw in the *sensei's* eyes.

'I will tell you a secret now,' Jacques held Alan by the shirt, 'and I want you to keep it that way, at least until tomorrow.'

And he unfolded his plans to Alan, of how he had designed the perfect scheme to ensure the money needed for Marie's operation, building an impossible stunt and convincing people that he could carry it through.

Under normal circumstances he would have been mocked as a mad man for devising such a stunt but he had gone about it very cleverly, demonstrating some of his new abilities, those he could produce by his weakening *Su*, to the hordes of rich and enthusiastic spectators. He had sponsors and a thickly paid life insurance and was pleased that he had been able to fool them all. All except Alan who was there when Jacques was preparing for the exploit and saw how far Jacques' skills were from what was required by the stunt. He had confessed to Alan yesterday that it was all about insurance money and that he didn't think he was going to make it! The words had released some of the pressure the secret held in his chest yet now he wished he had never said a word to Alan, now he only wished Alan was there.

One of the runners from the production office burst into the tent.

'Monsieur Jacques, everything is ready for you. The crowds, the TV networks, we can't wait any longer.' The young girl looked stressed and Jacques knew that she was under the thumb of the producers. He smiled softly at her, trying to relax her anxiety.

'I will be there in one minute,' he promised and excused her, hastily getting dressed. He would have to go through this alone; Alan had probably decided to stay away.

Jacques walked out of the tent, lifting the flapping doors, exploding into the unusually chill air of May and the commotion of the crowds.

'Jacques! Jacques!' they chanted loudly, thousands of them, the level of energy intoxicating. He looked at the TV cameras, knowing that Marie would be watching him perform and his heart pained him more than ever. She would have to watch him die on live TV and the thought was tearing at him from the inside. Jacques walked towards the catch ladder, ignoring the commentator who was describing in gory detail what would happen to Jacques should anything go wrong.

'My poor wife, please try and understand!' he pleaded and his eyes drifted to the ground. He knew Marie would never forgive him for what he was about to do yet he felt compelled to do it – saving her life was the only important thing in his. Jacques cursed at the needed detachment that was almost gone, touching his lower abdomen in despair. The stunt followed the options that the Strings presented yet he couldn't perform without possessing the *Skill* to its fullest and most effective implementation.

His lips curled down, moving the attention away from the eyes, holding back the tears. He inhaled against the tightness in his chest, clenching his teeth, wanting so badly to hold Marie in his arms just one last time; her image vividly accompanying his every move. Looking at the cameras and the crowds he managed to compose himself, stretching his back and his chin held high, looking smart and graceful one more time, smiling bravely towards what would probably be his very last show.

At the edge of the clearing, a car stopped and Alan jumped out, exchanging a few words with the woman in the back seat before rushing towards Jacques. He could see the big screens showing his *sensei* approaching the device of doom and he hastened his steps. Alan was bearing a message for Jacques and he needed to get it to him quickly, before he began the stunt.

He forced his way through the crowds, apologising as he pushed at them, sometimes with considerable brutal force. His eyes were focused on the ladder that would carry Jacques to the starting point of his stunt, to his certain death, and he listened to the commentator as he described Jacques' every move. Alan was breathing heavily, partly due to the physical exertion but mostly because of the emotional havoc that was cutting at his soul. He felt like a traitor, abandoning his master in his last precious moments of life and he swallowed hard, thinking of the news he bore for Jacques, should he reach him in time.

'Tell him that I died. Are you listening to me? Look at me when I am talking to you!' He heard the words as they scratched inside his head and he grimaced and looked down at his wrist and the marks that the fingernails had left on the delicate skin, a reminder of the conversation he'd just had.

'Ladies and gentlemen, please give a loud round of applause as we turn the stunt machine on,' the commentator called and the crowds went frantic. A giant screech of metallic hinges sounded as the device began to move and rotate. It was complex, bizarre and highly dangerous. Turning wheels, rolling pins, shifting platforms and much more.

Alan finally got to the inner fenced circle, surrounding and securing the space around the stunt machine. One of the security guards recognised him and allowed him in, and the man ran as if his life depended on it, towards Jacques who was at the bottom of the ladder, one hand reaching out.

'Stop!' Alan shouted as he ran. 'Stop, please!' Jacques couldn't hear him yet the unexpected sight of a man running beside the machine momentarily silenced the crowds and Jacques stopped in his tracks, his concentration broken. Alan approached and Jacques exhaled in relief, glad to see a familiar face in this sea of strangers. Alan reached and grabbed at Jacques' forearm, balancing himself on his mentor, shaken and short of breath.

'I'm glad you are here.' Jacques patted Alan softly, trying to cheer him up with a sad smile. 'Come, my friend, stay dignified. It is my last stance on earth, share it with me!' He was very dramatic.

'Something has happened, Jacques, something terrible!'

Jacques went limp, dreading what Alan was about to say. Never before in the ten years that he had known Alan had his student ever referred to him by his first name; it had to be serious.

'What is it?' he trembled, his back leaning against the ladder, the stunt almost forgotten. He could read the signs of disaster on the face of Alan, but he refused to analyse its cause.

'You don't need to do this stunt, you really don't.' Alan started with the same old argument but Jacques cut him short.

'I don't have time for it right now; I know what I am doing. Why can't you accept my decision, my friend?'

'*Sensei*, I beg of you,' Alan whispered, standing tight with Jacques. 'It's Marie ... I mean, you don't need to do it any more, really.' He was speaking through a coarse throat, as if it were a levy to stop the tears.

'What is with Marie?' Jacques asked and grabbed the catch ladder firmly; his fingers shining bony white from the tight grip.

The two were consumed by the conversation, disregarding the anxious crowds.

'Marie, she didn't make the routine treatment, something went wrong with the transfusion, I'm sorry ...'

It all became muffled around Jacques for a minute, the voice coming through a thick foamy cloud. He sensed the detachment unexpectedly trying to creep in and ironically he fought it off. Detachment was the recognition of his loss, allowing the emptiness to replace Marie, who had occupied his core for so long.

'I am going up there,' he finally said and turned to the ladder, composing himself for the climb.

The crowds were becoming really impatient now and the cheers were accompanied by a few nasty cries. Jacques placed a foot on the ladder and Alan jumped to stop him, clinging on to his padded suit.

'You don't need to do it now, please, there is no point. Marie herself asked me to beg of you not to do it – it was her last wish!'

Tears flowed down Jacques' cheeks and into his throat. He bit his bottom lip bloody and signalled for the security staff to approach.

He had spent the whole day preparing for the stunt while Alan took Marie for her weekly blood transfusion, a routine she had followed for months. Now Jacques understood Alan's delay and the horror struck him full on. Still he fought the detachment from entering, keeping his goals and Marie vivid more than ever inside. He turned to the ladder and started climbing, ignoring Alan's clinging grip.

'Don't, please ...' Alan continued to plead but security staff dragged him away, and in a few steps his cries mingled with those of the crowd, turning anonymous. There were a few things he said that Jacques might have liked to hear, but history chose otherwise.

Jacques heaved himself up the ladder instead, a hostage to his own dark thoughts. Limply and uncoordinated he climbed, fighting the urge to let the inner drive materialise. The steps of the ladder broke beneath him, leaving no chance of escape from the fall. The crowds responded with renewed enthusiastic calls.

'Master Jacques! Master Jacques!'

Jacques would have normally enjoyed their reaction, an entertainer deep at heart, but now he saw and heard none of them as there was only gloom left in his heart. He was a man who had lived in a dream, staring away from the harshness of life until life hit him straight in the face.

The pulsation inside him was impossible to ignore, like a drum that was begging to be played, yet he fought that sensation, wanting to hold Marie in her sacred place if only for a few seconds more. The more he thought about her, the further she was removed from his core and the raw detachment seeped through the gaps of her absence, soothingly replacing the throbbing pain.

Further he climbed and by the time he reached the starting point he could barely stand. Scared, nervous cries came from the crowds and the commentators were speculating whether medical intervention was required. It was dead silent otherwise; everyone held their breath, watching what appeared to be a terrified performer! Jacques himself was no longer there, but transferred to another world, the one that crossed dimensions. The detonator was about to explode beneath the platform and there was now serious concern for his well-being.

Jacques stood on the platform unprotected by the cables that had given him the extra push. Without those cables he had never been able to accomplish even the very first jump. Swaying, he was finally subdued by the primal calling of the Strings and the device that he had built was no longer an alien machine but a fine and dynamic form, harnessing together energy and matter in collaboration, like everything else in the universe.

He saw the unity of all that was around him and could sense the complexity of the Strings, their varying colours and resonance. *What a bloody waste of lives!* He thought bitterly as a window of opportunity appeared before him and he took it blindly, falling to the screams of the terrified viewers. He heard them not, sheltered in a longed for world and comforted beyond any measure that human resources could offer, not tackling the grief but rather using it.

36 The Rehearsal

JEROME CLUMSILY went through Jacques' stunt, the cables twisting into knots from the word go. Yves shook his head in annoyance, his left palm on his hip.

'Do it again from the beginning,' he bellowed and turned to face Max, who sat on the floor quietly, watching the two. 'Get up,' Yves growled at him. 'We have a demonstration to perform and you are not doing well enough to have a breather!' He circled the student and then launched forward, with a couple of quick blows hitting the target and echoing the hall with Max's cry of pain.

'You bastard!' Jerome cursed quietly from above, pulling and balancing himself on the first platform. It was difficult to concentrate on the stunt while his friend was being battered down below, the sounds of the battling strikes rumbling in Jerome's ears, distracting him from his goal. Yves and Max rehearsed their demonstration of the fight, the *uke* faithfully connecting with the *sensei's* every move, yet Yves was bullying Max shamelessly, striking painfully at his body with numerous surprise attacks and blaming Max for every blow.

'You should have seen it coming!'

'But *Sensei*, we never worked on thi—'

'Quiet, get up!'

Yves had a *jo* in his hands, the short staff, and he faced Max who held a *naginata*, long and sharp at its cutting edge.

'Are you ready?' Yves asked impatiently, watching Max rubbing his bruised rib, where the *jo* had recently struck. The youth nodded with a fixed expression, squinting his eyes. He moved in, hacking the *naginata* left and right, swift and strong, passionate with every blow.

Yves backed away, dodging the blows and waiting for his chance to enter. A window of opportunity opened in front of him and he expanded out, fizzing to the right and hitting Max's ribs with the rounded tip of the *jo*. A scream came from above and Yves motioned with his hand for Max to stop attacking, his eyes on Jerome once more, who was tangled up with the cables.

'What the hell are you doing? I told you not to think of the cables, to try and ignore their presence. I know that you can't do the stunt without them and that you are frustrated by that fact, but I don't care! Pretend that you can do it; it's the only way to get a reaction from the cables.'

'But I can't do it,' Jerome started to protest.

'Pretend,' Yves demanded and dropped the *jo*, climbing up the ladder to stand next to Jerome on the platform. He waited with a look of detestation until Jerome managed to tidy all the tangles of the cables and then he leaped out, demonstrating to Jerome yet again. It was the third time that he had done so but it still struck Jerome with wonder and awe. He watched the *sensei's* movements in the world of the *Su* and understood the logic; it was beautiful and poetic, the interaction with the *Skill* vivid and complete.

Yves explained while performing, as if exerting the most usual of tasks. 'You have to use full momentum on the first leap, extending all the way to the floating platform. Then you must collect into unity or risk being squashed by the "Twisting Rolls" in mid air. You can't survive this part if you are humanly shaped on impact.'

His body moved gracefully, the boys following his flight open mouthed, watching Yves' body cutting the air, changing angles and direction, using hidden levers and powers. The *Ki* played the song of the *Kotodama* on the human Strings, the *sensei's* movements a tangible mixture of sounds and sights.

The final moves Yves completed without a word. It was a succession of somersaults that gathered momentum towards the dais that marked the ending, far too advanced for Jerome to clutch at the moment. Yves waited as the pressure sensor switched on the engine that lowered the dais to the ground. He twisted his face at Max who was still staring at him, motioning to them both to resume training.

'These demonstrations are the pride of our school and I don't expect less than everything from you.' The admonishment was exchanged by blows that soon followed, shaking Max from his hazy stare.

* * *

A week before the demonstration Jerome was in the office trying to protest.

'It is impossible to perform, *Sensei*,' he reasoned, standing on the other side of Yves' desk, his face bright red. The *sensei* watched him, amused, his fingers interlocked on his muscular belly, taking his time before answering the heated youth.

'It has to be possible, don't you see, for the sake of Max if not for anyone else.'

'But I can't do it, you saw that I can't.'

'You will have to try harder; it is your task for the demonstration, it can't be changed!'

Jerome armpits were damp, sweat trickling down his sides, the words pounding on the *sensei's* wall of indifference and then bouncing off again. Yves was not really listening to what he had to say; from the *sensei's* point of view it was going according to plan and he was pleased if anything.

'You are to perform even if it's the last thing you ever do. You have no choice or say in the matter, so get on with it!' He stood up and gestured with his hand at the door, quietly waiting until the door closed behind Jerome's back.

Jerome walked down the stairs with his shoulders hunched, feeling small and defeated. He passed by Max who sat in the study, reading one of the books.

'Hey, J,' Max called and lifted his head up, a smile of satisfaction across his face. Jerome just gave him a quick look and continued to the bedroom, not wanting to converse.

'Wait up J,' Max demanded and Jerome reluctantly stopped and turned. 'Did you see me in action today?' he demanded, 'Wasn't it just awesome the way we looked?' Max was living under the strange impression that he and Yves had some bond between them – seeing that he was practising with the master on a daily basis. He was right, however, in describing them as an awesome sight. While Jerome's attempts were diminishing by the day, receding with the lost detachment, Max was improving to perfection, eagerly practising with Yves, his *uke* capacity allowing the master to look good and sharp. An *uke* is like the support musician, complementing the solo artist; the greater the back-up musician's knowledge and abilities the more options there are for the solo artist to perform.

Jerome couldn't share Max's enthusiasm but he managed to produce a little smile. 'You are a great *uke*,' he admitted.

'Thank you very much, sir,' Max said and jumped to his feet. 'Even the Grand Master Yves highly praised my efforts.' And he gave a little bow and chuckled.

'I'm sure he did but I wouldn't trust the man if I were you.'

The smile was wiped off Max's face and the old suspicious look was back in his eyes. 'Did he tell you anything up there? What's going on?' *Stupid idiot!* Jerome cursed at himself. *Why did I open my mouth at all?*

'Nothing unusual,' he said. 'I simply complained about the stunt and he listened. Say, what were you reading about?'

'Nothing unusual,' Max rebounded the same empty response and defiantly walked to the bathroom. Jerome was relieved; he didn't want to talk any more. He lay in bed and closed his eyes, trying to fall asleep.

'Don't let them kill me, J,' he heard Max mumbling from his bed. 'Get him if they do. Get him.' His words were passionate but there was little energy of resistance left – Yves cruelty was especially hard on the human spirit. 'Get him! You get him for me!' Max kept whispering through his clenched teeth, the words echoing in Jerome's head, hypnotising him and, like a mantra, sending him to sleep.

* * *

The Informer was on top of the Aikilibrium school, leaning against a wall in wait, watching the training. The roof was wide and mostly enclosed, creating open pathways that crisscrossed over the training halls. Between the paths there were large windows that gave a comprehensive view of what was going on below. The windows however, allowed only one-way viewing and for those who trained in the halls the ceiling looked like any other, keeping the observer concealed.

The Informer was waiting for the courier, waiting for the package he had mailed to himself weeks ago in Zurich. The timing was right as everyone was preoccupied with the demonstration; he could see them running around beneath. Sighing, he shifted his gaze to Jacques' stunt device, watching Jerome struggling and tangling with the cables, smiling as he heard Yves shouting at the unsuccessful youth.

You must be well frustrated by now, the Informer thought and chuckled, knowing how close Jerome was to success, so close but yet unaware of it. The *Skill* was a positive application of cruelty and part of its implementation tools were the frustration and the desperation of the student.

Yves scolded Jerome again and it sent the Informer giggling quietly. *Yves, you mean old bastard!* It was meaningless to try and talk people into performing the *Skill*, it wasn't something voluntarily done. Yves scolded Jerome just for the sake of anxiety because anxiety was what was needed most. 'Positive malice is a blessing, it's a teacher.' Yves always used to say. The Informer wondered if any long-term effects on the soul were left by the training, seeing that all the *Skilled* people he knew were a bit eccentric.

He was so consumed by his thoughts that the sound of the car approaching below surprised him. 'Shit!' Grimacing, he took his eyes away from the training, launching a rehearsed descent by way of the emergency staircase railing. He had to be quick and secretive going down the complex, to avoid anyone seeing him at it. 'Just on time, perfect!' A car stopped next to him in the side alley, engine turning off quietly. Informer approached quickly, opened the backseat door and jumped inside.

'Drive a couple of blocks away,' he ordered and sat back, keeping his face in the shadows. He had about an hour to follow his plan without anyone noticing his absence, and he had to be systematic, there was no room for mistakes. 'Hand me over the package!' he ordered impatiently as soon as they were far enough away. The driver snorted a laugh and passed the parcel to the Informer.

'Thanks,' he said and looked inside the large envelope, making sure that it was the real thing.

'Where to?' the driver asked a few seconds later. He was eager to drop the envelope and the passenger as soon as he could.

'Drive another block and stop the car.'

The Informer was looking out the window, consuming information with his eyes. He knew the area well enough but there were always details that changed locations and character, like the parked cars and the homeless people, he took a mental note of all. The driver pulled in to an industrial area, sheltered from the scrutiny of any of the passers-by.

'Here is good,' the Informer called and waited till the car stopped and the engine turned off.

'Monsieur Yves,' the driver started, 'I believe that everything is to your satisfaction.'

'Of course it is; thank you so much.' The Informer had his eyes on the parcel. 'Oh, em ... how many people know about our meeting?' he asked casually, not looking at the driver.

'The usual amount of people; the operator at the centre and the driver, that's me. Your man organised the deal and he is the third party to know.' The driver looked in the car mirror, his forehead wrinkled by a worrying thought. The passenger was asking too many questions, the kind he was supposed to know the answers to. The driver had seen the files at the operation centre and knew this wasn't the first time Yves had used their services. The driver squinted in the car mirror, thinking that the Informer looked way too young to be a master. The frown was gone after a quick consideration. *Curse them all!* he thought. *As if I care ...*

There was a long pause while the driver gaped at the Informer and then his eyes widened in a start, realising that the latter was staring back at him. The Informer smiled broadly into the car mirror and for a moment the driver relaxed, the innocence of the young person pacifying. Then he saw the eyes and fear and panic replaced the comfort. Hastily he reached for his hand gun, experience directing him to protect. He'd read the situation correctly but he was too late. The Informer was a *Skilled aikidoka* and a skilled killer as well. A nail appeared in his palm, sharp, wide and 20 centimetres long. The rounded end was hidden in the Informer's palm and he drove the sharp tip, quick as a flash, into the back of the driver's head, just underneath the skull and at an upward angle, in the direction of the forehead. The power and resolve were frightening and so was the expression on the Informer's face.

'Oh, can you feel me inside,' he coldly whispered to the driver, his eyes wide open, shining madly. He had pierced his way through flesh and brain matter, pulled the nail out and then punctured a second hole. It hit straight to the primal brain and the driver went limp, vital coordination of essential organs disrupted, sinking into a coma, death inevitable.

The Informer smiled, proudly scanning the clean kill and the minimum mess. Then his eyes looked up into the mirror and he winked at his reflection, satisfied, brushing his hair. 'Looking good,' he complimented himself then got out of the car, carefully removing any evidence of his presence. *Burn baby, burn* he thought and lit a match, setting the car ablaze before hurrying back to the school.

He didn't want anyone to see him, keeping himself well in the shadows. The package was his and there were three more days to the demonstration, three more days in which to complete his plan; it was more than perfect! He was back on the roof in ten minutes, back to the shadows of his conspiracies.

* * *

The day before the demonstration was as tense as ever, the boys practising their daily routine, their usual flow disrupted only in the afternoon, when the hall filled with the rest of the performers. The early hours of the morning were dedicated to a freezing *Misogi* session followed by the *Chinkon Kishin* rituals.

'Bloody cold!' Max whined before entering the water.
'You always complain about that.'
'Because it's cold.'
Yet he came out of the water clean and tuned.
'Come on boys, hurry up,' Yves called and walked out of the

meditation hall, hardly giving them time to dry off, leading the way to the Plain *Dojo*. They entered and practised basic Aikido for an hour, the martial art aspect that connects the individual to the world of the Strings.

'Nice one!' Max complimented Jerome on a *Kotegayshi* throw, considering himself an expert since he had begun practising with Yves.

'*Yame!*' the *sensei* called at the end of the practice and they bowed and left the *dojo*, struggling to keep up with Yves. They arrived at the demonstration hall, took a couple of sips of water and Jerome was ordered to sit and watch.

Yves faced Max. They bowed to each other and circled around, the *sensei* indicating the desired attack before entering in a powerful collision. He turned and connected with Max, controlling his balance, holding his wrist and throwing him down to the ground. Max changed the attacks by the commands, striking and falling, getting up and striking again.

The same pattern continued until Yves signalled gracefully with his palm. Max stopped attacking, bowed and quickly ran off the mats, returning with the weapons. It was difficult for Jerome to observe, Yves' blades coming way too close and too often to Max's throat. He swallowed hard, unconsciously reaching out and rubbing his own neck. His grimacing expressions did not escape the ever-watchful eyes of the *sensei*.

'Nothing will happen to Max because of his performance or mine. It is your performance that counts! Your friend's life is worthless without the success of the stunt.' He was standing close to Jerome, venomously whispering in his ear, waiting for Max to catch his breath. Max was ready and Yves cleared his throat, his attention back on the *uke*; smiling and diverting a couple of blows, winking at Jerome while resuming the threatening strikes of his blades.

'*Yame!*' Yves finally called and Jerome exhaled but only in semi relief; it was his turn to practise. He climbed up and went through the stunt surprisingly well, finally getting the hang of the timing and the flow, completing it to satisfaction but with the help of the cables. He knew that it would take a miracle tomorrow to perform properly without them but he had no choice.

In the afternoon the demonstration hall started to fill with entertainers and Yves had two giant *aikidoka* looking after the boys while he went around checking and rechecking that everything was ready for the show. Jerome noticed that Yves was taking part in a few demonstrations during the show, although his main presentation was with Max.

'Relax, J,' Max called, pulling in front of Jerome who was about to climb up the pole. 'You won't be improving anything that you didn't improve in the past few weeks; have a look around instead.' He rested his arm on Jerome's shoulder and motioned with his head towards their guards. The two *aikidoka* were concerned with keeping the boys in their places rather than actively schooling them, watching the preparations as well, casually checking on the boys from time to time.

'See, no one cares what we do now!' Max winked at Jerome who nodded to confirm. They could take their time, pretend to be busy but mainly look around and enjoy. The Aikilibrium demonstration wasn't limited to martial arts applications, encompassing a wide and colourful display of human abilities.

The show was popular, one of the only places in the world where the *Skill* could be viewed openly by the public. It drew performers from a variety of *Skills*, those who were vain enough to put themselves on display and those who were forced to do so by their masters. The hall was full of practising talents, acrobatic performers of Aikilibrium accompanied by music and light effects, female contortionists that bent and twisted themselves on the floor and the list went on.

'Look at that!' Jerome exclaimed, pointing to a group of *Skilled* dancers and singers that coloured and echoed the hall with sounds and images. Plenty of effort was made to bring every segment of the show to perfection, although the diversity of the *Skill* by itself was guarantee for success.

The boys sat quietly for a while and watched the acts, forgetting all about their own practice and displays. At a certain point Yves stopped the commotion and rehearsed the order of the demonstrations. Apparently all the performers knew their designated time slots beforehand, well prepared for the demonstration months in advance.

'Maybe His Grace will let us know when our turn to perform is,' Jerome whispered bitterly, Max chuckling in return. The boys, so it seemed, were the only ones to learn of their timing on the last day. It was insignificant information, as it turned out, since Yves and Max's martial art exhibition was near the end of the show, commencing right before Jerome was to perform the stunt, the act that traditionally closed the evening.

Yves approached the two and they rehearsed one last time, giving their best to the satisfied nods of the *sensei*. He bowed and released them from training. They were allowed to stay and watch.

A group of Greek *Kotodama* singers harmoniously coloured the atmosphere with their words, their voices serving as paint brushes, drawing lucid images of the spring.

'Do you see it too?' Jerome asked, enthralled by nature and the rejuvenation of spring. Max twisted his nose in annoyance, his palms on his ears.

'Don't like flowers,' he muttered.

Without the *Skill* it was hard to realise the mechanism with which the singers preformed and that fact was frustrating for some of the non-*Skilled*, who saw and felt it happening but could never grasp it from within.

Evening came surprisingly quickly, before they'd had time to reflect on the distress of the upcoming day. The gloomy mood, however, hit Jerome as soon as they arrived at their living quarters and he found it hard to sit, pacing up and down the room.

'What's up, J? Why are you looking so disturbed?' Max found himself having to repeat the question twice more. 'Hey, I'm speaking to you!'

'Forgive me.' Jerome smiled sadly. 'I couldn't hear you before. I'm very nervous about tomorrow.'

'I'm sure you can do the stunt,' Max tried to calm him. 'I have faith in you.'

'That's very kind of you, but I can't really perform the stunt without the cables. You saw it yourself.'

Max frowned and tilted his head to the right. 'I don't suppose Yves would let you get on with the stunt if he didn't think you are capable of performing it. Think of all the people that will be there watching. He has his reputation to consider; I can't imagine him risking something like that.'

There it was again, Max's blind trust in Yves, so foolishly based on the easiness with which the *sensei* treated him. *He treats you well because he needs your trust and loyalty for the demonstration, stupid!* Jerome thought angrily. *Yves' only interest is to look powerful and impressive.*

'You might be right about that,' Jerome said after a moment of silence, staring at his feet, not wanting to contradict or have a fight with the only friend he had. He considered the next day as his last on earth; there was no chance in hell of completing the stunt alive as far as he was concerned. 'Just do me a favour tomorrow and stay within my view the whole time, I want to make sure that we are both well.'

Max pulled on his shoulders and sighed, 'Whatever, J. You are such a paranoid creature.'

'Thanks man.'

'No problem, J.' They went to bed after that but Jerome found it hard to fall asleep. There was much to meditate on that night.

37 The Demonstration

MORNING BROUGHT a miserable blend of thoughts about the previous night. Jerome never really got any sleep, drifting between one tormented thought and another, tossing and turning in his bed the whole night long. He got up and ran straight to the shower, washing his face and looking in the mirror, his eyes piercing through his reflected image. Since the incident with George he would confront himself on a daily basis, looking deep into his own soul.

'I guess you are there to stay.' He smiled sadly, realising Max was still preoccupying his core. 'We are both doomed but I promise to give it my best try!'

It was a confusing contradiction, trying to save Max by using the *Skill* and detachment while that very thought of salvation was what pushed away the detachment and all hope for such a display. Max was at his centre, more strongly bound than ever before, and there was nothing he could do about it.

When he went back to the room Max was already up and dressed.

'No shower?' Jerome asked with a smile, trying to conceal his worries.

'No time for that, J, I'm too excited about the demonstration to be bothered with that.'

'Smelly!' Jerome teased and got dressed.

The demonstration was to begin at twelve noon yet the two had been pacing their living quarters impatiently since seven o'clock in the morning, looking at the door. At 8.30 the door finally opened and the two giant *aikidoka* escorted them without a word to the meditation hall, to start with the daily routines.

'I can't believe they expect us to go through all the usual stuff today,' complained Max, but his only choice was to comply.

They finished at 11.30 and after a short lunch break were taken to the artists' chamber located at the foot of the stage, where they were ordered to sit and wait their turn.

'It's going to be a long day,' Max impatiently complained.

'I think so too,' Jerome nodded and Max exhaled through his tightly squeezed lips, his cheeks inflating like a trumpet player; they had a good few hours to spend there.

The hall started to fill up at a quarter to twelve but the show was postponed a few minutes, until all the VIP spectators were seated. Yves stood at the nearest point to the stage doors, waiting to be called by the announcer to the centre of the platform to address the eager crowds.

The *sensei's* face was tensely stretched and lined; the news he had received today being more than alarming. The parcel with the lost book was supposed to be at the school by now; he had phoned and checked with the delivery centre and they'd promised him that the package was on its way. It wasn't easy to retrieve information from the centre, their secretive distribution system making it hard, even for them, to come up with a quick answer. He wanted to confront the Informer who had arranged the delivery, to see what he had to say in his defence, but he had no time for it at the moment; it had to wait.

Suddenly the lights in the hall were dimmed and a single beam of light shone straight to the centre of the stage. The crowds stomped with their feet, echoing the hall like a giant engine. Yves composed himself, his face changing to hospitable and friendly, and he stepped into the limelight.

'Yves! Yves!' the crowds chanted and went berserk.

Jerome raised his eyebrows in wonder. 'Idiots! Don't they know who they are cheering for?'

He didn't pay any attention to the speech but rather scanned the hall and the many people sitting around it, taking in the whole set-up. The performers were to come out of the stage doors group by group, finish their act and then leave the stage through another door, across from where they waited. Stairs climbed from the arena to the exits that were lit green, and the ceiling was dotted by hundreds of tiny lights, portraying the night and the stars above. Max tapped annoyingly at his knee and Jerome turned to face him.

'What?'

'Look!' Max pointed excitedly towards the exits with his finger, 'There is no one on the doors and the path is clear, we can take off, no one is looking,' he was whispering in Jerome's ear although he didn't need to, the noise coming from the hall suppressing the option of eavesdropping. Jerome lifted his eyes in hope and then slouched down again.

'Have a look who is standing near the stage door exit! They would never let us out of here freely.' Max peered out to find the two giant *aikidoka* standing tall and firm, one on each side of the door.

'Oh well, perhaps later on, when they won't be paying so much attention.' Jerome smiled at him and shook his head, pushing away hopeful thoughts and concentrating on what was real, of what would soon to come. He looked at Max who was still peering at the hall and bit his bottom lip, holding back from telling him of the sacrifice he was about to perform. He thought about his own life, tried to find some self-pity but only found resolve, and Max …

Time crawled slowly by for Jerome who preferred to keep to the shadows, his face hidden beneath the hooded school-issue sweatshirt, ignoring the spectacular show that played before him.

'Are you OK, J?'

He lifted his head and smiled, his eyes not joining in. 'Yes, bloody wonderful!'

A couple more hours went by and then the announcer called upon the martial art performers. The crowd's reaction was wild, knowing that the most exciting part of the show was about to commence. Drums thundered and wide and colourful beacons of light flashed and rolled through the hall, bouncing off the heads of the spectators, who reacted with further enthusiasm and waved their arms in the air.

The first group of performers was summoned and they rushed out of the stage door, long spears in their hands, somersaulting in synchronisation. Max was told to tidy and ready himself as it was almost time. He rose and started to warm up, sharp eyes blazing with passion and watering with excitement.

'Look after yourself,' Jerome begged, holding Max's sleeve. 'Keep your contact with me at all time and stay away from his blades.'

Max nodded his head but didn't even look at Jerome, his attention fixed on the act, waiting for his cue.

The eight speared warriors went through choreographed fighting forms, working as a unit with each and every stab or blow, to finish the act facing the back of the stage. 'Ladies and Gentlemen,' the speakers cried, 'Master Yves!' Yves came out of the shadows in a blur, rushing into the midst of the speared warriors. They closed in from all sides, the sharp tips almost puncturing the *sensei's* expensive *dogi* and *hakama*.

They circled Yves and he lead them by suggestion, turning his hips according to their moves, his core tempting the sharp edges to enter deeper and deeper into the vacancy of his detachment. In silent cooperation the spears were driven in, like an attack from a sword wielding octopus. 'Oh no,' some cried in the audience, others gasping or shading their eyes in their hands. As quick as a flash Yves extended from the deadly circle, holding one spear in his hand as he materialised away from the assailing group. 'Wow!' the crowd reacted, 'Amazing!' 'Superb!' The sharp points of the spears met at the centre, the metal protesting in a shrieking chink, frustratingly denied any flesh. The unexpected shift shattered the entire group's balance yet they soon regrouped and moved in again. Yves faced and subdued the fighters easily in the attacks that followed, explaining as he fought how to handle an organised band of enemies, and how the *Skill* presented him with the advantage of movement and further possibilities for attack.

The display was near its ending, almost time for Max's act. Jerome stood up and placed his arm warmly on his friend's shoulder. 'Remember what I told you!' he reminded him again and Max, who had just been called to enter the centre stage, turned his head with a jesting smile.

'See you on the other side!' he called, winked and rushed in.

Yves was waiting for him, in his hands the *jo* and Max closed in quickly, the *naginata* high and ready for the chop. Music played in the background, heavy drums shaking the foundations of the hall. Jerome swayed on his feet, holding the pillars of the stage door. He was like Samson among his foes, the muscles of his arms contouring into knots, forehead lined by morbid thoughts of doom.

The first strike was launched at Max's ribs to the exclamation of the crowds. He backed off momentarily and then regained his composure, clenching the *naginata* tightly, eyes narrowing in concentration on the *sensei*. 'Kiraiii!' he cried and chased Yves around the platform, the long reach of the weapon a clear advantage, but only a momentary lead against the presence of the *Skill*.

Yves backed off a couple of steps and then he dropped flat, his legs detaching from the floor, hovering through the air in a spin, the *jo* catching Max on his ankles. Max crashed down and immediately got up, his face contoured in pain.

'Bastard!' Jerome cursed as he watched from the door. His eyes bulging out in a terrified expression, knowing that the technique had not been part of the rehearsal.

'Keep a safe distance away,' he begged and shook his head, Max's slight limp not escaping his wide open eyes.

The *naginata* cut down in succession and the *sensei* judged the distance calmly, using the power of one of the chopping moves to connect with the weapon.

'Unbelievable!' the spectators cried as Yves, the Aikilibrium Master, blurred in the air for a fraction of a second, arching high before landing dramatically on the platform, Max's *naginata* in his hand. Even Jerome couldn't help admiring the timing and the grace of the moves, the power of his anger and worries couldn't shade his awareness of the *Skill*.

Max grimaced and reached over his shoulders, drawing the *jo* that was tied across his back. He got closer to Yves, cautious and a little less enthusiastic than before. Suddenly his eyes were lit on high beam and he charged forwards. 'Kiaiii!' he cried, cutting horizontally at the *sensei's* legs. The legs however, were already gone from the spot, extending sharply away. Max froze, the fine hairs at the back of his neck sending alarming shivers down his spine, realising that Yves had ended up behind him, springing through a window of opportunity that was hard to read.

You are toying with him, you coward! Jerome thought and fought the urge to burst onto the platform. *Max possesses no tool to counter your skilled surprise attacks and you know it!* To fight like Max did, in three-dimensional perspective against the multi-dimensions of the

Skill, was like the foils of a blind man chasing a person running through a crowded place.

The master stood behind Max motionless, allowing his *uke* to realise his inadequacy before hitting him again, on the same spot in the ribs. Max collapsed holding his sides, and Jerome bit his lip until he tasted blood. 'Hold on brother,' he mumbled, the clear pain on Max's face agonising him beyond control.

The spotlight was on the fighters who faced each other with the *jo* held across their middles. Their left hands pulled on the wooden tip of their *jo*, revealing with blinding flickers the sharp daggers that the two now held in their hands.

Jerome knew this was the last act, just before he would have to mount the device and perform. His heart dropped a beat and he swallowed spitless, his throat dry as sand. Yves and Max circled each other, judging the distance for the next move. A window of opportunity opened before the master and he took it, spiralling through the air and slicing at Max's left arm.

The dagger fell to the arena's floor and Max screamed in pain, a red spot appearing beneath his limp arm. He managed to maintain his grip on the *jo* with his right hand, the knuckles shining white both from strain and stress. Jerome was panting, opening and closing his palms, watching the *sensei* dangerously changing the patterns and the rules of conduct.

'Max!' he cried in frustration and tried to move in, his eyes never leaving the stage. The two giant *aikidoka* calmly held him back, easily restraining his intentions. With a scream of desperation Max collected all his might and charged at his mentor, his face white and drained of blood, loyal to the master regardless of the unjust treatment he was receiving. Yves spiralled backwards, allowing Max to close the distance and then his blade cut diagonally at the *uke's* throat. A mighty cry echoed the hall, the spectators reacting ecstatically to the danger, the suggestion of death serving as an adrenalin rush to the head.

The *jo* fell from Max's hand and his gaze turned to the stage door, opening his mouth soundlessly and bewilderedly reaching up to his throat. He flopped to the floor and the stage turned dark, accompanied by a blast from the speakers.

'Max! Max!' Jerome struggled in the arms of the giant *aikidoka*.

Suddenly the light was on again, the stage clean and empty, nothing to suggest what Jerome had witnessed, just a clean wet patch on the floor. The announcer was building up the tension towards the last act of the day and the two *aikidoka* suddenly let go of Jerome and he instinctively rushed in, the hall darkening around him, a beam of light focusing on his every move. Blinded he reached the spot where he had last seen Max, just about to lean and inspect the floor when he heard Yves' voice behind him.

'Come with me, I have to tell you something very important.'

Before he could think of any course of action, the master's hands grasped his shoulders gently, leading him away from the spot, following an illuminated path on the floor. In the background the announcer described the stunt to the excited onlookers and the hall shook with their inflamed roars.

Jerome wanted to pull away from the hands of the *sensei* but he wanted thousands of other things as well; resistance minimised by the disturbing and baffling situation. He sensed a hollow opening at his midst, allowing the detachment to return, but he fought it off with a clenched jaw, hoping that the display he had just witnessed was staged, that it was just another one of Yves' cruel deceptions.

'Where is Max?' he demanded of Yves. 'What have you done to him.' He looked at the *sensei* and the latter avoided his gaze, a distant expression on his face. Yves took his time before answering, continuing to walk until they reached the ladder beneath the stunt device. Yves let go of him.

'There has been an accident; something went very wrong with my demonstration—'

'Is Max OK?' Jerome cut him off with a shout, his voice muffled by the crowds.

'Shhh,' the *sensei* tried to calm him. 'We will talk about it later, after you have finished.'

'No, now!' demanded Jerome, one leg on the first rung of the ladder.

'Start climbing up and I shall tell you all about it, you must complete the stunt! The show must go on.' His voice was intoxicating and Jerome started to comply, climbing a few more steps before turning yet again to the *sensei*.

'Tell me now or I shall never complete the drill and jump straight to my death.' His face was red as burning amber, spit flying like venom with the final words. Yves looked around mystified, listening to the commentator giving irrelevant information, stalling, as everyone was waiting for the stunt to begin.

'Promise me that you will complete the stunt regardless of what you hear me say.'

'I promise,' said Jerome, tears in his eyes.

'I am sorry,' the *sensei* sighed as if pained, 'but Max is dead! He accidentally got too close and cut himself on my blade. There was nothing we could do to save him, although we did try.' He looked up with a grievous expression, eyes trustworthily wide. 'Now please finish what you have started, just as you promised. We will talk again, later on.'

Jerome looked at his mentor, his legs climbing intuitively, a body without thought. Yves' face was swallowed by the smoke effects and the darkening floor, the beam of light concentrating entirely on Jerome. He climbed up, forever the victim, accepting the cruelty of life.

Max is gone, Jerome nodded to himself as he climbed on. *And all these risky efforts were for nothing, nothing! For I've failed to save you, Max.* Eerie loneliness spread from head to toe, from the intellectual recognition of the loss to the emptiness at his core. He climbed another rung and his left knee buckled, as if made of jelly. The crowds reacted, some sighed, others shouted; he was at least 15 metres in the air. There was a stir inside him and he recognised the way the detachment was entering but he did not care any more. There was comfort in this unearthly place and Jerome sought its sheltering warmth, engulfed by its glow when he finally finished the climb and stood limply on the top platform.

The detonator beneath his feet was charged and Jerome had about a minute to move out before the platform would explode and shatter. He did not move yet, overwhelming sensations were spreading from his hub, like tentacles seeking connection with the surroundings.

The space around him was humming with the primal sounds of nature and he was like a semi-god, able to interact with the surroundings in an inspired way. Izanami and Izanagi, the divine creators of the world, were present within him and the resonance of their singing was inflaming the building blocks of creation, changing their shape and character with the vibration. It was a world of flux and opportunity and Jerome sensed the exact course that the stunt would take.

'To hell with everything; nothing is fair!'

Ironically, everything was coming together now that Max was gone, now that there was nothing to live for any more. Guided by instinct rather than thought he was determined to follow the course of the stunt, to fulfil the futile obligation that he had made.

Jerome closed his eyes and dived out, the first jump a true extension of his Strings. For a fraction of a second he lost his human form, long enough to apply the move and short enough so as not to lose his humanity for ever. His foot connected with the first floating platform and his body leaped out on impact.

No thought crossed his mind as to how he had suddenly received an advance in his abilities. It all made sense in its own context, his uncorked inhibition explosive as volcanic energy, surging out of the emptiness at his core. The rolling pins shot to meet him, but he squeezed through the narrow gap that they left, and rolled forward just in time to meet the spinning powers of the shifting platforms. In front of him he could see plenty of opportunities but in this game he could only choose the right ones, couldn't afford a mistake.

He solidified and melted accordingly, alternating the way he interacted with each and every move. To some of the platforms he connected with his feet and to others with his fingers or indeed any other part of his body that was present at the right timing. He travelled between plains and spaces and soon he reached the final stage where his body somersaulted upwards, against gravity and further away from the floor. Then suddenly he landed on the last platform and the stunt was over.

The crowds stood ecstatically on their seats, swinging their arms in the air, shouting and whistling, eager to connect and be a part of the unearthly show. Jerome heard all the commotion as a buzzing sound, the crowds a mere energy wave among the rest of the living world. Tears rolled down his cheeks, the pain pulsating with the detachment. He had accomplished his obligation but there was one more thing left for him to do. Jerome didn't bow or enjoy the throng calling but rather rushed out towards the stage door, looking for Max.

38 Sealing the Process

THE FINAL STAGE in acquiring the *Skill* is a delicate step to appease the turmoil and anxiety that the student has experienced, to bring him back to a normal level of social and psychological functioning.

Most schools used some sort of abuse throughout the studies and needed a pacifying mechanism before irreversible instability occurred. Only the *Kotodama* children from the mountains of Spain were taught differently, without abuse and strain, but they were an exception to the rule.

The time duration between the second shaking of the *Su* and the sealing process was a crucial element at this stage. Master Ueshiba waited a year from the time of his second detachment until his realisation came about and numerous attempts were made, throughout the short history of the *Skill*, by various *dojo* to follow his example. They all failed miserably, resulting in students losing their minds or even worse, committing suicide or crime.

That was the reason why almost all schools tended to seal the process as soon as the second detachment took hold, following Jacques *Sensei's* example. It is also one of the main reasons why Jacques is considered more than a mere *Skilled aikidoka* but rather an explorer and an innovator as well.

* * *

Paris, France, 2016

The platform declined slowly, the movement synchronised with the monotonous calls of the inflamed crowds, but Jacques heard none of it, couldn't, even if he wanted to. He was away, absent from his natural tools of perception. The world around him was that of shadows and sounds where a variety of cosmic applications occurred. He shook on his feet, gagging, nauseated and lost. Someone got hold of his arm and the familiar grip was trustworthy, leading him gently through the hordes. His legs were rubbery, and a few times he almost collapsed, the supporting arm saving him from an embarrassing fall.

The touch and its familiarity broke up some of the connection with the world of the Strings and part of the contemporary perception of humanity returned to Jacques. He could hear words but they sounded as if coming from afar, and for a while he couldn't make out any of their meaning. The sound of these words had a comforting quality and the positive tune didn't fit the situation. It puzzled him further and threw him out of the comforting shelter of the shadows and into the hectic reality around.

Lights were flashing at his eyes and the screams of the crowds were pounding at his ears. His eyes opened a fraction and reality started to sink in. Vaguely he noticed that he could let go of the detachment or move back into it voluntarily, as if it were already a matter of control.

'Ladies and gentlemen, the one and only, Master Jacques!' the announcer maintained the spectator's excitement and security staff had to fight their way to clear a path in front of Jacques. TV cameras monitored his every move, transferring his image to millions of households, an exposition on a global scale. The *Skill* was out in the open and history had been made.

'Come quickly, Master,' he heard Alan whispering behind him, the voice trembling in ecstasy and shame.

'What? Why?' he managed to mumble, not understanding anything, not knowing where he was led.

'So sorry Master, so sorry.' There was guilt in Alan's words and it puzzled Jacques.

What are you so sorry about? Jacques wondered. *You didn't do anything wrong!* He wanted to pacify the student but was confused and frail, couldn't bring himself to speak. There was no fault in the way Alan had behaved as far as Jacques was concerned, he had only been late, that's all, and Marie's illness had nothing to do with him. The thought of Marie brought a new wave of mental anguish and Jacques was tempted to move back into the comforting shadows, away from the human tragedy that was his life. The ring of spectators was finally broken and Jacques was led to a car that had the back door open.

'I am sorry,' he heard Alan saying again and he turned to face his student and trusted ally, his forehead lined with confusion.

Alan was smiling faintly but he didn't say a word, gently helping the master to take his seat, sheltering him from the horde of reporters that wanted to question the hero of the day. Jacques maintained his eyes on Alan as he was lowered down, afraid of the creeping sensations of loss that would engulf him as soon as he was left alone.

'Jacques!' he heard the loving whisper and he froze to the sound, so familiar and loved. His eyes shut closed involuntarily and he refused to believe its truth, dreading that it was only his mind playing cruel tricks on him.

'Jacques,' the voice called again and this time he opened his eyes and turned his head to face the caller, looking through a screen of tears. Marie reached out with her trembling hand, a move that took a great deal of her weak energy. 'I am so sorry,' she said as he clenched her in a hug, her tears mingling with his own.

'Shh … shh …' he calmed her and they savoured the moment quietly, tight as if they were one while the car broke away from the place, on its way home.

Only when they reached home did Marie tell him everything, of how she had forced Alan to lie to him, hoping that it might divert him from ever performing the stunt. They had both played a dangerous game with their well-being but now that it was over they could collect themselves and face a brighter future.

A week later Marie successfully underwent the expensive medical procedure and the couple gained a few more years of life together, this time living happily for a change.

As for the *Skill* and Aikido, Jacques sent a report worldwide about the second shaking of the *Su* and his unexpected success in sealing the process, a report which would help shape the way in which the *Skill* would be processed in the future throughout the world.

In a way he had been far more efficient than Master Ueshiba, the founder of Aikido. O Sensei's sealing process had been mysteriously dragged out for almost a year, something that none could comprehend or make use of. Master Jacques, in contrast, had found a quicker way to realise his dreams, although there was one thing he would never achieve. The *Skill* of Diversity, the most desired craft, remained an impossibility and a thorn in his side for the rest of his life. Neither he nor anyone that followed managed to grasp that ultimate goal.

* * *

Ayabe, Japan, April 1925

Spring was an awesome season in Ayabe, branches covered in young and freshly green leaves while the petals of the cherry trees finally opened, adding their beautiful pink flowers to the rejuvenated scene.

Master Ueshiba stood at the little clearing in front of his house and inhaled deeply, enjoying the fresh breeze that blew at his farming clothes. His eyes didn't miss the whiteness of the challenger's knuckles, clasping the *boken* tightly, ready for the cut. His adversary, a well-respected naval officer, was impatient and eager, waiting all through the morning while Ueshiba prepared himself for the fight.

These were arrangements that he couldn't avoid, necessary for what he believed to be his chance in finalising the personal quest that the great Onisaburo Deguchi had set him upon, to establish a new art. Now all the ingredients were ready and there was only one thing left to do. A challenge, a life-and-death situation, one final exercise in detachment that would hallmark the process permanently.

That morning he had undergone the *Misogi* and *Chinkon Kishin* rituals, cleaning and sterilising his mind and senses. He chanted and rehearsed *Kotodama*, taking each and every step with a careful amount of concentration. There was no room for mistakes as far as he was concerned; detachment, he already realised, was not something to be toyed with or to be taken lightly.

The naval officer was a man of *Kendo*, a martial art that practised sword fighting, and he had quite a reputation within the art. He was angered and insulted by Ueshiba who had made him wait all morning for the challenge and now refused even to raise a sword against him. The officer interpreted these conducts as a cowardly act by Ueshiba and he declined from using the real sword himself, planning instead to beat the coward with the wooden sword. Ueshiba regretted this decision, as he had hoped that the attacks would be more life-threatening, but he didn't want to press the issue, worried that the impatient officer would hamper the concentration necessary for the fight.

Ueshiba motioned with a slight nod that he was ready and the two watched each other for a second before bowing and assuming a fighting stance. Ueshiba's eyes were consuming in their glare, connecting with the mind of the opponent, becoming one with the man who was about to try and strike him to the ground. They walked in a small circle, looking for an opening in defence, not losing their awareness of the environmental factors, knowing that any little detail could change the outcome of the fight.

The officer stopped moving when the sun was at his back, a major advantage under normal circumstances. These were hardly normal circumstances but the naval officer couldn't know that, watching indifferently as Ueshiba took his favourite fighting stance, a 60 degree angle towards the front.

'Blend. Enter. Control.' Ueshiba rehearsed quietly, reciting the essence of his new principles of the fight, further registering its essence into his body and soul. He was connected with the officer and he waited for the first strike, eager for the threat that would inspire the truth from his core.

The *boken* was raised in a *Jodan* stance and the challenger closed some of the distance, knowing all too well where his effectiveness lay. He had heard of Ueshiba before, knew that the man used weaponry in an unorthodox fashion and he wanted to show him the power of the traditional art and its effectiveness.

'*Kiaiii*!' he cried, while cutting down the tip of the *boken*, aiming at Ueshiba's head that was resting proud and erect over the powerful shoulders.

Master Ueshiba almost shivered with delight, sensing how the strike was stimulating the inevitable to happen. He saw a flash of light before the blade came down, as if the sword were whispering its intention and he moved accordingly, gracefully avoiding the strike.

The officer was not daunted by the failure and he composed himself for the next attack, before moving in again. The aim of the next strike was registered long before the *boken* began its diagonal descent and Ueshiba had enough time to avoid it with ease, as if the attack were carried out by an amateur and not a professional fighter such as his antagonist. The tempo was raised and the strikes were crashing down like an avalanche, becoming fiercer and with further murderous intention as the officer kept missing the illusive master.

Ueshiba found his detachment and with each and every turning motion of his body he increased the sensation that radiated from within him and without. He didn't want to strike back at the officer, wishing the man to drain himself of his deadly energy by his own accord. There were numerous opportunities for him to hit back but he kept avoiding until the officer finally started to slow down. There was recognition of defeat and bewilderment on his face but he tried a few more forlorn strikes, hoping they would hit the target and save him a world of embarrassment.

Ueshiba sensed that the deadly intention was declining and he sought a dignified way out for the opponent, wanting to be true to his new principles of non-resistance fighting. He acknowledged the importance people held for their petty pride and its dangers when ignored and he suddenly lifted his hand up, motioning the officer to halt. The man stopped and bowed to the master, his eyes silently exposing the gratitude for the honourable release. He was lucky to leave without harm to body and soul, the usual outcome of such encounters.

Ueshiba waited patiently until the officer went away and then he exhaled loudly, walking behind the house to wash himself in the well. There was a hum in his ears, an electric current that buzzed at his centre, looking for a way out. He felt light-headed and aloft, knowing that he was finally there, solidly connected with the *Su*.

Reaching the well, he hurled the bucket down, his hands shaking slightly as he lifted it filled to the brim. He washed his body ecstatically, enjoying the clear and freezing water as it coated him coolly – it was the purest *Misogi* that he ever experienced. 'Ahhha,' he sighed, 'I am one with all!' The water interacted with the delicate surface of his human form and his mind acknowledged the resonating building blocks of his body, the same building blocks that composed the universe.

He saw the option of *Kotodama* and for the first time it was meaningful and stable; like a master mason he knew exactly how to place and work the bricks of creation. Knowledge was pouring in, rich and consuming, and his body started to glow. *I am finally there*, Ueshiba thought, then chuckled in euphoria, feeling deserving and ready.

He heaved as wave after wave of golden light showered his soul, drowning him in a wave of a spiritual *tsunami*. It was as if he had found the download button and information was flowing freely to his core, file after file of understanding, his body shaking like a leaf. In a matter of seconds he grew as a human being, physically, mentally and spiritually, attaining *Satori* – the ultimate goal, the enlightenment.

When he got off the dusty ground he was smiling as a proud mother would, rewardingly watching her baby taking its first breath of life, a moment's compensation for the painful hours of labour and torment when the baby tore its way out of her womb. Finally Ueshiba could marvel at his own creation and the art of Aikido was born.

39 The Final Act

ON THE VERGE of collapse he pushed his way to the stage doors, oblivious to his surroundings, his mind set to find Max. He walked through the backstage corridor and peered in to each and every door that stood to its sides, looking for his last bond to comfort and sanity but Max was nowhere to be found.

Most of the performers had climbed up a flight of stairs that took them to a seating place in the arena, ready for Yves' speech that would conclude the day. Jerome climbed up and searched among those who sat there but a moment later he was down again, his desperation mounting to insanity. He ran all the way to the end of the corridor and kicked open the only door that was bolted, hoping that his worries would prove faulty, that what he had seen in the demonstration hall was another misconception. It took a tremendous amount of effort to fight off the detachment that wanted to move in, yet for the first time he could somewhat control it and he pushed it away with passion.

The door gave way with a loud noise and he rushed in to find what he was dreading the most. In the overly empty room stood a bed and a little chair with basic medical equipment around it. The bed itself was vacant but the alarming red stains on the sheet drew Jerome's attention. He reasoned it to be blood yet he knew that it could be anybody's blood and after a moment of confusion he searched for further clues, his heart racing in his chest. On first inspection he saw nothing significant and he scanned the room once more until he noticed the fighting staff. He froze! Mouth semi-open, eager to move away and obey the calling of the *Su*.

Slowly he composed himself and walked towards the staff, recognising its shape and unmistaken master. It was the staff Yves used for the demonstration and Jerome ran his fingers across its surface until he reached the tip and drew it out. He looked at the bloodstained blade and immediately started to hyperventilate, the room spinning around. Despair was moving in quickly and the tears were piercing at the corners of his eyes. 'Max,' he whispered with renewed agony, 'Oh no Max.'

It was tempting to let the detachment move in and take all the pain away, to lift him over the petty turmoil of the human soul. He fought it off vigorously, just as he had fought off the sorrow and despair. There was nothing else to use as a drive for his soul and he looked at the bloody blade with renewed interest that frightened him.

Let's end this shit now!

Killing himself was a convenient solution to the problems he had in hand, revenge at the institute that had spent so much time and finance on his training. He knew that it would be a satisfying retaliation against Yves' cruel efforts and he reached out and held the blade firmly, bringing it close to his throat.

Don't let them kill me, J! Max's demanding voice suddenly whispered inside his head and slowed down his determination. *Make them pay for what they did!* It was a demand for an oath to be fulfilled and it refreshed Jerome's sense of purpose, forcing him to focus on a course he was suddenly obliged to take.

I have fulfilled my obligation to my enemy and now comes the time to fulfil what I have promised to a friend.

He moved the blade away from his throat and pushed it back into the staff, hearing it click into position. A new sensation was creeping in, tainting everything in red, like ripples on the surface of a pond spreading with each and every heart beat. He remembered abusive images from the past year and a half, adding new stimulants to his growing rage. Jerome was almost a man now; over seventeen years old and he had no desire left in him to live. His new determination demanded of him to take a life instead, to avenge the death of his friend.

Sure, he ground his teeth, *Yves said that Max's death was a mistake, but it's not reasonable that the master couldn't control his blades. It was intentional and I can't accept that!*

He heard the announcer calling for Yves to take the centre stage and the crowd cheered in return, a fact that made Jerome cringe.

They are all wrong! he thought and composed himself for his final act, knowing that it would probably mean death for himself as well; it was a small price to pay at the moment.

Jerome lifted the staff and started to walk back towards the stage, his grit fusing with the rage. He pulled the hood of the school-issued sweatshirt over his head and covered his face in the shadows; chin tucked against the chest, seeing mostly the ground and the path back to the stage doors. Somebody called him to stop, but he ignored the caller, almost reaching the entrance to the stage. The call for him to stop was accompanied by a firm hand that suddenly grabbed at his shoulder, forcing him to slow down.

He did not stop but swung the *jo* backwards, hearing the unmistakably loud crack as the fingers that held his shoulder were broken and crushed. His shoulder was free, and determined he entered the stage, walking quietly towards the centre where Yves stood and addressed the crowds. Jerome was less than three metres away from the *sensei* when he was finally noticed.

'Not now,' Yves whispered, quietly gesturing with his hand for Jerome to leave.

Never before had the *sensei* been disturbed in the middle of the final speech. Jerome peered at him from beneath the hood and assumed a fighting stance, the *jo* held across his body. Yves eyes narrowed in misunderstanding yet he recognised the intent by the way the staff was held.

A tremor ran through the crowd, the newcomer presenting a change to the pattern they were accustomed to. Yves didn't recognise Jerome although the school-issue sweatshirt was more than familiar. He frowned and looked around for something or someone that he could not find.

'Very well then,' he finally said and took his own fighting stance, knowing that he couldn't back away from the fight in front of all the spectators. No one knew if the man holding the staff was sincere or if it was an out-of-the-blue innovation that Yves was so famous for.

Jerome started to circle the *sensei* just as he had seen Max doing during the demonstration, not as well but with an attitude for the kill that made him far more dangerous than Max had ever been. Yves reacted according to Jerome's movements, facing him and lifting his arms to defend against the armed opponent.

Jerome didn't wait for the master to get ready, charging forward with the *jo* swinging diagonally, forcing Yves to somersault back. The great spotlight followed the fight and the crowds cheered uncontrollably, enjoying the fantastic and unexpected finale!

Jerome stopped swinging and instead stabbed twice with the *jo*, forwards, in the direction of the *sensei's* head. The first stab Yves avoided while the second he used to his advantage. As the tip neared his head he collected inwards and then twirled head first, parallel to the *jo* and spiralling around it. He ended up connecting to Jerome's body with his clenched fists, sending him backwards rounded in pain, his ribs almost fractured by the impact. Jerome lifted up and shook his head, the *jo* stretched in front of him, ready for the next assault.

From the shadows the Informer watched curiously at the action unfolding; in his arms he held the box with the supposed lost book of Ueshiba, his book and no other's. He clutched the old box tightly to his chest, eyes blazing in excitement.

On stage the battle was raging and Jerome, who got up from yet another strike to his body, composed himself and charged at the *sensei*, screaming in passion. Yves lifted in the air, reacting to a window that opened before him. Jerome read the motion too, swinging the staff up, crossing the path that Yves had taken.

It was another trick of diversion and Yves changed direction, knocking the *jo* out of his student's grip, his legs connecting with Jerome's back. He fell face down and the crowds cried out in return, their confidence re-established by witnessing the grace and control in the *sensei's* moves.

Yves waited for Jerome, confidently watching him lifting up and reaching for the *jo*. Jerome couldn't comprehend why the *sensei* didn't remove the *jo* from him as it was his for the taking through most of the attacks. He watched Yves, the master showman, performing to the pleasure of the crowds and his eyes narrowed in disbelief; it seemed as though the *sensei* was not taking him seriously, confidently knowing that his *Skill* was way beyond that of his adversary. If Yves thought that would deter Jerome, he was mistaken, and the boy went back to face him, deadly serious in his intention. Yves turned to meet him, an annoying smile spreading across his face.

'You think you can fight against my abilities, young one?' he asked and Jerome's blood chilled by the remark; it was obvious that the master realised who he was by now, a fact that gave him an extra hold on the boy, a remnant of his past authority. Jerome did not reply but tried his best to keep focused as the *sensei* kept talking, sensing that his words were hitting the right spot.

'So, you are out to get me, to avenge whatever wrongs you may think I have done to you. You are more than welcome to fight me but you are wrong about the whole thing!' His speech was echoed through the speakers for all the audience to hear and they sighed in compassion, supporting the *sensei's* words.

'Tell that to Max,' Jerome replied and charged forward, his answer muffled by the shouting crowds.

There was arrogance in the way Yves stood straight and exposed, his chin held high, his neck stretching long. Jerome, however, only read it as an impression that the *sensei* was trying to impose, an impression to shield over the truth of his fears. He didn't wait to contemplate what was prowling beneath the *sensei's* gestures and attacked instead, cutting the staff sharply down, aiming at Yves's head.

With perfect timing the master was gone from the spot, deceiving Jerome as he shuffled sideways, connecting to the boy's body with a punch from his left while his right pulled the *jo* sharply, and hauled it out of Jerome's grasp. Jerome grimaced from the strike, bending sideways with the impact but he kept his hold on the tip, the blade protruding from his palm.

Yves towered over him with a smile, instinctively nodding to the sounds of the cheering crowds. Jerome's body was twisted from the strike to his side but he used the gap in the *sensei's* attention to untwirl himself upward, cutting brusquely at the exposed neck with the bloodstained blade. The move was too quick to notice, hazing without resistance in an arc.

The hall went deadly silent and for a moment Jerome was sure that he had missed.

Yves remained standing but did not move, suddenly his

expression changed to that of dreadful expectation. The sharp blade had sliced through the soft tissue with such precision that the neck held its alignment, the body frantically trying to fix itself. Then Yves gasped and the delicate structure was broken, blood pouring from the ripped arteries and veins, draining into the *sensei's* sliced windpipe, splattering his *dogi* and the arena floor. Life was leaving the body of the bewildered master, with each effort to draw a breath resulting in further damage to his throat.

The teacher and tormentor struggled to stay composed, his palms clasping the neck until the jets of blood from the severed arteries forced him to collapse. A pool of blood formed around the twitching head of the master and the sickly sweet odorous liquid started to spread, closer and closer to where Jerome stood. Jerome held his face behind the hood, the mad intensity of the eyes hidden from the hordes of spectators.

'Murder!' someone finally screamed, 'The Master is dead!' The loud cry triggered the whole audience to react in panic and disorder.

The *sensei* stopped twitching on the floor and that pulled Jerome away from his fascination, suddenly very aware of the commotion around. He expected to be cut down at any moment by one of Yves' faithful disciples but nothing like that happened. He looked around the hall and saw the panic-driven crowds pushing their way out towards the exits and he recognised among them some who fought the human flow, desperately trying to get to him and the dead or dieing *sensei*.

He calculated his options, saw his chance for salvation and he took it, instinctively reacting to a window of opportunity, a caged animal that had finally found a way out. He mingled with the crowds and their destination, making the efforts of his chasers futile. One minute he was on the inside and on the next he was at the exit doors, the Informer watching satisfied from the shadows as Jerome squeezed his way outside.

The human flood spilled him into the Parisian night and the fresh air of late summer. He stood outside for a second, observing the huge building that had been his jail and torment for the better part of the past two years. Then he spat, turned and ran away, his process disrupted, fused with the shadows of the night.

Epilogue

A NOT SO YOUNG and colourful Onisaburo Deguchi sat one evening after the great war and watched the skies. He was waiting for someone, his body barely moving, only the lips chanting away, composing songs and spelling visions. Deguchi looked tired from long and wild years, his body consumed by diabetes and pain, the only remnant of his famous passion was the hypertension that vigorously thumped at his temples. He coughed and his whole body shook but he soon composed himself.

'Please enter, Morihei,' he called to the sound of the door sliding open behind him. 'Come and sit by me.'

But how did you know it was me? Ueshiba, the famous master of Aikido, was tempted to ask but decided otherwise. 'Thank you Master,' he politely answered and obediently sat down. Ueshiba was the founder of the new martial art of Aikido and his fame was growing fast yet he was still considering himself as a student of the *Omoto Kyo* leader.

They sat and watched the sunset in silence, trying to bridge over time wasted, two victims of the late imperial ruling. During the war Master Deguchi had been choked in jail, charged, and convicted with treason, while Ueshiba, who thinly escaped the jail sentence, was forced to teach how to maim and kill in the notorious school for spies – against his own will and nature.

The colours of the sky intensified, the wind whispering as it gently pushed at the tree tops. The two men watched and listened in concentration, just like they had done so many years ago in Ayabe.

'I have failed you, Master.' Ueshiba at long last spoke, his throat hoarse by the sharpness of the words.

Deguchi reached out with his frail hand and rested it on Ueshiba's shoulder. He didn't look at his ageing student, his eyes fixed on the dieing glow.

'I have failed you, Master,' Ueshiba said again, convinced that the meaning of his words were not detected. 'I thought that I had succeeded in creating what you ordered me to do, but now I know that is not so.' He looked at the *Omoto Kyo* director and spiritual leader, waiting hungrily for his reply.

'Shhh ...' Deguchi quietened Ueshiba, his hand not leaving the powerful shoulder of his previous bodyguard. 'Your efforts, Morihei, were neither a mistake nor a waste of time. You are merely frustrated by the fact that the conclusion to your quest will only manifest itself long into the future, never in your lifetime or mine. Be proud though, your achievements are important stepping stones on the very steep climb for human development.'

Ueshiba drank the words thirstily, accepting their conclusive meaning. He knew from personal experience that Deguchi's powers of foresight were true. After all, his own superhuman abilities were foretold years ago by the great Onisaburo Deguchi himself. Ueshiba eagerly waited for the master to tell him more, trying to capture Deguchi's attention with his eyes.

The sun had almost set, painting the sky in dramatic strokes of pink, yellow and red; offering inspiration to the ever-creative Onisaburo. Ueshiba gave up on connecting with Deguchi's enchanting eyes and he turned his head to face the sunset, polite and not pressing the master, giving him the necessary space. Onisaburo's lips moved silently, following his restless mind that streamed out *waka* after *waka*, within them hidden secrets of things to come.

'You have done your share, Morihei, and now it's time to sit back and let it roll. The world must wait patiently for a time in which the elements are ready and the dragon is reborn.'

Deguchi rose up as if suddenly his former powerful self and stood with his back to Ueshiba, the latter watching him in awe. The old master spread his arms and the wind rushed through his loose garments, helping him to stand, like reinforcement from the universe.

'This is just the beginning, nothing more!' he rumbled and collapsed, straight into the attentively waiting arms of his former student.

They were quiet for a little longer, the crocodile and the dragon, two visionaries of humanity interacting without a word.

When they parted Ueshiba bowed humbly low, tears in his eyes, knowing this would be the last time they would ever meet in life.

Deguchi did not change the direction of his stare, nodding to his student, sitting and watching the now greying skies, a little smile on his face. And as Morihei turned to leave he could swear he saw the lips of the master moving soundlessly and suddenly Morihei could read what Deguchi was saying, the words thundering without a sound.

'It has only just begun,' the lips chanted, passionate eyes staring into the darkening skies – Deguchi, a man engulfed in a storm of vision; forever the prophet.

Glossary

Aiki Healer Skill: One of the many styles of the 'Aiki Skills'. The supernatural abilities of the Aiki Healer allows him or her to connect with their patients through Aiki breathing and 'hands on' therapy. The Aiki Healers can analyse and cure medical conditions by a mere touch, conditions which would otherwise need invasive therapy.

Aiki: Literarily means 'flowing energy'; part of the name of the art of Aikido.

Aikidoka: A practitioner of Aikido.

Aikilibrium: One of the many styles of the 'Aiki Skills', developed by Master Jacques Patye during the twenty-first century.

Baka: Fool.

Boken: A wooden sword.

Budo: 'Bu' literarily means 'Martial' and 'Do' means 'Way'. Together they mean 'Martial Ways'.

Bushido: The way of the warrior.

Chinkon Kishin: Literarily means 'calm the spirit and return to the divine'; a general name given for meditation.

Cocha: Tea.

Dai Ichi Kihon Waza or Dai Ichi Kihon: First level of techniques.

Dai Ni Kihon: Second level of techniques.

Dai San Kihon: Third level of techniques.

Daito Ryu Aikijujitsu: The transitional name which Ueshiba used to distinguish his art from that of Daito Ryu, before calling it Aikido.

Daito Ryu: A Japanese martial art which was headed during the early years of the twentieth century by Master Sokaku Takeda. The founder of Aikido learned and practised Daito Ryu prior to the development of Aikido. Most Aikido techniques are derived from Daito Ryu.

Dogi: Training uniforms; the traditional clothing in the dojo.

Dojo: The school; the place in which Aikido is practised.

Hajime: A call in Japanese to begin training; a widely used command in the dojo.

Hakama: Uniquely designed Japanese 'trousers' which aikidoka traditionally wear in the dojo. The hakama is composed of many folds of fabric which allow the wearer to obscure the movement of their legs and hips, movement considered by many as the key behind Aikido techniques. The hakama is secured to the waist of the wearer by long strips of fabric and it also benefits from a small back rest which aids the practitioner in keeping their posture erect.

Ikkyo: Lock or Control Number One. A technique which aims to control the balance of the opponent by bending his arm at the elbow.

Iriminage: An Aikido throw in which the tori connects with uke's body from the front, taking him off balance and then throwing him down by entering the hips behind him and by using the arms in unison to throw him down.

Itaii: Literarily 'itai' means pain. Also used as a call to indicate one's pain.

Jiyu Waza: Free techniques. A unique system of training in which a student performs techniques under quick and ongoing attacks. It is a good method to develop performance under extreme physical and mental stress.

Jo: A staff, approximately the size of a walking stick.

Jodan: High stance; usually refers to the way one holds a sword.

Kamai: Fighting stance.

Kami Dana: The miniature shrine in the dojo; traditionally placed at the front of the dojo to represent the spirits and guardians of the place.

Kami: The divine; the beyond; god.

Kamikaze: Literarily means 'Divine Wind' but is also a popular term to describe Japanese suicide pilots during World War II.

Kata: A fixed and rehearsed form of practice.

Katana: A Japanese sword.

Kendo: The Japanese martial art of sword fighting. It is traditionally practised with full body armour and bamboo swords.

Ki: Energy in its purest manifestation.

Kiaii: A loud and powerful cry that accompanies a strike or a throw in order to increase the power and intensity of the attack.

Kobudo: Weaponry.

Kojiki: The writings of Japanese mythology.

Kokyu: Breath.

Kokyunage: Literarily means 'Breath Throw'; a general name given to techniques which use the momentum of uke's attack and the connection with his body as the only means to throw him.

Kotegaeshi: A technique which bends uke's wrist forcefully backwards, forcing his whole body to topple to the floor.

Kotodama: Words or sounds of power. In Japanese mythology Kotodama are considered to be the sounds with which the universe was created.

Misogi: Ritual cleansing of the body with water; a part of many spiritual Aikido rituals.

Misogi No Jo: A purification technique without water, choreographed by the founder and which is carried out using the staff – the jo.

Naginata: A weapon composed of a spear-like body and extended curved tip, coming in three forms: solid wood, bamboo and live blade.

Nikajo: The original name for the Aikido technique Nikyo.

Nikyo: Lock or Control Number Two. A technique in which the opponent's arm is compressed firmly at the wrist, a motion which turns his arm into a fixed lever through which he is then cut down in a sharp, sweeping movement; a move similar to the way one would cut down with a sword.

O Sensei: Literarily means 'Great Teacher'; a term normally used to describe the founder of Aikido, Morihei Ueshiba.

Ocha: Green tea.

Omoto Kyo: A shamanistic religion established at the turn of the twentieth century by Nao Deguchi and later on run under the supervision of the visionary Unisaburo Deguchi.

On a Yahashano: Part of a chant of the Shingon religion.

Onsen: A natural hotspring.

Osu: The word one is most likely to hear in an Aikido dojo or indeed in any dojo of Japanese martial arts. Osu has many useful and ethical meanings; it is used as a greeting, to indicate understanding, gratitude to the training partner and so on.

Rei: The command to bow, frequently used in the dojo.

Ronin: A master-less Samurai.

Sakaki: The evergreen leaves that are placed on the miniature shrine in the dojo.

Samurai: A traditional Japanese warrior, famous for their strict code of conduct and for their great devotion in the service of their masters.

Sankyo: Lock or Control Number Three. A technique in which the tori twists the palm of the uke inwards and by doing so causes the uke to lose his balance and collapse to the ground.

Satori: Enlightenment; the ultimate spiritual goal of the Aikido practitioner.

Seeker Skill: One of the many styles of the 'Aiki Skills'; often referred to as the Skill of the Tracker; a supernatural ability to connect and find people without any physical touch, based on the principles of Zanshin.

Seiza: The proper Japanese way of sitting; in the dojo it is practised by sitting on the knees with erect back, palms placed neatly on top of the thighs.

Sensei: A teacher.

Sento: Man-made hot baths, traditionally used for communal bathing.

Shihonage: An Aikido technique in which uke's wrist is bent backwards and then used to throw him to the ground. Shionage literally means 'Four Direction Throw'.

Shimai: A shamanistic dance.

Shingon Ryu: A Japanese Buddhist sect which was the official religion of Japan until the end of the nineteenth century.

Shinto: One of the original Japanese religions.

Shomen Ni Rei: A call to bow to the front; in the dojo it means to bow in the direction of the shrine; usually performed at the beginning and end of the class.

Shomen Uchi: A front cut with the 'blade' of the hand towards the forehead of the enemy; a similar motion to the forward cut with a sword.

Skill of the Aiki Grappler: One of the many styles of the 'Aiki Skills'; an art which combines the common abilities of the grappler with the unique supernatural qualities of the Skill.

Skill of the Uke: One of the many Skills derived from the art of Aikido. A Skilled Uke is the master of the receiving end of a technique; knowingly cooperating with the attacker's intention and blows to such a degree that it in turn allows the Skilled Uke to reverse almost any lock or throw being initiated upon him.

Skill: The supernatural abilities developed and derived through the practice of true Aikido.

Su: The primary sound of the universe, according to Onisaburo Deguchi; the primal sound from which everything in the universe emerged.

Sumo: The traditional Japanese art of 'Ring Wrestling'.

Suri Ashi: A unique system of sliding along the ground rather than stepping; the way in which Aikido techniques are executed in the dojo. Suri Ashi is a great way to learn how to keep stable and how to maintain good connection to the floor.

Tatami: The tightly packed straw mats which are traditionally used as flooring in the dojo.

Tegatana: Literarily means 'The Blade of the Hand'; a term referring to the forearm as a blade.

Tori: The aikidoka whose role is to execute a technique on his training partner, on his uke. In Aikido training, the roles of tori and uke switch in a balanced way, allowing both partners to practise both roles.

Tsunami: A powerful tidal wave which often unleashes itself on the coasts of Japan.

Uchi Deshi: A live-in student; traditionally in a Japanese dojo there are students who live and care for the place.

Uke: An uke is a training partner, the person upon which the technique is executed. It is important to note that by definition an uke is not an opponent but rather a partner who helps the tori learn and achieve his goals.

Ukemi: Break fall; a controlled way of falling in which one avoids harm to the body.

Waka: A traditional Japanese poem composed of five lines of lyrics and 31 syllables, in the order 5:7:5:7:7. These poems are supposed to possess either supernatural power or meaningful insight.

Yame: A call in Japanese to stop all training; a widely used command in the dojo.

Yokomen: A diagonal strike to the temple with the side of the hand.

Yonkyo: Lock or Control Number Four. It is a technique in which the tori presses sharply with his palm against the inner part of the uke's forearm, immediately above the wrist, and by doing so controlling his balance through severe yet harmless pain.

Yukata: A Japanese bathrobe.

Zanshin: A connection maintained at the end of a throw between the tori and the uke. It is a principal which serves as a base to the art of the Seekers.